WATERDEEP
DRAGON HEIST™

CREDITS

Lead Designer: Christopher Perkins
Designers: James J. Haeck, James Introcaso, Adam Lee, Matt Sernett
Rules Development: Jeremy Crawford, Ben Petrisor, Kate Welch
Story Consultants: Matthew Mercer, Charles Sanders

Managing Editor: Jeremy Crawford
Lead Editor: Christopher Perkins
Editors: Michele Carter, Scott Fitzgerald Gray, Kim Mohan

Art Director: Kate Irwin
Additional Art Direction: Shauna Narciso, Richard Whitters
Graphic Designer: Emi Tanji
Cover Illustrator: Tyler Jacobson
Interior Illustrators: Mark Behm, Eric Belisle, Zoltan Boros, Clint Cearley, Sidharth Chaturvedi, Daarken, Eric Deschamps, Olga Drebas, Leesha Hannigan, Ralph Horsley, Tyler Jacobson, Sam Keiser, Julian Kok, Alayna Lemmer, Christopher Moeller, Scott Murphy, Jim Pavelec, Claudio Pozas, Vincent Proce, Ned Rogers, Craig J Spearing, Jason Thompson, Cory Trego-Erdner, Richard Whitters, Mark Winters, Shawn Wood, Bayard Wu, Kieran Yanner
Interior Cartographer: Dyson Logos
Poster Map: Jason Engle

Producers: Daniel Tovar, Matt Warren, Stan!
Product Engineer: Cynda Callaway
Imaging Technicians: Carmen Cheung, Kevin Yee
Art Administration: David Gershman
Prepress Specialist: Jefferson Dunlap

Other D&D Team Members: Bart Carroll, Pelham Greene, Ari Levitch, Chris Lindsay, Jeremy Martin, Shelly Mazzanoble, Mike Mearls, Hilary Ross, Liz Schuh, Nathan Stewart, Greg Tito, Trish Yochum

Gratitude to Elliott Zastrow for his extensive research.

Special thanks to the hundreds of playtesters whose feedback made this adventure more fun at every turn.

FOREWORD

A simple question began rattling around in my head over two years ago as I was bidding farewell to Barovia, dragging myself out of the depths of Maelstrom, and planning a yearlong expedition to Chult. Where do we go next? After mulling over several options, we decided it would be refreshing to return to civilization.

Waterdeep: Dragon Heist is a treasure hunt with an urban backdrop. We've visited Waterdeep before, but not like this. Clever heroes will respect the city's rules. Those who get on the city's bad side are in for a rough time, as the City of Splendors is home to some of the most powerful figures in the Forgotten Realms.

Charlie Sanders, a lifelong D&D player, brought his experience writing for television to the project by helping flesh out the story bible months before work on the adventure was scheduled to begin. Matthew Mercer, whom you might know from the livestreamed show *Critical Role*, lent us his boundless imagination and helped flesh out the villains and their motives. A D&D adventure is only as good as its villains, and *Waterdeep: Dragon Heist* has multiple baddies to choose from.

Before I pull back the curtain and lead you into the heart of Waterdeep, I wish to thank Ed Greenwood for making the City of Splendors what it is: the kind of magical place you wish in your heart was real.

Chris Perkins
December 2017

ON THE COVER

In Waterdeep, a gold coin is called a dragon, and someone has hidden half a million dragons in the City of Splendors. Tyler Jacobson illustrates the villains hunting for the treasure. May the gods protect any adventurer who stands in their way!

Disclaimer: The Lords of Waterdeep cannot be held responsible for the flogging, banishment, incarceration, or execution of adventurers who violate the Code Legal, nor are the Lords responsible for the actions of beholder crime lords, unscrupulous nobles, drow swashbucklers, and evil clones. Also, don't be alarmed by the colossal statues scattered throughout the city. They're quite safe and haven't gone berserk in years.

620C4658000001 EN
ISBN: 978-0-7869-6625-7
First Printing: September 2018

9 8 7 6 5 4 3 2 1

CONTENTS

PRONUNCIATION GUIDE

This guide shows how to pronounce many of the non-English names that appear in this adventure.

Name	Pronunciation	Name	Pronunciation
Agorn Fuoco	AY-gorn foo-OH-koh	Marro Qaz'arrt	MAW-row kah-ZART
Ahghairon	ah-GAIR-awn	Mattrim Mereg	MAT-trim MAIR-egg
Ahmaergo	ah-MAIR-go	Melannor Fellbranch	MEL-ah-nor
Alcedor Kolat	awl-SEE-door KOH-lat	Meloon Wardragon	may-LOON
Alturiak (month)	awl-TUR-ee-ak	Mirt	MERT or MEERT
Amath Sercent	AH-math SER-sent	Mirtul (month)	MER-tul
Ammalia Cassalanter	ah-MAW-lee-ah KAS-ah-lan-ter	Nar'l Xibrindas	NAR-ul zeh-BRIN-das
Arn Xalrondar	ARN zal-RON-dar	Nihiloor	NYE-heh-lure
Aurinax	OR-ah-nax	Obaya Uday	oh-BYE-yah oo-DAY
Avareen Windrivver	ah-vah-REEN	Orond Gralhund	oh-ROND GRAWL-hoond
Bregan D'aerthe	BRAY-gan DAIRTH	Raelyn Auvryndar	RAY-lin ah-VRIN-dar
Corylus Thann	KOR-eh-luss	Remallia Haventree	reh-MAW-lee-ah
Davil Starsong	DAH-vil	Renaer Neverember	reh-NAIR
Duhlark Kolat	doo-LARK KOH-lat	Rishaal	ree-SHAWL
Eleasis (month)	eh-LEE-sis	Rongquan Mystere	RONG-kwan mis-TAIR
Eleint (month)	eh-LAINT	Saeth Cromley	SAYTH KROM-lee
Esvele Rosznar	EZ-veh-lay RAWJ-nar	Savra Belabranta	SAV-rah bel-ah-BRAN-tah
Fala Lefaliir	FAH-lah LEF-ah-leer	Seffia Naelryke	SEF-yah NAIL-rike
Fel'rekt Lafeen	FEL-rekt lah-FEEN	Sidra Romeir	SID-rah roh-MEER
Fenerus Stormcastle	FEN-er-us	Skarn Zarphoul	SKARN ZAR-fool
Flamerule (month)	FLAME-rool	Skeemo Weirdbottle	SKEE-moh
Floon Blagmaar	FLOON BLAG-mar	Soluun Xibrindas	soh-LOON zeh-BRIN-das
Hlam	huh-LAWM	Talisolvanar Fellbranch	tal-iss-AWL-van-ar
Holvan Ebberek	HOLE-van EBB-er-ek	Tarsakh (month)	TAR-sack
Hrabbaz	hrah-BAWZ	Tashlyn Yafeera	TASH-lin yah-FEER-ah
Hyustus Staget	HEW-stus STAG-it	Tissina Khyret	teh-SEE-nah KYE-ret
Iokaste Daliano	i-oh-KAW-stay daw-lee-AH-noh	Tylan Ilueph	TYE-lan ill-OO-eff
Istrid Horn	ISS-trid	Umbero Zastro	um-BAIR-oh ZASS-troh
Jalester Silvermane	JAH-less-ter	Urlaster Ghann	ur-LASS-ter GAN
Jarlaxle Baenre	jar-LAX-ull BANE-ray	Urstul Floxin	UR-stool FLOX-in
Jelenn Urmbrusk	juh-LEN URM-brusk	Vaelle Lurval	vay-ELLE lur-VAWL
Jeryth Phaulkon	JAIR-ith FAWL-kon	Vajra Safahr	VOJ-rah sah-FAR
Jezrynne Hornraven	JEZ-rin	Velgos Ephezzrin	VEL-gohs eh-FEZ-rin
Kaevja Cynavern	CAVE-yah SIN-ah-vern	Vevette Blackwater	veh-VET
Kalain	kah-LAIN	Vhaspar Holmdreg	VASS-par HOLM-dreg
Karabal L'enz	KAWR-ah-bawl LENZ	Victoro Cassalanter	vik-TOR-oh KAS-ah-lan-ter
Khafeyta Murzan	kah-FAY-tah mur-ZAWN	Volkarr Kibbens	VOAL-kar KIB-enz
Korgstrod Uxgulm	KORG-strawd UX-gulm	Volothamp Geddarm	VOH-loh-thamp geh-DARM
Krebbyg Masq'il'yr	KREH-big MASK-il-eer	Westra Moltimmur	WES-trah MOLT-im-ur
Kythorn (month)	KY-thorn	Xanathar	ZAN-ah-thar
Laeral Silverhand	LAIR-awl	Yagra Stonefist	YAG-raw
Laiba Rosse	LAY-bah ROSS-uh	Yalah Gralhund	YAW-law GRAWL-hoond
Llorath Pharn	LOR-ath FARN	Yaliek Iltizmar	yah-LEEK ill-TIZ-mar
Losser Mirklav	LOSS-er MER-klav	Zaibon Kyszalt	ZYE-bawn kij-ALT
Manshoon	man-SHOON	Ziraj the Hunter	zeer-AWJ
Margo Verida	MAR-go veh-REE-dah	Zorbog Jyarkoth	ZOR-bog jee-AR-koth

INTRODUCTION

 **W**ELCOME TO WATERDEEP, THE CROWN OF the North, where a wondrous tale of urban adventure is about to unfold. Our story begins with the gathering of adventurers at the Yawning Portal Inn and Tavern. Volothamp Geddarm, the famous explorer and raconteur, has a quest for them—one that entangles the characters in a bitter conflict between two nefarious organizations. If the adventurers complete his quest, Volo rewards them handsomely. Yet a much greater prize lies hidden somewhere in the City of Splendors, waiting to be claimed.

Waterdeep: Dragon Heist is a DUNGEONS & DRAGONS adventure designed for characters starting at 1st level. By the end of the story, the characters will be at least 5th level. If you're planning to run through the adventure as a player, stop reading now!

If you're looking for higher-level adventure content set in Waterdeep, a companion product titled *Waterdeep: Dungeon of the Mad Mage* explores the vast dungeon under Waterdeep known as Undermountain and is designed for characters of levels all the way up to 20th.

STORY OVERVIEW

Waterdeep: Dragon Heist is a treasure hunt set against an urban backdrop. The adventure's plot can be summarized as follows:

- Half a million gold coins are hidden somewhere in Waterdeep. Many individuals know about the cache and are looking for it. Adventurers can join the hunt and prevent the cache from falling into evil hands.
- The city is threatened by escalating tension between two power groups that is on the verge of flaring into violence. The Zhentarim, a shadowy network of mercenaries, and Xanathar, the beholder crime lord of Waterdeep, are at odds, and when they clash, the characters are pulled into the conflict.

CACHE OF DRAGONS

In Waterdeep, a gold coin is called a *dragon*. Before he was ousted from his position as the Open Lord of Waterdeep, Dagult Neverember embezzled half a million dragons and hid them in a secret vault. As a security precaution, he arranged for all knowledge of the vault's location and defenses to be magically erased from his mind and the minds of his subordinates. The wizard who performed the procedure trapped this knowledge within an artifact called the *Stone of Golorr*. The wizard disappeared shortly thereafter, and Dagult hid the stone in the Palace of Waterdeep.

Dagult was off rebuilding the city of Neverwinter when the other Lords of Waterdeep voted him out of office. He immediately made plans to retrieve the *Stone of Golorr* and smuggle his cache of dragons out of Waterdeep. His spies plucked the stone from the palace but were killed while trying to leave the city. The stone was stolen and passed from one hand to another like a common jewel until it wound up in the clutches of Xanathar.

USING THE POSTER MAP

The map in the back of this book has the city of Waterdeep on both sides. One side can be shown to players. The other side is for the DM and includes tags marking important locations in the adventure.

The *Stone of Golorr* is actually an aboleth transformed by magic. In this inanimate state, the aboleth can read the mind of any creature that attunes to the stone, as well as modify that creature's memory. A creature attuned to the stone can also extract information from the aboleth, including lore about Neverember's vault.

Built long ago by dwarves, the vault is warded against all forms of magical detection and intrusion. Its current protector is an adult gold dragon named Aurinax, who is also the current wielder and guardian of the *dragonstaff of Ahghairon*, which has the power to prevent other dragons from entering the city. In exchange for the staff, Aurinax promised to guard the gold until such time as Neverember or his appointed vassals removed it.

WAR IN THE STREETS

Beneath the city streets lurks a criminal underworld, its leader a beholder called Xanathar. Hoping to gain a political foothold in Waterdeep, agents of the Zhentarim (also known as the Black Network) recently tried to ally their organization with the Xanathar Guild. The architect of this attempt was a clone of the wizard Manshoon, a founder of the Black Network long thought dead.

While the two sides were negotiating in Xanathar's lair, the *Stone of Golorr* suddenly disappeared from where Xanathar had hidden it. The paranoid beholder accused the Black Network of stealing it and slew the Zhentarim envoys who were present. When the Zhents retaliated by attacking Xanathar Guild outposts, Xanathar took their actions as confirmation of the Black Network's vile intentions. Now the bad blood between the Zhentarim and Xanathar has begun to spill into the streets, threatening peace throughout the city.

Who actually stole the *Stone of Golorr*? The answer: a rock gnome named Dalakhar. After Lord Neverember used magic to discern the gemstone's location, he sent forth a succession of spies to infiltrate Xanathar's lair and obtain it. Dalakhar succeeded where many others before him had failed, but his success turns out to be short-lived.

VOLO'S QUEST

The Yawning Portal serves as the default starting point for this story. One of the first people the adventurers meet there is Volothamp Geddarm. He has just returned from a tour promoting his latest book, *Volo's Guide to Monsters*, and he has a quest for the characters.

One of Volo's friends, a handsome simpleton named Floon Blagmaar, has disappeared, seemingly kidnapped. The search for Floon leads to the revelation that he was caught up in a case of mistaken identity, and the characters are actually looking for two victims. The intended target was Lord Neverember's estranged son,

AHGHAIRON'S DRAGONWARD

Waterdeep is blanketed by an undispellable magical effect called *Ahghairon's dragonward*. The effect originates from somewhere under Ahghairon's Tower in the Castle Ward and is permanent. Dragons and all other creatures of the dragon type are physically unable to enter the city (or its sewers) as long as the *dragonward* persists. The effect doesn't extend to the harbor or into Undermountain.

A creature of the dragon type that is touched by the *dragonstaff of Ahghairon* (see appendix A) can ignore *Ahghairon's dragonward* and move through the city freely. The effect lasts until the creature is touched again by the staff, or until the passage of a period of time specified by one who is attuned to the staff.

The *dragonstaff* is currently in the possession of an adult gold dragon named Aurinax (see appendix B), who guards a hidden vault under the city.

Renaer Neverember. Agents of the Zhentarim waylaid him because they want to know everything that Renaer knows about the cache of dragons. (Unfortunately for them, Renaer is ignorant of the cache and its whereabouts.) If the characters rescue him, Renaer proves to be a worthy ally to adventurers hoping to make a name for themselves in Waterdeep.

As a reward for rescuing Floon, Volo gives adventurers the deed to a building in the North Ward that looks out onto a wide cul-de-sac hemmed in by old residences and shops. The property used to be a tavern with a residence on the upper floors. The tavern has been closed for years, and the residence is haunted by a poltergeist that the characters can lay to rest.

FIREBALL!

As time goes on, the characters attract the attention of local factions hoping to recruit them while they settle into the city. Eventually, these relatively peaceful times are shattered when a fireball detonates near their new residence. The characters are swept up in the aftermath of this horrific event and can try to get to the bottom of it. Who cast the *fireball* spell and why? Who was the intended target? They can investigate the incident on behalf of a guild or a faction, or they can become involved for reasons of their own.

One casualty of the fireball is in fact its intended target: Lord Neverember's spy, Dalakhar. Whoever killed the gnome now has the *Stone of Golorr*, the key to finding the lost cache of dragons. One way or another, depending on the alliances—and the enemies—they have made in the city, the characters become embroiled in the chase for the stone and the hoard it protects.

CHOOSE YOUR VILLAIN

When you run this adventure, you choose its main villain at the outset. Your choice determines the season of the year in which the story takes place, as well as the antagonists in several of the encounters in chapter 4. The villain you choose opposes the player characters, while the villains you don't choose become part of the backdrop and could help the characters or hinder them.

As another unusual feature of this adventure, the villains aren't meant to be killed, nor are they out to kill the player characters. The villains are after a treasure

hoard, and the adventurers' ultimate goal is to keep the treasure out of their clutches.

You can swap out one villain for another at any time. For example, if you decide halfway through the adventure that because of how the story has progressed Jarlaxle Baenre would make a better antagonist than Xanathar, you can make that change on the fly and run subsequent encounters accordingly.

Each villain is fully described in appendix B and summarized below.

XANATHAR

Xanathar is a paranoid, megalomaniacal beholder crime lord whose goal is to wipe out anyone it perceives as a Zhentarim operative or sympathizer, retrieve the *Stone of Golorr*, and secure the cache of dragons. Its base is a dungeon under Skullport, a subterranean settlement beneath Waterdeep. This lair is described in chapter 5.

Xanathar has a healthy fear of Laeral Silverhand and is inclined to spare those in her employ, to avoid provoking a conflict with Waterdeep's Open Lord. Adventurers who incur the wrath of the beholder can use its fear of Laeral to escape certain death.

If you choose Xanathar as the villain, the adventure takes place in the spring.

THE CASSALANTERS

Victoro and Ammalia Cassalanter are Waterdavian nobles and secret devil worshipers. The Cassalanters plan to use the cache of dragons to buy back the souls of their children, which they traded to Asmodeus for power. Their estate, Cassalanter Villa, has a temple of Asmodeus hidden underneath it, as described in chapter 6.

The Cassalanters try to misdirect and discredit the characters rather than murder them. Victoro and Ammalia rely on their noble status to protect them, and the last thing they want is the City Watch on their doorstep.

If you choose the Cassalanters as the villains, the adventure takes place in the summer.

JARLAXLE BAENRE

Jarlaxle Baenre is a drow swashbuckler and the secret lord of Luskan, the City of Sails. Jarlaxle plans to use the cache of dragons to buy his way into the Lords' Alliance, a confederation of cities and towns that band together against common threats. Jarlaxle also wants the *dragonstaff of Ahghairon* for leverage in his negotiations. In the magical guise of a human sea captain named Zardoz Zord, Jarlaxle runs a traveling carnival called the Sea Maidens Faire and lairs aboard a ship in Waterdeep's harbor that has a submarine (the *Scarlet Marpenoth*) underneath it, as described in chapter 7.

Jarlaxle delights in thwarting his enemies, enjoys the complications that arise when adventurers try to meddle in his affairs, and loves to see the looks on their faces when he finally gets the better of them. He doesn't suffer fools who threaten him, however. If forced into a violent confrontation, he swiftly and brutally kills someone to make an example of them and then walks off.

If you choose Jarlaxle as the villain, the adventure takes place in the autumn.

Manshoon

A clone of the wizard Manshoon, one of the founders of the Zhentarim, is hiding in Waterdeep. He wants to rule the city, by claiming the cache of dragons and by using that wealth to bribe the Masked Lords into making him the new Open Lord. He also wants to regain control of the Black Network. Manshoon lurks in Kolat Towers, a pair of wizards' towers in the Trades Ward. This residence is described in chapter 8.

Manshoon creates copies of himself using the *simulacrum* spell and takes great pains to conceal his identity, since his success hinges on not attracting the attention of others who would seek to thwart him before his plans come to fruition. Manshoon avoids unnecessary confrontations with adventurers; only those who enter his extradimensional sanctum are likely to incur his wrath.

If you choose Manshoon as the villain, the adventure takes place in the winter.

Seasons

The adventure unfolds in a particular season depending on the villain you choose at the outset. If you switch to a new villain midway through the adventure, don't change the season to match unless the characters take enough downtime for seasons to change naturally.

Spring

In Waterdeep, early spring tends to be cold and damp. Misty rain falls for days on end. It's common for fog to settle at night and last through the day. As the weather improves, the city attracts more visitors, and the streets become increasingly crowded as summer approaches.

Summer

Summers in Waterdeep are quite comfortable, and it's a great time for citizens and visitors to congregate outside. The markets are busier than at any other time of year. Sometimes, though, warm air pushes up from the south and settles in the valleys north and east of the city. This air gets trapped, creating a hot spell that might last days or weeks. Activity in the city slows to a crawl, since Waterdavians are unaccustomed to such heat.

Autumn

Throughout autumn, wagonloads of food arrive in Waterdeep from outlying farms. Without this bounty, city folk would starve during the winter. Cold, howling sea winds remind Waterdavians that winter is near.

Winter

Waterdavian winters are harsh. As snow piles up around the city and ice fills the harbor, trade grinds to a halt and the city seals its gates. Citizens willing to brave the cold still gather in local taverns and festhalls, but few venture outside the city walls.

Running the Adventure

To run this adventure, you need the D&D fifth edition core rulebooks: *Player's Handbook*, *Dungeon Master's Guide*, and *Monster Manual*. The *Sword Coast Adventurer's Guide* is helpful, but not necessary.

> Text that appears in a box like this is meant to be read aloud or paraphrased for the players when their characters first arrive at a location or under a specific circumstance, as described in the text.

The *Monster Manual* contains stat blocks for most of the creatures found in this adventure. All the necessary stat blocks are included there or in appendix B. When a creature's name appears in **bold** type, that's a visual cue for you to look up the creature's stat block in the *Monster Manual*, unless the adventure's text instead refers you to the monster appendix in this book.

Spells and equipment mentioned in the adventure are described in the *Player's Handbook*. Magic items are described in the *Dungeon Master's Guide*, unless the adventure's text directs you to an item's description in appendix A.

Abbreviations

The following abbreviations appear in this book:

hp = hit points	LG = lawful good
AC = Armor Class	CG = chaotic good
DC = Difficulty Class	NG = neutral good
XP = experience points	LN = lawful neutral
pp = platinum piece(s)	N = neutral
gp = gold piece(s)	CN = chaotic neutral
ep = electrum piece(s)	LE = lawful evil
sp = silver piece(s)	CE = chaotic evil
cp = copper piece(s)	NE = neutral evil
NPC = nonplayer character	DM = Dungeon Master

THE SUN GLOWS OVER WATERDEEP'S HARBOR.

ADVENTURE STRUCTURE

Waterdeep: Dragon Heist consists of an introductory adventure designed to familiarize player characters with the city of Waterdeep and provide them with a base of operations (chapters 1 and 2), followed by a citywide treasure hunt (chapters 3 and 4) and descriptions of the villains' lairs (chapters 5 through 8).

In chapter 1, the characters arrive at the Yawning Portal, where Volo gives them a quest. It's a straightforward rescue mission with a twist involving a case of mistaken identity. If the adventurers complete the quest, Volo rewards them with a valuable piece of property.

In chapter 2, the characters explore their new home in Trollskull Alley and attract the attention of factions interested in recruiting them for special missions.

Chapter 3 begins days or weeks later, allowing characters time to adjust to city life and pursue their own interests. An explosion tears through Trollskull Alley, prompting an investigation that hurls the characters into conflict with some secondary villains, culminating in a bloody confrontation at a noble estate.

In chapter 4, the characters race to find the gold. The encounters in this chapter and the order in which they occur change depending on the villain you've chosen. The chapter concludes with the discovery of Lord Neverember's treasure vault and a showdown with its gold dragon guardian. The characters' ultimate goal is to prevent the gold from falling into the hands of the bad guys. If all goes well, some of the gold will find its way into the characters' pockets. Characters will have a hard time claiming it all for themselves, however.

Chapters 5 through 8 describe the lairs of the story's villains and can be used at any time, in any order, or not at all. The characters might have reason to visit one or more of these lairs in the course of the adventure. Thwarting the villains doesn't require the characters to invade their lairs or defeat them in combat, so it's possible to complete the adventure without these chapters coming into play.

Be prepared to make adjustments on the fly if the characters find themselves in a villain's lair prior to completing chapter 4, as the challenges within each lair are difficult for characters of lower than 5th level to overcome. You can gently steer characters in a different direction, drop hints that urge them to use extreme caution, or make deadly encounters easier. It also bears remembering that the villains are meant to be thwarted, not killed, and they are rarely spoiling for a fight. Adventurers who get in over their heads can be knocked unconscious rather than killed. Such characters might awaken in an alley, a sewer tunnel, or a prison cell, with or without their gear. Conversely, they might awaken safe and sound with all their gear in a private residence, being cared for by friendly NPCs who took them in.

VOLO'S WATERDEEP ENCHIRIDION

The special chapter of this book titled "Volo's Waterdeep Enchiridion" is a tour of the City of Splendors. If you're unfamiliar with Waterdeep, review this section before running the adventure. You can also share this section with players whose characters would know general information about the city.

LIFE IN WATERDEEP

City-based adventures can be challenging to run, especially if your player characters are inclined to wander. Keeping the characters in Waterdeep, where the action is, requires that they feel at home. To that end, here are some points to keep in mind:

- Almost anything can be bought or sold in Waterdeep. There's no need for adventurers to shop elsewhere.
- Waterdavians generally hold adventurers in high regard, given that many of the city's most esteemed citizens are former adventurers and that the city has been saved countless times by adventurers over the years.
- Adventurers who are invested in the city are less likely to want to leave it. As your players flesh out their characters' backgrounds, encourage them to establish roots in Waterdeep. The adventure further invests the characters by awarding them property in the city and giving them opportunities to join local factions and guilds.

BREAKING THE LAW

Waterdeep is a city of firm laws and swift justice. Adventurers hell-bent on slaughter and plunder won't fare well in the City of Splendors. The punishments for assault, arson, theft, and murder are severe, regardless of the reason for the crime.

If the characters express interest in knowing more about crimes and punishments in Waterdeep, give them the Code Legal handout in appendix C.

Characters who overtly engage in criminal behavior are quickly cornered and arrested by members of the City Watch. Those charged with committing a crime are brought before a magister to be judged. Advocates might intercede on behalf of the characters if they have allied themselves with influential NPCs and factions. For example, characters who become agents of the Lords' Alliance are more likely to be excused for crimes if Laeral Silverhand, the Open Lord of Waterdeep, has cause to let them off the hook.

Given how strictly laws are enforced in Waterdeep, it's possible that the adventure could end with one or more of the characters being exiled, sentenced to several years of hard labor, imprisoned, or put to death. If that's how their adventure ends, so be it. Hopefully, your next group will fare better.

ARRESTING CHARACTERS

When the authorities show up to arrest one or more player characters for breaking the law, you can handle the arrest in one of two ways.

The first approach is to roleplay the encounter with the arresting officers of the City Watch. The benefit

ADVENTURE FLOWCHART

CHAPTER 1:
A FRIEND IN NEED
Volo gives the adventurers a quest and an estate as their reward.

CHAPTER 2:
TROLLSKULL ALLEY
Adventurers settle into their new estate and meet the neighbors.

CHAPTER 3:
FIREBALL
A fireball explodes in Trollskull Alley, setting off an investigation.

CHAPTER 4:
DRAGON SEASON
Adventurers join the race to find and unlock the Vault of Dragons.

VILLAIN LAIRS

CHAPTER 5:
SPRING MADNESS
Adventurers invade Xanathar's dungeon under the city and confront the beholder in its lair.

CHAPTER 6:
HELL OF A SUMMER
Adventurers storm House Cassalanter and make a diabolical discovery.

CHAPTER 7:
MAESTRO'S FALL
Adventurers board Jarlaxle's ships and learn the sinister secrets of the Sea Maidens Faire.

CHAPTER 8:
WINTER WIZARDRY
Adventurers search Kolat Towers for Manshoon's clone and find his extradimensional den.

ADVENTURE BACKGROUND

GOLD EMBEZZLED
Lord Dagult Neverember embezzles half a million gold pieces and hides them in the Vault of Dragons.

STONE CRAFTED
Dagult hires a wizard to create the *Stone of Golorr*, then hides the artifact in the Palace of Waterdeep.

DAGULT OUSTED
Dagult leaves Waterdeep to rebuild Neverwinter and is ousted as Open Lord of Waterdeep.

STONE STOLEN
The *Stone of Golorr* is stolen from the Palace of Waterdeep and ends up in Xanathar's possession.

STONE STOLEN AGAIN
As Zhents loyal to Manshoon try to forge an alliance with Xanathar, the *Stone of Golorr* is stolen.

ALLIANCE ENDED
War erupts when Xanathar accuses the Zhents of stealing the *Stone of Golorr*, which they didn't do.

DALAKHAR FLEES
Dalakhar, a gnome thief working for Dagult, tries to smuggle the *Stone of Golorr* out of Waterdeep.

DALAKHAR DIES
Dalakhar is killed by a *fireball* spell. Urstul Floxin steals the *Stone of Golorr* from Dalakhar's corpse.

of this approach is that characters can choose to go quietly or resist. The drawback is that the encounter might devolve into a fight-or-flight situation, leading to one or more characters becoming fugitives. If the party includes one or more characters who aren't lawful, such an outcome is likely. To mitigate this drawback, you might allow fugitive characters to forge alliances with NPCs who can help clear their names.

If the threat of arrest becomes tedious, you can switch to the second approach, which is to merely inform the players that one or more characters have been arrested. You can describe the arrest, the subsequent detention, and the events leading up to the trial. The drawback to this approach is that player characters have no control over the situation. (This sense of helplessness has the virtue of being realistic, if not fun.) To mitigate this drawback, you might allow characters to make ability checks to influence the outcome; for example, a successful Charisma (Persuasion) check might enable a character to bribe an official or sow enough doubt in the mind of a magistrate to have the case thrown out.

> ### Naming NPCs
> Important NPCs in the adventure are given names, but many of the secondary NPCs aren't named. *Xanathar's Guide to Everything* contains an appendix of tables you can use to randomly generate names for human and non-human NPCs if you have trouble coming up with names on your own.

Character Creation

If your players are creating 1st-level characters for this adventure, consider setting aside the first game session for character creation. That way, the players can flesh out their adventuring party together and come up with reasons why their characters are friends.

Bringing the Party Together

The Yawning Portal is a popular adventurers' hangout. Unless you have a better idea, assume that the characters are familiar with the establishment and have met there before. If any of the characters are new to the city, they can be drawn to the Yawning Portal by its reputation or summoned there by Volo.

To make the Yawning Portal feel like a familiar, welcoming place, give the players a copy of the Yawning Portal Familiar Faces handout in appendix C and allow each player to select one NPC as a friendly acquaintance. Additional information about these NPCs can be found at the end of this introduction.

Buying Equipment at 1st Level

All the equipment in chapter 5 of the *Player's Handbook* is available for purchase in Waterdeep at normal prices.

Character Backgrounds

Players looking for background options beyond those described in the *Player's Handbook* can find several appropriate ones in the *Sword Coast Adventurer's Guide*: City Watch, cloistered scholar, courtier, faction agent, far traveler, inheritor, mercenary veteran, urban bounty hunter, and Waterdavian noble. If you have access to this book, consider making its background options available to your players' characters.

WATERDAVIAN NOBLE FAMILIES

Waterdeep contains well over a hundred noble families. The following noble houses are fine choices for any character with the noble background from the *Player's Handbook* or the Waterdavian noble background from the *Sword Coast Adventurer's Guide*.

House Amcathra. The Amcathras are a Tethyrian family that specializes in horse breeding and training, cattle ranching, wine-making, and weaponsmithing. The family motto is "We trample our troubles." The family has a large villa in the North Ward, on the east side of the High Road between Hassantyr's Street and Tarnath Street.

House Margaster. The Margasters are an Illuskan family whose business interests lie in land-based shipping and bulk goods trading. The house also has a quiet history of wizardry. The family motto is "Nothing is beyond our grasp." The Margaster family estate is situated between Stabbed Sailor Alley and Shattercrock Alley in the North Ward.

House Phylund. The Phylunds are a Tashlutar family that captures and sells monsters. Monsters that can't be trained as pets or guard beasts are sold to arenas or harvested for their meat, bones, and skins. The Phylunds sponsor adventuring parties and monster-hunting expeditions, and their motto is "What you fear, we master." House Phylund has an estate on Copper Street, west of the High Road between Julthoon Street and Trader's Way in the North Ward.

House Rosznar. Once banished from Waterdeep for smuggling, slavery, and other crimes, this Tethyrian house has returned and is trying to overcome its dark past and disgraceful reputation by focusing on legitimate business ventures such as wine-making and gem trading. The family motto is "We fly high and stoop swift." Rosznar Villa is situated on Thunderstaff Way between Copper Street and Shield Street in the Sea Ward, west of the High Road.

Lady Esvele Rosznar (see "The Black Viper" in appendix B) is a member of this house, though she keeps her masked identity and thieving escapades a secret.

GUILD MEMBERSHIP

Any characters with the guild artisan background are assumed to have free membership in one Waterdeep guild of their choice. Arcane spellcasters living in the city are required by law to register with the Watchful Order of Magists and Protectors, so that they can be called on to defend the city with their magic in times of need.

Waterdeep's most prominent guilds appear on the Guilds of Waterdeep list. By law, there are no active thieves' guilds in Waterdeep, and the Xanathar Guild isn't an actual guild but a faction (see "Factions in Waterdeep," page 14).

To join a guild, one must possess a background, a proficiency, or a status that the guild values. For example, a character with the sailor background is welcome to join the Master Mariners' Guild. One can practice a profession and not be a guild member, but such autonomy carries a cost. The guilds do everything they can to entice new members to join and pay for membership, and they go out of their way to hinder independent business owners, up to and including driving them out of business. A baker who refuses to join the Bakers' Guild might find her flour supply cut off, while a wizard who refuses to

GUILDS OF WATERDEEP

- Bakers' Guild
- Carpenters', Roofers', and Plaisterers' Guild
- Cellarers' and Plumbers' Guild
- Coopers' Guild
- Council of Farmer-Grocers
- Council of Musicians, Instrument-makers, and Choristers
- Dungsweepers' Guild
- Fellowship of Bowyers and Fletchers
- Fellowship of Carters and Coachmen
- Fellowship of Innkeepers
- Fellowship of Salters, Packers, and Joiners
- Fishmongers' Fellowship
- Guild of Apothecaries and Physicians
- Guild of Butchers
- Guild of Chandlers and Lamplighters
- Guild of Fine Carvers
- Guild of Glassblowers, Glaziers, and Spectacle-makers
- Guild of Stonecutters, Masons, Potters, and Tile-makers
- Guild of Trusted Pewterers and Casters
- Guild of Watermen
- Jesters' Guild
- Jewelers' Guild
- Launderers' Guild
- League of Basket-makers and Wickerworkers
- League of Skinners and Tanners
- Loyal Order of Street Laborers
- Master Mariners' Guild
- Most Careful Order of Skilled Smiths and Metalforgers
- Most Diligent League of Sail-makers and Cordwainers
- Most Excellent Order of Weavers and Dyers
- Order of Cobblers and Corvisers
- Order of Master Shipwrights
- Order of Master Tailors, Glovers, and Mercers
- Saddlers' and Harness-makers' Guild
- Scriveners', Scribes', and Clerks' Guild
- Solemn Order of Recognized Furriers and Woolmen
- Splendid Order of Armorers, Locksmiths, and Finesmiths
- Stablemasters' and Farriers' Guild
- Stationers' Guild
- Surveyors', Map-, and Chart-makers' Guild
- Vintners', Distillers', and Brewers' Guild
- Wagon-makers' and Coach Builders' Guild
- Watchful Order of Magists and Protectors
- Wheelwrights' Guild

join the Watchful Order of Magists and Protectors might be denied access to sages, libraries, and other useful resources.

Guilds charge members monthly or yearly dues that vary. For simplicity, you can have a guild charge 1 gp per month or 10 gp for a year's dues paid in advance. A guild can expel a member for any number of reasons, not the least of which is failing to pay dues.

FACTION MEMBERSHIP

A character with the faction agent background (described in the *Sword Coast Adventurer's Guide*) must choose a faction to belong to (see "Factions in Waterdeep" below). Characters without this background can join factions once they reach the end of chapter 1 of this adventure.

CHARACTER ADVANCEMENT

You can track experience points or simply allow characters to level up when they reach certain points in the adventure. Ideally, the characters should fall within the desired level range as they experience each chapter, as shown in the Suggested Character Levels table.

SUGGESTED CHARACTER LEVELS

Chapter	Suggested Level
1. A Friend in Need	1st–2nd
2. Trollskull Alley	2nd
3. Fireball	3rd
4. Dragon Season	3rd–4th
5. Spring Madness	5th or higher
6. Hell of a Summer	5th or higher
7. Maestro's Fall	5th or higher
8. Winter Wizardry	5th or higher

If you decide to track experience points, you can slow the rate of advancement by banking XP until you're ready for the party to level up. Conversely, you can hasten level advancement by awarding ad hoc XP for completing goals, roleplaying well, and surviving or avoiding deadly traps. Any such award should be no more than

what the characters would earn for defeating a monster with a challenge rating equal to their level. For example, a fair ad hoc award for a party of 2nd-level adventurers would be 450 XP, which is what the characters would earn for defeating a challenge rating 2 monster.

If you dispense with XP tracking and allow characters to gain levels as the adventure progresses, use the Suggested Character Levels table as your guide.

FACTIONS IN WATERDEEP

Various factions have roots in Waterdeep, and any character with the faction agent background (described in the *Sword Coast Adventurer's Guide*) can choose to belong to one of the factions described below, provided the character meets the faction's prerequisites.

If you're using the optional renown rules described in chapter 1 of the *Dungeon Master's Guide*, allow a player whose character has the faction agent background to roll a d4 to determine that character's renown at the start of the adventure. See the "Tracking Renown" sidebar for more information.

Characters of other backgrounds will have opportunities to join a faction later in the adventure. Any such character must meet a faction's prerequisites to be eligible to join it, and the character's starting renown is 0.

Characters who have renown greater than 0 in a faction can gain its support in times of need by reaching out to an influential NPC member of that faction. As a character's renown improves, so does the quality of the support. A faction might also help non-members who further its interests. The descriptions of the factions that follow include suggestions for how support from a faction can manifest.

You decide the extent to which a faction will assist the adventurers, based on each faction's perception of how important or valuable the adventurers are. For example, if the characters earn Laeral Silverhand's trust and her support of them becomes public knowledge, members of Bregan D'aerthe might aid the characters so that Jarlaxle Baenre can curry favor with the Open Lord of Waterdeep.

BREGAN D'AERTHE

A character must be a drow, preferably a male, to join this faction.

Bregan D'aerthe is a company of mercenaries originally made up of the much-derided and dishonorable castaways of destroyed drow houses. The group's leader, Jarlaxle Baenre, is always looking for new members to fill the ranks, and loyalty is what matters to him most.

Almost all Bregan D'aerthe members are male because female drow rarely condescend to take orders from a male. A female drow can earn a place in the faction by decrying the drow matriarchy and convincing Jarlaxle that she would be an asset to the brotherhood. Jarlaxle employs non-drow operatives as well, none of whom know they're working for him; such individuals aren't considered members of the faction.

Bregan D'aerthe is using one of Jarlaxle's legitimate business enterprises—the Sea Maidens Faire—as a front in Waterdeep. The Sea Maidens Faire consists of

three carnival ships (the *Eyecatcher*, the *Heartbreaker*, and the *Hellraiser*) crewed by disguised drow and a host of non-drow performers (musicians, acrobats, actors, and the like). The ships' cargo consists mostly of wagons and floats that can be hastily assembled and paraded through the city. The drow use these parades to draw attention away from their illicit activities.

In the magical guise of a flamboyant Illuskan captain named Zardoz Zord, Jarlaxle oversees things from the *Eyecatcher*, his flagship, and the *Scarlet Marpenoth*, a submarine mounted underneath it. He relies on three drow gunslingers—Fel'rekt Lafeen, Krebbyg Masq'il'yr, and Soluun Xibrindas—to do most of his dirty work in the city. For more information on Jarlaxle and his lieutenants, see appendix B.

Bregan D'aerthe is skilled at infiltrating criminal organizations. Xanathar's drow advisor, Nar'l Xibrindas (see appendix B), is actually a Bregan D'aerthe spy.

Bregan D'aerthe support comes in these ways:

- The adventurers receive small, unmarked black pouches of coins from an anonymous source.
- The adventurers receive an invitation to dine with Zardoz Zord aboard his flagship, during which Jarlaxle takes their measure and offers assistance if they impress him.
- Bregan D'aerthe members buy off or quietly dispose of individuals who threaten the adventurers (usually without asking).

EMERALD ENCLAVE

A character must demonstrate an interest in protecting nature or the natural order to join the Emerald Enclave. Druids and rangers are especially welcome.

Waterdeep harbors a few members of the faction, which seeks to foster harmony between nature and civilization. Members living in Waterdeep help guard the city against unnatural threats, including aberrations and undead. They also watch over the City of the Dead (Waterdeep's public cemetery) and the city's parks.

Members of the Emerald Enclave can be found in Phaulkonmere, a noble villa in the Southern Ward, and at the Snobeedle Orchard and Meadery in Undercliff.

The walls of Phaulkonmere enclose fabulous gardens, and the buildings are covered with moss and ivy. The place is owned by descendants of two wealthy families—the Tarms (longtime Waterdavians) and the Phaulkons (who are of Cormyrean descent). They spend most of the year traveling abroad and entrust the estate to a half-elf groundskeeper named Melannor Fellbranch. He is joined by Jeryth Phaulkon, a noblewoman turned demigod who serves Mielikki, divine lady of the forest.

The Snobeedle Orchard and Meadery is run by the Snobeedle family of halflings, among them an old druid named Blossom Snobeedle. Blossom's youngest son, Dasher, disappeared in Waterdeep about six months ago. He was infected with lycanthropy and is now a member of a wererat gang called the Shard Shunners.

Emerald Enclave support comes in these ways:

- Enclave members share information they've gathered from magical conversations with animals in the city.
- Melannor Fellbranch (see "Emerald Enclave," page 35) provides free food and care for the adventurers' animals at Phaulkonmere.
- One adventurer receives a supernatural charm (see "Supernatural Gifts" in chapter 7 of the *Dungeon Master's Guide*) bestowed by Jeryth Phaulkon (see "Emerald Enclave," page 35).

FORCE GREY

To join Force Grey, one must first become a member of the Gray Hands. An individual who has served in the City Watch or the City Guard is eligible to join, as are characters who are willing to swear oaths to defend Waterdeep, its citizens, and its laws with their lives. Adventurers who show promise might be invited to join the Gray Hands, a faction overseen by the Blackstaff, Vajra Safahr. Members of the Gray Hands complete assignments dictated by Vajra.

Force Grey is an elite cadre of specialized adventurers, drawn from the ranks of the Gray Hands, whose fighting prowess is matched only by their loyalty to the city. Force Grey attracts the best of the best. Characters don't begin their adventuring careers as members of Force Grey, but they can work up to that status.

Whenever Waterdeep has a problem that can't be handled by diplomats or the city's other armed forces, the Open Lord has the option to mobilize Force Grey. Such action is usually taken as a last resort, since some past members of the group have exhibited a tendency to indulge in wanton violence, causing as much damage as they ostensibly prevent.

Although the Open Lord sets mission goals and parameters whenever the unit is activated, the Force Grey team needed to complete any given assignment is made up of individuals handpicked by the Blackstaff.

If members of Force Grey (and, in some cases, the Gray Hands) are arrested for a crime, the Open Lord or the Blackstaff will usually intervene on their behalf and facilitate their release.

Force Grey support comes in these ways:

- Adventurers who are arrested are released under the loose supervision of Vajra Safahr (see appendix B).
- The adventurers receive a helpful uncommon or rare magic item that they're allowed to use for a time (until it mysteriously disappears).
- Meloon Wardragon (see appendix B) or some other respected member of Force Grey helps the adventurers out of a tough situation.

HARPERS

Any smart, non-evil character can join the Harpers of Waterdeep. Bards and wizards are especially welcome.

Harpers are altruists who work behind the scenes to keep power out of the hands of evil tyrants. In the cur-

rent situation, it doesn't take long for them to suspect that the Zhentarim is wholly or partially responsible for the escalation of violence in Waterdeep. Harper spies might use the adventurers as instruments to get at the truth. Various nobles and guildmasters in the city are Harper sympathizers.

The Harpers have several secret gathering places in Waterdeep, among them Ulbrinter Villa, an estate located on Delzorin Street between Vhezoar Street and Brondar's Way, in the North Ward (just south of Trollskull Alley). The elf lady of the house, Remallia Haventree ("Remi" to her friends), the widow of Lord Arthagast Ulbrinter, is a high-ranking member of the faction. Other key members include Renaer Neverember, the estranged son of Lord Dagult Neverember, and Mirt, an advisor to Open Lord Laeral Silverhand. See appendix B for more information on these NPCs.

Harpers prefer to conduct their business in bustling inns and taverns such as the Yawning Portal, or in quiet locations such as the City of the Dead.

Harper support comes in these ways:

- The Harpers make common and uncommon potions and scrolls available to the adventurers at a reduced or deferred cost depending on the circumstances.
- Remallia Haventree (see appendix B) feeds useful bits of information to the adventurers and might also offer them temporary shelter.
- If the adventurers are accosted and overwhelmed, one or more Harpers come to their rescue. A Harper rescue team usually consists of a **bard** (see appendix B) or a **mage**, plus 1d4 + 3 **spies** or **veterans**.

LORDS' ALLIANCE

To become a member of the Lords' Alliance faction in Waterdeep, a character must be a Waterdavian citizen. Those with criminal records can also join, provided they demonstrate their allegiance to the city.

The Lords' Alliance is a confederation of cities and towns up and down the Sword Coast and throughout the North, including (among others) Baldur's Gate, Mirabar, Mithral Hall, Neverwinter, and Silverymoon. Members of the alliance must come to one another's aid in times of need, and the organization uses field operatives (diplomats, spies, and assassins) to safeguard its interests.

Waterdeep is one of the most influential and invested members of the Lords' Alliance. Waterdeep's Open Lord, Laeral Silverhand, uses spies to keep tabs on adventurers in the city, rewarding those who place Waterdeep's interests above their own. Laeral employs adventurers as agents of the Lords' Alliance, among them Jalester Silvermane. See appendix B for more information on these NPCs.

Laeral spends most of her time in the Palace of Waterdeep. Within walking distance of the palace are well-maintained government residences set aside for the use of representatives of other Lords' Alliance cities and towns.

Lords' Alliance support comes in these ways:

- City Watch officials are notified that the characters are on "official business" for the Lords' Alliance and instructed to provide support whenever they can.
- Mirt (see appendix B), a Masked Lord who serves as Laeral Silverhand's advisor, invites the adventurers to dinner at his dilapidated mansion as a pretense for sharing rumors and imparting pearls of wisdom.
- The characters are granted a brief audience with Laeral Silverhand (see appendix B).

ORDER OF THE GAUNTLET

Any non-evil character can join the Order of the Gauntlet in Waterdeep. Clerics, monks, and paladins are especially welcome, particularly if they worship Helm, Torm, or Tyr.

The order's mission is to seek out and destroy evil before it gains a foothold. The surge of violence in Waterdeep spurs members of the order to find adventurers who can help return peace to the city.

An individual can be a member of the faction and also a member of the clergy or a knight pledged to a specific god or temple. Members of the order act alone or in small groups. Some are Waterdavian natives; others hail from distant settlements and have come to the city on temple business.

Order of the Gauntlet support comes in these ways:

- If the adventurers require healing or other magic, a member of the order can facilitate meetings with local priests who worship non-evil deities.
- If the adventurers get in trouble with the law, a member of the order puts in a good word for them and tends to their affairs while they're incarcerated.
- **Hlam** (see appendix B) might show up and help the characters in an impending battle.

XANATHAR GUILD

Anyone can join the Xanathar Guild, which, despite its name, doesn't have official guild status in Waterdeep. Before membership is granted, however, an applicant must pass a test that always involves the perpetration of a serious crime. Possibilities include murdering a guild member who has failed Xanathar in some fashion, kidnapping a Waterdavian citizen, collecting a ransom, robbing a hire-coach, or looting a warehouse.

Among low-ranking guild members, rampant speculation goes on about the true nature of Xanathar. Few have any inkling that their boss is a beholder, and fewer still have seen or spoken to the eye tyrant.

Given that the faction is fundamentally evil, advancement is based on one's wiles or one's ability to dispose of rivals. Competition within the organization is fierce and often deadly. Evil characters can thrive in this environment, but the risks are seldom worth the reward.

Xanathar Guild support comes in these ways:

- Any member given an assignment might receive a monstrous bodyguard or assistant (such as a bugbear, a kenku, or a wererat), who has secret instructions to kill the guild member if they fail to complete the assignment as ordered.
- The guild grants access to secret tunnels and safe houses (hidden cellars) underneath Waterdeep.
- Xanathar might send a **gazer** (see appendix B) to help (and spy on) an up-and-coming guild member.

ZHENTARIM

The Black Network has an open recruitment policy. Anyone can join. Tenacity and loyalty are highly valued (but not essential) traits in new members.

The Zhentarim is a shadow organization that trades mercenaries and goods (including weapons) for profit. It has long sought to gain political influence in Waterdeep, but the strength of the city's Masked Lords, nobility, and professional guilds makes that difficult.

The Zhentarim in Waterdeep is a fractured organization. Those who support Manshoon want to destroy Xanathar and seize political and economic control of the city. Those who oppose Manshoon want to expose and destroy him before they are themselves apprehended or driven out of the city by the local authorities.

Adventurers can't join Manshoon's cause, but they can join and receive aid from the Zhents who are opposed to him. The leaders of this branch of the Black Network are retired adventurers who have become business entrepreneurs. Their adventuring party was called the Doom Raiders because their specialty was plundering lich lairs (which are called "dooms"). They are desperately trying to gain a legitimate economic foothold in Waterdeep, which requires making alliances with local guilds and nobles. Manshoon's war against the Xanathar Guild has thrown their plans into upheaval.

The Doom Raiders (described in appendix B) consider themselves the true Zhentarim of Waterdeep. The group's leaders are Davil Starsong (Master of Opportunities and Negotiations), Istrid Horn (Master of Trade and Coin), Skeemo Weirdbottle (Master of Magic), Tashlyn Yafeera (Master of Arms and Mercenaries), and Ziraj the Hunter (Master of Assassination).

Zhentarim support comes in these ways:

- Davil can arrange meetings with influential nobles and members of city guilds.
- Adventurers can procure discounted potions and poisons from Skeemo's shop, Weirdbottle's Concoctions, which is located in the Trades Ward.
- Tashlyn offers affordable mercenaries, either **thugs** costing 2 sp per day each or **veterans** costing 2 gp per day each.
- Istrid offers loans of up to 2,500 gp with an interest rate of 10 percent per tenday.
- Adventurers can hire Ziraj to assassinate someone, in return for some undisclosed favor to be called in later.

THE INN OF THE YAWNING PORTAL

The Yawning Portal attracts adventurers from every corner of the Forgotten Realms and the D&D multiverse. Not sure who a numbered character is? Go to page 224 for the answer key.

THE YAWNING PORTAL

The Yawning Portal is a famous inn and tavern located in the Castle Ward of Waterdeep. Adventurers can meet all sorts of colorful characters here.

The place is a stone building with a slate roof and several chimneys. Most of the ground floor is taken up by the tavern's common room, which contains a 40-foot-diameter open well (actually the outer shell of a sunken stone tower) that descends 140 feet to the first level of Undermountain, the sprawling dungeon under Waterdeep. A rope-and-pulley mechanism is used to lower adventurers into the well and hoist them out. More information about this entrance to Undermountain can be found in *Waterdeep: Dungeon of the Mad Mage*.

The upper floors of the Yawning Portal contain comfortable, nicely appointed rooms for guests.

Durnan, the proprietor, charges standard prices for food, drink, and lodging (see chapter 5 of the *Player's Handbook* for costs).

FAMILIAR FACES

Give the Yawning Portal Familiar Faces handout in appendix C to the players, and allow each of them to select one NPC as a friendly acquaintance—someone the player's character knows and trusts. More than one player can select the same NPC. The information below should be withheld from the players until their characters learn it.

DURNAN
N male Illuskan human innkeeper

The proprietor of the Yawning Portal is a retired adventurer and a man of few words. **Durnan** (see appendix B) bluntly warns adventurers of lower than 5th level that entering Undermountain "isn't a good idea." He keeps a magic greatsword hidden behind the bar just in case something monstrous crawls up out of the entry well.

"BONNIE"
N doppelganger disguised as Tethyrian human barmaid

This **doppelganger** posing as a friendly barmaid is the leader of a gang of five doppelgangers that arrived in Waterdeep over a year ago. To help the gang make ends meet, she works for Durnan as a barmaid. Mattrim Mereg (see below) knows her secret.

MATTRIM "THREESTRINGS" MEREG
LG male Illuskan human bard

This socially awkward **bard** (see appendix B) performs at the Yawning Portal and is a better musician than he pretends to be. He's called "Threestrings" because he plays a lute that has only three strings remaining. His secret is that he's a Harper spy, and he's far more eloquent and composed than he lets on. He lives at the inn, where he spends his afternoons and evenings spying on Zhentarim agents and gathering information on other potential troublemakers. He recently befriended Bonnie and wants to help her doppelganger gang settle into the city.

JALESTER SILVERMANE
LG male Chondathan human fighter

Jalester Silvermane (see appendix B) is an agent of the Lords' Alliance who reports directly to Laeral Silverhand. The Open Lord of Waterdeep has asked him to spy on adventurers who might, through their actions, aid or imperil the city and its citizens. Since the Yawning Portal attracts adventurers of all sorts, Jalester spends a lot of time here, usually seated by himself in a quiet corner. Durnan knows that Jalester works for Laeral and leaves the young man alone.

Jalester is often distracted by thoughts of Faerrel Dunblade, his boyfriend, who was killed in a street fight last year. When not engaged in alliance business, Jalester is lonely and looking for love.

MELOON WARDRAGON
NE male Chondathan human adventurer under the control of an intellect devourer

Meloon Wardragon (see appendix B) comes across as a cheery, optimistic, warm-hearted man eager to fight alongside those he considers his friends. The Yawning Portal staff and many of the regular guests know that Meloon is a skilled fighter with ties to Force Grey.

An **intellect devourer** in league with Xanathar ate Meloon's brain several months ago. Now under the monster's control, Meloon actively discourages adventurers from exploring Undermountain and urges them to focus on conflicts in the city instead. He also hunts down and kills Zhentarim operatives for his secret beholder master. He has his eye on Davil Starsong (see appendix B) but won't kill the elf in plain view of witnesses.

OBAYA UDAY
NG female Chultan human priest of Waukeen

Obaya, a **priest**, has traveled from Chult to sponsor expeditions into Undermountain, with the goal of bringing its magical treasures back to her employer, the merchant prince Wakanga O'tamu of Port Nyanzaru. She discourages low-level adventurers from exploring Undermountain but is happy to help them with her magic until they gain enough experience to be useful to her.

If you plan to run *Waterdeep: Dungeon of the Mad Mage* after this adventure, Obaya can take on a more prominent role as an advisor and a source of quests.

YAGRA STONEFIST
N female half-orc thug-for-hire

Yagra is a Black Network mercenary who gets paid to protect a Zhent negotiator named Davil Starsong (see appendix B for more information on him). Yagra finds the job boring and likes to pass the time by challenging adventurers to arm wrestle. (Resolve such contests using contested Strength checks.) If the characters express their opposition to the Xanathar Guild, Yagra might urge them to speak to Davil about joining forces with the Zhentarim to destroy the beholder crime lord.

Yagra is a half-orc **thug**. When reduced to 0 hit points, she drops to 1 hit point instead (but can't do this again until she finishes a long rest). She has darkvision out to a range of 60 feet. She speaks Common and Orc.

Chapter 1: A Friend in Need

A BAR BRAWL IN THE YAWNING PORTAL PROVES that nowhere is safe from the gang war between the Zhentarim and the Xanathar Guild. In this atmosphere of danger, the characters are offered a quest by Volothamp Geddarm. Volo promises a reward if they can rescue his missing friend, Floon Blagmaar, who he fears has been caught up in the conflict. Volo's quest is a straightforward introduction to the streets of Waterdeep, providing the characters with an excuse to explore the city.

In their hunt for Volo's friend, the characters might make allies and enemies who can resurface throughout the adventure. Following the completion of Volo's quest, the characters gain a home base with an address in Trollskull Alley, in Waterdeep's North Ward. From their new base, the characters can plot their own course, whether it involves interacting with Waterdeep's people, joining one of the city's many factions, or simply poking around for danger.

Where to Start

This adventure assumes that the characters have already formed a party and are presently in the Yawning Portal, perhaps knocking back a pint of Shadowdark ale and wolfing down a plate of quipper and chips. Alternatively, you can begin this adventure as the characters first enter the raucous tavern, or by having them all meet for the first time as Volo hands them their initial quest.

Tavern Brawl

As the characters are relaxing in the taproom of the Yawning Portal, a fistfight breaks out. Read the following to set the scene:

> You sit around a sturdy wooden table lit by a brightly burning candle and littered with plates cleared of food and half-drained tankards. The sounds of gamblers yelling and drunken adventurers singing bawdy songs nearly drown out the off-key strumming of a young bard three tables over.
>
> Then all the noise is eclipsed by a shout: "Ya pig! Like killin' me mates, does ya?" Then a seven-foot-tall half-orc is hit by a wild, swinging punch from a male human whose shaved head is covered with eye-shaped tattoos. Four other humans stand behind him, ready to jump into the fray. The half-orc cracks her knuckles, roars, and leaps at the tattooed figure—but before you can see if blood is drawn, a crowd of spectators clusters around the brawl. What do you do?

The human combatants are five members of the Xanathar Guild (CE human **bandits**). The one with the eye-shaped tattoos on his bald pate is their leader, Krentz. Their foe, Yagra Strongfist, is a half-orc employed by the Zhentarim (see the Yawning Portal Friendly Faces handout in appendix C). Yagra fights for her pride.

Getting Involved

If the characters choose to join the fray, have everyone roll initiative. But the fight is almost over by the time they push through the rowdy spectators. Krentz has only 3 hit points remaining and is trying to escape from underneath Yagra, but the four other Xanathar Guild members are poised to tackle her.

Pulling Yagra away from Krentz requires a successful Strength check contested by Yagra's Strength check. Yagra thanks the characters if they help her, but is disappointed that they interfered in the fight.

Remember how the characters deal with Krentz in this scene. If he survives, the characters might meet him again in one of the Xanathar Guild's sewer hideouts (see area Q5, page 28).

Hanging Back

If the characters don't interfere in the brawl, Yagra knocks Krentz out cold but is then beaten unconscious by his companions. Durnan, the proprietor of the Yawning Portal, points toward the door. "Out!" he snarls, and the Xanathar Guild members flee carrying Krentz's unconscious form.

Troll and Friends

In the third round of the brawl, trouble arises from out of the gaping well in the middle of the Yawning Portal's taproom:

> Shouts of alarm suddenly ring out as a hulking creature climbs up out of the shaft in the middle of the taproom—a monster with warty green skin, a tangled nest of wiry black hair, a long, carrot-shaped nose, and bloodshot eyes. As it bares its yellow teeth and howls, you can see that a half-dozen bat-like creatures are attached to its body, with three more circling above it like flies. Everyone in the tavern reacts in fear except for the barkeep, Durnan, who shouts, "Troll!"

The **troll**, which currently has 44 hit points, has crawled up from the first level of Undermountain to feed on tasty humanoid flesh, bringing nine **stirges** with it. Once in the taproom, the troll rises to its full height of 9 feet and rolls initiative. The stirges also roll initiative, but only the three flying above the troll pose a threat. The remaining stirges are bloated, having drained copious amounts of the troll's blood, and fly back down the shaft to digest their meal. As the troll regenerates, the effects of its blood loss become less apparent.

Most tavern patrons and staffers flee or take cover at the sight of the troll. The stirges attack the nearest characters as **Durnan** (see appendix B) draws his greatsword, springs over the bar, and confronts the monster himself. As he attacks, he calls on the characters to focus on slaying the stirges and then douse the troll with lamp oil and set it on fire when it falls. Yagra joins the fight if she's conscious. To any characters who help defeat the troll, Durnan says matter-of-factly, "You fought well."

If any of the characters are reduced to 0 hit points during the fight, employees of the Yawning Portal step forward to stabilize them.

Meeting Volo

Once the troll and the stirges are dealt with, Volo pushes against the tide of patrons staying clear of the monster to greet the characters, lavishing praise on them for their bravery (whether justified or not): "You be adventurers, am I right? I could use your help. Let's find a table to talk, shall we?"

Volothamp Geddarm is known to most Waterdavians as a braggart and a notorious embellisher of facts. For all his faults, though, Volo is a soft-hearted sort who cares for nothing as much as his friends. At present, he is grievously concerned for the well-being of one of them. He begins his request with an air of charm and mystery, but it quickly devolves into tearful sincerity.

> The figure who approached you strokes his mustache, adjusts his floppy hat, and tightens his scarf. "Volothamp Geddarm, chronicler, wizard, and celebrity, at your service. I trust you've noted the violence in our fair city these past tendays. I haven't seen so much blood since my last visit to Baldur's Gate! But now I fear I have misplaced a friend amid this odious malevolence.
>
> "My friend's name is Floon Blagmaar. He's got more beauty than brains, and I worry he took a bad way home a couple nights ago and was kidnapped—or worse. If you agree to track him down with all due haste, I can offer you ten dragons apiece now, and I can give you each ten times that when you find Floon. May I prevail upon you in my hour of need?"

Volo gives each character a small pouch containing 10 gp simply for accepting his quest. Characters who want to discover his intentions must make a DC 10 Wisdom (Insight) check. On a success, a character discerns that Volo is honest but might be stretching the truth about how much he can pay. (Currently low on cash, Volo is awaiting royalty payments from *Volo's Guide to Monsters*. To make more coin, he began work on a new book, *Volo's Guide to Spirits and Specters*. As it happens, his knowledge of spirits mostly concerns the alcoholic variety, and the writing has not been going well.) If pressed, Volo urges the characters to trust him, and promises he'll have the rest of the reward, 100 gp per character, ready to deliver once Floon is returned to him alive.

Volo describes Floon as a handsome human male in his early thirties with wavy red-blond hair. He was dressed in princely garb when Volo last saw him. Two nights ago, before Floon disappeared, he and Volo were drinking and merrymaking at the Skewered Dragon, a dark, bawdy tavern in the Dock Ward. Volo recommends that the characters start their search there.

What Happened That Night?

Volo is embarrassed to admit he might have gotten his friend Floon in trouble, and he resists providing all the details of what happened the night Floon disappeared.

Beset by writer's block, Volo met Floon Blagmaar for drinks at the Skewered Dragon two nights ago. They drank and gambled for a few hours, and then Volo left. That's the last he saw of Floon.

Unbeknownst to Volo, not long after he departed, a drunken Floon met another acquaintance, Lord Renaer Neverember, at the tavern. The two left together, with Renaer offering to walk Floon home. Five Zhentarim thugs working for Urstul Floxin (see appendix B) jumped both Floon and Renaer. They took them to a warehouse in the Dock Ward, so they could question Renaer—the son of Lord Dagult Neverember—about the whereabouts of the *Stone of Golorr* and his father's hidden cache of dragons. Before the interrogation could begin, members of the Xanathar Guild ambushed and killed the Zhent guards in the warehouse. The new arrivals mistook Floon for Renaer, knocked Floon unconscious, and dragged him away while Renaer hid and escaped their notice.

Floon was taken to a Xanathar Guild hideout in the sewers. A small gang of kenku was left behind at the Zhentarim warehouse to kill any other Zhents who might show up at the warehouse. The presence of the kenku has prevented Renaer from trying to leave the warehouse.

Finding Floon

Volo last saw Floon outside the Skewered Dragon, a dubious (and Zhentarim-owned) tavern between Net Street and Fillet Lane in the Dock Ward. The following encounters kick off the characters' investigation.

En route to the tavern, "Blood in the Streets" is a chance for characters to see the City Watch in action. If the characters decide to look around, "Searching the Dock Ward" gives them a feel for their surroundings, and they might discover a strange place, "Old Xoblob Shop," that warrants further exploration. Once they arrive at their destination, "The Skewered Dragon" is an opportunity for the characters to get information from the patrons, which leads them to "Candle Lane," where their quest continues.

Blood in the Streets

As the characters travel through the Dock Ward, they come upon the aftermath of a bloody clash between the Xanathar Guild and the Zhentarim:

> As you turn a corner, you find yourselves on a street that has been cordoned off by the City Watch. Lying on the cobblestones are a half-dozen corpses, seemingly the victims of some terrible skirmish. Watch officers have disarmed and arrested three blood-drenched humans and are in the midst of questioning witnesses. One of the officers sees you. "Get on," she says. "Nothing to see here."

The skirmish that occurred here has nothing to do with Floon's disappearance but represents an escalation in the conflict between the Zhentarim and the Xanathar Guild. A dozen **guards** of the City Watch have arrested three **bandits** and are questioning witnesses while waiting for wagons to take away the criminals and the corpses. The survivors of the skirmish have been stripped of their weapons and forced to kneel with their hands on their heads. All three, loyal Zhentarim agents (employed by Urstul Floxin; see appendix B), are likely to be accused of murder. They coldly catch the eye of anyone who passes by, but the City Watch won't let the characters anywhere near the prisoners.

Searching the Dock Ward

The Dock Ward is unsafe. You can set the mood by reading the following to the players:

> Tall, densely packed tenements leave most of the neighborhood in shadow at ground level. Most of the streetlamps have had their glass smashed and their candles stolen, and the smells of salt air and excrement linger as you pass by rows of run-down buildings.

On the corner of Zastrow Street and Fillet Lane is a shop with a peculiar window display:

> One nearby shop stands out from the others. It has a deep purple facade, and in its window hangs a stuffed beholder. Above the door hangs a sign whose elaborate letters spell out "Old Xoblob Shop."

If the characters check out the shop, continue with "Old Xoblob Shop." If they don't, they find the tavern without further incident; see "The Skewered Dragon" below.

Old Xoblob Shop

When the characters enter, they quickly get a sense of the strangeness of the place:

> A cloud of lavender-scented purple smoke trails out of the shop's door as you peer inside. Every wall is painted purple, and every dusty knickknack on the shelves is dyed a deep violet. The hairless old gnome sitting cross-legged on the counter wears plum-colored robes. His cheeks are decorated with nine purple face-painted eyes.
>
> The gnome lowers a pipe and exhales a cloud of lavender smoke before raising a hand. "Hail and well met! Come browse the shelves of the most curious curiosity shop in the world!"

The shop is named after the stuffed beholder in the window—a fixture that is actually a magical sensor, through which Xanathar can peer whenever it wishes.

The shopkeeper is a wizened **deep gnome** who spies for the Xanathar Guild. A few years ago, he survived the detonation of a gas spore in Undermountain and inherited some stray beholder memories. Driven by a compulsion to carve out his own domain, the gnome settled in Waterdeep, bought the Old Xoblob Shop from its previous owner, and tried renaming it after himself, yet everyone kept calling it the Old Xoblob Shop. He therefore restored the old name and changed his name to Xoblob. "No relation to the eye tyrant hanging in the window!" he says.

Trinkets. The gnome sells an assortment of trinkets. As the characters search the shelves, roll on the Trinkets table in chapter 5 of the *Player's Handbook* to determine what catches their eye. Xoblob sells any trinket for 1d6 gp.

Floon's Fate. The gnome doesn't know Floon by name, but he recognizes his description. He is reluctant to share information, but offering him a new purple item or succeeding on a DC 13 Charisma (Intimidation or Persuasion) check loosens his tongue. He says that Floon and a well-dressed fellow of similar appearance and bearing (Renaer Neverember, though the gnome doesn't know his name and didn't recognize him) were jumped outside the shop by rough-looking men in black leather armor. Xoblob thinks there were five attackers, but none of them looked familiar. One of them had a black tattoo of a winged snake on his neck.

The Skewered Dragon

The Skewered Dragon faces an alley that runs between Net Street and Fillet Lane in the Dock Ward, not far from the Old Xoblob Shop. When the characters approach it, read:

> The Skewered Dragon looks like a ruin. Both of its front-facing windows are smashed, and a ship's anchor is lodged in the roof. Through the windows, you can see a group of haggard patrons drinking from huge tankards.

Floon has not been at the Skewered Dragon since the night of his disappearance, and the dive's dockworker patrons are loath to talk to strangers. A bribe or a successful DC 13 Charisma (Intimidation or Persuasion) check gets them to open up.

Floon's Fate. Several of the regulars remember seeing Volo and Floon drinking together a couple of nights ago. After Volo left, Floon stuck around long enough to meet with another friend: Renaer Neverember, the son of Waterdeep's previous Open Lord, Dagult Neverember. "Chip off the old block, that one!" sneers one patron. "Just another spoiled, rich noble who likes to rub our noses in it!" says another.

The two drank and played a few rounds of Three-Dragon Ante before leaving around midnight. Five men followed them out, and no one in the tavern knows what happened after that. The men who left shortly after Floon and Renaer haven't returned to the tavern since, but they're known to frequent a warehouse on Candle Lane. "Look for the snake symbol on the door," says one of the tavern regulars.

Candle Lane

The buildings on either side of Candle Lane are so tall and so tightly packed together that light touches the street only at highsun.

> Gloom envelops a narrow alley as dark as a dungeon—and as odorous as one, too. Nearly all the streetlamps have been smashed. The only light that pierces the darkness is a faint flickering from down the lane, like a distant candle.

The flickering comes from the one streetlamp still intact on Candle Lane, kept alight by a *continual flame* spell. A warehouse is directly across the street from the lamp, which illuminates a black winged snake (the symbol of the Zhentarim) painted above the door's handle. Characters who have ties to the Zhentarim recognize the symbol, while others can recall its significance with a successful DC 10 Intelligence check.

Zhentarim Hideout

The hideout on Castle Lane (see map 1.1) is a ramshackle two-story warehouse. The Black Network has other sanctuaries in run-down buildings like this one throughout Waterdeep (meaning that the floor plan of this locale can be reused for other Zhent hideouts).

The warehouse stands at the back of an outer yard behind a high fence. The gate on the fence isn't locked. The building's three points of entry—a front door, a large warehouse loading door, and a painted-over window—are locked. The front door has a sliding peephole that can be opened from the inside. Either of the doors or the window can be unlocked by a character who makes a successful DC 12 Dexterity check using thieves' tools, or can be forced open with a successful DC 10 Strength (Athletics) check.

Knocking at the doors or the window alerts a group of kenku inside that someone is coming. The kenku scramble to hide behind toppled furniture, making a ruckus that any character who has a passive Wisdom (Perception) score of 16 or higher can hear. These kenku are all that remain of the Xanathar Guild force that murdered almost everyone in the warehouse after the five Zhentarim thugs captured Renaer Neverember and Floon Blagmaar and brought them here. Floon was taken away, but Renaer succeeded in staying alive by hiding. Now, the young noble is trying to figure out how to slip past the kenku, who are lazily searching the warehouse for loot while waiting to see if any more Zhents show up.

Z1. Main Room

The Black Network's main business is recruiting, training, and equipping sellswords. Crates packed with weapons, rations, boots, black uniforms, and other gear fill the warehouse.

When the characters try to enter, determine if the four **kenku** inside are aware of their presence before reading the boxed text.

A character with thieves' tools can pick the lock on a door or the window with a successful DC 10 Dexterity check. Characters who enter quietly can try to catch the kenku by surprise. If the characters knock before entering or announce their arrival in some other way, the kenku hide as described above.

> Tables and chairs have been carelessly tossed across the floor. The corpses of a dozen men lie along the walls, their rapiers and daggers lying nearby. On the north side of the area, stairs rise to an open level above.

If the kenku aren't hidden, add:

> Four short, avian creatures with long beaks and black feathers look over in surprise from where they stand in the middle of the warehouse. Each wears a hooded cloak and wields a shortsword.

The corpses belong to five human Zhentarim sellswords (the same ones who kidnapped Floon and Renaer) and seven human Xanathar Guild thugs, all of them clad in leather armor. Each Zhent has a black tattoo of a winged snake on his neck or forearm, and one of the Xanathar Guild members has a black tattoo on the palm of his right hand that looks like a circle with ten spokes radiating out from its circumference (the symbol of Xanathar).

The kenku fight until two of them are incapacitated or killed, whereupon the survivors try to flee. A successful DC 10 Charisma (Intimidation) check forces captured kenku to divulge what they know.

What the Kenku Know

When kenku speak, they mimic sounds and voices they have heard before. Under interrogation, they repeat the following phrases:

- In a deep voice with an orcish accent: "Xanathar sends its regards."
- In a thin, nasally voice: "Tie up the pretty boy in the back room!" and "Follow the yellow signs in the sewers." (This remark refers to tunnels in the sewers that are marked with Xanathar's symbol where they lead to the Xanathar Guild hideout.)
- In a scratchy voice: "No time to loot the place. Just get him to the boss."

Z2. Storage Closet

The door to this back room hangs loosely on broken hinges. The cramped chamber beyond smells strongly of sour fish and vinegar. It is filled with discarded ropes, canvas tarpaulins, and splintered wood from smashed barrels. Renaer Neverember (see appendix B) is hiding here, having slipped free of his rope bonds. The characters can hear his ragged breathing coming from under a tarpaulin at the north end of the room.

Roleplaying Renaer

Renaer is unarmed. Marred by grime and the lingering stench of rancid pickled herring, he speaks with grace and articulation, as befits his noble upbringing. His trust is easily gained but impossible to restore once broken.

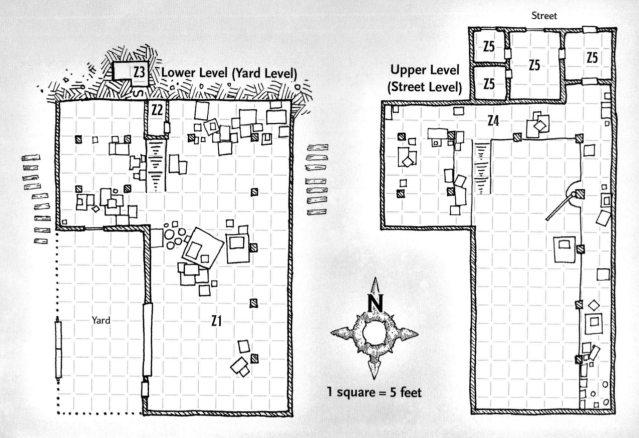

Map 1.1: Zhentarim Hideout (Dock Ward)

On the night of the abduction, Renaer was concerned that Floon was too intoxicated to find his way home by himself and offered to escort him. The two were jumped by five thugs as they left Fillet Lane and headed north on Zastrow Street.

Renaer feels guilty that Floon was taken, since he believes (correctly) that they mistook Floon for him. If the characters ask Renaer to join their search for Floon, he agrees to do so, arming himself with a dagger and a rapier scavenged from the dead Zhents in the warehouse.

If a character asks Renaer why the Zhents kidnapped him, he gives the following truthful reply:

> "The Zhentarim thinks that my father embezzled a large amount of gold while he was Open Lord, and that he hid the dragons somewhere in the city. They think they can find it by using an artifact called the *Stone of Golorr*, which was in the hands of the Xanathar Guild until recently. Apparently, someone stole it. The Zhents thought I knew something about all of this, but I don't. My father and I haven't spoken in years."

Z3. SECRET ROOM

This room is hidden behind a secret door that can be found with a successful DC 15 Wisdom (Perception) check. When the secret door is opened, the characters can hear the faint sound of a bell ringing in the offices above them (area Z5).

TREASURE

The Zhents have stashed two wooden crates here. The first, stolen from the docks, contains four wood-framed paintings wrapped in leather. The paintings depict the cities of Luskan, Neverwinter, Silverymoon, and Baldur's Gate and are worth 75 gp each.

The second crate, stolen from a caravan on the High Road, contains fifteen 10-pound silver trade bars, all black from corrosion but still worth 50 gp each.

Z4. BALCONY

The open second level is stacked with crates where it overlooks the main warehouse. Characters who search through the crates find all sorts of junk, including moth-eaten bolts of cloth, bottles of spoiled olive oil, and hundreds of pairs of wooden-soled sandals that were all the rage last summer but are now out of fashion. None of this junk is valuable.

Z5. OFFICES

The upper floor contains a suite of offices that get little use by the Zhents. The rooms have desks, chairs, and bare shelves covered with dust and draped in cobwebs. Harmless **rats** skitter about.

Mounted above each office door is a steel alarm bell. The bells are connected by wires to the secret door in area Z3, and they ring loudly when that door is opened.

TREASURE

A character who searches the offices finds an unused *paper bird* (see appendix A).

The Watch Arrives

Shortly after the characters find Renaer, a captain of the City Watch named Hyustus Staget (LG male Illuskan human **veteran**) leads a dozen **veterans** to the warehouse. Having received a report of suspicious activity, they barge in and try to prevent anyone from leaving. Kenku that are still alive and present are taken into custody, and it doesn't take long for the City Watch to conclude that the dead men are members of the Zhentarim and the Xanathar Guild, since violent encounters between the two factions are becoming ever more frequent. While his constables search the warehouse, Captain Staget questions the characters.

Captain Staget is an uptight man who helps keep the peace in the Dock Ward. Every shopkeeper, guild member, innkeeper, and tavern keeper in the Dock Ward knows him, and most respect him regardless of their opinions of the City Watch in general. Staget doesn't believe in rumors or gossip, he doesn't drink, and he doesn't let anger get the better of him. His job is to curb the violence in the Dock Ward, but he has been dragging his heels. After all, he reasons, if the Xanathar Guild and the Zhentarim want to destroy each other, why not let them?

Staget once had the warehouse under surveillance, but elected to pull the detail to bolster patrols throughout the Dock Ward—a decision he now regrets. That surveillance was part of an attempt to catch a known Zhent instigator named Urstul Floxin, a "big fish" rumored to be responsible for much of the recent strife. Staget doesn't share this information with strangers.

Staget and Renaer recognize each other, though they aren't well acquainted. The involvement of a Neverember noble prompts the captain to be on his best behavior. He is prepared to overlook any crimes committed by the characters as long as Renaer is with them, but he gives them a folded sheet of parchment with the Code Legal written on it and encourages them to read it. (Give the players a copy of the Code Legal handout in appendix C, if you haven't done so already.)

If the characters ask for the Watch's help in locating Floon, Staget makes it clear that he won't send a force into the sewers in search of someone who might well be a Zhent or Xanathar Guild spy. If they appear intent on involving themselves further in the conflict between the Zhentarim and the Xanathar Guild, Staget imparts some free advice before letting them go:

- "Best not to meddle in criminal matters. Leave this dirty business to the City Watch."
- "Not all City Watch officers are as nice as me."
- "Keep the blood off the streets, okay?" (This is a common saying among City Watch officials, who care more about what happens in the city above than what happens in the sewers below.)

Characters who stir up trouble in the Dock Ward are likely to run into Captain Staget again. Though he is secretly pleased to have adventurers doing some of his work for him, he can't let them overshadow his own efforts to keep the peace without risking a reprimand from his superiors.

Tracking Floon

At this point, the characters likely know that Floon was kidnapped by Xanathar Guild members who mistook him for Renaer Neverember, and that he was taken to a hideout in the sewers. If the characters didn't learn from the kenku where Floon was taken, asking questions of the locals can reveal that many people saw him being dragged off. A successful DC 15 Intelligence (Investigation) check or 5 gp in bribes allows the characters to trace the kidnappers' path through back alleys to a circular metal cover inset in the pavement. The cover is easily lifted, revealing a ladder down into the sewers.

Navigating the Sewers

The sewers have no natural light. Characters without darkvision need light sources to see.

> A putrid stream flows along this sewer tunnel, which leads in two directions. In one direction, you see a tiny symbol drawn on the wall in yellow chalk: a palm-sized circle with ten equidistant spokes radiating out from its circumference.

The hideout of the Xanathar Guild operatives who snatched up Floon is deep in the city's labyrinthine sewers. At every location where characters must make a decision about which direction to go, a symbol scrawled in yellow chalk—a stylized representation of Xanathar—is marked next to the tunnel that leads in the right direction. The symbols are erased by members of the Xanathar Guild or the Dungsweepers' Guild every few days, but these markings have yet to be removed.

Gazer Guard

Before arriving at the Xanathar Guild hideout, the characters have an encounter in the sewers:

> After an hour of following signs through the tunnels, you come to a three-way intersection where a ladder leads up into a stone shaft capped by a circular metal cover. One of the familiar chalk symbols is marked on a wall nearby, and floating near the symbol is a spherical, grapefruit-sized creature with a bulging central eye and four stumpy eyestalks. It bares its teeth at you.

A hostile **gazer** (see appendix B) that is in league with Grum'shar, the local Xanathar Guild boss, guards this intersection. Once the characters defeat it, they can press on, following the corridor where the chalk symbol is located; they reach the hideout after following the correct tunnel for 5 minutes.

Ladder. Characters who climb the ladder and push open the metal cover find themselves in the cellar of the Spouting Fish, a tavern in the Dock Ward.

Xanathar Guild Hideout

The Xanathar Guild has hideouts throughout Water-deep's sewers. The floor plan of this locale (see map 1.2) can be reused for other hideouts.

The boss of this hideout is a half-orc named Grum'shar. When the characters arrive, Grum'shar is interrogating Floon Blagmaar in area Q7. His display of torture techniques is a ploy to impress his other guest: a mind flayer named Nihiloor (see appendix B).

All the doors in the hideout are unlocked. Grum'shar assumes that only those who have guild business will be able to find their way here.

Q1. Central Hub

The characters approach this area from the east, slog-ging through 1-foot-deep water and sewage.

> The main sewer tunnel expands into a circular hub with a pair of arrow slits carved into its outer walls, directly across from each other. Two passages continue on to the north and south. A stone door is set into the back wall of a stone ledge to the west.

If the characters talk loudly or otherwise make a lot of noise here, the goblin sentries in areas Q2a and Q2b awaken and shoot arrows at them through the arrow slits. The slits provide the goblins with three-quar-ters cover.

Secret Door

A secret door in the wall of the tunnel that leads south can be found with a successful DC 15 Wisdom (Percep-tion) check.

Q2. Watch Posts

Two **goblins** are stationed here, one in area Q2a and one in Q2b. Allies of the Xanathar Guild, they came here from Undermountain. The goblins rely on darkvision to see and are supposed to be watching area Q1, but both have dozed off. Characters who succeed on a DC 9 Dexterity (Stealth) check can sneak past the sleeping goblins without waking them.

Treasure

Each goblin carries 1d6 cp in a small pouch.

Q3. Messy Room

Rusty weapons and threadbare clothing litter the floor of this area, which serves as a coat room and armory. It contains nothing of value.

Q4. Empty Sleeping Area

This room contains six tattered, straw-stuffed mat-tresses and nothing of value. If the occupant or occu-pants of area Q5 have not been dealt with already, the characters hear the sounds of activity in that room through the thin wooden door that separates these two chambers.

Q5. Sleeping Area

This room contains six tattered, straw-stuffed mat-tresses and a hostile member of the Xanathar Guild, a **duergar** named Zemk. If Krentz (CE human **bandit**) escaped from the Yawning Portal after the tavern brawl that kicked off the adventure, he's here as well.

When the characters arrive, Zemk is using pieces of furniture to barricade the door to area Q6. If Krentz is here, he's trying to explain that Zemk's approach won't work, and is telling him to plug the gap at the bottom of the door with blankets. Neither of them notices intrud-ers right away unless the interlopers make a lot of noise.

Once combat starts, Zemk fights to the death. How Krentz reacts to the adventurers depends on how they treated him earlier. If they helped him, he gives them a chance to leave in peace, but he fights alongside Zemk if they refuse to withdraw. If the duergar is killed, Krentz flees if he can or surrenders if he must.

Neither Zemk nor Krentz carries any treasure. Both report to Grum'shar (see area Q7).

Q6. Lavatory

This room has a hole in the floor that opens into a cess-pit. A **gray ooze** has emerged from the pit and killed two goblins that were sent into the room to dispose of it. The goblins' bones float amid the ooze's gooey form, and their pitted weapons lie on the floor nearby. None of the gear is salvageable.

Q7. Boss Fight

> Threadbare curtains hang on the east wall of a long hall, in the middle of which a muscular half-orc in dingy robes stands with his foot on the chest of a male human with wavy red-blond hair. Fire burns around the orc's clenched fist, and his victim cries and squirms helplessly beneath him.
>
> Seated on a raised platform to the south is a nightmar-ish figure wearing black robes. It has large white eyes and rubbery purple skin, with four tentacles encircling its in-human mouth. It cradles and gently caresses what looks like a disembodied brain with feet.

The tentacled creature is Nihiloor (see appendix B), a **mind flayer** that is caressing an **intellect devourer**. Upon seeing the adventurers, Nihiloor rises from the stone chair, sets its pet down, and glides across the room, intending to leave through the double door in the west wall. The mind flayer expects Grum'shar and the intellect devourer to cover its escape.

Nihiloor carries a 3-inch-diameter stone orb carved to resemble an eyeball, similar to what one might see at the end of a beholder's eyestalk. This stone eye is the key to activating the magic portal in area Q11. The mind flayer uses it to return to Xanathar's lair (described in chapter 5). It uses *dominate monster* to control some-one who gets in its way and turns any such individuals against their allies.

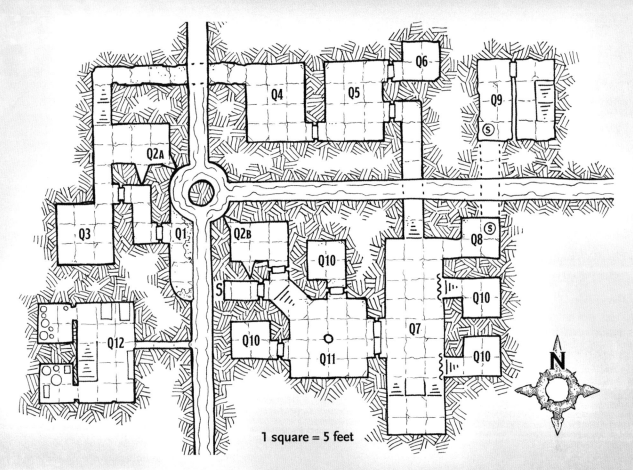

Map 1.2: Xanathar Guild Hideout (Southern Ward)

1 square = 5 feet

The half-orc is Grum'shar, a low-end Xanathar Guild boss. As soon as his minions retrieved who they thought was Renaer Neverember, the half-orc begged Nihiloor let him witness the interrogation of the captive, not realizing until after he did so that he had mistaken the prisoner's identity. Grum'shar attacks the characters in the hope of salvaging his reputation. He is an **apprentice wizard** (see appendix B), with these changes:

- Grum'shar is chaotic evil.
- He has these racial traits: When reduced to 0 hit points, he drops to 1 hit point instead (but can't do this again until he finishes a long rest). He has darkvision out to a range of 60 feet. He speaks Common and Orc.

ROLEPLAYING FLOON

As a result of Grum'shar's torture, Floon Blagmaar (see appendix B) has 1 hit point left. If he is healed by the characters, he is eternally grateful and shows his affection by hugging them. He stays close to them, trusting in their ability to protect him. If Renaer is with the party, he can shoulder the burden of protecting Floon.

TREASURE

In a satchel, Grum'shar carries his spellbook, which contains the following spells: *burning hands*, *disguise self*, *false life*, *shield*, *unseen servant*, and *witch bolt*.

Tucked behind the stone chair is a small, unlocked wooden chest containing two *potions of healing*, 16 gp, 82 sp, and 250 cp.

Q8. GETAWAY PASSAGE

This room looks empty, but a thorough search accompanied by a successful DC 10 Wisdom (Perception) check reveals a rough-hewn tunnel hidden beneath a loose flagstone. The low tunnel leads north to area Q9.

Q9. PRIVATE CELLAR

An innocent halfling family, the Peabodys, brews beer in this cellar, which lies beneath their home on Fishgut Alley in the Dock Ward. Their cellar contains brewing supplies and lots of worthless clutter.

The halflings haven't noticed the secret tunnel that leads to the Xanathar Guild hideout; it's concealed beneath a large flagstone that requires a Strength score of 10 or higher to be lifted.

DEVELOPMENT

If the characters ascend out of the cellar and enter the Peabodys' small house, the halflings are initially alarmed but can be easily calmed. Upon learning of the secret trapdoor, they vow to seal it up again but allow the characters to make use of it if the need arises.

Q10. SLEEPING QUARTERS

Straw pallets lie on the floor, and rusty manacles are bolted to the walls.

Q11. BACK DOOR

This hideout contains a secret route to Xanathar's lair.

> In the middle of this otherwise empty room is a stone pillar carved with a small symbol: a perfect circle with ten equidistant spokes radiating outward from its circumference. In the middle of this circle is a smaller circular indentation that bears a passing resemblance to a lidless eye.

If the stone eye in Nihiloor's possession is pressed into the circular indentation, an opaque black doorway magically opens in the south wall. The opening is 8 feet tall and 4 feet wide. Any creature that passes through it appears in area X22 of Xanathar's lair (see chapter 5). The door is a one-way portal, and it closes again 1 minute after the stone eye is removed from the pillar.

NOT-SO-SECRET DOOR

The secret door is plainly visible to anyone who approaches it from the east.

Q12. HOSTEL CELLAR

A narrow passage leads to the cellar of a halfling-owned hostel on Spices Street in the Dock Ward. Medium characters must squeeze to reach this area from the tunnel. The hostel is used as a base by the Shard Shunners, a gang of halfling wererats. They are aware of the Xanathar Guild hideout, and the two gangs are tenuous allies.

Roscoe Underbough, a Shard Shunner in hybrid form, guards the cellar. He hides in the northwest storeroom, ready to jump out and scare away anyone who heads for the stairs. Not eager to commit murder, Roscoe allows retreating characters to flee back to the sewers. He is a **wererat**, with these changes:

- Roscoe is Small and has 27 (6d6 + 6) hit points.
- He has these racial traits: He can move through the space of a Medium or larger creature. He has advantage on saving throws against being frightened. He speaks Common and Halfling, and he knows thieves' cant.

DEVELOPMENT

If the characters defeat Roscoe or slip past him, they can make their way up into the hostel, which caters to a mostly halfling clientele. With none of the other Shard Shunners currently present, the characters are greeted warmly by staff and patrons, who point them in the direction of the nearest bathhouse.

COMPLETING VOLO'S QUEST

Returning to the Yawning Portal with Floon Blagmaar in tow marks the end of this introductory quest. All that remains is for the characters to collect their reward.

REWARDS

Volo is drinking alone in the Yawning Portal while anxiously awaiting news of Floon's fate. He springs up and runs to embrace the characters and his friend as soon as he sees them.

A GOOD DEED

If the characters reunite Volo with Floon, Volo gives them a rather sheepish look as he explains their reward:

> "I confess that I have but few coins to spare. But never let it be said that Volo reneges on a promise. Allow me to present something much more valuable." He holds out a scroll tube. "The deed to a remarkable property here in Waterdeep! We'll need a magistrate to witness the transfer of ownership. I'll arrange a meeting with one after you've inspected the estate and deemed it satisfactory."

The tube contains a deed to Trollskull Manor, a historic building in the North Ward that the characters can claim as a home base. The deed has been notarized and appears legitimate (because it is). Volo recently bought the property because it is rumored to be haunted, and he was hoping that investigating it might yield a chapter for his next book, *Volo's Guide to Spirits and Specters*.

If the characters accept their reward, Volo sets up a meeting with a tiefling magistrate named Kylynne Silmerhelve. The brief session takes place at a courthouse in the Castle Ward at highsun. Magistrate Silmerhelve witnesses the transfer of the deed, rendering the new ownership official, with the impatience of one who has more important matters to attend to. She also collects an estate transfer tax of 25 gp, which is normally paid by the new owners. If the characters can't afford this fee or don't want to pay it and they have befriended Renaer Neverember, he makes sure that Volo has a pouch of coins to cover the expense.

FINE FRIENDS

Volo, Floon, and Renaer all express their gratitude through camaraderie. If the characters need to call upon their new friends for an occasional favor, any of them are happy to oblige. Floon has little to offer the characters, but friendship with Volo and Renaer has its perks.

Volo knows the best places to eat and find merriment. He can also give characters a tour of Waterdeep. If the characters accept his offer, share the information in chapter 9, "Volo's Waterdeep Enchiridion," with the players.

Although Renaer is estranged from his rich and powerful father, he still has friends in high places, including Harpers who can come to the characters' rescue if they need it. If the characters are looking for an audience with influential persons in Waterdeep, Renaer can set up meetings with Mirt, Remallia Haventree (see appendix B for both), or just about any other Waterdavian noble, if he thinks the characters will comport themselves well.

LEVEL ADVANCEMENT

If you're using milestone level advancement instead of tracking experience points, the characters advance from 1st to 2nd level when they return to Volo after having explored the Xanathar Guild hideout.

Chapter 2: Trollskull Alley

ROLLSKULL ALLEY IS FILLED WITH PEOPLE who can shape the characters' day-to-day lives in Waterdeep. The characters will likely return to Trollskull Alley many times during the adventure and get to know their neighbors as time passes.

The locations described below are keyed to the map of Trollskull Alley (map 2.1, page 33). Buildings not specifically identified on the map are rowhouses that serve as private residences for upper-middle class Waterdavians who can afford housekeepers, groundskeepers, and nannies.

T1. Trollskull Manor

See appendix C for a handout showing the floor plan of this building. Give a copy of this handout to your players as their characters begin to explore Trollskull Manor.

Four stories tall and boasting balconies, a turret, and five chimneys, the abandoned building is one of the grandest in Trollskull Alley. Characters can refurnish, rebuild, rename, and otherwise personalize their new stronghold to their hearts' content.

Tavern Rooms

When the characters first arrive, the tavern's taproom is filled with broken furniture, tarnished silverware, casks of wine that have turned to vinegar, and worthless detritus. The tavern's other rooms are all empty, except for cobwebs, dust, and harmless rats.

Spirit on Tap

The former tavern is haunted by the poltergeist (**specter**) of the tavern's previous barkeeper, a half-elf named Lif. Maintaining the tavern was his life's work, and he couldn't abandon the place in death.

The poltergeist understands Common and Elvish, but it can't speak. It invisibly causes mischief at the expense of the new owners by smashing plates, breaking beer barrels, and so forth. If the characters don't take the hint, it writes not-so-subtle warnings (such as "Closing time!" and "Last call!") on dusty floors and grimy windows. To truly claim the tavern as their own, the characters must either appease the poltergeist or destroy it.

Appeasing Lif. If the characters work to repair and renovate the tavern with the goal of opening it to the public again, the poltergeist begins to accept them as the new owners and gradually becomes quite accommodating: pulling out a chair when a character wants to sit down, pouring a beer and delivering it to a character, taking coats when folks come in from the rain, and so forth. Once the business is up and running, Lif can also perform other helpful functions, such as locking doors, sweeping floors, and so forth.

Destroying Lif. Lif's poltergeist is destroyed if its hit points are reduced to 0. If attacked, it flees to the uppermost level of the turret when reduced to half its hit points. From there it fights to the bitter end.

T2. The Bent Nail

A small wooden sign above this shop's main door is bare except for a large, bent nail sticking out of it. The front room contains displays of ornate wooden furniture, as well as a selection of bows and crossbows. The wall behind the counter is lined with rows of finely carved wooden canes, quarterstaffs, and shields.

Talisolvanar "Tally" Fellbranch, the owner and chief artisan of the Bent Nail, is a male half-elf carpenter and woodcarver. He is a **commoner**, with these changes:

- Tally is chaotic good.
- He has these racial traits: He has advantage on saving throws against being charmed, and magic can't put him to sleep. He has darkvision out to a range of 60 feet. He speaks Common and Elvish.

Services

Tally sells wooden weapons and shields at normal cost. He also crafts and sells furniture and wood sculptures.

T3. Steam and Steel

During daylight hours, smoke and steam billow from the many windows around this indoor forge where metal weapons, armor, and tools are made. The forge is owned and operated by a married couple: a fire genasi named Embric and a water genasi named Avi. Both are members of the Most Careful Order of Skilled Smiths and Metalforgers. As an armorer, Avi also belongs to the Splendid Order of Armorers, Locksmiths, and Finesmiths.

Embric tends the forge and is an expert weaponsmith. He claims descent from the efreet of Calimshan and is prone to extreme mood swings. He has the statistics of a **bandit captain**, with these changes:

- Embric is neutral good.
- He has these racial traits: He can cast *produce flame* at will. (Constitution is his spellcasting ability, and he has a +4 bonus to hit with spell attacks.) He has darkvision out to a range of 60 feet and resistance to fire damage. He speaks Common and Primordial.

Avi worships Eldath, god of peace, and uses his magic to quench hot steel. He is an expert armorsmith. Avi is laid back and speaks plainly. He has the statistics of a **priest**, with these changes:

- Avi is neutral good.
- He has these racial traits: At will, he can control the flow and shape of water in a 5-foot cube, or cause the water to freeze for up to 1 hour. He has a swimming speed of 30 feet, and he can breathe air and water. He has resistance to acid damage. He speaks Common and Primordial.

Services

The genasi couple sells all metal weapons, armor, and shields listed in chapter 5 of the *Player's Handbook* at normal cost.

T4. Corellon's Crown

Fala Lefaliir, an herbalist and a member of the Guild of Apothecaries and Physicians, operates out of this stately, three-story town house, the third floor of which has been converted into a greenhouse. Its translucent glass walls allow anyone on the street to see the rainbow of flowers blossoming within.

Fala Lefaliir is an outgoing wood elf with long, braided hair. Like the elven god Corellon Larethian, Fala is neither male nor female. If referred to as "he" or "she," Fala gently requests to be addressed by name or as "they." Fala is friends with a member of the Zhentarim named Ziraj, who saved Fala's life. He visits Fala from time to time, and Fala has set aside a room for him on the second floor.

Fala is a **druid**, with these changes:

- Fala is chaotic good.
- Fala has these racial traits: Fala has advantage on saving throws against being charmed, and magic can't put Fala to sleep. Fala has a walking speed of 35 feet and darkvision out to a range of 60 feet. Fala speaks Common, Druidic, and Elvish.

Services

In addition to nonmagical herbal remedies, Fala sells potions of the types listed in the Fala's Potions table. Fala keeps 1d6 vials of each potion in locked cabinets behind the shop counter.

Fala's Potions

Potion	Cost
Potion of animal friendship	125 gp
Potion of climbing	50 gp
Potion of greater healing	250 gp
Potion of healing	50 gp
Potion of water breathing	250 gp

T5. Tiger's Eye

This private detective's business is unremarkable on the outside, its only distinguishing mark an orange-and-black sign featuring a cat's eyes. Inside is a regal apartment dimly lit by flickering oil lamps. The door is locked, and visitors must knock or ring the bell before being let in.

They are met by Vincent Trench, a human detective and the owner of the Tiger's Eye. He speaks concisely, dresses in a sharp suit, and smokes a slim pipe. Vincent is in fact a **rakshasa** named Valantajar that always casts *disguise self* on itself before seeing visitors. The rakshasa has lived in Waterdeep for years, switching identities as often as needed to keep its true nature hidden. It has grown accustomed to living among mortals and, much to its own astonishment, is rather fond of Waterdeep and its citizens.

Services

Trench can discover any secret in Waterdeep, for a fee. Use your judgment when pricing its services; 50 gp is sufficient for most investigations, but if the characters want to learn secrets relating to the major antagonists

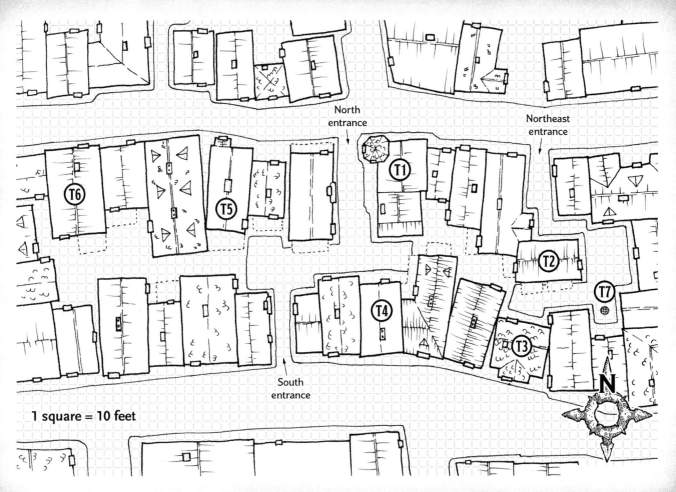

MAP 2.1: TROLLSKULL ALLEY (NORTH WARD)

of this adventure, the rakshasa might require a service in payment, such as slaying enemies that are hunting it, posting advertisements for its business in their tavern, or keeping tabs on someone Vincent has been hired to spy on.

T6. Book Wyrm's Treasure

The front of this bookstore is adorned with a charming sign of a gold dragon curled around a treasure hoard of books and scrolls. Inside, the shop is decorated with beautiful hardwood, and the earthy scent of old books permeates the air. The library fills two floors of this three-story building, and it somehow seems to contain more shelves than the building should be able to hold.

The shop is managed by a short dragonborn of gold dragon ancestry named Rishaal the Page-Turner, who lives on the third floor. Rishaal, a member of the Watchful Order of Magists and Protectors, is a **mage**, with these changes:

- Rishaal is neutral.
- He has these racial traits: He can use his action to exhale a 15-foot cone of fire (but can't do this again until he finishes a short or long rest); each creature in the cone must make a DC 10 Dexterity saving throw, taking 2d6 fire damage on a failed save, or half as much damage on a successful one. He has resistance to fire damage. He speaks Common, Draconic, Dwarvish, and Elvish.

Services

The shop contains books of all sorts. In addition, Rishaal has a small collection of spellbooks and allows wizards to copy spells from them at the cost listed in the Spells for Sale table. He can scribe any of these spells as a *spell scroll* but charges twice the listed cost for this service.

Spells for Sale

Spell	Cost per Spell
Comprehend languages, detect magic, feather fall, find familiar, mage armor, magic missile, shield, unseen servant	25 gp
Arcane lock, continual flame, darkvision, invisibility, magic weapon, misty step, rope trick, suggestion	75 gp
Clairvoyance, counterspell, dispel magic, fireball, fly, nondetection, water breathing	150 gp
Arcane eye, fabricate, greater invisibility, ice storm, locate creature, polymorph	300 gp
Bigby's hand, cone of cold, modify memory	750 gp

T7. Sewer Access

At the east end of Trollskull Alley is a removable metal grate that covers an opening. Below the grate, a ladder descends 20 feet into the Waterdeep sewer system.

Joining Factions

Word begins to spread throughout Waterdeep that a group of adventurers helped Volothamp Geddarm and rescued Renaer Neverember. Within days, faction representatives begin to approach the characters and try to recruit them. This book's introduction describes the various factions and what they look for in recruits. The characters need not all join the same faction, and some might not want to join a faction at all.

A character who belongs to a faction is given a mission upon gaining a level, from 2nd through 5th level. Completing the mission increases that member's renown in the faction. Other characters who aren't faction members can assist in the mission's completion. A character who belongs to a faction other than the Lords' Alliance can turn down a mission without consequence.

Each faction has a representative who serves as its primary contact. This NPC delivers mission briefings and dispenses the tangible rewards for completing a mission. An increase in renown quickly follows. The missions and the manner in which they can be completed are described in the tables throughout this section. You can use missions from these tables or replace any of them with ones of your own creation.

If a mission ends in failure, the characters can try again after 24 hours, unless the failure has created circumstances where doing so is impossible.

Bregan D'aerthe

If one or more characters are drow, Jarlaxle Baenre has his lieutenants, three **drow gunslingers**, shadow these potential new recruits while keeping a safe distance. Fel'rekt Lafeen and Krebbyg Masq'il'yr watch the characters at night, and Soluun Xibrindas watches them during the day (doing his best to stay out of the sunlight). See appendix B for details on these lieutenants.

Characters who have a passive Wisdom (Perception) score of 18 or higher see fleeting glimpses of the drow spies over a period of several days and can, with a suc-

Bregan D'aerthe Missions

Party Level	Mission Brief	Mission Requirements and Reward
2nd	"I'd like you to steal a silk handkerchief from a Waterdavian noble and give it to a tiefling girl who lives in a crate at the corner of Net Street and Dock Street, by the wharf."	Finding a noble isn't hard, but snatching one's handkerchief without being detected requires a successful DC 12 Dexterity (Sleight of Hand) check. One can also convince a noble to surrender it with a successful DC 12 Charisma (Deception, Intimidation, or Persuasion) check. The tiefling girl in the crate thanks the characters for the hanky. *Reward:* Each Bregan D'aerthe character gains 1 renown.
3rd	"This mission is so easy, a gang of street urchins could pull it off. I want you to deliver an exposé to Gaxly Rudderbust, the publisher of a local broadsheet called *The Waterdeep Wazoo*, without his knowing who wrote it or where it came from. You'll find his office at the corner of Immar Street and Stallion Street, in the North Ward. Leave the story on his desk."	Jarlaxle has written an exposé on devil worship among unnamed Waterdavian noble families. The story mentions orgies and secret deals happening behind closed doors. (Jarlaxle never passes up a chance to rattle the nobility and sow political unrest.) A character can break into Gaxly's office while it's closed, either during lunch hour or after hours. Getting in and out without being seen requires two successful DC 15 Dexterity (Stealth) checks, and getting past a locked door requires a successful DC 10 Dexterity check using thieves' tools (or a *knock* spell or similar magic). *Reward:* Each Bregan D'aerthe character gains 1 renown.
4th	"We've captured a member of the Xanathar Guild, and I'd like you to guard him for three nights until I or another member of Bregan D'aerthe reclaims him. You'll find him trapped in your basement."	Characters who search the basement of their Trollskull Alley tavern find Ott Steeltoes (see appendix B) bound by *iron bands of Bilarro*. How he got there is anyone's guess; even he doesn't know. On the first night, Xanathar sends a gang of six **bugbears** to attack the tavern and rescue Ott. If the characters have moved Ott elsewhere, the bugbears attack the tavern anyway. On the second night, four members of the Dungsweepers' Guild (**commoners**) with **intellect devourers** in their skulls visit the tavern. They order drinks and scope out the tavern, attacking if they find Ott or leaving if they don't. On the third night, a **beholder zombie** attacks. After the third attack, Ott disappears as mysteriously as he arrived, along with the *iron bands of Bilarro*. *Reward:* Each Bregan D'aerthe character gains 2 renown.
5th	"We have a spy deep within Xanathar's organization, but I fear he has been compromised. It breaks my heart to do this, but I'm sending you to eliminate him. Make it quick and painless, and for Lolth's sake, be discreet."	Jarlaxle identifies the traitor as a drow mage named Nar'l Xibrindas (see appendix B) and furnishes the characters with a route to Xanathar's lair through underground passageways. (Xanathar's lair is described in chapter 5. Characters who follow Jarlaxle's route arrive at area X1.) *Reward:* Each Bregan D'aerthe character gains 2 renown. Each party member who contributes to the mission receives a trophy bearing a gold statuette of Jarlaxle (worth 250 gp).

cessful DC 15 Wisdom (Insight) check, ascertain that these spies are paying particular attention to the activities of the drow party members.

Jarlaxle Baenre

If the party reports the drow to the City Watch, Jarlaxle ends the surveillance and breaks off all contact with the characters for the time being.

On the other hand, if the characters try to confront the drow spies, they avoid contact but leave behind a black eye patch as a calling card. The next day, **Jarlaxle Baenre** (see appendix B) shows up at the party's headquarters, using his *hat of disguise* to appear as a haberdasher named J.B. Nevercott. In this guise, he asks to speak privately with drow characters who he thinks might make suitable Bregan D'aerthe recruits. Only drow are given serious consideration, but Jarlaxle doesn't care if they're male or female. As a test, he offers them their first mission.

Jarlaxle is a consummate actor who never lets down his guard. Even if the characters discern his true identity, he never admits to being anything other than what he pretends to be.

Emerald Enclave

The Emerald Enclave takes an interest in characters who seek to preserve the balance within Waterdeep (particularly clerics of nature, druids, and rangers). Any such character is visited by a white cat that speaks the following message in a melodious male voice:

> "Interested in joining the Emerald Enclave? Come meet us at Phaulkonmere in the Southern Ward."

The cat is an ordinary animal upon which an *animal messenger* spell was cast. It dashes away after delivering its invitation.

Melannor Fellbranch

The characters' main contact in the Emerald Enclave is Melannor Fellbranch, the friendly but humorless groundskeeper of Phaulkonmere, a compound located one block south of Kolat Towers (see chapter 8). Phaulkonmere is owned by the Tarm and Phaulkon noble families. Melannor delivers missions by way of *animal messenger* spells and is partial to using cats and pigeons as couriers. He quickly assigns new members their first mission.

Emerald Enclave Missions

Party Level	Mission Brief	Mission Requirements and Reward
2nd	"Outlying farms are being terrorized by a scarecrow come to life. It has slaughtered livestock, chased horses, and spooked farmers. No people have been killed as yet, so the City Guard is dragging its heels. Something must be done!"	Not one but three **scarecrows** are terrorizing Undercliff. One wears a sackcloth hood, another has a rotting pumpkin head, and the third is covered with a threadbare blanket. Characters who camp in a field for the better part of a day or night have a 10 percent chance of encountering one of the scarecrows. The attacks continue until all three scarecrows are destroyed. *Reward:* Each Emerald Enclave character gains 1 renown for ending the threat.
3rd	"Sir Ambrose Everdawn, a grizzled old champion of Kelemvor, has offered to help the City Guard catch a necromancer who's stealing bones from the City of the Dead and animating them as skeletons. Sir Ambrose could use your help, if you're not too busy."	Convincing Ambrose Everdawn (LG male human Tethyrian **knight**) that the party intends to help requires a successful DC 13 Charisma (Persuasion) check. If the check succeeds, Sir Ambrose asks the party to patrol the southern half of the cemetery for ten consecutive nights while he patrols the north half. The characters have a cumulative 10 percent chance each night of encountering six **skeletons**, but there's no sign of the necromancer who animated them. Once the skeletons are destroyed, no further encounters occur. After a tenday, Sir Ambrose releases the characters from service. *Reward:* Each Emerald Enclave character gains 1 renown. Each party member who patrolled the cemetery for all ten nights receives 100 gp.
4th	"Doppelgangers threaten the balance of power in Waterdeep. Rumor has it a group of them are hiding in the Yawning Portal. Root them out and rid the city of them if you can."	The characters need to confront "Bonnie" the **doppelganger** and, with a successful DC 15 Charisma (Intimidation or Persuasion) check, convince her to leave Waterdeep and take her gang with her. *Reward:* Each Emerald Enclave character gains 2 renown.
5th	"The Xanathar Guild is releasing monsters to distract the City Watch and the City Guard while its members stir up trouble elsewhere. The authorities are having trouble catching and killing a flying horror known as a grell. This aberration was latest seen snatching up an old woman in the Dock Ward. Unless we intervene, she won't be the last."	Locating the grell requires a successful DC 18 Intelligence (Investigation) check followed by a successful DC 18 Wisdom (Survival) check. Each check, whether successful or not, represents 1 hour of gathering information or tracking spoor. In fact, there are two **grells**. One grell tries to flee if the other is killed. *Reward:* Each Emerald Enclave character gains 2 renown. Jeryth bestows a *charm of heroism* (see "Supernatural Gifts" in chapter 7 of the *Dungeon Master's Guide*) on each party member who helped slay the grells.

Melannor is a half-elf **druid**, with these changes:

- Melannor is chaotic good.
- He has these racial traits: He has advantage on saving throws against being charmed, and magic can't put him to sleep. He has darkvision out to a range of 60 feet. He speaks Common and Elvish.

Jeryth Phaulkon

When the characters arrive at Phaulkonmere for the first time, Melannor introduces them to the lady of the estate: a noblewoman-turned-demigod and Chosen of Mielikki named Jeryth Phaulkon. Jeryth, the only member of her family who currently resides at Phaulkonmere, manifests as a disembodied female voice that can be heard by anyone in the villa gardens. She offers membership in the enclave and bestows on each new member a *charm of restoration* (see "Supernatural Gifts" in chapter 7 of the *Dungeon Master's Guide*). Jeryth also offers Phaulkonmere as a safe haven for enclave members and their friends.

In her disembodied state, Jeryth can't be harmed. If the need arises, Jeryth can cast any spell on the druid spell list. She uses her spells in defense of her estate and its beautiful gardens. A member of the Emerald Enclave can petition Jeryth to cast a spell, which she is happy to do if that character's renown in the enclave equals or exceeds the spell's level.

Force Grey (Gray Hands)

The Blackstaff, **Vajra Safahr** (see appendix B), is friends with Renaer Neverember, and word of his rescue quickly reaches her ears. She uses a *sending* spell to deliver the following short message to one of the characters:

> "I am Vajra Safahr, the Blackstaff. Come to Blackstaff Tower in the Castle Ward at once. Bring your friends."

Despite her insistent tone, Vajra doesn't take offense if the character refuses her invitation. A day later, she casts another *sending* spell and reaches out to a different party member. If she is refused a second time, she doesn't contact the party again until the characters gain a level.

Force Grey (Gray Hands) Missions

Party Level	Mission Brief	Mission Requirements and Reward
2nd	"Seek out Hlam, a monk who lives in a cave on the side of Mount Waterdeep. Ask him what he's heard about threats to the city, but try not to annoy him or overstay your welcome."	Those who climb the mountainside to reach the cave must succeed on a DC 12 Constitution saving throw or arrive with 1d4 levels of exhaustion. Trying to get **Hlam** (see appendix B) to share information requires a DC 12 Charisma (Persuasion) check. If the check succeeds, he tells the characters, "Evil's twin hides its face for now. Expect that to change before winter's end." (This is an oblique reference to Manshoon.) The characters can descend the mountain safely. *Reward:* Each Gray Hand character gains 1 renown.
3rd	"A young bronze dragon has taken up residence in Deepwater Harbor. It startled a few sailors recently but hasn't hurt anyone. Confront the dragon and learn its intentions."	Vajra gives each character a *potion of water breathing* to complete this mission. They find a **young bronze dragon**, Zelifarn, swimming around a barnacle-covered shipwreck at the bottom of the deep harbor. The friendly dragon tries to coax as much treasure as it can from the characters. Those who converse with Zelifarn can make a DC 13 Wisdom (Insight) check. A successful check reveals that the dragon poses no danger to Waterdeep. If no one succeeds on the check, the dragon's true intentions can't be gleaned. *Reward:* Each Gray Hand character gains 1 renown.
4th	"A member of Force Grey has been acting strangely of late. His name is Meloon Wardragon, and his happy-go-lucky demeanor has soured. He's been hanging around the Yawning Portal more than usual. Observe him for a tenday, then report back to me."	Characters can befriend **Meloon Wardragon** (see appendix B) or watch him from afar. Each day at dawn, Meloon engages in a telepathic contest of wills with his magic axe, *Azuredge* (see appendix A), before leaving his room at the Yawning Portal. The axe wants a new wielder, but Meloon refuses to part with it. Characters who observe Meloon during this exchange can ascertain what's going on with a successful DC 15 Wisdom (Insight) check. *Reward:* Each Gray Hand character gains 2 renown. If the characters rid Meloon of the **intellect devourer** in his skull, Vajra gives the party a *wand of secrets*.
5th	"Xanathar is using intellect devourers to take control of Waterdavians in key positions throughout the city. We must deal with this problem at once. Infiltrate Xanathar's lair and destroy whatever is responsible for creating these creatures."	The characters must slay Nihiloor the **mind flayer** (see appendix B). They can stake out a Xanathar Guild hideout (see chapter 1) and wait for Nihiloor to show up there, or confront the mind flayer in Xanathar's lair (see chapter 5). *Reward:* Each Gray Hand character gains 2 renown. Every character who participated in the raid receives a *potion of resistance*. In addition, Vajra covers the cost of any *raise dead* spells needed to bring back dead characters.

Vajra Safahr

Blackstaff Tower is a fortress and a wizard training academy all in one. From here, Vajra Safahr watches over the city and asserts herself as Blackstaff. *Sending* spells are her preferred way of communicating with her operatives.

Vajra offers the characters membership in the Gray Hands, a private security force under her command. She doles out missions designed to tax the characters' resources and test their loyalty to Waterdeep. Characters who complete these missions won't gain enough renown to join Force Grey yet, but they will gain something valuable: the Blackstaff's patronage. Vajra continues to take an interest in their adventuring careers, helping out when she can.

Harpers

The Harpers approach good-aligned characters who show promise as spies. One such character receives the following message, written on a *paper bird* (see appendix A):

> "Renaer tells us you are a good bet. He bought you tickets to the opera tonight at the Lightsinger Theater in the Sea Ward. If you are interested, meet Mirt at intermission. Private Box C. Formal attire is required for admittance."

Harper Missions

Party Level	Mission Brief	Mission Requirements and Reward
2nd	"One of the drays working in the city is pulled by a talking mare named Maxeene. Locate her, find out if she's learned the identity of any Zhent operatives, and if so, determine their whereabouts."	Characters can find Maxeene, a **draft horse** with an Intelligence score of 10, with a successful DC 13 Intelligence (Investigation) check. Maxeene speaks Common, and characters must try to convince her that they're Harpers by making a DC 13 Charisma (Persuasion) check. If the check succeeds, the horse recalls giving a ride to a sun elf and his half-orc bodyguard two days ago; she picked them up at an intersection (she doesn't recall which one) and dropped them off at the Yawning Portal. They talked about hiring spies to root out Xanathar Guild hideouts in the city. Maxeene's descriptions of the passengers match the appearances of Davil Starsong and Yagra Stonefist. *Reward:* Each Harper character gains 1 renown.
3rd	"Uza Solizeph is an old woman who sells books out of a narrow three-story building on Sorn Street in the Trades Ward. She claims to have trapped a monster in her shop and fears for the welfare of her books and her cat. The City Watch isn't likely to lend a hand, given Uza's propensity for tall tales, but the Harpers owe her a favor. You'll find her sobbing at Felzoun's Folly, a tavern on the corner of Sorn Street and Salabar Street. Make haste!"	Uza (LG female human Mulan **commoner**) describes the threat as a "monstrous orb of many eyes" that chased her cat, Fillipa, into the shop. The monster is, in fact, a **gazer** (see appendix B). If the characters met a gazer in chapter 1, they know what they're up against. Uza lends them the keys to the front and back doors of her shop. Characters find the interior in shambles and hear a cat meowing on the third floor. The sounds are coming from the gazer, which is hunting Fillipa. The **cat** has so far eluded the nasty little predator. *Reward:* Each Harper character gains 1 renown if the gazer is defeated. Uza also gives the party a used spellbook containing four 1st-level and three 2nd-level wizard spells.
4th	"One of our members, Mattrim Mereg, has allied himself with a gang of doppelgangers and believes the Harpers should recruit them. We need an unbiased opinion. Track down and speak with each of the doppelgangers, and gauge their trustworthiness."	The characters must speak with five **doppelgangers**, starting with their leader, "Bonnie," who works at the Yawning Portal. She needs a few days to round up the other doppelgangers, who agree to meet at the tavern in human guises. Characters must interview each doppelganger and succeed on a DC 16 Wisdom (Insight) check to ascertain its trustworthiness. Only "Bonnie" is trustworthy. *Reward:* Each Harper character gains 2 renown. Every contributing party member receives 50 gp.
5th	"Lady Remallia Haventree is hosting a party at House Ulbrinter, her villa on Delzorin Street, located between Vhezoar Street and Brondar's Way in the North Ward. We have reason to suspect that drow spies have infiltrated the guest list. Attend the party and root out the disguised drow. Dress sharply."	Remallia Haventree (see appendix B) knows of the mission, but it's not revealed to the characters that she's a Harper. There's one drow spy in attendance: **Jarlaxle Baenre** (see appendix B). He uses his *hat of disguise* to appear as a young actor from Luskan named Erystian Demarne. A successful DC 24 Wisdom (Insight) check is needed to out Jarlaxle. Impressed by the perceptive adventurers, he thanks Lady Haventree for an entertaining evening and dashes off, but not without first tipping his hat to the character or characters who exposed him. *Reward:* Each Harper character gains 2 renown. Every party member who attended the party receives 200 gp.

Enclosed are tickets for the entire party to *The Fall of Tiamat*, an opera sung in Giant describing the evil dragon queen's defeat at the Well of Dragons.

MIRT

If any of the characters join the Harpers, **Mirt** (see appendix B) becomes their main Harper contact throughout the adventure.

Lightsinger Theater is a high-end establishment located in the Castle Ward. If the characters meet Mirt in his private box during the opera's intermission, he describes the Harpers and offers membership to eligible characters. Characters who accept receive a silver pin of a harp within a crescent moon, along with their first mission (see the Harpers Missions table). Mirt also tells them that if they ever need to speak with him directly, they are welcome to visit his manor in the Sea Ward. If the characters do visit Mirt's manor, there's a 90 percent chance that Mirt isn't home and no one answers the door.

LORDS' ALLIANCE

Characters who place the security of the city and the realm ahead of their own interests are invited to join this faction. Potential recruits must be residents of Waterdeep.

JALESTER SILVERMANE

The characters' primary contact is **Jalester Silvermane** (see appendix B), a field agent who reports to Open Lord Laeral Silverhand. Jalester spends much of his time in the Yawning Portal and other taverns that adventurers are known to frequent.

Jalester offers membership in the Lords' Alliance to those who qualify. Members are expected to complete whatever missions are assigned to them in a timely, professional manner. Refusing to accept or complete a mission can result in suspension or dismissal. An alliance member who is suspended receives no alliance missions until the suspension ends, while dismissal from the alliance means a loss of membership and the loss of all renown in the faction.

LORDS' ALLIANCE MISSIONS

Party Level	Mission Brief	Mission Requirements and Reward
2nd	"A gang war is causing unrest throughout the city. We have offered protection to members of the Dungsweepers' Guild, and you have been assigned to protect a group of them. Meet them at the Muleskull Tavern, on Ship Street in the Dock Ward, at six bells and guard them while they work. Do this every day for a tenday."	Each morning, the characters meet with a team of four dungsweepers (**commoners**) and head to the Trades Ward, where the sweepers spend the day cleaning up waste in the streets. It's boring work. On the ninth day, around highsun, a **carrion crawler** emerges from a nearby alley, pursued by two City Watch **guards**. The characters can help slay the carrion crawler, which came up from the sewers. *Reward:* Each Lords' Alliance character gains 1 renown.
3rd	"Harko Swornhold, an evil adventurer who was exiled three years ago for attempting to bribe a city magistrate, has returned to Waterdeep illegally. We think the Xanathar Guild is using him to incite violence. He was last seen recruiting kenku in the Dock Ward. Find him and quietly put him to the sword."	Whichever character leads the search must succeed on three DC 14 Intelligence (Investigation) checks before gaining three failures, with each check representing 8 hours of investigation. Other characters can assist, granting advantage on the checks. Harko (**bandit captain**) has two **kenku** companions that fight by his side. *Reward:* Each Lords' Alliance character gains 1 renown.
4th	"The Zhents are courting a Red Wizard of Thay named Esloon Bezant, trying to add his gang of thugs to their ranks. All we know about him is that he fled his homeland a few years back and is too smart to get caught doing anything illegal. He and his gang of bullies prowl the Dock Ward. Scuttle the deal, and do it fast!"	The characters can create a rift between the Zhentarim and Esloon's gang by sowing rumors of betrayal. They must spend 25 gp in bribes and succeed on a DC 16 Charisma (Deception or Persuasion) check. Conversely, they can confront Esloon Bezant (LE male Thayan human **mage**) and his gang of five **thugs** and either defeat them or bribe them with at least 500 gp. *Reward:* Each Lords' Alliance character gains 2 renown. The characters can also deprive Esloon of his spellbook, which contains all the spells he has prepared.
5th	"The City Watch is overwhelmed by the recent surge in violence and needs our help. We have reports of an assassin prowling the rooftops, picking off targets with arrows and alarming citizens. My sources say he goes to ground somewhere near Trollskull Alley. Find him, alert the City Watch to his whereabouts, and aid in his arrest if you can. Don't kill him, since doing that could escalate the violence further."	Whichever character leads the hunt must succeed on three DC 18 Intelligence (Investigation) checks before gaining three failures, with each check representing 8 hours of investigation. Other characters can assist, granting advantage on the checks. If the search succeeds, characters corner the assassin, **Ziraj the Hunter** (see appendix B), in the greenhouse of Corellon's Crown in Trollskull Alley (area T4). Ziraj surrenders to the City Watch without a fight, believing that his fellow Zhents will find a way to free him. *Reward:* Each Lords' Alliance character gains 2 renown. Every character who aids in Ziraj's capture receives 50 gp.

ORDER OF THE GAUNTLET

The Order of the Gauntlet looks for members who seek to fight evil in all its forms. Adventurers who worship Helm, Torm, or Tyr are especially sought after.

SAVRA BELABRANTA

If the party includes one or more likely recruits, Savra Belabranta (NG female Tethyrian human **knight**) visits the characters' residence and invites them to the Halls of Justice, the temple of Tyr (located west of the Market in the Castle Ward), where they can be sworn into the order. The swearing-in ceremony involves the recitation of an oath to find and destroy evil in all its forms. The oath is spoken while every candidate wears a silver gauntlet (a symbol of the order). After the ceremony, Savra gives new recruits their first mission.

The Belabrantas are a Waterdavian noble family that raises griffons for the Griffon Cavalry. Savra is trying to regain her honor by serving Tyr, thus atoning for the evil acts she committed as a member of an evil elemental cult called the Howling Hatred. Savra's sins are irrelevant to this adventure, but you can learn more about her past in *Princes of the Apocalypse*. Whenever she has a mission for the characters, she communicates the missive to them herself.

ZHENTARIM

The Doom Raiders try to contact evil-aligned or morally ambiguous characters. A **flying snake** with a parchment tied about its body visits one character in the dead of night. The message reads:

> "Want to be part of something big? Speak to Davil Starsong at the Yawning Portal."

If the characters seek out Davil, Yagra Stonefist (see "Familiar Faces," page 20) greets them and leads interested parties to a table in the center of the Yawning Portal's taproom, where her boss waits with drink in hand.

ORDER OF THE GAUNTLET MISSIONS

Party Level	Mission Brief	Mission Requirements and Reward
2nd	"We hear that the Zhents are paying gangs in the Field Ward to attack suspected Xanathar Guild members. Fights are breaking out in the ward daily. Stop a fight before it happens. We need to send a message to these thugs that further altercations won't be tolerated."	The characters must visit the Field Ward and, as a fight threatens to break out, make three successful DC 12 Charisma (Intimidation) checks before failing three checks, or else defeat four **thugs** (preferably without killing them) to disperse the would-be brawlers. *Reward:* Each Order of the Gauntlet character gains 1 renown.
3rd	"A notorious thief called the Black Viper, long thought dead, has apparently returned to Waterdeep. She has already robbed at least a dozen noble estates. No one knows her identity because she wears a mask, but it was reported in *The Waterdeep Wazoo* that she's a noble. Find out what else the broadsheet's publisher knows about her and report back to me."	The characters can meet with Gaxly Rudderbust (N male Illuskan human **commoner**), the publisher of *The Waterdeep Wazoo*, and either succeed on a DC 12 Charisma (Intimidation or Persuasion) check or bribe him with at least 50 gp. If they do so, Gaxly shares his suspicions that the Black Viper is the secret, evil twin sister of Ammalia Cassalanter (see appendix B), and that she wears a mask to hide a disfigurement. Interviewing the Cassalanters at their villa (see chapter 6) or conducting a day-long investigation and succeeding on a DC 15 Intelligence (Investigation) check reveals that no such person exists. *Reward:* Each Order of the Gauntlet character gains 1 renown for reporting what Gaxly said.
4th	"Guards at the Endshift Tavern, located on Endshift Street in the Field Ward, are being robbed nightly, and the innkeeper says he's seen giant rats prowling around the back alleys. Sounds dull, but it's a plea for help that we can't ignore."	The inn is being harassed by the Shard Shunners, a gang of halfling wererats, because the innkeeper's guards once threatened a gang member. To end the harassment, the characters must defeat three **wererats** or scare them off with a successful DC 17 Charisma (Intimidation) check. *Reward:* Each Order of the Gauntlet character gains 2 renown and receives a *potion of healing*.
5th	"I just received a report that spined devils are terrorizing citizens in Twelvedog Court, in the Field Ward. Come, let us slay them together and find their evil summoner!"	The characters must help Savra defeat five **spined devils**, which have locals pinned down in nearby buildings. Right afterward, Gysheer Omfreys (LE female Tethyrian human **cult fanatic**) emerges from an alley and attacks Savra. Gysheer is an overzealous member of a devil-worshiping cult led by Victoro Cassalanter (see appendix B). Savra tries to subdue and question her, but only magical compulsion can force her to implicate Victoro. Since devil worship isn't illegal in Waterdeep, Savra has no grounds to stir up trouble with the Cassalanters, and she advises characters not to do so, either. *Reward:* Each Order of the Gauntlet character gains 2 renown. Every character who took part receives a *potion of greater healing*.

Davil Starsong

Davil Starsong (see appendix B) is the characters' primary contact in the Black Network, at least initially. Over drinks, he shares the following information:

- Davil is a retired adventurer. He and his adventuring companions joined the Zhentarim a few years back. They help people in need. (More specifically, they provide loans, mercenaries, and other services.)
- Another Black Network gang has recently infiltrated the city and tried to take over the Xanathar Guild. They failed, setting off a war in the streets. Davil and his colleagues want to end the violence and restore the peace.

Davil offers membership in the faction to interested characters, then assigns them their first mission (see the Zhentarim Missions table). Subsequent mission briefings are written on scrolls and delivered by flying snakes.

Tashlyn Yafeera

After the characters complete two missions for Davil, he is arrested by the City Watch and held in Castle Waterdeep while he waits to be questioned by the Lords

Zhentarim Missions

Party Level	Mission Brief	Mission Requirements and Reward
2nd	"Someone is killing elf and half-elf sailors in the Dock Ward—three dead so far, each one decapitated by a blade in the dead of night. Look into it, will you? Methinks the City Watch could use a little help."	Characters who spend three consecutive nights loitering around the docks spot Heldar, a drunk half-elf sailor (**bandit**), leaving the Muleskull Tavern (on Ship Street in the Dock Ward). Characters who follow Heldar can save him from Soluun Xibrindas, a renegade **drow gunslinger** (see appendix B). Soluun hides in the shadows, blade drawn, waiting for the half-elf to stumble by. Spotting him before he strikes requires a successful DC 18 Wisdom (Perception) check. Soluun flees if reduced to half his hit points or fewer. *Reward:* Each Zhentarim character gains 1 renown. If Heldar survives Soluun's attack, each character receives 50 gp.
3rd	"There's a shop in the Trades Ward called Weirdbottle's Concoctions. The gnome who runs it is a friend of ours named Skeemo. He's made some *potions of mind reading* for a client. Pick up the potions and deliver them to the God Catcher, one of the enormous statues in the Castle Ward. Give the potions to the lady in the purple cloak, and keep the tip."	**Skeemo Weirdbottle** (see appendix B) has placed four *potions of poison* in a small silk-lined coffer. The potions look, smell, and taste like *potions of mind reading*. Awaiting delivery near the God Catcher is Esvele Rosznar, the **Black Viper** (see appendix B). She wears a hooded purple cloak and is seated in the back of a hire-coach. She exchanges the coffer for a black velvet pouch, then orders her driver to depart. The coach delivers Esvele to her estate in the Sea Ward. *Reward:* Each Zhentarim character gains 1 renown. Esvele's pouch contains 15 pp, which the characters can keep.
4th	"Waterdeep's richest halfling family, the Snobeedles, is offering 500 gold pieces for information leading to the safe return of a missing family member named Dasher Snobeedle. Those dragons sure would look good in our coffers! Investigate and see what you can learn, but don't get in any trouble. The City Watch already has it out for us."	Any character who spends at least three days asking pertinent questions and pursuing leads in the Southern Ward or the Dock Ward can, at the end of that time, make a DC 18 Charisma (Persuasion or Intimidation) check. On a success, the character convinces some tight-lipped halflings to arrange a meeting with Dasher. The meeting is scheduled to occur at highsun in Waymoot the next day. Dasher shows up to hear what the characters have to say, but he has no intention of going home. He recently joined a gang of halfling wererats called the Shard Shunners (so named because they detest silver) and has since become a wererat himself (see chapter 1 for halfling wererat statistics). The Shard Shunners are his family now. *Reward:* Each Zhentarim character gains 2 renown.
5th	"Skeemo Weirdbottle has betrayed us! The little worm has been feeding information to our enemies. He must be eliminated. Make it look like an accident."	**Skeemo Weirdbottle** (see appendix B) manages to stay one step ahead of the characters. As they approach his shop, they see him ride off in a dray with five other passengers and a driver (all **commoners**). If Skeemo realizes he's being followed, he casts *fly* and takes to the air. If the effect is dispelled or the characters maintain pursuit, he casts *greater invisibility* on himself and uses crowds to cover his escape. If the characters fail to nab him, he takes refuge in Kolat Towers (see chapter 8). *Reward:* Each Zhentarim character gains 2 renown if Skeemo is eliminated without implicating the Black Network. In addition, characters who snatch Skeemo's satchel find that it holds his spellbook (containing all the spells he has prepared), a *potion of mind reading*, and 150 gp in a silk coin purse.

of Waterdeep about the Black Network's operations in the city. The characters continue to receive missions, but they come from **Tashlyn Yafeera** (see appendix B). Characters first become aware of this change when they receive their next mission briefing, since it's written in a different hand.

If the characters want to speak with Tashlyn directly, Yagra can arrange a meeting in the City of the Dead or some other quiet place. By the time the characters see her, Tashlyn has learned the following information:

- The rumored leader of the renegade Zhent faction is Urstul Floxin, a known Black Network assassin.
- A warrant has been issued for Urstul's arrest, but his current whereabouts are unknown. Even magical scrying has failed to reveal his location.
- The botched kidnapping of Renaer Neverember won't sit well with Urstul. He might try again. (Tashlyn doesn't actually believe this, but she knows that Renaer has ties to the Harpers and might share information of interest with the characters.)

Weeks after his arrest, Davil is released from custody once the Lords of Waterdeep are satisfied that neither he nor his associates are responsible for the recent violence.

OPEN FOR BUSINESS?

If the characters intend to fix up and reopen the tavern in Trollskull Alley, they can expect to deal with various guilds without whose support the business is likely to fail. Repairs to the walls and the roof require the approval and oversight of the Carpenters', Roofers', and Plaisterers' Guild. The Cellarers' and Plumbers' Guild is best equipped to handle the refurbishing of the basement and plumbing. Clean bedsheets are provided by the Launderers' Guild. The streets around the establishment are kept up by the Dungsweepers' Guild and the Loyal Order of Street Laborers. Meat must come from the Guild of Butchers; ale and wine from the Vintners', Distillers', and Brewers' Guild; and bread and pastries from the Bakers' Guild. The list goes on.

The "Tavern Keeping Expenses" sidebar lists the costs that the characters must pay to get their place ready for business, as well as the recurring obligations they must meet while the tavern is open for business.

SAMPLE GUILD REPRESENTATIVES

Once it becomes known around the city that the tavern in Trollskull Alley is planning to reopen its doors to the public, the adventurers receive visits from guild representatives interested in the tavern's welfare. This section describes a handful of these representatives.

BROXLEY FAIRKETTLE
Fellowship of Innkeepers

Broxley (LG male strongheart halfling **commoner**) is a laid-back, law-abiding halfling with mutton chops and bushy eyebrows. Inns and taverns are few and far between in the North Ward, so he makes frequent visits to the characters' place to see how it's doing and to offer his well-wishes. If none of the characters are

members of the guild, he strongly urges them to join "to avoid further harassment." The cost of membership in the Fellowship of Innkeepers is included in the regular expenses outlined in the "Tavern Keeping Expenses" sidebar.

Broxley has long believed the tavern to be haunted and is glad to see living souls in it once more. While lamenting the burdens of being a father of nine, he is quick to point out that the characters' continued compliance with guild rules and regulations makes his rather difficult life "just a bitty bit easier."

HAMMOND KRADDOC
Vintners', Distillers', and Brewers' Guild

Hammond (N male Illuskan human **commoner**) doesn't like adventurers, but he likes their coin. This effete, well-dressed man is always seen in the company of a young scribe, Jinny (NG female tiefling **commoner**), who wears spectacles and silently records notes and conversations in a small book as Hammond speaks.

Hammond likes to stop by in the middle of the month to inform the characters of new spirits that the guild has to offer, and to give them a list of which ones to push hard. To test the extent of their willingness to cooperate, he chastises them for their current selection of beverages, even if he previously sold them those goods.

JUSTYN RASSK
Guild of Butchers

Dead-eyed, slack-jawed Justyn (NE male Illuskan human **thug**) grew up in the toughest neighborhood in the Field Ward and has the scars to prove it. The guild doesn't pay him enough for him to afford a residence in the North Ward, and going to that part of the city fills his heart with resentment. He darkens the characters' doorstep once a month to deliver a cartload of chopped meat for the tavern's larder. Although delivery fees are covered by the guild's monthly dues, Justyn always demands some extra coin for his service. If the characters don't give him a gratuity of at least 3 gp, he says, "Maybe next time the meat will be someone you know." He lets the threat hang in the air, then departs.

TAVERN KEEPING EXPENSES

This sidebar summarizes the one-time payments and continuing expenses associated with running the tavern in Trollskull Alley, as well as providing rules for determining how much coin the business makes or loses.

One-Time Expenses
- 1,000 gp to renovate the tavern over 12 days
- 250 gp for guild licenses and contracts (paid up front)

Regular Expenses
- 50 gp per tenday for maintenance and wages of hirelings
- 10 gp per tenday for all other guild expenses

Profit or Loss
At the end of every tenday, roll a d100 + 10 and consult the Running a Business table in chapter 6 of the *Dungeon Master's Guide* to determine whether the tavern lost money or earned profit. If the characters spent coin on promoting their business during that tenday, add 1 to the roll for each 1 gp they spent. If the characters have unpaid expenses, subtract 1 from the roll for each 1 gp they owe.

ULKORIA STONEMARROW
Watchful Order of Magists and Protectors

Ulkoria (NG female shield dwarf **archmage**) has defended Waterdeep with her magic more times than she can recall. She's known as "the Gargoyle" because her face is frozen in a scowl that frightens adults and children alike. No one knows where she lives, but it's believed to be underground, possibly a cellar or dungeon under one of the city's oldest estates. She uses *teleport* spells to enter and leave her home, and she's never seen without her **shield guardian** close by.

A little known fact is that Ulkoria once owned the tavern in Trollskull Alley. She sold it to a family of shield dwarves, who fell on hard times and sold it to a woman who made it into an orphanage. "Turned out to be a hag who was cooking and eating the children," Ulkoria recalls. The estate passed through several more hands in the years that followed. Ulkoria hopes the new owners make something good of it.

Anytime she passes through the North Ward, Ulkoria stops by the tavern for a drink and to check out the place while her shield guardian waits outside. If she doesn't like what the characters have done with the establishment, she keeps her criticisms to herself. The characters can hire her to cast *glyphs of warding* on the place, for which she charges 300 gp apiece.

BUSINESS RIVAL: EMMEK FREWN

Emmek Frewn, a salty northerner (NE male Illuskan **commoner**), recently tried to buy the tavern in Trollskull Alley but was outbid by Volothamp Geddarm. Stung by the loss, he bought a smaller, less impressive building in the same alley and turned it into a pub, which he calls Frewn's Brews. If you decide to introduce Emmek as a business rival, choose an unmarked building on map 2.1 to serve as the pub.

Emmek's family migrated to Waterdeep after its holdings in Neverwinter were destroyed by the eruption of Mount Hotenow in 1451 DR. The family struggled to make ends meet by tanning leather in the Trades Ward. After Emmek's parents died, his sisters took over the business and bought him out. He never liked the work anyway, and he particularly hated dealing with the League of Skinners and Tanners.

Emmek is on shaky financial footing because he has sunk most of his wealth into this latest endeavor. He's also in trouble with two of the guilds. First, he tried to save coin by fixing the roof himself, in defiance of the Carpenters', Roofers', and Plaisterers' Guild. Then he offended a member of the Cellarers' and Plumbers' Guild by comparing the dwarf's beard to barnacles on a ship.

GOALS

Emmek wants his pub to be the most successful tavern in the North Ward, and he wants the characters' business to fail spectacularly.

ASSETS

Emmek is stingy when it comes to certain kinds of expenses and foolish with his coin in other ways. He tends to spend a lot on big, showy items and cut corners on the little amenities. Because he doesn't have much coin to throw around right now, his plan to ruin the characters' establishment begins with borrowing some money.

PLANS

Emmek secures a 150 gp loan from Istrid Horn (see appendix B). He spends 50 gp for the services of the Shard Shunners, a gang of halfling wererats with which he has had nefarious dealings in the past. He pays the halflings to hinder the characters' efforts while he works feverishly to manage his own business.

Four gang members have been assigned to work with Emmek: two males named Kelso Fiddlewick and Dasher Snobeedle, and two females named Danika Fiddlewick (Kelso's younger sister) and Brynn Hilltopple. These halflings are **wererats**, with these changes:

- Each wererat is Small and has 27 (6d6 + 6) hit points.
- It has these racial traits: It can move through the space of a Medium or larger creature. It has advantage on saving throws against being frightened. It speaks Common and Halfling, and it knows thieves' cant.

Emmek's strategy for ruining the competition and the consequences for putting it into action are summarized in the table below.

EMMEK'S PLANS

Element	Description
Event	The wererats scope out the characters' tavern in halfling forms and might try to get jobs there.
Event	The wererats plant morsels of food inside the characters' place and bore tiny holes in the outside walls to attract rats, creating an infestation.
Action	Emmek spreads rumors that the characters' tavern is rat-infested, which is why he didn't buy it. Apply a –10 penalty on the next three rolls characters make on the Running a Business table (see "Tavern Keeping Expenses," page 41).
Event	The Shard Shunners claim they've done enough for their coin and demand more.
Action	Emmek pays the wererats another 50 gp to creep around the characters' tavern at night in hybrid and rat form, carve rat faces into the doors of neighbors, and otherwise draw attention to themselves.
Action	Emmek convinces several local residents to sign a letter he has drafted, then dispatches it to the City Watch. The letter accuses the characters of running a front for a guild of wererat thieves and urges the Watch to close their establishment.

LEVEL ADVANCEMENT

In this section of the adventure, the characters should advance to 3rd level by engaging in faction missions, dealing with Emmek Frewn, or partaking in self-directed activities. This period of time represents an opportunity for the characters to make friends and gain a reputation (for good or ill) in Trollskull Alley—and in Waterdeep itself—before the events of chapter 3 embroil them in a greater plot.

CHAPTER 3: FIREBALL

R ESIDENTS OF TROLLSKULL ALLEY ARE SHAKEN by a loud whoosh, rattling windows, and the screams of city folk. A *fireball* spell has just detonated in the street, and the neighborhood is thrown into chaos. As members of the City Guard, the City Watch, and the Watchful Order of Magists and Protectors rush to the scene, the characters are afforded a chance to assess the damage and investigate further. This incident sets into motion the main plot and puts the characters on a collision course with those who want to find and claim Lord Neverember's hidden cache of gold.

The fireball goes off early in the morning, at a time when all the characters are in Trollskull Manor. Read aloud the following text to set the scene:

> Windows rattle as the roar of an explosion fills Trollskull Alley. Charred bodies and anguished screams fly through the air. A thick cloud of acrid smoke billows outward from the blast, which seems to have occurred right outside your door.

Let the players tell you what their characters are doing at this moment and how they react to the explosion. Those who want to guess the nature of the explosion can, with a successful DC 13 Intelligence (Arcana) check, conclude that someone just cast a *fireball* spell outside.

WHAT'S HAPPENING HERE?

Dalakhar, a rock gnome spy working for Lord Dagult Neverember, was on his way to see the characters when the fireball went off, killing him and ten other people. The gnome is important because he was carrying the *Stone of Golorr* (see appendix A)—the key to finding Lord Neverember's hidden cache of gold.

Hounded by agents of the Zhentarim, the Xanathar Guild, and Bregan D'aerthe, Dalakhar was unable to escape from Waterdeep with the artifact, so he planned to entrust it to the characters briefly, for surely the folk who rescued Lord Neverember's son could keep it safe where he could not.

By the time the events of this chapter have played out, the *Stone of Golorr* has changed hands a few times and the characters have learned more about the big picture—though they still have a long chase ahead of them.

ZHENTS CAUGHT IN THE ACT

Three members of the Black Network, including the Zhent assassin Urstul Floxin (see appendix B), were close to nabbing Dalakhar when they were caught in the blast. Of the three, only Urstul survived. Though he was wounded, he was able to pluck the *Stone of Golorr* from Dalakhar's pocket before fleeing the scene. While other survivors were coming to their senses, Urstul stumbled through the smoke and haze and eventually made his way back to Gralhund Villa a short distance away.

House Gralhund

The heads of the Gralhund noble family, Yalah Gralhund and her husband, Orond, are providing coin and shelter to Urstul and his fellow Zhents in exchange for the promise of getting their fair share of the hidden cache of gold. But the Gralhunds aren't willing to put their trust entirely in the Black Network; they sent out their own agent to shadow the Zhents, eliminate Dalakhar, and obtain the *Stone of Golorr* on their behalf. Yalah gave the would-be assassin a *necklace of fireballs* with instructions on how and when to use it. When it seemed as though Dalakhar might give Urstul Floxin the slip, this agent hurled one of the beads from the necklace to stop the gnome in his tracks.

The Gralhunds' assassin is a nimblewright (see appendix B) that escaped from the House of Inspired Hands, the temple of Gond in the Sea Ward, a month ago. The construct hitched a ride on House Gralhund's coach. Yalah Gralhund befriended it, offered it shelter, and used it as a servant until she and her husband found a more sinister use for it.

The incident with the fireball has strained the alliance between the Gralhunds and the Black Network. Urstul Floxin is refusing to hand over the *Stone of Golorr* until he speaks to his secret master, Manshoon. Meanwhile, the Gralhunds are weighing the risks of betraying and murdering Urstul in their own house. If the characters' investigation go well, they'll blunder into this den of snakes before the chapter is done.

Unraveling the Plot

During their investigation, the characters should learn who or what cast the fireball (a nimblewright), why the attack was committed (to steal the *Stone of Golorr*), and where the stone was taken (Gralhund Villa). If the investigation stalls, friendly NPCs might step forward to help in exchange for compensation. One such figure is Vincent Trench, the private detective, who lives in Trollskull Alley (see chapter 2, area T5). The characters can also consult with friendly factions such as the Harpers.

The Crime Scene

In the wake of the explosion, people emerge from their houses and shops to survey the devastation. The fireball didn't set any buildings ablaze, but it left eleven people dead:

- One elderly female human who was out for a walk (no one recognizes her)
- Two cloaked male humans (Zhentarim sellswords) clad in leather armor with sheathed longswords
- Two female humans and one male half-elf dressed in plain clothes (servants of wealthy North Ward families, killed while running errands)
- One male gnome (Dalakhar) wearing a burned cloak and clutching a dagger
- Two female halflings who were playing a flute and a fiddle, and two male halflings who were dancing

The characters have only a few minutes to search the crime scene before members of the City Guard arrive. After that, they aren't allowed anywhere near the bodies, although invisible and similarly hidden characters can search the crime scene further. A search of the bodies accompanied by a successful DC 15 Wisdom (Perception) check reveals the following:

- One of the dead male humans has a black, winged snake (the symbol of the Black Network) tattooed on his right forearm.
- The dead gnome has dry waste on his boots and cloak, suggesting he has spent time in the sewers recently. He also has a pouch containing five 100 gp gemstones.

A character can try to snatch Dalakhar's pouch without being seen by NPC onlookers, doing so with a successful DC 13 Dexterity (Sleight of Hand) check. On a failed check, the character still acquires the pouch, but someone observes the theft and reports it to City Watch constables once they show up (see "The Watch Arrives" below). This witness to the theft can be silenced with a bribe of 50 gp or more.

After the Blast

The characters have a few minutes to examine the crime scene before the City Guard arrives and cordons off Trollskull Alley, posting six **guards** at each entrance. The guards don't allow anyone in or out without permission from a superior officer. Another six **guards**, including a sergeant with 18 hit points, make their way to the crime scene and watch over the dead bodies until the City Watch arrives. Lingering smoke from the fireball also attracts a **Griffon Cavalry rider** (see appendix B). As its **griffon** mount circles the neighborhood, the rider watches the streets and alleys for suspicious figures.

The Watch Arrives

Twenty minutes after the explosion, a City Watch sergeant named **Saeth Cromley** (see appendix B) escorts a member of the Watchful Order of Magists and Protectors named **Barnibus Blastwind** (see appendix B) to the crime scene. Barnibus quietly takes charge of the investigation at that point, while Sergeant Cromley directs a force of twenty constables (**veterans**) to knock on doors and question locals.

Before allowing the corpses to be removed and taken to local temples, Barnibus inspects the scene closely and reaches the following conclusions, which he prefers to keep to himself but might share with other members of the Watchful Order:

- The gnome was running from armed pursuers, of which there were three. The third person who was chasing the gnome isn't among the dead.
- The gnome and his pursuers were moving toward the tavern in Trollskull Alley (which Barnibus will soon come to realize is the characters' property).
- Neither the gnome nor his pursuers saw the blast coming.

Given these findings, Barnibus decides to question the tavern's owners and occupants, with Sergeant Cromley by his side as a witness and bodyguard. Specifically, Barnibus wants to find out the gnome's identity and whether he was known to anyone. The characters, having never met Dalakhar, have little information to offer unless they decide to lie.

Neither Barnibus nor Sergeant Cromley is quick to jump to conclusions. They both prefer to have ironclad evidence and testimony from reliable witnesses before making any arrests. Even though the characters are suspects by virtue of their proximity to the crime scene, it hardly seems plausible that they would unleash destructive magic so close to their place of business in broad daylight. Consequently, Barnibus intends not to take up too much of their time.

Barnibus and Sergeant Cromley refuse requests by characters to join the investigation. "That would introduce too many new variables into an already confounding equation," replies Barnibus with a frown. "Trust in the Watch," Cromley adds dismissively. Characters who seem truthful and honest can press Barnibus for further information by making a DC 15 Charisma (Persuasion) check. On a success, they nudge Barnibus into revealing what he has discovered, as outlined above.

EYEWITNESSES

Many other people witnessed the fireball without being caught in the blast. Three of them have important information to share. Any character who spends at least 1 minute talking to one of them learns what that person saw or heard. (No ability checks are required, since the eyewitnesses are eager to talk.)

FALA LEFALIIR

Fala, the owner of Corellon's Crown (see chapter 2, area T4), relates the following information:

> "I was watering plants in the greenhouse on the second floor of my shop when the blast blew out some of the windows. Lucky I wasn't injured! Through the smoke, I saw a cloaked man take something from the body of a dead gnome, then start limping away. He was badly burned and casting glances over his shoulder, like he was afraid someone might be following him. He was headed toward the Bent Nail."

Fala saw Urstul Floxin fleeing the scene with the *Stone of Golorr* in his clutches. He circled around the Bent Nail (see chapter 2, area T2) on his way out of Trollskull Alley.

JEZRYNNE HORNRAVEN

A Waterdavian born of wealth and privilege, Jezrynne was leaving the Tiger's Eye (see chapter 2, area T5), having just hired Vincent Trench to spy on her philandering husband, when she witnessed the following:

> "I tell you, it was not a man. More like a puppet shaped like a man. A puppet without strings. It was on the rooftop. It hurled something into the crowd below that caused the explosion. I saw those halflings burned alive! I saw them!"

SAETH CROMLEY AND BARNIBUS BLASTWIND

Jezrynne doesn't know what the "puppet" hurled to cause the fireball. She took her eyes off the thing during the chaos and doesn't know where it went.

MARTEM TREC

This 12-year-old boy watched as his halfling friends perished in the flames. He didn't see much beyond that, but he found something important after the blast went off:

> "Right after the explosion, I ducked behind a rain barrel. Then I heard a 'plop' and found this in the barrel."

Martem produces a *necklace of fireballs* with two beads remaining and a broken clasp. As it fled across a rooftop, the nimblewright accidentally yanked on the necklace, which came off, fell to the roof, slid off the edge, and plopped into the rain barrel next to Martem.

He doesn't know what to make of this object but was planning to keep it. A character can snatch it from him or convince Martem to relinquish it with a successful DC 8 Charisma (Intimidation or Persuasion) check.

Characters who withhold the necklace, and knowledge of it, from the City Watch are guilty of a crime in Waterdeep. Hampering justice by concealing evidence can result in a fine of up to 200 gp and hard labor for up to a tenday.

Speaking with the Victims

The dead are taken to a City Watch station in the North Ward and kept in a cellar morgue. Clerics from local temples are brought in to cast *gentle repose* spells on the corpses, to preserve them while the investigation is ongoing. Any character who has a renown of 1 or higher in Force Grey (the Gray Hands), the Harpers, the Lords' Alliance, the Order of the Gauntlet, or the Zhentarim can petition their faction representative to hire a cleric to cast *speak with dead* on one or more of the fatalities. The characters can hire a cleric themselves by making a donation of at least 25 gp to the cleric's temple for each casting of the spell. They must also provide a list of questions they want answered.

A *speak with dead* spell can pry some or all of the following information from Dalakhar's corpse if the right questions are asked:

- Dalakhar stole an artifact called the *Stone of Golorr* from the lair of a beholder known as Xanathar, in a dungeon deep below the city.
- Dalakhar worked for the Open Lord of Waterdeep. (Here he refers to Lord Dagult Neverember, whom he believes is the rightful Open Lord, not Laeral Silverhand.)
- The *Stone of Golorr* is the key to finding a hoard of dragons hidden in the city.
- Dalakhar heard about a group of adventurers who rescued Lord Neverember's son from the Zhentarim and thought the *Stone of Golorr* would be safe in their hands for the time being. He was on his way to deliver it to them, planning to come back and reclaim it after he had eluded his pursuers. Then the fireball went off.

The following information can be learned by casting *speak with dead* on one or both of the dead Zhentarim sellswords:

- Their names were Bashekk Ortallis and Wern Malkrave. They worked for Urstul Floxin and resided at Gralhund Villa.
- Their job was to help catch a gnome named Dalakhar.
- Dalakhar had some kind of artifact in his possession which, according to Urstul Floxin, would make them as rich as kings.

Nim's Secret

Characters who question Jezrynne Hornraven (see "Eyewitnesses" above) can get a description of the creature that set off the fireball. It bears a striking similarity to the automatons that sometimes march in the Day of Wonders parade, as anyone who has lived in Waterdeep during the fall season knows. Because the Day of Wonders parade is sponsored by the local temple of Gond, characters might want to visit the temple and investigate a possible connection.

House of Inspired Hands

The House of Inspired Hands, Waterdeep's temple of Gond, sits on the corner of Seawatch Street and Shark Street in the Sea Ward. If the characters visit the temple, they see the following:

> The House of Inspired Hands looks like a cross between a temple and a workshop. The symbol of Gond, a toothed cog with four spokes, is displayed prominently. You see the silhouette of a humanoid shape perching on the rooftop. It extends an arm, releasing a tiny metal sparrow into the sky. The bird does a few loops in the air, then veers right toward you.

The creature atop the temple is Nim, a **nimblewright** (see appendix B). Nim was given to the temple as a gift from a visiting Lantanese wizard and has been creating its own inventions on the sly. One of those inventions was the nimblewright that detonated the fireball in Trollskull Alley. Another less-dangerous invention, a mechanical sparrow, is on an accidental collision course with the party.

Have the characters roll initiative. Nim's mechanical bird acts on initiative count 10, has a flying speed of 60 feet, and starts 60 feet away from the characters. It has AC 15, 1 hit point, and immunity to poison and psychic damage. On its turn, it flies toward one party member at random and makes a melee weapon attack (+0 to hit) against that character. On a hit, the bird deals 2 (1d3) piercing damage as it slams into the character with surprising force. On a miss, it crashes. Either way, it's destroyed on impact.

After the attack, Nim withdraws into the temple's attic through a secret hatch in the roof and lies low, hoping the characters don't report the incident to the temple's acolytes.

Inside the Temple

The temple of Gond is open and abuzz with activity during daylight hours, then closes from sunset until sunrise. At night, acolytes retire to their private quarters to work on pet projects.

Hall of Exemplary Inventions

The main hall of the temple holds two dozen marble pedestals. Each one bears a prize-winning invention or a miniature model of some other extraordinary creation. Among the displays are several that stand out:

- A 4-foot-tall working model of a clock tower rings at the top of every hour. It is made of wood, iron, bronze, and glass, with brass bells and delicate hands formed from solid gold.
- A wooden flying machine has wings that flap when it becomes airborne.
- A miniature model of a mechanical dragon turtle has a brass plate affixed to its pedestal that reads, "Big Belchy. Sank in Deepwater Harbor on the Day of Wonders in 1363 DR."
- A functional "waking helmet" equipped with small, articulated metal arms and hands that gently slap the wearer if he or she falls asleep.
- A miniature model of a red submarine shaped like a manta ray has a brass plate affixed to its pedestal that reads, "The *Scarlet Marpenoth*. Lantanese submersible. Launched in 1489 DR."

Meeting Valetta

The characters are met by Valetta, a dragonborn **priest** of bronze dragon ancestry, with these changes:

- Valetta is neutral.
- She has these racial traits: She can use her action to exhale a 5-foot-wide, 30-foot line of lightning (but can't do this again until she finishes a short or long rest); each creature in the line must make a DC 11 Dexterity saving throw, taking 2d6 lightning damage on a failed save, or half as much damage on a successful one. She has resistance to lightning damage. She speaks Common and Draconic.

If the characters mention the figure they saw on the roof of the temple, Valetta identifies it as Nim, a nimblewright that was gifted to the temple by a Lantanese wizard. If they describe the incident involving the mechanical bird, Valetta sighs and leads them up a spiral staircase to an attic that Nim uses as a lair—only to find the attic's door fitted with a new lock. Valetta doesn't recognize the lock or have a key to open it, but a character using thieves' tools can pick the lock with a successful DC 20 Dexterity check. A *knock* spell or similar magic also opens the door. Valetta won't allow characters to break down the door, but she does permit them to speak to Nim through the door. A character can persuade Nim to unlock the door with a successful DC 17 Charisma (Persuasion) check. Valetta grants advantage on the roll by strongly urging Nim to comply.

Meeting Nim

Nim understands Common but can't speak. It has developed a simple sign language that Valetta and other members of the temple staff understand. After the incident with the bird, Nim hides amid the clutter in its lair, but it emerges if the characters find their way inside or coax it into unlocking the door. If the characters ask about the other nimblewright, Nim admits (through gesturing to Valetta) that it built the other nimblewright to ease its loneliness. But then Nim's creation fled in confused terror a month ago, and Nim hasn't seen it since. In light of this revelation, Valetta angrily orders acolytes to remove Nim's tools and unfinished inventions from the attic, while she forces Nim to look on.

Nimblewright Detector. Characters who search Nim's attic or watch the area as it's being cleaned out can find a 1-foot-long copper contraption with an umbrella-like metallic protrusion at one end. A *detect magic* spell reveals an aura of divination magic around it. If asked about it, Nim tells Valetta that it built this device to find the errant nimblewright and tried to seek it out, only to discover that Nim couldn't leave the temple grounds. Once Nim explains how the *nimblewright detector* works, Valetta allows the characters to take it.

To activate the *nimblewright detector*, a character must hold down its trigger. When the activated device comes within 500 feet of a nimblewright other than Nim, the umbrella begins to spin, whir, and click. The spinning, whirring, and clicking accelerates as the distance to the target lessens, reaching maximum velocity and volume when a nimblewright other than Nim is within 30 feet of the device.

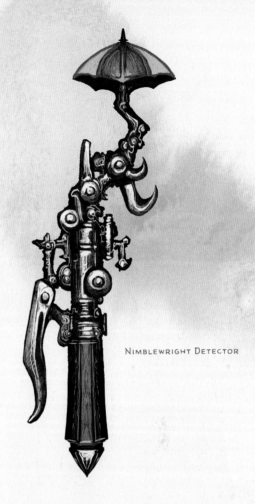

NIMBLEWRIGHT DETECTOR

Reward

If the characters want to track down the wayward nimblewright themselves, Valetta says that the House of Inspired Hands will pay them 500 gp to destroy it. If they return with proof of its destruction, Valetta sees that they receive the promised reward and also offers them one each of the following nonmagical inventions:

Adjustable Stilts. The stilts take 1 minute to put on or remove. They increase the height of any humanoid wearing them by 2 to 5 feet. Each stilt weighs 8 pounds and is 1 foot long when fully collapsed.

Backpack Parachute. A humanoid wearing this piece of gear can deploy the parachute as a reaction while falling, or as an action otherwise. The parachute requires at least a 10-foot cube of unoccupied space in which to deploy, and it doesn't open fast enough to slow a fall of less than 60 feet. If it has sufficient time and space to deploy properly, the parachute allows its wearer to land without taking falling damage. Once it has been used, the parachute takes 10 minutes to repack.

Barking Box. This metal cube, 6 inches on a side, has a crank on top. Using an action to wind the crank activates the box for 8 hours. While activated, the box barks whenever it detects vibrations within 15 feet of it, as long as the box and the source of the vibrations are in contact with the same ground or substance. A switch on one side of the box sets the device to emit either a small dog's bark or a large dog's bark.

JARLAXLE BAENRE

Matchless Pipe. A switch made of flint is built into the bowl of this fine wooden smoking pipe. With a few flicks of the switch, the pipe lights itself.

FINDING NIM'S CREATION

Equipped with the *nimblewright detector*, the characters can search for Nim's escaped creation. A ward-by-ward search is the best approach, but let the players tell you how their characters conduct the search. Depending on where they go, the search could take days.

A character mounted on a griffon can complete a city-wide search in a couple of hours. To secure the use of a griffon, a character must either be a member of the Order of the Gauntlet on good terms with Savra Belabranta or a member of the Lords' Alliance on good terms with Jalester Silvermane. As it happens, a young **griffon** named Bonesnapper is being trained to serve as a mount in the Griffon Cavalry. If Savra or Jalester is inclined to help the party, the characters can arrange to meet the griffon and its trainer outside the River Gate the following morning shortly after dawn. (The griffon and its trainer normally reside in Peaktop Aerie atop Mount Waterdeep, but most civilians aren't welcome there.) To gain Bonesnapper's trust, a character must succeed on a DC 16 Wisdom (Animal Handling) check. The griffon won't allow any character who fails the check to ride it.

Nim's errant nimblewright is in Gralhund Villa on Saerdoun Street, in the North Ward. It isn't, however, the only nimblewright to be found outside the House of Inspired Hands. If the characters decide to search the Dock Ward, the *nimblewright detector* starts to whir when it comes within range of a couple of the ships in port.

DOCK WARD DISTRACTION

Zardoz Zord, owner of the Sea Maidens Faire, has brought his three ships to Waterdeep. Two of these galleons, the *Heartbreaker* and the *Hellraiser*, are docked. Zord's flagship, the *Eyecatcher*, is anchored in Deepwater Harbor. Each of the three ships (described in chapter 7) has at least one nimblewright aboard.

The docks are bustling and chaotic during the day, except in winter. At night, darkness provides sufficient cover for characters to approach the docked vessels unseen. If one or more characters are caught aboard a ship, the crew tries to corner them until the ship's captain can have words with them. The nimblewrights, they say, are "attractions and nothing more." If the characters ask to speak to the owner of the fleet, a *sending* spell is used to contact Zord, who invites the characters to dine with him aboard the *Eyecatcher*.

Dining with Zardoz Zord. Characters who accept Zord's offer are shuttled by dinghy to his flagship, welcomed aboard by drow crew members magically disguised as attractive humans (see chapter 7 for more information), and led to the captain's dining cabin (area J10):

The dining cabin is bedecked with golden filigree, the purple curtains festooned with silken tassels, the wood paneling scented with perfume. A magnificent feast laid out on golden platters sprawls atop a mahogany table of exquisite craftsmanship. Even the doilies are something to behold. Standing behind it all with wine glass in hand is a well-built, scantily clad man, his scarlet apparel designed to accentuate his trim figure and bountiful chest hair. A flashy rapier hangs from his stylish belt.

"Welcome aboard the *Eyecatcher*," he says, flashing his pearly white teeth. "Zardoz Zord, at your service."

This dashing figure is none other than **Jarlaxle Baenre** (see appendix B) magically disguised as Zardoz Zord.

The characters have piqued Jarlaxle's curiosity. He doesn't know much about them (yet) and wants to determine whether they pose a threat (they don't). To win them over, he shares the following information over dinner and wine:

- The Sea Maidens Faire, owned and operated by Zord, is a seafaring carnival based in Luskan that travels along the Sword Coast. It provides good, wholesome entertainment in the form of fantastic street parades.
- The *Heartbreaker* and the *Hellraiser* are used to transport entertainers, wagons, and parade floats. The *Eyecatcher* is Zord's command ship and private yacht. All three ships are built for comfort and speed.
- Zord visits the distant island of Lantan about once a year. During his last visit, he purchased four nimblewrights from a Lantanese wizard. He keeps two aboard his flagship, and one aboard each of the other two vessels.
- When they're not marching in a parade, Zord's nimblewrights remain aboard his ships. "They're perfectly harmless," he attests, whereupon a nimblewright holding a decanter enters the dining cabin and quietly refills everyone's wine glasses.

If the characters mention the *Stone of Golorr*, Zord shrugs his shoulders in a manner that suggests he doesn't know what they're talking about. He also feigns disinterest in Waterdeep politics, saying, "Every city has problems, I suppose. My job as an entertainer is to make people forget about politics for a while." Characters who are suspicious of Zord can make a DC 24 Wisdom (Insight) check. Any character who succeeds on the check senses that there's much more to him than meets the eye.

Jarlaxle owns a *hat of disguise* but doesn't need it to hide his true form while he's aboard any of his ships. His disguise (and the disguises of his drow subordinates) can be dispelled only by destroying the ship's figurehead (see chapter 7). If the characters somehow discern his true form, Jarlaxle gives the party a slow nod of his head, dryly says "Bravo!" and lets them make the next move.

When dinner is concluded, Zord bids the characters farewell and sees that they are escorted safely back to the docks.

DROW CHARACTERS

If the adventuring party includes one or more drow characters, Captain Zord pays close attention to what they do and say, but doesn't treat them any differently from the other party members.

WHAT RENAER KNOWS

At some point during their investigation, the characters might want to speak to Renaer Neverember about the fireball, given his own recent brush with the Zhentarim. Conversely, he could decide to pay them a visit at their tavern. If he's told that a gnome and two Zhents were killed in the blast, Renaer drops a bombshell:

"When the Lords of Waterdeep ousted my father, I thought his long, dark shadow was finally gone for good. The truth is, I want nothing to do with him. But his spies hound me. One of them, a gnome named Dalakhar, had been watching me for months. Then, about two tendays ago, the spy was suddenly nowhere to be seen. My father didn't trust many people, but he trusted that gnome.

"I spoke to a few of Dalakhar's friends. Apparently, he was on a special mission to retrieve the *Stone of Golorr* and was afraid that the Zhentarim and the Xanathar Guild were close to catching him. When he heard about my kidnapping, he wanted more information about the adventurers who had rescued me. I think Dalakhar was planning to pay you to deliver the *Stone of Golorr* to my father in Neverwinter."

Any attempt to follow up with Dalakhar's friends proves futile, since they have gone into hiding in the wake of the gnome's sudden demise.

If the characters tell Renaer that Fala Lefaliir saw a man fleeing Trollskull Alley (see "Eyewitnesses," page 45), Renaer reaches out to his friends in the Harpers. A day later, he returns with the following information:

- The man Fala saw matches the description of Urstul Floxin, a suspected member of the Black Network.
- Another North Ward resident claims he saw Urstul enter Gralhund Villa, in the North Ward, shortly after the fireball incident. The resident reported him to the City Watch because Urstul looked suspicious.
- Two City Watch constables spoke to Lord Gralhund. He assured them that no one had broken into the estate and that everything was fine. The constables had no grounds to get a search warrant, so they didn't pursue the matter.

GRALHUND VILLA

After fleeing Trollskull Alley with the *Stone of Golorr* in his clutches, the Zhent assassin Urstul Floxin returned to Gralhund Villa to confront Yalah Gralhund about sending the nimblewright to meddle in his mission. Lady Gralhund decides she no longer likes Urstul and, taking advantage of his injuries, wrests the *Stone of Golorr* from him at swordpoint and orders her guards to lock him up until she decides what to do with him.

Your choice of main villain determines Lady Gralhund's motivation, which is a secret held by her and Hrabbaz, her loyal half-orc bodyguard:

- If Xanathar is the main villain, Yalah Gralhund has secretly cut a deal with the beholder crime lord, offering to return the *Stone of Golorr* to it if the beholder helps her create a vacancy on the council of Masked Lords.
- If the Cassalanters are the main villains, Yalah is a fawning member of their Asmodeus-worshiping cult and intends to deliver the *Stone of Golorr* to them as a demonstration of her fealty and friendship.
- If Jarlaxle is the main villain, he and Yalah are secret lovers. He has promised to facilitate her rise in power after he uses Lord Neverember's lost hoard to buy Luskan's way into the Lords' Alliance.
- If Manshoon is the main villain, he promised not to destroy Yalah's family if she allowed her villa to be used as a staging area for his secret plots. Believing that Urstul Floxin is after the gold for himself, Yalah plans to cut Urstul out of the deal and deliver the *Stone of Golorr* to Manshoon herself.

Having gravely misjudged and underestimated Lady Gralhund once, Urstul isn't about to do so again. Rallying despite his injuries, he manages to kill the two inattentive Gralhund guards who were watching over him and alert the other Zhents on the estate, who begin dispatching the other guards and servants. Urstul's goal is to capture Lord or Lady Gralhund, force the surrender of the *Stone of Golorr*, and deliver it to his master Manshoon in Kolat Towers (described in chapter 8).

Urstul's plans—unbeknownst to him—are dashed when Lady Gralhund orders her nimblewright to take the *Stone of Golorr* elsewhere. Amid the chaos, the nimblewright flees the estate.

SHOULD THEY OR SHOULDN'T THEY?

The characters must proceed carefully, since they have no evidence that directly implicates the Gralhunds in the attack in Trollskull Alley. Their two basic choices are to share what they know with the City Watch or to visit Gralhund Villa themselves.

LET THE WATCH HANDLE IT

The characters can go to any City Watch station in the North Ward and report what they have learned to the constables there. Shortly thereafter, the characters receive a visit from **Barnibus Blastwind** and **Saeth Cromley** (see appendix B), who have no reason to suspect the characters are lying. Their own investigation corroborates much of what the characters said. Barnibus concludes the meeting by saying, rather brusquely,

"Thank you for the information." Cromley adds, "Rest assured, we'll have this case resolved in no time."

A magistrate provides the City Watch with a warrant to search Gralhund Villa. Sometime afterward, Cromley visits the characters by himself and, as a courtesy, tells them what happened:

- Officers arrived to find Lord Gralhund unconscious, Lady Gralhund in shock, and their half-orc bodyguard bloodied but unbowed.
- Apparently, the Gralhunds had been held hostage for more than a tenday by agents of the Black Network. Most of the Zhents were killed during a bloody revolt led by Lord Gralhund himself.
- The Zhent leader, Urstul Floxin, was among those who got away. He's still at large. The Watch plans to step up its search for him.
- Of the nimblewright, there was no sign. According to the Gralhunds, the construct was delivered to Gralhund Villa weeks earlier. The family took it in, not realizing it was a Zhentarim spy. Lady Gralhund reported that it stole her *necklace of fireballs*.

Cromley's summary of events is based on information given to the City Watch by the Gralhunds and is riddled with falsehoods. The hostage situation, Lord Gralhund's heroism, and the theft of Lady Gralhund's *necklace of fireballs* never happened. The nimblewright's affiliation with the Zhentarim is also a lie. The Gralhunds' account further doesn't explain why the nimblewright would use the *necklace of fireballs* to inflict harm on the Zhents if it was working with them. If characters raise that question, Cromley thinks for a moment and then ventures the guess that the nimblewright underestimated the necklace's explosive power.

INVESTIGATE THE VILLA

The characters can insert themselves into Gralhund Villa and accost its residents with impunity if they're careful to pin the violence on the Zhents or if they're able to enter and leave unseen before the City Watch shows up to arrest everyone.

Sneaking in or out of the villa without being seen or heard by neighbors and passersby requires each character to succeed on a DC 15 Dexterity (Stealth) check. A character who has proficiency in the Stealth skill can take disadvantage on the check to grant advantage on another party member's check (essentially compensating for a less stealthy companion).

If the characters side with the Gralhunds in the conflict, Lady Gralhund is inclined to overlook their trespass. Her demeanor sours, however, if they start asking too many questions. She vigorously denies accusations that her family is involved with the Black Network and claims the Zhents were holding her family hostage (a false claim also parroted by her husband, her bodyguard, her children, and her staff). If the characters assault any member of the household or brandish weapons in an attempt to intimidate, the Gralhunds inform the City Watch of the party's crimes.

During the characters' invasion of Gralhund Villa, the nimblewright flees the estate with the *Stone of Golorr* (see chapter 4 for more information on its destination). If

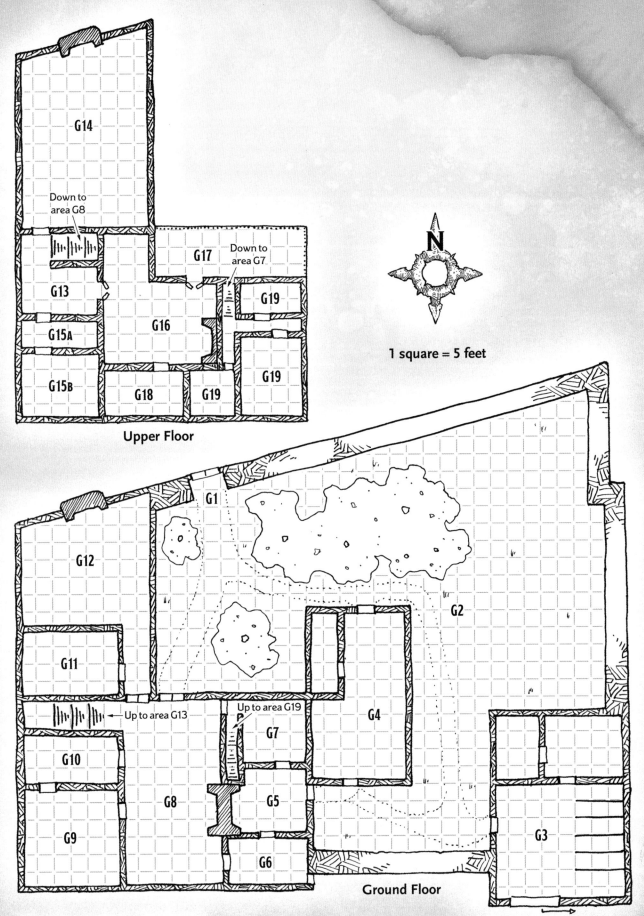

G14

Down to
area G8

Down to
area G7

G17

G13

G19

G15A

G16

G19

G15B

G18

G19

Upper Floor

N

1 square = 5 feet

G1

G12

G2

G11

Up to area G13

Up to area G19

G7

G4

G10

G8

G5

G3

G9

G6

Ground Floor

the characters are using Nim's *nimblewright detector* to track the nimblewright, the device lets them know that the nimblewright has fled the scene, but not the direction it went.

OVERVIEW

Gralhund Villa sits in the middle of an upper-class residential neighborhood in the North Ward. Here are some general facts to keep in mind:

- The streets around the villa have pedestrians and coaches traveling along them at all hours, though traffic is heavier during the day.
- The estate is enclosed by 12-foot-high stone walls that require a successful DC 15 Strength (Athletics) check to negotiate without the aid of climbing gear or magic.
- Neighbors and bystanders alert the City Watch if they hear loud, disturbing noises (such as a *thunderwave* spell) coming from the estate or if they see anything suspicious. The Watch sends a **mage** and six **veterans** (one sergeant and five constables) to investigate, and it takes 1d6 + 4 minutes for this force to arrive.
- All ceilings in the mansion are 20 feet high.

ENCOUNTERS IN THE VILLA

The following encounter locations, keyed to map 3.1, describe the Gralhund estate as it stands when the characters first arrive. The Zhents have taken over the downstairs level of the mansion; the Gralhunds are fighting to hold the upstairs.

G1. LOCKED GATES

Through a set of ornate iron gates, the characters can see a yard with several large trees, as well as two footpaths that lead to a two-story brick mansion and eastward toward a detached coach house.

An *arcane lock* spell is cast on the gates. Forcing them open requires a successful DC 25 Strength (Athletics) check, while picking the lock requires a successful DC 20 Dexterity check using thieves' tools. The spell doesn't bar members of the Gralhund family, their staff, their guards, or Lady Gralhund's nimblewright from opening the gates.

G2. YARD

The estate is well tended. In spring and summer, large trees provide shade. The trees begin shedding leaves in the fall. By winter, their branches are stripped bare.

Balcony. Through the trees, the characters can see a large balcony (area G17) enclosed by an iron railing above the mansion's main entrance. The balcony is 20 feet above ground level, and scaling the mansion's brick walls to reach it without the aid of climbing gear or magic requires a successful DC 15 Strength (Athletics) check.

Evil Groundskeeper. The yard is looked after by a menacing groundskeeper named Hurv Taldred (LE male Illuskan **cult fanatic**) and his two quiet **mastiffs**. The Gralhunds paid a necromancer to perform a ritual on Hurv and his mastiffs. After sundown, the physical forms of these figures melt away, and they become three **shadows** until dawn. Characters who succeed on a DC

13 Dexterity (Stealth) check can cross the yard without being detected. Otherwise, Hurv and his hounds detect the characters and attack, day or night.

G3. COACH HOUSE

This stone building contains a beautifully maintained coach and clean stables that house four **draft horses** and Lady Gralhund's jet-black **riding horse**, named Maladar. A sliding wooden door bars access to the street and has a padlock on the outside that holds it shut. Picking the lock requires a successful DC 20 Dexterity check using thieves' tools.

The larger room north of the stables contains tack and harness for each horse, as well as bales of hay and yard tools. The smaller room in the northwest corner has two cots: one for the groundskeeper, Hurv (see area G2), who sleeps during the day, and one for a stableboy named Ike (**commoner**), who sleeps here at night. Ike is away (either picking up food for the horses or out drinking with friends) if the characters arrive during the day.

Treasure. Lady Gralhund's horse is outfitted with *horseshoes of speed* and two saddlebags, each of which holds four 5-pound gold trade bars worth 250 gp each.

G4. GUARD BARRACKS

This one-story stone building attached to the mansion serves as quarters for twenty house guards. The main room contains ten bunk beds. Each comes with a pair of footlockers containing folded clothes and worthless personal effects.

The room in the northwest corner contains wooden mannequins and racks designed to hold armor and weapons. Since there are no guards present, the mannequins and racks are bare.

G5. KITCHEN

An unlocked wooden door leads from the yard to the mansion's kitchen, which is stocked with cookware and utensils. A large fireplace is used for cooking meals.

G6. PANTRY

This pantry is lined with shelves containing dry foodstuffs, spices, folded tablecloths, and jars of preserves. Casks of fresh water, ale, and wine are also stored here.

Barred Door. A back door leads out to the street. This sturdy wooden door is barred shut on the inside. Forcing it open from the outside requires a successful DC 20 Strength (Athletics) check and makes a lot of noise.

Corpses. The Zhents have killed two servants, an older male human (the head butler) and a younger male halfling (a cook), and left their bodies on the floor.

G7. LAUNDRY ROOM

This room is where servants wash clothing. It contains scrub buckets, wash basins, soap, mops, and chamber pots.

Corpses. The Zhents have killed a servant, a middle-aged female human (the head maid), and left her body on the stairs leading up to the servants' quarters (area G19). The maid has a ring of keys on her belt that opens all the locked doors in the mansion as well as the cabinets in area G8.

G8. Great Hall

Characters who enter this hall for the first time notice the following:

- The floor is strewn with bodies. Two **thugs** holding bloody maces stand over them.
- The sound of fighting can be heard coming from the top of a wide staircase in the northwest corner (see area G13).
- Two iron chandeliers hang from the dark mahogany ceiling above a long dining table carved from red larchwood. Chairs surround the table, with a particularly tall and elaborate chair at each end.
- Lining the wood-paneled walls are tapestries and locked wooden cabinets that contain fine dishes, silverware, and candlesticks.
- A fireplace with a black marble mantelpiece has a framed family portrait mounted above it. (The portrait depicts Lord and Lady Gralhund, their three young children, and a family dog that died three years ago.)

Corpses. Lying about the room are the bodies of eight guards wearing bloody and tattered House Gralhund livery over their chain shirts, as well as two dead Zhents in black leather armor. All are humans.

Thugs. The two figures with maces are Zhents clad in black leather armor. Their orders are to hold the room. They attack strangers, including members of the City Watch, on sight. They carry no treasure.

G9. Parlor

Urstul Floxin was confined here when he returned to the villa, but shortly thereafter he killed his guards and escaped. The room is furnished for comfort and contains dainty chairs, a chaise longue, a wine cabinet, and framed paintings of various long-dead members of the Gralhund family.

Corpses. The bodies of the two guards lie atop blood-soaked rugs. The guards wear chain shirts and the livery of House Gralhund.

G10. Den and Trophy Room

Lord Gralhund's den has the heads of various beasts mounted on the walls and gleaming suits of armor standing at attention in the corners. Bearskin rugs and overstuffed chairs fill the room.

Lord Gralhund recently took up falconry as a hobby. In the middle of the room, resting on a table, is a cage containing a hooded falcon (use **hawk** statistics).

G11. Orond's Study

The door to this room is locked. The lock can be picked by a character who makes a successful DC 15 Dexterity check using thieves' tools. The room has these features:

- A 10-foot-square canvas wrestling mat is sprawled on the floor in the middle of the room.
- Velvet armchairs, small statues of naked men on pedestals, and tall mahogany bookshelves are arranged neatly around the room.
- A mahogany desk in one corner doesn't look like it sees much use.

Books. Most of the books are fake boxes made of painted cardboard. A few have bawdy drawings and salacious poems hidden inside them.

G12. Family Library

The wood-paneled library includes these features:

- Tall bookshelves are packed with tomes. Sliding wooden ladders mounted on rails allow easy access to higher shelves.
- In one corner stands an iron lectern with a closed, locked, leather-bound tome resting on it.
- Two padded chairs face a large fireplace. One has a wolf skin draped over it.

Books. Many of the books were handed down to Lady Gralhund by her parents, and they are well kept. They include historical texts, play scripts, novels, and poetry collections.

Locked Tome. Although it looks like it might be a spellbook, the tome on the lectern is a chronicle of the Gralhund family's accomplishments, embellished or recast to paint the family in the most favorable light. A *detect magic* spell reveals an aura of abjuration magic emanating from the tome.

The tome is meant to be unlocked using a key that Lady Gralhund wears on a chain around her neck. The lock can be picked by a character who succeeds on a DC 15 Dexterity check using thieves' tools, or it can be opened with a *knock* spell or similar magic. Opening the book by any means other than using the proper key causes three **specters** to appear within 10 feet of the book and attack its opener. The magic that binds the specters has weakened over time; they can exist on the Material Plane for only 1 minute, after which time they are banished to the Ethereal Plane (unless destroyed first). The specters manifest as ghostly tieflings with elongated fingers.

The Gralhund family crest appears on the book's title page. The rest of the book is written in Common and describes births, deaths, and other family events between 1239 DR, the Year of the Bloodied Sword, and 1422 DR, the Year of Advancing Shadows. Of particular note is the little-known fact that the Gralhunds forged pacts with devils in years past, giving rise to a strain of tieflings. All such members of the house were sent to live on a Gralhund estate in Yartar, a city far to the north (or so the book claims in its epilogue), and there are passing references to some Waterdavian family members having been born with tails.

G13. Upstairs Foyer

A lot is happening in this elegant foyer:

- A battle rages between several Zhents and house guards, and the floor is strewn with dead bodies.
- Doors to the master bedroom (area G16) stand open. (If Lady Gralhund is in the master bedroom, she shouts, "The City Watch is on the way!")
- The door to area G15a is ajar. Beyond it, characters can hear someone putting a boot to another door.

Corpses. Lying on the floor are the corpses and weapons of six guards wearing House Gralhund livery over chain shirts and two Zhents in black leather armor.

URSTUL FLOXIN

Fight in Progress. Four **veterans** of House Gralhund (each with 30 hit points remaining) are fighting off an attacking force of Zhents consisting of three **thugs** (each with 20 hit points remaining). The Zhents are trying to get to area G16, but the guards are blocking them.

If the characters do nothing to affect the outcome of this fight, assume that it ends with three House Gralhund veterans still alive and all the Zhents dead.

G14. BALLROOM

The door to this room is locked. A character using thieves' tools can pick the lock with a successful DC 15 Dexterity check. The ballroom is unoccupied and contains the following features:

- Gilded mirrors, tasseled tapestries, and stained-glass lamps festoon the walls. Mounted above a fireplace is a stag's head made of blown glass.
- The veined marble floor is polished to a mirror-like sheen.
- Tacky crystal chandeliers dangle from the ceiling, which has a mural depicting an orgy painted on it.

G15. GUEST SUITE

Until recently, this suite was set aside for the use of Urstul Floxin. Lord Gralhund has barricaded himself in area G15b, using heavy furniture to block the door. Forcing it open requires a successful DC 18 Strength (Athletics) check.

The characters encounter **Urstul Floxin** (see appendix B) in area G15a. Urstul is wounded with 50 hit

points remaining and has no poison coating his weapons, reducing his challenge rating to 3 (700 XP). He's trying to kick open the door to area G15b in a desperate attempt to capture Lord Gralhund and trade him for the *Stone of Golorr*. If he is accosted before reaching Lord Gralhund, Urstul tries to flee the villa and uses any other surviving Zhents to cover his escape. He knows the same information that Lord Gralhund does (see "Orond Gralhund" below) but won't divulge it or the name of his master, Manshoon, unless he's magically compelled to do so.

Area G15a is a bathroom. A curtain to the east has been drawn back, revealing a claw-footed bathtub.

Area G15b is a wood-paneled bedchamber with a birdcage on a table and a permanent teleportation circle inscribed on the floor. The birdcage contains three **flying snakes** that Urstul uses to deliver messages to his spies throughout the city. The circle is used by Manshoon to meet secretly with Urstul Floxin and to teleport Zhents to and from Kolat Towers (see chapter 8). See the *teleportation circle* spell description in the *Player's Handbook* for more information on how the circle functions.

Orond Gralhund. Having blocked the bedroom door with a wardrobe, a desk, and an overstuffed chair, Orond Gralhund (see appendix B) cowers behind a bed in the southwest corner of area G15b. Although he's armed with a rapier, Orond throws himself at the mercy of the first person to bust through his barricade.

Characters who have Lord Gralhund at their mercy can pry the following information from him with a successful DC 10 Charisma (Intimidation) check, but the check is made with disadvantage if Lord Gralhund has reason to believe his wife can see or overhear the conversation:

- "The *Stone of Golorr* is some kind of ancient creature transformed into an artifact. It knows the location of a hidden vault in Waterdeep containing half a million dragons."
- "House Gralhund has been bankrolling Black Network operations in Waterdeep, including the plot to kidnap Renaer Neverember and the plot to steal the *Stone of Golorr* from his father's gnome spy, Dalakhar."
- "My wife was frustrated with the Zhents and their inability to secure the artifact. She gave a *necklace of fireballs* to her mechanical servant and sent it out to help retrieve the stone. It was careless and caught the Zhents in the fireball by mistake."

G16. MASTER BEDROOM

The doors to this room have been thrown open. The room contains the following occupants and features:

- **Yalah Gralhund**, wearing a breastplate and armed with a rapier, stands next to her well-dressed half-orc bodyguard, **Hrabbaz** (see appendix B for their statistics).
- A locked wooden trunk rests at the foot of a large, canopied bed in the southwest corner.
- A claw-footed bathtub sits in the northwest alcove near a freestanding mirror and a privacy screen.
- Hanging above a fireplace in the southeast corner is a shield that bears the Gralhund coat of arms. Logs are stacked neatly next to the hearth.
- A tall mahogany wardrobe stuffed with expensive gowns and dress clothes stands next to a pair of open glass doors leading out to a balcony.

Yalah Gralhund. Lady Gralhund gave the *Stone of Golorr* and a map of where to take it to her nimblewright servant, who has left the villa by the time the characters reach this chamber. Its escape is crucial, since it sets into motion the events in chapter 4.

Lady Gralhund and Hrabbaz are the only people who know where the nimblewright has gone, but they feign ignorance when questioned about it.

Yalah carries a ring of keys that open all locked doors in the mansion, as well as the locked wooden trunk at the foot of the bed. If her situation turns dire and Hrabbaz is unable to protect her, Yalah unlocks the door to area G18, rushes inside, and locks the door behind her with her next action. She makes her final stand there, with her children cowering behind her.

Wooden Trunk. The lock on the trunk can be picked with thieves' tools and a successful DC 15 Dexterity check. The trunk appears to contain folded clothes and shoes. A secret compartment in the bottom can be detected by someone who examines the outside of the trunk and makes a successful DC 15 Wisdom (Perception) check. The compartment holds two holy symbols of Asmodeus and two robes, each red and gold in color.

Lord and Lady Gralhund are both secret members of a cult of Asmodeus worshipers popular among select nobles in Waterdeep. The cult is led by Lord Victoro Cassalanter (see appendix B), though the Gralhunds won't divulge this information willingly.

G17. BALCONY

This large balcony is enclosed by an ornate wrought-iron railing and has lounge chairs neatly arranged on it. The ground is 20 feet below, and open glass doors lead to the master bedroom (area G16).

G18. CHILDREN'S ROOM

The door to this room is locked. The lock can be picked with a successful DC 15 Dexterity check using thieves' tools.

Three beds line the south wall, and an empty cradle rests against the east wall. Other furnishings include squat wardrobes, play rugs, and children's desks.

Children. Confined here for their safety are the Gralhunds' two youngest children, a 13-year-old boy named Zartan and a 10-year-old boy named Greth. Both are noncombatants. Their 18-year-old sister, Tomassin, is visiting a tiefling cousin in Yartar.

G19. SERVANTS' WING

Three rooms in the southeast area of the upper floor are where the servants sleep at night. The head butler and head maid have rooms to themselves, but those places are currently unoccupied. The largest of the three chambers is a common room containing six bunk beds for the junior staff. A total of nine maids, cooks, and valets (**commoners**) are holed up here, waiting for someone to rescue them. They are armed with improvised weapons (rolling pins, mops, brooms, and the like) that are treated as clubs.

AFTERMATH

After fleeing Gralhund Villa with the *Stone of Golorr*, Lady Gralhund's nimblewright hides the artifact in a secret location in Waterdeep, setting the stage for chapter 4.

Even if the bloody conflict at Gralhund Villa goes unnoticed outside the walls of the estate, the carnage can't be hidden from the City Watch for long. There are too many murdered servants and guards for anyone to conceal what has transpired. The arrival of the City Watch foreshadows the return of **Barnibus Blastwind** and **Saeth Cromley** (see appendix B), who arrive in due course with twenty constables (**veterans**) and two **Griffon Cavalry riders** (see appendix B) astride **griffons**. The griffons and their riders remain airborne, providing aerial support and reconnaissance.

Barnibus thoroughly investigates the Gralhund Villa crime scene and questions neighbors and bystanders. Characters who are seen leaving the scene become suspects. If the characters killed any members of the Gralhund family and left witnesses or evidence of the act, Barnibus instructs Sergeant Cromley to arrest them for the crime of murdering a noble, which carries a death sentence if they're found guilty.

Loose Ends

You can use the following optional event to address what happens to the Zhentarim in the aftermath.

Bad Time to Be a Zhent

Within days after the events that local broadsheets dub the "Gralhund Villa Bloodbath," the City Watch cracks down on the Black Network. Even members of the Zhentarim who have no known criminal ties are rounded up and interrogated, including Davil Starsong (see appendix B). Characters who are members of the faction are safe for the time being, as long as they keep a low profile. Otherwise, they too are rounded up and questioned over a period of several days, until the Lords of Waterdeep ascertain their level of involvement in the violence at Gralhund Villa. The broadsheets jump on the bandwagon by portraying the Black Network in the most unflattering light, thus dealing a crippling blow to the faction's already questionable reputation.

Encounter with Istrid Horn

This encounter occurs only if the characters were directly involved in the events that transpired at Gralhund Villa. After Davil Starsong is taken in for questioning, **Istrid Horn** (see appendix B) sends a message to the characters by way of a **flying snake**. The message, written in Common, reads as follows:

> I would like to know more about what happened at Gralhund Villa. If you can spare the time, meet me at Ahghairon's Statue in the City of the Dead at highsun tomorrow. You'll be paid generously for your time and trouble.
> —Istrid Horn

If the characters attend the meeting, use the following boxed text to help set the scene, embellishing it to reflect the season:

> Ahghairon's Statue is a well-known landmark in the city's parkland cemetery: a tall, marble sculpture of a bearded, robed wizard standing atop concentric steps and facing west toward the skyline of Waterdeep, his hands outstretched and a broad smile on his face. At the foot of the statue stands a female dwarf clad in plate armor.

If the weather is fair, characters can see pedestrians, picnickers, and frolicking children throughout the cem-etery grounds. It's clear that Istrid chose a safe, public place for the meeting. Characters who succeed on a DC 15 Wisdom (Insight) check can tell that she came alone.

Istrid fears being arrested by the City Watch. Although she wasn't involved in the matters concerning Gralhund Villa, she is worried that the Watch will uncover her illegal currency-lending operation in the course of its investigations. She offers the characters 10 pp just for meeting with her and promises another 40 pp if the characters agree to help her lie low for a tenday—half to be paid once a deal is struck and half at the end of her stay. If they decline her offer and the party includes one or more Zhentarim members, she threatens that if she's arrested and charged with a crime, she will reveal their affiliation and bring them down with her.

Hiding Istrid. If the characters decide to let Istrid hide out at their tavern, she uses a disguise kit to make herself up to be a male dwarf named Jorn. If asked to do so, she's willing to perform chores around the place once she settles in. Ultimately, no one comes looking for her, but the longer she stays hidden, the more testy and demanding she becomes.

If the characters tolerate her bad behavior, Istrid leaves at the end of the tenday as promised and pays characters the remainder of what she owes. Characters who are members of the Zhentarim gain an added benefit for harboring Istrid in her time of need: their renown in the faction increases by 2.

If, on the other hand, the characters throw her out or rat her out to the City Watch, Istrid becomes their mortal enemy and tries to undermine them at every turn.

Harming Istrid. As a precaution against being double-crossed, Istrid shared her plan concerning the characters with at least one other member of the Doom Raiders (see appendix B). If the characters betray or harm Istrid, her former adventuring companions use every resource at their disposal to ruin the characters. The laws of Waterdeep discourage them from attacking the characters openly, but they can damage the party's business by scaring off their clientele, and characters might find themselves the targets of worse if they dare to leave the confines of the city.

Level Advancement

If you're leveling up characters using story milestones instead of tracking experience points, the characters advance from 3rd to 4th level if they conducted their own investigation into the fireball incident and affected the outcome of events in Gralhund Villa. Otherwise, they are still 3rd level at the start of chapter 4.

CHAPTER 4: DRAGON SEASON

OLD MAKES PEOPLE DO STRANGE THINGS, AND Lord Neverember's hidden cache of dragons is up for grabs. The *Stone of Golorr* knows where the treasure vault is located and how to get inside, and much of this chapter focuses on the characters' hunt for the artifact. The challenges before them depend on the villain (or villains) that you selected to oppose them. Whatever the season, a villain's goals are simple: obtain the stone, find the Vault of Dragons, and claim the treasure within.

SETTING THE STAGE

In chapter 3, Lady Gralhund's nimblewright took the *Stone of Golorr* and fled with it. The nimblewright delivers the artifact to a location and leaves it there for the main villain or villains to retrieve:

- If Xanathar is the villain, the stone is delivered to a mage named Grinda Garloth. She owns an *apparatus of Kwalish* and lives in Mistshore, a seedy neighborhood built on a dock in the Dock Ward.
- If the Cassalanters are the villains, the stone is left in their family crypt in Waterdeep's cemetery, the City of the Dead. A halfling necromancer gets to it before the Cassalanters or the characters do.
- If Jarlaxle is the villain, the stone is delivered to Fenerus Stormcastle, a lamplighter in the Trades Ward. Fenerus has a criminal history and is currently in trouble with the law.

- If Manshoon is the villain, the stone is brought to Thrakkus, a dragonborn butcher in the Field Ward who chops up bodies for the Zhentarim.

FINDING THE NIMBLEWRIGHT

If the characters can't pick up the trail after the nimblewright escapes with the *Stone of Golorr*, they might turn to the City Watch, the City Guard, or a friendly faction for help, which comes forth in 1d4 days. If it occurs to none of the characters, an NPC suggests that the party visit the House of Inspired Hands to see whether the priests of Gond know a way to find it (see "Nim's Secret," page 46). Thereafter, armed with Nim's *nimblewright detector*, the characters can sweep the city. But by the time they find the nimblewright, it has already delivered the *Stone of Golorr* to its intended destination.

CAUGHT AT LAST!

When it is finally found, the **nimblewright** (see appendix B) is wearing a stolen cloak and hiding under a pile of uncollected garbage in an alley. Exactly where and when the characters stumble upon it is up to you. With nowhere to go and no other purpose, it fights until destroyed. Regardless of where and when this event takes place, six members of the City Watch (**veterans**) arrive as the fight ends. Drawn by the commotion, the Watch couldn't care less about the nimblewright and believes any plausible story the characters tell them. (As a construct, it had no rights to speak of.) The officers are near the end of their shift and eager to move on; they urge the characters to go home and cause no further mischief.

Lady Gralhund's Map

Lady Gralhund gave her nimblewright a map showing where to take the *Stone of Golorr*, but she forgot to tell it to destroy the map once the stone was delivered. Characters who search the nimblewright's remains find the folded-up map, which depicts one of Waterdeep's wards. Written on the map is an X with a name next to it. This map points the characters to where they need to be, setting off a sequence of encounters (see "Encounter Chains" below). The main villain determines which ward the map depicts and what name is written on it:

- If Xanathar is the villain, "Grinda Garloth" is written by the X on a map of the Dock Ward. (The X marks the dock neighborhood of Mistshore, where Grinda lives.)
- If the Cassalanters are the villains, the name "Cassalanter" is written by the X on a map of the City of the Dead. (The X marks the location of the Cassalanter mausoleum.)
- If Jarlaxle is the villain, "Fenerus Stormcastle" is written by the X on a map of the Trades Ward. (Residents of the Trades Ward know Fenerus. He's a lamplighter with an alley dwelling. The X marks the alley.)

OBTAINING THE STONE OF GOLORR

The *Stone of Golorr* possesses an intelligent, alien intellect and has enough prescience to realize that the characters are destined to find it. The stone doesn't want to be found too easily, though.

If the characters obtain the stone earlier than expected, it proves uncooperative and tries to separate itself from the party as quickly as possible, refusing to share any knowledge with characters in the meantime. The stone tries to take control of anyone who attunes to it, triggering a conflict (see "Sentient Magic Items" in chapter 7 of the *Dungeon Master's Guide*). If the stone fails to take control, it can't try again against that character until the next dawn. If the stone succeeds in taking control of its owner, it orders that character to deliver it to whichever location sets into motion the sequence of encounters discussed in this chapter (see "Encounter Chains"). Once the stone divests itself of its current owner, it tries to erase all knowledge of itself from that character's mind (see the item's description in appendix A). Any player whose character is forced to forget about the stone carries the burden of roleplaying that memory loss. You can award inspiration to that character as a way to acknowledge the player's good roleplaying.

As chapter 4 unfolds, you decide when it's time for the characters to have a chance of securing the *Stone of Golorr*. Try to keep it out of their hands for as long as possible to maximize the suspense.

Once the characters have earned the *Stone of Golorr*, it no longer tries to take control of them. A character can attune to it and learn the following information:

- The location of the Vault of Dragons (see "Vault of Dragons," page 94)
- The three keys required to unlock the vault's doors (see "Vault Keys," page 90)
- The name of the vault's gold dragon guardian, and the powers of the staff in its possession (see the description of the *dragonstaff of Ahghairon* in appendix A)

- If Manshoon is the villain, "Thrakkus" is written by the X on a map of the Field Ward. (The X marks the location of Thrakkus's butcher shop and residence.)

ENCOUNTER CHAINS

Eight encounters comprise the characters' hunt for the *Stone of Golorr* and the Vault of Dragons. They form a chain, and their order is determined by your choice of villain and season. The diagram on the facing page illustrates the order of encounters in each chain. If Xanathar is the villain, for example, the chain begins with encounter 2, "Mistshore," and ends with encounter 6, "Theater."

Don't feel bound by an encounter chain. Let the characters' decisions and actions drive the story. You can change the order in which encounters happen, remove encounters you don't need, or create new encounters. You can also modify encounters to suit your tastes.

If the characters stray, they might find themselves at a loss for what to do next. You have a couple of easy ways to guide them back on track:

- A friendly faction that has information about the whereabouts of the *Stone of Golorr* whereabouts can bring that knowledge to the characters.
- A treacherous underling of the villain reveals the location of the *Stone of Golorr* for a price.

SPRING ENCOUNTER CHAIN

Ah, springtime—when beholder eyestalks are in bloom. The *Stone of Golorr* was originally snatched from Xanathar, and the eye tyrant wants it back. It sends monsters and minions to do its dirty work.

SUMMARY

The stone is delivered to Grinda Garloth, a mage who has worked for Xanathar in the past. When she refuses to give up the stone, members of the Xanathar Guild try to take it by force (encounter 2, "Mistshore"). After the characters defeat these attackers, they learn that Grinda told her rat familiar to hide the stone in her family's crypt in the City of the Dead. From this point on, the characters are followed by a gazer (see appendix B), through whose eyes Xanathar can see. If this gazer is killed, Xanathar doesn't send another one to replace it.

Losser Mirklav, a halfling necromancer, raids the Garloth mausoleum and takes the stone shortly before the characters arrive (encounter 4, "Mausoleum"). As they emerge from the mausoleum, members of the Xanathar Guild attack them, believing they have the stone. A clue left behind in the mausoleum leads the characters to an old windmill in the Southern Ward and a pair of grave robbers (encounter 10, "Converted Windmill"). Fearing arrest, the grave robbers point them to a cellar complex under the Trades Ward (encounter 9, "Cellar Complex"). When the characters arrive, they find Losser surrounded by foes and kenku working for the Xanathar Guild making off with the stone. A chase through the streets on or before Trolltide (encounter 3, "Street Chase") ends when the kenku, fearing capture, duck into an old tower (encounter 7, "Old Tower"). If they are caught and confronted, the kenku hand over the stone.

ENCOUNTER CHAINS BY SEASON

SPRING
Xanathar

- ENCOUNTER 2: MISTSHORE
- ENCOUNTER 4: MAUSOLEUM
- ENCOUNTER 10: CONVERTED WINDMILL
- ENCOUNTER 9: CELLAR COMPLEX
- ENCOUNTER 3: STREET CHASE
- ENCOUNTER 7: OLD TOWER
- ENCOUNTER 1: ALLEY
- ENCOUNTER 6: THEATER

SUMMER
The Cassalanters

- ENCOUNTER 4: MAUSOLEUM
- ENCOUNTER 10: CONVERTED WINDMILL
- ENCOUNTER 5: ROOFTOP CHASE
- ENCOUNTER 1: ALLEY
- ENCOUNTER 3: STREET CHASE
- ENCOUNTER 9: CELLAR COMPLEX
- ENCOUNTER 8: COURTHOUSE
- ENCOUNTER 7: OLD TOWER

AUTUMN
Jarlaxle Baenre

- ENCOUNTER 1: ALLEY
- ENCOUNTER 9: CELLAR COMPLEX
- ENCOUNTER 6: THEATER
- ENCOUNTER 8: COURTHOUSE
- ENCOUNTER 7: OLD TOWER
- ENCOUNTER 5: ROOFTOP CHASE
- ENCOUNTER 2: MISTSHORE
- ENCOUNTER 10: CONVERTED WINDMILL

WINTER
Manshoon

- ENCOUNTER 10: CONVERTED WINDMILL
- ENCOUNTER 1: ALLEY
- ENCOUNTER 5: ROOFTOP CHASE
- ENCOUNTER 6: THEATER
- ENCOUNTER 3: STREET CHASE
- ENCOUNTER 2: MISTSHORE
- ENCOUNTER 7: OLD TOWER
- ENCOUNTER 4: MAUSOLEUM

WATERDEEP
SEA WARD

The Xanathar Guild makes one last attempt to regain the stone (encounter 1, "Alley"). Any character who becomes attuned to the stone learns that the Vault of Dragons lies beneath a theater in the Castle Ward (encounter 6, "Theater").

WEATHER EFFECTS

Until the encounter chain is complete, the following weather effects are in play.

Heavy Rain. Heavy rain falls from noon until midnight. Creatures in the rain have disadvantage on Wisdom (Perception) checks that rely on hearing or sight. The rain also extinguishes open flames. Visibility is reduced to 60 feet.

Thick Fog. From midnight until noon, the city is engulfed in thick fog. Creatures in the fog have disadvantage on Wisdom (Perception) checks that rely on sight. Visibility is reduced to 30 feet.

SUMMER ENCOUNTER CHAIN

As Waterdavians contend with sweltering heat, the Cassalanters send disciples of their Asmodeus-worshiping cult to seize the *Stone of Golorr* while deftly avoiding entanglements with local authorities.

SUMMARY

The characters arrive at the Cassalanter mausoleum to find several dead cultists inside (encounter 4, "Mausoleum"). A left-for-dead survivor reveals that these cultists were betrayed by two of their own. The characters head to an old windmill in the Southern Ward where the cult fanatics practice their diabolical faith (encounter 10, "Converted Windmill"). Spined devils swoop in, snatch the stone, and flee, setting up a rooftop chase (encounter 5, "Rooftop Chase").

The spined devils deliver the stone to a hire-coach parked in an alley (encounter 1, "Alley"). Inside the coach is Victoro Cassalanter's valet, Willifort Crowelle, a doppelganger in tiefling form. As the hire-coach flees, a street chase ensues (encounter 3, "Street Chase"). When a crowd cuts off his escape route, Willifort leaps out of the hire-coach and tries to lose himself in the crowd. In the confusion, street urchins snatch the stone. The characters catch up to the children in their cellar hideout (encounter 9, "Cellar Complex").

With the *Stone of Golorr* in their possession, the characters emerge from the cellar complex only to find themselves surrounded by members of the City Watch. They are arrested for one or more crimes and taken to a courthouse in the Dock Ward to face sentencing by a

---

magister (encounter 8, "Courthouse"). Meanwhile, the doppelganger tries to get the stone back.

Any character who becomes attuned to the *Stone of Golorr* learns that the Vault of Dragons is hidden under an old tower in the Sea Ward (encounter 7, "Old Tower"). When they arrive at the tower, they encounter its new owner, who is discussing renovations with various local guild members.

WEATHER EFFECTS

Until the encounter chain is complete, the following weather effect is in play.

Heat Wave. During the day, a character without access to drinkable water must succeed on a DC 10 Constitution saving throw at the end of each encounter in the chain or gain one level of exhaustion. The saving throw is made with disadvantage if the character is wearing medium or heavy armor. Characters who have resistance or immunity to fire automatically succeed on the saving throw.

AUTUMN ENCOUNTER CHAIN

Deception and misdirection are Jarlaxle's forte, and he likes to trick his rivals into working for him. He steers the characters toward the *Stone of Golorr* and lets them think they're always one step ahead. Drow player characters who are members of Bregan D'aerthe might find their loyalty to the party put to the test.

SUMMARY

The characters visit the residence of Fenerus Stormcastle, a lamplighter and retired brigand who funnels information to Bregan D'aerthe. They arrive to find the place ransacked (encounter 1, "Alley"). The duergar who looted the residence work for the Xanathar Guild, and Bregan D'aerthe spies have tracked them to a cellar complex in the Southern Ward. In the guise of Laeral Silverhand, Jarlaxle steers the characters in that direction (encounter 9, "Cellar Complex"). A search of the cellar complex yields a fake stone, but not the real *Stone of Golorr*. With no other leads, the characters can follow up with "Laeral" at a theater in the Dock Ward (encounter 6, "Theater"). Jarlaxle makes the characters an offer they can't refuse, setting his agents on them if they dare to do so.

Once he realizes the Xanathar Guild doesn't have the stone, Jarlaxle asks the characters to interrogate Fenerus to find out where he hid it. Jarlaxle has learned that Fenerus is awaiting trial at a courthouse in the Castle Ward (encounter 8, "Courthouse"). Fenerus wants immunity for all of his past crimes. The characters are in no position to grant his wish, but they might threaten him, persuade him, or use magic to charm him. If he is compelled to reveal the stone's location, Fenerus points the characters to an old tower in the Dock Ward (encounter 7, "Old Tower").

Jarlaxle's lieutenants reach the stone first and flee across the rooftops in the Dock Ward to escape the characters (encounter 5, "Rooftop Chase"). They go to ground in Mistshore (encounter 2, "Mistshore"). Once the characters wrest the stone away from these drow, they can use it to guide them to the home of a famous

---

IF A VILLAIN GETS THE STONE

If a main villain acquires the *Stone of Golorr*, it takes that villain 2d6 days to find the Vault of Dragons and its keys. During this time, the characters have a chance to steal the stone from the villain's lair. If the characters don't steal the stone in time, the villain sends forces into the vault to defeat Aurinax and recover the gold, which takes another 2d6 days. Once the gold is recovered, the villain moves forward with a master plan as detailed in the introduction. If the characters are still alive, they could oppose the villain by stealing the gold from the villain's lair.

painter in the Sea Ward (encounter 10, "Converted Windmill"), beneath which is a tunnel that leads to the Vault of Dragons.

Weather Effects

Until the encounter chain is complete, the following weather effect is in play.

Autumn Wind. Wind whistling through the streets imposes disadvantage on ranged weapon attack rolls and Wisdom (Perception) checks that rely on hearing. The wind also extinguishes open fires smaller than a torch flame.

Winter Encounter Chain

Now is the winter of Waterdeep's discontent. The Zhents who serve Manshoon believe their master to be all-powerful, which has made them reckless. Against a frigid backdrop, they're willing to thumb their noses at local authorities and risk death in pursuit of the *Stone of Golorr*.

Summary

The stone is delivered to Thrakkus, a dragonborn butcher in the Field Ward (encounter 10, "Converted Windmill"). Thrakkus hides the stone in one of his meat deliveries. The characters follow the delivery cart to an alley in the Trades Ward where Zhents meet in secret (encounter 1, "Alley"). Before the characters can lay hands on the stone, a Zhent named Vevette Blackwater grabs it and flees, initiating a chase across icy rooftops (encounter 5, "Rooftop Chase"). She hands off the stone to Agorn Fuoco, a bard who is attending a play in a nearby theater (encounter 6, "Theater"), before leading her pursuers on a merry chase through the snow-covered streets (encounter 3, "Street Chase"). The characters learn that the stone has been taken by hire-coach to Mistshore. The characters can catch up to Agorn there (encounter 2, "Mistshore").

If he is captured and questioned, Agorn reveals that he made one stop on his way to Mistshore. He dropped off a lady friend, a priest of Bane allied with the Zhentarim, and left the stone with her and her acolytes for safekeeping. The characters can find them in an old tower in the Castle Ward (encounter 7, "Old Tower"). Before they leave that place, the characters are confronted by Manshoon's simulacrum, which arrives by way of teleportation circle to collect the stone. Once the simulacrum is defeated, the characters can use the stone to learn that the entrance to the Vault of Dragons is hidden below a mausoleum in the City of the Dead (encounter 4, "Mausoleum").

Weather Effects

Until the encounter chain is complete, the following weather effects are in play.

Blizzard. Shrieking wind and falling snow impose disadvantage on Wisdom (Perception) checks that rely on hearing or sight. The wind also extinguishes open fires smaller than a torch flame. Visibility is reduced to 60 feet. Snow on the ground creates difficult terrain in areas that are not heavily trod.

Extreme Cold. A character exposed to the cold must succeed on a DC 10 Constitution saving throw at the end of each encounter in the chain or gain one level of exhaustion. Characters who have resistance or immunity to cold automatically succeed on the saving throw, as do those wearing cold weather gear (thick coats, gloves, hats, and the like).

Encounter 1: Alley

Use map 4.1 for this encounter. The buildings that border the alley are 30 feet (three stories) high unless you decide otherwise. Since this encounter occurs outdoors, be mindful of any weather effects in play.

Areas of the Alley

The following locations are keyed to map 4.1.

L1. Alley Residence

This old, one-story, windowless stone house with a slate roof is tucked in the middle of the alley, surrounded by taller buildings. Its doors are made of sturdy wood, and the outer door can be barred shut from within. Breaking down the barred door requires a successful DC 18 Strength (Athletics) check.

The interior is divided into two rooms, a kitchen with a fireplace and a plainly furnished bedroom.

L2. Store

This stone building is a store of one kind or another. If an encounter doesn't specify the goods sold here, roll a d20 and consult the Store Goods table to determine what the store sells.

A small room serves as a cloakroom, where visitors can hang their heavier overgarments. Past the cloakroom is the store proper, with wares on display. The room to the north is a storeroom or a workshop. The store owner (**commoner**) has keys to all doors.

Store Goods

d20	Goods	d20	Goods
1	Art	11	Hats
2	Books	12	Hunting traps
3	Candles	13	Locks and keys
4	Cartwheels	14	Musical instruments
5	Costumes	15	Pets
6	Dolls	16	Pots
7	Fresh meat	17	Rations
8	Furniture	18	Rugs
9	Games	19	Umbrellas
10	Glass	20	Wine

MODIFYING ENCOUNTERS

You can adjust the difficulty of a combat encounter by adding or subtracting monsters. If you need to increase the difficulty of an encounter that has already begun, have enemy reinforcements arrive during the battle. If you find an encounter too deadly, reduce the antagonists' hit points, have NPCs arrive to help the characters, or have the bad guys cut their losses and flee.

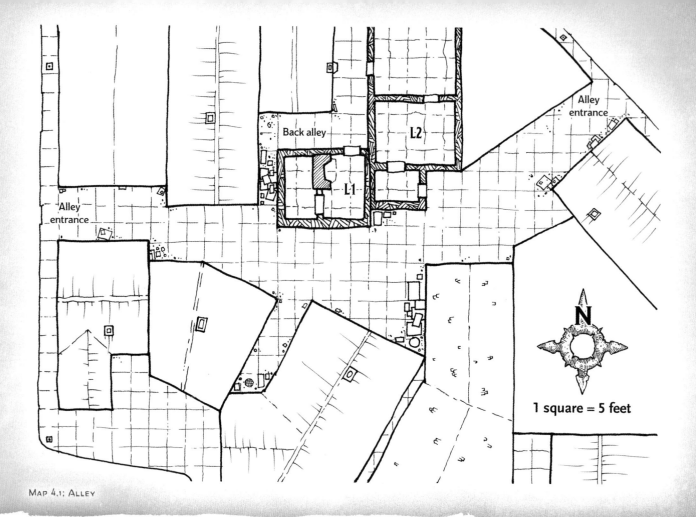

ALLEY: SPRING

When this encounter begins, either the characters have the *Stone of Golorr* in their clutches, in which case they're jumped as they move through an alley near the tower—or it was taken from them by Xanathar's gazer spies, in which case they catch up with the gazers in the alley before the creatures can descend into the sewers.

BEAR TRAPS

Choose five squares on the map. These squares contain deep puddles of muddy water. Hidden within each puddle is a spring-loaded bear trap. A creature that has a passive Perception score of 13 or higher spots a trap before accidentally stepping in it.

Any creature that steps into a trap's square must make a DC 10 Dexterity saving throw. On a failed save, the creature takes 3 (1d6) slashing damage as the trap snaps shut around its ankle, and the creature is restrained until the trap is removed. As an action, a creature can try to pry open the trap, doing so with a successful DC 12 Strength (Athletics) check.

AMBUSHERS

The characters enter the alley followed by eight **kobolds** disguised as children wearing troll masks. A **bugbear** named Morga and an **intellect devourer** hide in a doorway halfway down the alley and can be spotted with a successful DC 16 Wisdom (Perception) check.

When the characters reach Morga's hiding spot, the bugbear and the kobolds attack. The intellect devourer stays hidden and tries to take control of a character. Given the chance, Morga tries to shove a character into the nearest trap. If these creatures obtain the stone, they bring it to Xanathar in its lair (see chapter 5).

NEXT ENCOUNTER

If a character becomes attuned to the *Stone of Golorr*, it reveals the location of the Vault of Dragons, below a theater in the Castle Ward called the Pink Flumph, and the three keys that are needed to enter it. When the characters are ready to visit the location, proceed with encounter 6, "Theater."

ALLEY: SUMMER

The characters begin this encounter on the rooftops overlooking the alley. If any characters went to ground during the rooftop chase, start them at one end of the alley instead.

HIRE-COACH

Parked in the middle of the alley is a hire-coach pulled by two **draft horses**. The driver, Haru Hamatori (LG male Kozakuran human **commoner**), wears a feathered cap and matching outfit.

Lord Cassalanter's **doppelganger** valet, in the guise of an elderly tiefling named Willifort Crowelle, sits in the passenger cab, which grants half cover. Standing next to the hire-coach is a **bearded devil** disguised as a cloaked human bodyguard wearing a wide-brimmed hat, and perched on the coach are three invisible **imps**. Any

spined devils that survived the previous encounter are also present, having just delivered the *Stone of Golorr* to Willifort.

When he sees the characters, Willifort orders the imps and the spined devils to attack. The bearded devil stays close to Willifort and engages any character who tries to reach the hire-coach.

The hire-coach has AC 14, 45 hit points, and immunity to poison and psychic damage.

If there's any chance that the characters might obtain the *Stone of Golorr* as the encounter progresses, Willifort orders the driver to move the hire-coach out of the alley as quickly as possible. If the driver is incapacitated or killed, the bearded devil climbs into the driver's seat on the back of the coach and steers the vehicle. If the bearded devil is unable to replace the driver, the doppelganger takes the reins. Willifort flees on foot if the hire-coach is destroyed or its horses are unable to move.

Next Encounter

If Willifort escapes and the characters pursue him, proceed with encounter 3, "Street Chase."

Alley: Autumn

The characters' quest for the *Stone of Golorr* first leads them to Fenerus Stormcastle, a lamplighter who rents a small house in the Trades Ward (area L1).

Apple Cart

The characters enter the alley from either end. Determine their marching order, then read the following text once they reach the alley's midpoint:

> A cart laden with apples comes careening toward you from the opposite direction, rolling downhill. Riding on the cart is a tiefling boy with an eye patch, screaming at the top of his lungs. "Look out!" he shouts.

A character in the path of the apple cart must succeed on a DC 10 Dexterity saving throw or be struck for 5 (2d4) bludgeoning damage and knocked prone. A character can forgo the Dexterity saving throw and try to stop the cart bodily, doing so with a successful DC 15 Strength saving throw. On a failed save, the character is struck by the cart and falls prone as it continues to roll. After plowing through the party, the cart flips on its side, sending apples tumbling down the alley. The tiefling boy is thrown from the cart but not seriously hurt.

The boy is one of three street urchins who teamed up to steal the apple cart from a nearby street corner. The other two children lost control of the cart at the crest of the alley before they could hop on. They catch up to their friend after the crash, make sure he's all right, and then apologize profusely to anyone who was hurt. The urchins, harmless troublemakers, are detailed in the sidebar "The Three Urchins."

If they are asked about Fenerus, the children know who he is. They describe him as a big man with graying hair who looks like he has been in many fights, based on "the scars he wears on his face." They know nothing more about him, other than that he lives alone.

If the characters don't frighten them away, the children loiter around the alley, eating apples and picking through garbage piles.

Fenerus's House

The door to Fenerus's house stands open, and the place has been ransacked. Painted in blood on the kitchen wall is a circle with ten equidistant lines radiating outward from its circumference: the sign of Xanathar. A thorough search accompanied by a successful DC 12 Wisdom (Perception) check reveals small pools of blood on the kitchen floor. A successful check also verifies that the blood on the floor and wall is fresh.

Fenerus's Story

Fenerus Stormcastle was the founder of the Blood Hawk Posse, a gang of horse-riding brigands that, to this day, harries travelers on the road to Amphail. When he was drummed out of the gang after a botched raid, Fenerus "retired" to Waterdeep and joined the Guild of Chandlers and Lamplighters.

Until recently, Fenerus supplemented his income by spying for the city of Luskan and providing his contacts with information on the political climate in Waterdeep, as well as juicy bits of news overheard on his nightly rounds through the Trades Ward. He has no clue that his contacts are drow members of Bregan D'aerthe, since they wear cloaks and keep to the shadows.

Agents of the Lords' Alliance recently labeled Fenerus as a wanted brigand and notified the Lords of Waterdeep, who sent the City Watch to arrest him. Fenerus had the good sense to hide the *Stone of Golorr* elsewhere and hopes to use it as leverage to gain his freedom as well as forgiveness for past crimes.

Shortly after Fenerus's arrest, drow agents of Bregan D'aerthe showed up to collect the stone and were waylaid by invisible duergar hiding in the alley. The duergar were members of the Xanathar Guild that had been sent by Nar'l Xibrindas (see appendix B) to retrieve the stone. After searching Fenerus's home and finding nothing, they were waiting for Fenerus to return when the drow showed up. The drow barely got away with their lives.

Jarlaxle in Disguise

Before the characters leave the alley, **Jarlaxle Baenre** (see appendix B) uses his *hat of disguise* to approach

---

> #### The Three Urchins
>
> Three street urchins, described below, appear in several of this chapter's scenes:
>
> **Nat** is a lanky, 10-year-old deaf Illuskan girl with a wooden toy sword. She is the leader of the group and communicates using a sign language that she invented and taught to her friends.
>
> **Jenks** is a portly 9-year-old Turami boy with a cloak, a toy wand, and a stuffed owlbear "familiar." He's shy around strangers but brave when it comes to helping his friends.
>
> **Squiddly** is a slim 9-year-old tiefling boy with an eye patch, a small bow, and a quiver of toy arrows. He rarely thinks before he talks or acts.

them in the guise of Laeral Silverhand, the Open Lord of Waterdeep:

> A tall, graceful woman in an emerald green cloak approaches you, her long, silver hair billowing out from under her hood. "If you've come looking for Fenerus Stormcastle, I'm afraid you're too late," she says. "It appears Xanathar has gotten to him first. Fenerus had something in his possession that I desire. Perhaps you can help retrieve it."

"Laeral" tells the characters that Fenerus had a sentient magic item in his possession called the *Stone of Golorr*, which knows the location of a large cache of gold that was embezzled from the city by its previous Open Lord. She asks the characters to retrieve the stone, for the good of Waterdeep, and deliver it to her at the Seven Masks Theater in the Dock Ward. "Laeral" offers no reward other than the gratitude of Waterdeep's Open Lord.

Jarlaxle suspects that Nar'l Xibrindas, his spy in the Xanathar Guild, has betrayed him and is now using the resources of Bregan D'aerthe to help the beholder retrieve the stone. Jarlaxle also knows that the Xanathar Guild has a refuge fairly close by, in a cellar complex under the Southern Ward. "Laeral" suggests that the characters search for the stone there. (Jarlaxle doesn't want Nar'l to know that he's onto him, which is why he would rather send a small group of adventurers than call upon a Bregan D'aerthe attack force.)

Characters who are suspicious of Laeral's intentions can ascertain that she's hiding something with a successful Wisdom (Insight) check contested by Jarlaxle's Charisma (Deception) check. If the characters somehow penetrate Jarlaxle's disguise, he smiles and offers them 10,000 gp if they promptly deliver the stone to him at the Seven Masks Theater. He assures them, in all honesty, that he plans to give the gold back to Waterdeep in exchange for some political goodwill.

NEXT ENCOUNTER

If the characters invade the Xanathar Guild refuge, proceed with encounter 9, "Cellar Complex."

ALLEY: WINTER

The characters' search for the *Stone of Golorr* leads them to a snow-covered alley in the Trades Ward that contains a windowless Zhentarim safe house (area L1) and a meat shop called Cuttle's Meat Pies (area L2).

The characters approach from either end of the alley. Hoofprints and wheel ruts in the snow testify that Justyn Rassk's delivery cart passed through the alley recently after a brief stop outside the meat shop. A character who inspects the tracks and succeeds on a DC 10 Wisdom (Survival) check can tell that the deliverer visited both the shop and the alley residence. Before the characters can investigate further, they are assaulted by members of the Xanathar Guild.

BUGBEARS ATTACK

At the end of a dead-end side alley south of areas L1 and L2 is an iron grate that covers an opening to the sewers under the North Ward. Five **bugbears** have quietly climbed up through the grate and concealed themselves in the side alley. They pour out and attack the characters, hoping to gain surprise in the blizzard. Characters who have a passive Perception score of 16 or higher aren't surprised.

The bugbears were sent by Xanathar to retrieve a prisoner being held in the Zhent safe house, but they're too bloodthirsty to pass up the chance to murder a band of adventurers standing in their way. The wind and snow render the City Watch oblivious to the danger.

CUTTLE'S MEAT PIES

Characters who speak to the proprietor of the meat shop, a portly middle-aged woman named Sora Cuttle (LG female Illuskan human **commoner**), learn that she received an unexpected delivery from Justyn Rassk of the Guild of Butchers. Given that fresh meat is in short supply in winter, Sora could hardly turn it down. If the characters see fit to tell her that the meat came from chopped-up humanoids, Sora falls ill. She has no knowledge of Thrakkus's nasty handiwork and promises to bring the matter to the attention of the Guild of Butchers and the local magister. Until then, she won't use any of Thrakkus's meat to make her famous meat pies.

Sora is suspicious of her two neighbors in area L1. They come and go at strange hours, sometimes returning from a night's sojourn with blood on their leather armor. If the characters do Sora the courtesy of warning her about the meat, she happily shares her concerns about her naughty neighbors, along with descriptions of them. One is a pale, gaunt woman in her twenties with dark, stringy hair. The other is a much older, dark-skinned man with a bald head, a half-missing ear, and a short white beard.

ZHENTARIM SAFE HOUSE

This windowless house is occupied by two Zhents loyal to Manshoon—the same individuals that Sora describes. Their names are Avareen Windrivver (LE female Illuskan human **spy**) and Zorbog Jyarkoth (NE male Turami human **thug**).

When the characters first enter the alley, Avareen is in the front doorway of the house, handing the *Stone of Golorr* to a high-ranking Zhent named Vevette Blackwater (CE female Tethyrian human **swashbuckler**; see appendix B). Zorbog is stoking a fire in the fireplace while quietly observing the transaction. With stone in hand, Vevette scrambles up to the rooftops, leaving Avareen and Zorbog to deal with the survivors of the conflict between the characters and the bugbears.

Gagged and tied to a chair in the back room of the house is a known member of the Xanathar Guild—a shield dwarf who wears a leather skullcap stitched with fake beholder eyestalks. The dwarf, Ott Steeltoes (see appendix B), was captured while buying fish food in a Dock Ward market. After the Zhents interrogated Ott, it became clear to them that Xanathar would want him back. He is being held until a ransom is paid, but

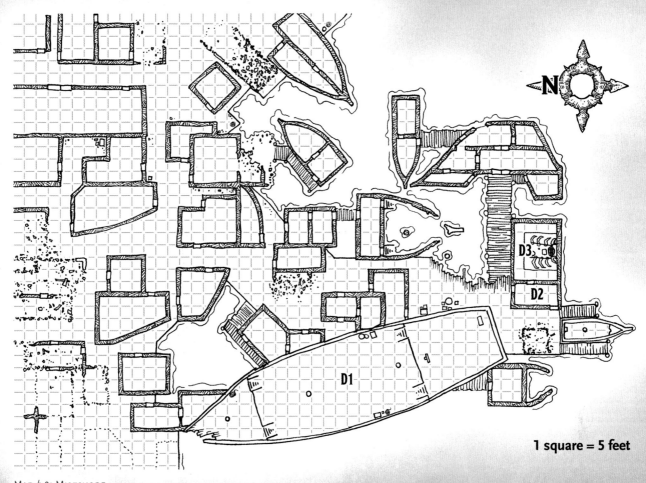

Xanathar has learned where he is being kept. Any bugbears that survived the initial attack try to rescue Ott, while Avareen and Zorbog do their best to fight them off. If Ott is set free, he runs back to the waiting eyestalks of his insane beholder master. Characters who follow him are led straight to Xanathar's lair (see chapter 5).

NEXT ENCOUNTER

Any characters within 10 feet of the Zhents' front door can make a DC 14 Wisdom (Perception) check. Those who succeed on the check hear a mocking laugh above the howling wind and glimpse a cloaked figure on a nearby roof, darting away through the blizzard. If the characters chase after this figure, proceed with encounter 5, "Rooftop Chase."

ENCOUNTER 2: MISTSHORE

Mistshore is a run-down Dock Ward neighborhood that reeks of fish and scorched timber. A fire swept through the area a little over a year ago, and most of the buildings are now burned-out shells with (at best) sails for roofs. Fishing poles and nets line the dock, and the 15-foot-deep water is covered by a thick layer of ice during the winter.

AREAS OF MISTSHORE

Mistshore is a riotous assemblage of ramshackle homes made of wood from old ships and inhabited by impoverished Waterdavians. Several buildings were reduced

to ash by the fire last year. Although some were rebuilt, others were ruined beyond repair and are now used as roofless dens by homeless children and rats.

The following locations are keyed to map 4.2.

D1. KRAKEN'S FOLLY

The *Kraken's Folly* is a beached pirate ship that some residents of Mistshore use as a tenement. At any given time, 4d6 **bandits** loiter on deck, hoping that someone who needs muscle will offer them work. These ruffians live in the rat-infested cabins belowdecks. They are willing to come to the aid of anyone who asks—for a price. Each demands 1 gp to get involved in a fight or create a distraction on behalf of their employer.

D2. GRINDA'S RESIDENCE

A mad treasure hunter named Grinda Garloth (CN female Illuskan human **mage** who speaks Common, Dwarvish, Halfling, and Undercommon) lives here. Her ramshackle home contains an unmade bed, an alchemist's laboratory, a small stove, a coat rack, a table, a stool, a stuffed chair in poor condition, a wash basin, and a locked wooden sea chest with a *glyph of warding* spell cast on it. Grinda carries the key, and the glyph triggers an explosive runes effect (see the spell description in the *Player's Handbook*) if anyone other than Grinda lifts the lid of the chest.

Chest. Grinda's chest contains a heavy iron key that locks and unlocks the Garloth family mausoleum in the City of the Dead (see "Mistshore: Spring" below).

GRINDA GARLOTH AND HER APPARATUS OF KWALISH

D3. GRINDA'S APPARATUS

Grinda Garloth keeps her *apparatus of Kwalish* here when she's not using the vehicle to hunt for treasure in Deepwater Harbor. While the apparatus is here, it floats in an enclosed dock. Underwater metal doors leading out to the harbor are kept shut by an iron bar across the inside. The apparatus can lift the iron bar automatically; a creature inside the bay can lift it with a successful DC 20 Strength (Athletics) check.

Borrowing the Apparatus. Grinda allows the characters to borrow her *apparatus of Kwalish* on the condition that they first use the device to search the bottom of Deepwater Harbor for treasure and give her half of whatever they find. To meet the mage's demands, the characters must spend a day searching the harbor. At the end of the day, the pilot makes an Intelligence (Investigation) check. Multiply the total of the check by 10 to determine the gold piece value of any treasure found. Grinda sells the bounty and gives half to the characters.

As the characters search the harbor for treasure, roll any die. If an even number is rolled, an awakened shark named Obliteros attacks them. Grinda has had several close encounters with the shark recently, but fails to mention this to the characters for fear of scaring them off. Obliteros is a **giant shark**, with these changes:

- The shark's alignment is chaotic evil.
- Its Intelligence score is 10 (+0), and it can speak and understand Aquan.

MISTSHORE: SPRING

Xanathar has sent forces to collect the *Stone of Golorr* from Grinda Garloth, known up and down the wharf as an eccentric wizard who owns a submersible contraption that she uses to hunt for treasure on the bottom of Deepwater Harbor. The characters have no trouble getting directions to her Mistshore residence (area D2).

When the characters arrive at her home, Grinda is holed up inside, having barricaded the doors with furniture. Trying to break down the doors are four members of the Xanathar Guild (CE male human **bandits**) under the command of a dwarf enforcer named Noska Ur'gray (see appendix B). A **merrow** also under Noska's command swims beneath the docks. It surfaces to attack when the characters arrive.

If the characters come to Grinda's defense, Noska orders his thugs to attack them while he takes potshots at the characters with his crossbow. Two rounds later, eight more **bandits** leap down from the *Kraken's Folly* (area D1) and join the fray. These hooligans were paid 1 gp each to watch Noska's back. The characters can turn them against Noska by offering a larger bribe (at least 5 gp each).

If the characters turn the hooligans against Noska or reduce the dwarf to half his hit points or fewer, Noska flees. Any remaining Xanathar Guild members cover his escape. Grinda emerges from her residence to thank the characters once the fight has concluded.

Where's the Stone?

Grinda admits that she has done business with the Xanathar Guild in the past. Her orders were to protect the stone until Noska arrived to claim it, but she changed her mind and decided to keep the stone for herself. She now realizes that decision was a mistake.

Grinda tells the characters that she gave the stone to her rat familiar and told the creature to stash it in her family's mausoleum in the City of the Dead. The mage gives the characters directions to the site and a key to the mausoleum. (They won't need the key, since the mausoleum is open when they arrive.)

Spy in the Sky

As the characters leave Mistshore, a **gazer** (see appendix B) begins to follow them, staying at least 60 feet away. Xanathar uses it to spy on the characters. Characters who have a passive Perception score of 15 or higher can spot the gazer shortly after the party enters the City of the Dead. The gazer defends itself if attacked.

Next Encounter

Armed with directions to the Garloth mausoleum, the characters can head for the City of the Dead. The spring chain continues with encounter 4, "Mausoleum."

Mistshore: Autumn

At the end of their pursuit, the characters corner Fel'rekt Lafeen and Krebbyg Masq'il'yr in Mistshore. The two **drow gunslingers** (see appendix B) lurk behind the *Kraken's Folly* (area D1) and wait to be rescued. When the characters confront them, Fel'rekt and Krebbyg stall for time until their escape vehicle arrives. If either drow falls, the other tosses the stone into the harbor to keep it from falling into enemy hands. A character can recover the sunken stone by using a *detect magic* spell to help pinpoint its location.

Big Belchy

A mechanical dragon turtle, dubbed Big Belchy, sank in Deepwater Harbor almost a century ago. Lantanese gnomes working for Jarlaxle have managed to repair the construct. Two rounds after the characters corner Fel'rekt and Krebbyg, Big Belchy surfaces next to the dock on initiative count 5, close enough that the drow can leap onto its barnacle-encrusted back on their next turns.

In the round after it surfaces, the mechanism breathes a cloud of steam onto the docks in a 30-foot cube, then begins to move away at a swimming speed of 20 feet. Any creature in the cloud of steam must make a DC 14 Dexterity saving throw, taking 22 (4d10) fire damage on a failed save, or half as much damage on a successful one. Big Belchy can breathe steam only once. On each of its turns thereafter, it swims a total of 40 feet toward Jarlaxle's flagship, the *Eyecatcher*, which is anchored in the middle of the harbor 1 mile away.

Big Belchy has AC 18, 75 hit points, and immunity to poison and psychic damage. If it is reduced to 0 hit points, it sinks once more to the bottom of Deepwater Harbor. If the drow are still on its back when it goes down, they swim the rest of the way to the *Eyecatcher* but gain two levels of exhaustion from the cold water and exertion.

If the drow are defeated while on Big Belchy's back, the *Stone of Golorr* tumbles off the mechanical dragon turtle's shell and drops into Deepwater Harbor. If the water is deep enough, the characters might need to borrow Grinda Garloth's *apparatus of Kwalish* to recover it.

Next Encounter

If a character becomes attuned to the *Stone of Golorr*, it reveals the location of the Vault of Dragons, beneath an old stone windmill in the Sea Ward, and the three keys needed to enter it. When the characters are ready to visit the location, proceed with encounter 10, "Converted Windmill."

Mistshore: Winter

The characters head to Mistshore in search of the man they believe has the *Stone of Golorr*. En route to that destination, the man had his hire-coach make a brief stop in the Castle Ward to drop off his lady friend. She now has the stone—a fact that characters can discover by questioning the man, a bard named Agorn Fuoco.

Agorn made such a good impression on Manshoon that he was elevated quickly through the ranks of the organization, but his life is full of disappointment otherwise. He has not achieved the fame he craved nor earned the wealth he felt he was entitled to. He has adopted the Zhentarim credo that power comes to those who deserve it and has come to see the Black Network as a new family of sorts. Agorn has come to Mistshore to visit a member of his actual family—his mother, who is gravely ill and lives in abject poverty.

A Waiting Coach

Waiting at the edge of the neighborhood is the hire-coach that bore Agorn Fuoco through the blizzard to Mistshore. Two **draft horses** stamp their hooves impatiently in the snow. The driver, Rowan Evenwood (LG female Chondathan human **commoner**), was paid extra to wait for Agorn to return. He left in a hurry, and she doesn't know how long she is expected to wait, but her patience has limits.

A Cold Reception

A blizzard is tearing through Mistshore, turning its rotten tenements into dark, looming shapes behind veils of blowing snow. The water around the docks is frozen solid, and impoverished **commoners** clad in tattered garments gather around sputtering campfires for warmth. These folk are suspicious of anyone they don't recognize and far from welcoming, even toward those who show them charity. These people would tear the clothes from the characters' backs given half a chance.

Ice Escapades

Playing on the ice underneath the docks are three street urchins wearing frayed cloaks and gloves. They dart in and out of view, hurling snowballs at each other and laughing as the blizzard batters the structures above them (see "The Three Urchins," page 63).

When the children see the characters for the first time, their interest is piqued. The children fancy themselves adventurers of sorts, and they are quick to idolize and emulate real-life ones. Squiddly even has the audacity to hurl a snowball at one of them (+0 bonus to hit). The children know who Agorn Fuoco is because he used to live and play music in Mistshore. They offer to lead characters to his mother's residence.

MOTHER AND SON

Pick one of the unmarked buildings on map 4.2 to serve as the Fuoco residence. Agorn Fuoco (NE male Turami **bard**; see appendix B) is inside, trying to smother his bedridden mother, Marta (N female Turami human **commoner** with 1 hit point), with a sack she uses as a pillowcase. With tears born of joy and sadness streaming down his face, Agorn is cutting loose his old family ties and embracing his new family: the Zhentarim. The characters can stop him from committing matricide by pulling him away from his mother before she suffocates.

Agorn was moved to perpetrate this act by the play he saw at the theater and by his lady friend, Amath Sercent, to whom he entrusted the *Stone of Golorr*. He won't give up her location willingly, though magic can be used to pry the information from his lips. Characters can also speak to the hire-coach driver, Rowan Evenwood, who dropped off Agorn's lady friend before transporting Agorn to Mistshore. Amath lives in an old tower in the Castle Ward called Yellowspire.

ZHENTS IN THE WIND

As the characters leave the Fuoco residence, with or without Agorn as their prisoner, they are surrounded by nine Zhentarim **thugs**. The thugs fight to the death while Agorn tries to escape. If he gets away, the characters might encounter him again in chapter 8.

As the Zhents attack and Agorn attempts to flee, the characters hear a child's scream coming from the opposite direction. Through the blowing snow, they can see that one of the urchins, Jenks, has fallen through a thin patch of ice and is in danger of sinking to the bottom of the harbor. His two friends are trying to pull him out of the hole, but he's too heavy. The children are roughly 30 feet away. A character within arm's reach of Jenks can use an action to try to pull the boy from the cold water, doing so with a successful DC 11 Strength (Athletics) check. If no adult comes to Jenks's aid within 1 minute of his falling through the ice, he sinks below the surface and begins to drown as the cold water overcomes him.

If the characters find themselves outmatched by the Zhents, help comes in two forms. Two Harper **spies** sent by Remallia Haventree (see appendix B) appear on the scene. Their names are Salazar Lorrance (CG male Tethyrian human) and Mavia Oxlander (NG female Chondathan human). If the battle doesn't turn quickly in the party's favor, Grinda Garloth (see area D2) appears and uses her magic to aid them.

NEXT ENCOUNTER

Armed with information from Agorn Fuoco or his hire-coach driver, the characters might feel compelled to pay a visit to Yellowspire in the Castle Ward. Proceed with encounter 7, "Old Tower."

ENCOUNTER 3: STREET CHASE

For this encounter, use the chase rules and the Urban Chase Complications table in chapter 8 of the *Dungeon Master's Guide*. The chase plays out as a "theater of the mind" experience. Consequently, you don't need a map to run the encounter. The chase occurs outdoors, so be mindful of any weather effects in play.

STREET CHASE: SPRING

A **kenku** in cahoots with the Xanathar Guild has the *Stone of Golorr* and is running through the streets with it. The kenku is 60 feet away from the characters at the start of the chase.

If at any point the kenku is incapacitated, another **kenku** previously hidden by the rain or fog joins the chase, acting next in the initiative count. It suddenly appears, snatches the stone, and flees with it.

NEXT ENCOUNTER

When the characters are close to catching the kenku, or when you want the chase to end, the creature ducks into an old tower. Proceed with encounter 7, "Old Tower."

STREET CHASE: SUMMER

The characters are pursuing Lord Cassalanter's doppelganger valet, Willifort, as he flees in a hire-coach or on foot. The chase takes place on crowded streets, in front of agog spectators.

If you haven't been tracking the distance between the doppelganger and the characters, assume the characters are 120 feet away from their quarry at the start of the chase if Willifort is traveling by hire-coach, or 60 feet away if the doppelganger is on foot. The hire-coach has an initiative modifier of +0, and Willifort moves with it. A creature in the hire-coach doesn't need to roll on the Urban Chase Complications table on its turn.

CROWDED STREET

If Willifort flees in a hire-coach, his getaway is thwarted on the third round of the chase when a large crowd blocks the road, forcing the hire-coach to stop. (If the chase occurs on Founders' Day, the crowd is part of the holiday celebration.) The doppelganger jumps out of the hire-coach on his next turn and makes his way through the crowd on foot.

Any creature in the crowd has half cover, and any attack that misses the creature because of the cover hits an innocent **commoner** instead.

If Willifort is incapacitated, a raven abruptly swoops down, acting next in the initiative count. It snatches the stone and flees with it. This raven is a shapechanged **imp** that works for Lady Cassalanter.

STREET URCHINS

The chase ends when three street urchins (see "The Three Urchins," page 63) steal the stone, either by pickpocketing it from the doppelganger or by shooting a toy arrow at the raven and causing it to drop the stone.

Once they have the stone, the street urchins quickly lose themselves in the crowd. If Willifort the doppelganger is still around, he tries to slip away, believing he still has the stone. The imp, if present, turns invisible and circles above the crowd in a futile attempt to find the stone.

A character can use an action to search the crowded street by making a DC 17 Wisdom (Perception) check. On a successful check, the character spots an iron grate in the street that wasn't closed properly. Lifting it reveals an iron ladder that descends 10 feet to an underground sewer tunnel. Characters who lower themselves into the tunnel can hear the sounds of splashing water and children's voices in the distance and might decide to follow them. (The children are holding hands in the dark and being guided by Squiddly, who has darkvision.)

Next Encounter

If the characters follow the street urchins into the sewer, proceed with encounter 9, "Cellar Complex."

Street Chase: Winter

After leaving the theater, the characters resume their pursuit of the elusive Zhent spy, Vevette Blackwater (CE female Tethyrian human **swashbuckler**; see appendix B). She leads them on a merry chase through snowy streets until she is finally caught or until the characters give up the chase. She starts 30 feet away from the characters. If forced to make an ability check or saving throw because of a chase complication, she has advantage on the roll. Also, she can use the Dash action during the chase without having to make Constitution checks to avoid exhaustion.

Where's the Stone?

If she is caught, Vevette surrenders. She's counting on the law to protect her from serious harm, and she knows she has done nothing to warrant arrest. Vevette no longer has the *Stone of Golorr*, after parting with it back in the theater. She doesn't willingly divulge who has the stone, though the characters can pry the information from her using a *charm person* spell or similar magic.

If the characters return to the theater, **Remallia Haventree** (see appendix B) waves them over and tells them that she saw two people exit the theater shortly after they did and then depart together in a hire-coach shortly thereafter. One of them is a bard named Agorn Fuoco, the other a woman unknown to Lady Haventree.

Both Remallia and Vevette know that Agorn spends time around the dangerous dockside neighborhood of Mistshore.

Next Encounter

Proceed with encounter 2, "Mistshore."

Encounter 4: Mausoleum

The City of the Dead is a public park dotted with mausoleums. The place is closed at night, with two City Guard soldiers (**guards**) stationed at each entry gate. A character can slip over a wall undetected with a successful DC 15 Dexterity (Stealth) check.

At dusk, hundreds of *driftglobes* make their way from the inhabited part of the city and congregate in the City of the Dead. They spend the night here, then disperse and return to the waking city at dawn—for a reason no one knows.

Sir Ambrose Everdawn (LG male human Tethyrian **knight**), an aging servant of Kelemvor (god of the dead), patrols the cemetery from sunset to sunrise, chasing off grave robbers and making sure the dead stay buried. Characters who creep around the cemetery in the dark have a 30 percent chance of running into him. If that happens, he escorts them out and alerts the City Guard if they refuse to leave.

Areas of the Mausoleum

Rooms in the mausoleum have 8-foot-high ceilings, with 6-foot-high passages and doorways connecting them.

The following locations are keyed to map 4.3.

M1. Ground Level

Unless the text of an encounter says otherwise, the stone double door to the mausoleum is locked. The lock can be picked by a character who makes a successful DC 15 Dexterity check using thieves' tools, or the door can be forced open with a successful DC 25 Strength (Athletics) check.

Inside, a family emblem is emblazoned on the floor between four ostentatious marble coffins. The coffins, engraved with the names of those interred within, contain nothing but dust and bones.

M2. Underground Crypts

Empty sconces adorn the walls. Cobwebs and dust indicate that no one has tended to this place in a long time. Stone coffins in alcoves contain dust and bones.

Mausoleum: Spring

This encounter begins when the characters come to the Garloth mausoleum seeking the *Stone of Golorr*. The double door to the mausoleum is open when they arrive.

Earlier, Grinda Garloth's rat familiar arrived to find the mausoleum open and grave robbers inside. They killed the rat, took the stone, and fled along with the skeletal remains of Grinda's ancestors. Characters who search the plundered crypts find neither the rat nor the stone, but they do find a clue left behind by one of the grave robbers (see "Crypt Clue" below). As the characters make their way out, Xanathar Guild members attack them in an attempt to retrieve the stone.

Crypt Clue

Characters who search the underground crypts can find a shiny steel key lying in the dust on the floor. One of the grave robbers dropped it while looting the crypts.

The characters can take the key to the Metal House of Wonders, the guildhall of the Splendid Order of Armorers, Locksmiths, and Finesmiths in the Dock Ward, or to any local locksmith. In either place, someone can identify the key as the handiwork of a dwarf locksmith in the Trades Ward named Elaspra Ulmarr. Characters who visit Elaspra's shop can learn from her that she made a key for a client who bought one of her excellent locks. She even installed the lock for him. Elaspra won't easily divulge the name of the client or his place of residence. She has great respect for the Harpers, however; a character who belongs to this faction and produces a Harper pin to prove it can pry the information from her with a successful DC 13 Charisma (Persuasion) check. A character pretending to be a Harper can fool her with a successful DC 16 Charisma (Deception) check.

Otherwise, the characters must either compel Elaspra to release the information using magic, or they must sneak a peek at her records, which she keeps in an iron safe that can be opened with a *knock* spell or similar magic. To pick the combination lock on the safe, a character must succeed on three DC 20 Dexterity (Investigation) checks in a row. Each attempt made to pick the lock requires an action.

From Elaspra or her records, the characters learn that she sold the key to a man named Volkarr Kibbens, whose address is an old windmill in the Southern Ward. The key unlocks the door to his apartment, which he shares with another man named Urlaster Ghann.

Xanathar Guild Ambush

As the characters leave the mausoleum, they are jumped by four **duergar**, members of the Xanathar Guild, who slipped past the cemetery guards using their invisibility. The leader, Gorath, accosts the characters in Dwarvish, demands the *Stone of Golorr*, and refuses to believe that they don't have it. If the stone isn't turned over to them promptly, the duergar enlarge themselves and attack. Xanathar watches the battle unfold through the eyes of a **gazer** (see appendix B), which stays out of the fight and tries to remain unseen.

If this encounter occurs at night, there's a 50 percent chance that Ambrose Everdawn hears the disturbance and investigates, arriving after two duergar fall in battle. The characters can convince him that they're not grave robbers with a successful DC 15 Charisma (Persuasion) check. If they're polite, Ambrose escorts them out of the City of the Dead and warns them not to trespass again. Otherwise, he attempts to subdue them and turn them over to the City Guard.

Next Encounter

Once they trace the key to its owner, the characters can head to the Southern Ward in search of Volkarr Kibbens. The spring chain continues with encounter 10, "Converted Windmill."

Villain Lairs

Chapters 5 through 8 describe the lairs of the main villains. The characters might want to explore the lairs for a variety of reasons, including the following:

- Disrupting the villain's operation
- Gaining an audience with the villain (perhaps to forge a truce or an alliance)
- Completing a special mission for a faction (see "Joining Factions," page 34)
- Investigating a false clue given to them as part of a scheme concocted by another villain
- Stealing the *Stone of Golorr* if the villain has it, or finding leads on its whereabouts when the trail goes cold

---

Mausoleum: Summer

The characters travel to the City of the Dead, which is open to the public from dawn until dusk. One well-maintained mausoleum has the name CASSALANTER engraved above its entrance. The outer door is locked when the characters arrive in search of the *Stone of Golorr*. A successful DC 20 Intelligence (Investigation) check reveals that it has been opened recently, as evidenced by dirt smears on the door. A character can try to pick the lock using thieves' tools, doing so with a successful DC 15 Dexterity check. A *knock* spell or similar magic also opens the door.

Human footprints crisscross through the dust on the upper level. A search of the underground crypt reveals the bodies of three humans—two males and a female, all dressed in hooded robes. Further inspection reveals that the woman is still breathing (unconscious with 0 hit points).

Left for Dead

The three cultists were low-ranking members of Victoro Cassalanter's cult of Asmodeus. They were betrayed by two cult fanatics acting on orders from Lord Cassalanter, who not only wants the *Stone of Golorr* but also, as a security precaution, intends to eliminate cult members who know too much about it. These three cultists were felled by daggers and *inflict wounds* spells.

The survivor is Vaelle Lurval (LE female Tethyrian human **cultist**), a 30-year-old Waterdavian florist. She was brought into the cult by her boyfriend, Holiver Tornrudder, who lies dead nearby. The other dead cultist is named Kaeth Warloon.

If she is healed, Vaelle regains consciousness. She reveals that the cult fanatics, Arn Xalrondar and Seffia Naelryke, would likely have taken the stone to an old windmill in the Southern Ward, where they hold their own ceremonies worshiping Asmodeus. Vaelle can provide directions, or she can lead characters there if she is healed fully, for the sake of avenging her murdered lover.

Vaelle believes that the cult fanatics acted on their own, not under Lord Cassalanter's orders. She won't reveal the Cassalanters as the leaders of the cult unless magically compelled to do so.

Next Encounter

Proceed with encounter 10, "Converted Windmill."

Mausoleum: Winter

The *Stone of Golorr* has revealed that the Vault of Dragons lies beneath the Brandath family mausoleum in the City of the Dead. The characters are unlikely to know it, but the Brandath family is an old one. Lord Dagult Neverember married into it for its wealth, and Lady Brandath gave birth to his son, Renaer. It's a dark irony that Neverember entrusted the location of his embezzled gold to his dead wife's family. Renaer Neverember would be horrified but not surprised to learn the truth.

The cemetery is buried in snow, and though some visitors are drawn to its scenic beauty even in winter, the blizzard keeps most of them away. The crumbling

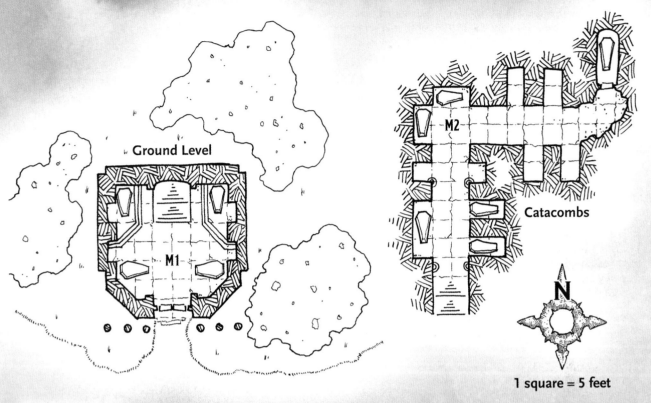

Ground Level

M1

M2

Catacombs

N

1 square = 5 feet

MAP 4.3: MAUSOLEUM

mausoleum is sealed tight, and the name BRANDATH is etched above its entrance. Large elm and birch trees grow around the structure, sheltering it as best they can with their leafless boughs.

GUARDIAN TREANT

The largest tree growing in front of the entrance is a **treant**. It awakens when one or more creatures approach the entrance and growls, "Only those of Brandath blood are welcome here! Begone!" The treant is particularly surly, it being winter and all.

If someone other than a Brandath descendant tries to open the mausoleum, the treant animates two nearby trees and then attacks. The treant and its animated allies are too big to enter the mausoleum.

The characters can kill the treant, try to slip past it, or retreat until they learn more about the Brandath family. A day's research followed by a successful DC 10 Intelligence (Investigation) check reveals that the characters know one such person: Renaer Neverember. If they ask Renaer to admit them to the Brandath family mausoleum, he agrees to do so. Because the treant can sense that Renaer has Brandath blood in his veins, it allows him and those he calls his friends to enter unmolested, and says to Renaer in passing, "Your mother was a lovely person."

GLYPH OF WARDING

A *glyph of warding* spell has been cast on the first step leading down to the underground level, set to trigger when a humanoid creature passes over the step. The glyph can't be spotted unless the dust on the floor is cleared away by a *gust of wind* spell or some other means. Once the dust is swept aside, a character who searches the stairs notices the glyph with a successful DC 15 Intelligence (Investigation) check.

If the glyph is triggered, it erupts with magical fire in a 20-foot-radius sphere centered on it. The fire spreads around corners. Each creature in the area must make a DC 15 Dexterity saving throw, taking 22 (5d8) fire damage on a failed saving throw, or half as much damage on a successful one. The glyph disappears after it is triggered.

ULD'S RESTING PLACE

A *detect magic* spell reveals an aura of transmutation that emanates from one of the stone coffins on the underground level. This crypt contains the shattered bones of Uld Brandath, a Waterdavian magister who died in a freak accident decades ago. (A gargoyle broke off the corner of a government building and fell on Uld, crushing him.) Guarding his remains are six **crawling claws** made from the hands of murderers who were sentenced to death by Uld. These undead hands spring out and attack when the lid is lifted or shoved aside.

Treasure. Lying amid the bones is Uld's *headband of intellect*, which the characters can retrieve once the crawling claws are dealt with.

PATH TO THE VAULT

The collapsed eastern end of the underground level is actually an illusion that conceals an intact, 10-foot-wide passageway that slopes down. The characters can walk right through the illusion, which has no substance, and a *dispel magic* spell destroys it. The tunnel wends downward for several hundred feet, gradually widening to 20 feet where it ends at the doors to the Vault of Dragons.

Rooftop Chase Complications

d20	Complication
1	You come to a 10-foot-wide gap between rooftops. You can jump over the gap if your Strength is 10 or higher (each foot you clear costs 1 foot of movement), and you must succeed on a DC 10 Dexterity (Acrobatics) check or fall prone on the far rooftop. Or you can cross the gap using a 10-foot-long rope line that stretches between the two rooftops; each foot of rope line costs 2 feet of movement.
2	You come to a rooftop that's 10 feet higher than the one you're on. Make a DC 10 Strength (Athletics) check. On a failed check, the height change counts as 10 feet of difficult terrain.
3	You come to a rooftop that's 10 feet lower than the one you're on. Make a DC 10 Strength (Athletics) check to jump down safely. On a failed check, you take damage from the fall and land prone.
4	A roof is slippery. Make a DC 10 Dexterity saving throw. On a failed save, you fall prone.
5	You step on a rotten section of roof, and it collapses underneath you. Make a DC 15 Dexterity saving throw. On a failed save, you fall partway into the hole in the roof and become stuck. While stuck, you are prone and restrained. You can use an action on your turn to make a DC 10 Strength (Athletics) or Dexterity (Acrobatics) check, ending the effect on a success.
6	Roof shingles or tiles give way as you step on them. Make a DC 15 Dexterity saving throw. On a failed save, you fall prone and slide 10 feet back.
7	A rooftop protuberance such as a chimney or weather vane gets in your way. Make a DC 10 Dexterity (Acrobatics) check. On a failed check, the obstacle counts as 5 feet of difficult terrain.
8	You startle a flock of birds nesting on the rooftop, and they flutter all around you. Make a DC 10 Dexterity saving throw. On a failed save, the birds count as 10 feet of difficult terrain.
9	You trigger a *glyph of warding* spell placed on the roof to discourage burglars. Make a DC 13 Wisdom saving throw. On a failed save, you are targeted by a *Tasha's hideous laughter* spell, the effect of which lasts 1 minute.
10	Someone on the ground throws a rock, a snowball, or a similar projectile at you. Make a DC 10 Dexterity saving throw. On a failed save, the attack deals no damage but distracts you and counts as 5 feet of difficult terrain.
11–20	No complication.

Encounter 5: Rooftop Chase

This encounter uses the chase rules in chapter 8 of the *Dungeon Master's Guide*. It also uses the Rooftop Chase Complications table, which applies only to creatures moving across rooftops on foot. Flying creatures needn't roll on the table.

Rooftop Chase: Summer

The characters are trying to catch up with three **spined devils** that keep low above the rooftops, so as not to be seen by Waterdeep's Griffon Cavalry. The devils are 100 feet away from the characters at the start of the chase.

If the devil carrying the *Stone of Golorr* becomes incapacitated, another devil snatches the stone and flees with it.

Next Encounter

When the characters are close to getting the stone, or when you want the chase to end, all remaining spined devils duck into an alley. If the characters lose their quarry, they can question city folk on the ground who saw where the devils went. Continue with encounter 1, "Alley."

Rooftop Chase: Autumn

The characters are chasing two **drow gunslingers** (see appendix B) across windy rooftops in the Dock Ward. The drow stick together as they run, but each one acts on his own initiative count.

Fel'rekt Lafeen and Krebbyg Masq'il'yr start out 40 feet ahead of their pursuers. They do nothing but move on their turns, trying to put as much distance between themselves and the characters as possible. Fel'rekt has the *Stone of Golorr* at the start of the chase, but one drow gunslinger can pass the stone to the other as a reaction as long as the two drow are within 10 feet of each other.

Next Encounter

The drow keep running across the rooftops until they get to the run-down dockside neighborhood known as Mistshore. Characters who remain in pursuit can follow them all the way there. If all the characters lose their quarry, they can question city folk on the ground who saw the drow heading toward Mistshore. In either case, proceed with encounter 2, "Mistshore."

Rooftop Chase: Winter

A Zhent named Vevette Blackwater (CE female Tethyrian human **swashbuckler**; see appendix B) has snatched the *Stone of Golorr* and is fleeing as fast as she can across icy rooftops during a blizzard. Characters who intend to pursue her are 60 feet away from their quarry at the start of the chase and must also take to the rooftops or lose sight of her.

Vevette was a vicious pirate before she joined the Zhentarim and rose to become one of Manshoon's favored lieutenants. She cackles madly in the face of

danger and loves a good chase. She knows the streets, alleys, and rooftops of Waterdeep well. If forced to make an ability check or a saving throw because of a chase complication, she has advantage on the roll. Also, she can take the Dash action during the chase without having to make Constitution checks to avoid exhaustion.

Next Encounter

The chase lasts no more than 5 rounds, after which Vevette drops to the ground and ducks into a theater. Characters who lose sight of her can ask people along her path to help them out. Continue with encounter 6, "Theater."

Encounter 6: Theater

Whether the theater is open for business or shut down, it has the following features:

- Ceilings in the rooms are 10 feet high except in area P5, which has a 20-foot-high raftered ceiling. Connecting the rooms are 8-foot-high passages and 7-foot-high doorways.
- The theater is lit by lanterns that have *continual flame* spells cast on them. Speaking a command word inside the theater causes the lights in the theater and backstage to dim; speaking another command word inside the theater restores them to full brightness. All the stage managers know the command words.

Areas of the Theater

The following locations are keyed to map 4.4.

P1. Lobby

This plush lobby is decorated with red carpet and ornate wallpaper. On display here are several painted wooden mannequins dressed in fancy costumes, each one representing a character from a famous play.

P2. Ticket Booths

The western door on each booth is locked. The lock can be picked by a character who succeeds on a DC 15 Dexterity check using thieves' tools, or the door can be forced open with a successful DC 13 Strength (Athletics) check. The ticket sellers and the stage manager have keys to these doors.

A stack of torn tickets sits on a shelf beneath a counter inside the booth. Prior to a show, each booth holds a ticket seller (**commoner**). Admission to the theater is 1 sp per person.

P3. Ticket Offices

A desk near the far wall in each of these rooms contains notebooks, papers, and a lockbox.

Treasure. The house managers hold the key to each lockbox. A lock can be picked by someone who makes a successful DC 12 Dexterity check using thieves' tools, or a lockbox can be forced open with a successful DC 15 Strength (Athletics) check. During a performance,

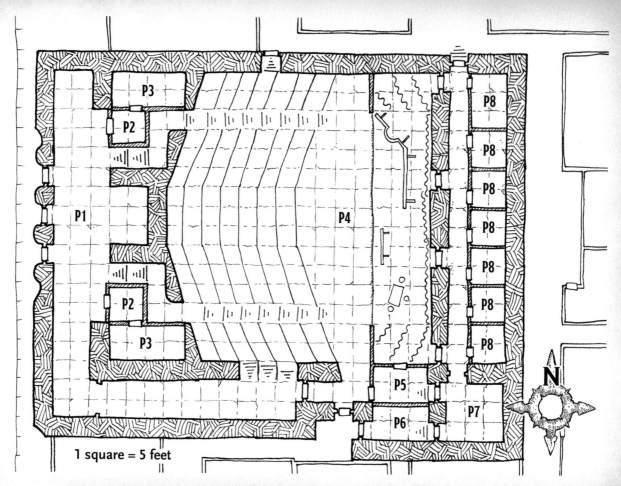

MAP 4.4: THEATER

each lockbox holds 10d10 sp. After a performance, both boxes are empty.

P4. AUDITORIUM

The auditorium has the following features:

- Cushioned seats are arranged in seven tiered rows facing a 5-foot-high wooden stage. Each row has twenty seats.
- Behind a raised red curtain are painted backdrops and stage props for the current production.

During a performance, a stage manager (**commoner**) watches from the back of the seating area.

P5. WING

This small offstage area is painted black and has a table that holds fake daggers, swords, and other props. Prop weapons can be used in combat but deal only 1 bludgeoning damage on a hit.

P6. STAGE MANAGER'S OFFICE

This room holds a desk covered in papers. The stage manager (**commoner**) stays here between performances.

P7. GREEN ROOM

A trio of mismatched couches and a stained beige rug are the main features of this room, whose walls are covered with light green paint. This is where the actors congregate when they aren't on stage or in their dressing rooms.

P8. DRESSING ROOMS

This room contains clothes racks, tables lined with makeup, and long wall mirrors. During or immediately before a performance, each dressing room holds 1d3 actors (**commoners**).

THEATER: SPRING

The name of the Pink Flumph theater is displayed on a sign mounted to the building's facade. Posters on the outside walls advertise the latest shows, *Meet the Goodberrys* and *Kiss of the Lamia*. The former is a comical glimpse into the travails of a large halfling family engaged in illicit criminal activity. The latter is a tragic play about an evil Mulhorandi prince who is banished to a desert, charmed by a lamia, and sent back with powerful magic items to conquer his homeland in her name.

In the early hours of the morning, the backstage area is abuzz with halfling actors donning costumes, wigs, and makeup in preparation for the afternoon's show. As that show wraps, the cast and musicians for the evening's tragic fare arrive. The actor who plays the evil prince is a woman named Yaliek Iltizmar (N female Rashemi **bard**; see appendix B), who is also a member of the Harpers. She pays close attention to characters who nose around backstage, then shares any interesting revelations with Remallia Haventree (see appendix B) at the earliest opportunity. If Remallia learns the location of the Vault of Dragons, she sees that the information reaches the Lords of Waterdeep by conveying it to Mirt.

Theater Owner

The owner of the Pink Flumph, Iokaste Daliano (N female Tethyrian **commoner**), is a selfish, middle-aged widow with no great love of theater. The Pink Flumph was her husband's passion; for Iokaste, it's strictly a means through which she can rub shoulders with the city's elite. She requires the directors to choose plays and hire actors, while she spends her time "on the job" greeting important guests and promising them the finest entertainment. She treats her actors and staff like half-forgotten children, and she turns away characters who come to the theater seeking the Vault of Dragons unless there's something in it for her. Appealing to her greed backfires, since Iokaste wants all the treasure for herself.

Path to the Vault

One of the dressing rooms (area P8) contains a secret trapdoor in the floor that no one knows about. It can be found with a successful DC 20 Wisdom (Perception) check. This stone door has an *arcane lock* spell cast on it and can be pulled open with a successful DC 30 Strength (Athletics) check. A *knock* spell or similar magic also does the trick.

Below the trapdoor is a 30-foot-deep shaft containing a wooden ladder. Characters who descend the ladder find themselves at one end of a 20-foot-wide stone passageway that gradually slopes down 100 feet before ending at the entrance to the Vault of Dragons.

Wishes the Faerie Dragon

Iokaste's late husband, Algondar Daliano, had a violet **faerie dragon** companion named Wishes. The faerie dragon detests Iokaste but remains on the payroll, begrudgingly using its magic to enhance performances for the sake of preserving Algondar's legacy. It prefers to remain invisible and unseen otherwise. Iokaste refers to it derisively as "the flying serpent."

If the characters threaten it or endanger the theater, Wishes uses its magic to confound and neutralize them. As they make their way to the Vault of Dragons, it follows them invisibly. Once it learns about the gold in the vault, the faerie dragon casts *mirror image* on itself, turns visible, and addresses the characters telepathically. It demands a share of the hoard (at least 5,000 gp), threatens to tip off the City Watch if the characters refuse, and makes good on its threat if the characters don't share the wealth. The faerie dragon doesn't have a hoard of its own, since it gives its earnings to unfortunate Waterdavians by invisibly flying around the city at night and leaving coins on doorsteps, window sills, nightstands, and pillows.

Theater: Autumn

At the end of their previous encounter, the characters are no closer to finding the *Stone of Golorr*. Jarlaxle is waiting for them at the Seven Masks Theater in the Dock Ward. The theater caters to a lower-class clientele, and ship captains and sailors are admitted for free. The owner of the theater is a burly and jovial Shou man with a braided goatee named Rongquan Mystere—another of Jarlaxle's many disguises. When Jarlaxle is away, he entrusts his stage managers to look after things.

Sapphiria's Booty

When the characters first arrive, all doors except the ones leading backstage are locked. Characters who slip in through the back see actors and stagehands bustling about and the director arguing with the playwright while the stage manager looks on helplessly. On the stage, actors walk through their scenes and read their lines to a mostly empty theater. Watching the rehearsal from the front row while smoking a pipe is **Jarlaxle Baenre** (see appendix B), disguised as Rongquan. Hidden in the shadows in various spots are four **drow elite warriors** ready to fight by Jarlaxle's side.

The play, *Sapphiria's Booty*, is a romantic comedy about a blue-haired madam named Sapphiria who runs a thieves' guild out of a festhall. When a charming sea captain arrives with a hold full of booty from a faraway land, Sapphiria decides to steal it. Zaniness ensues when she falls in love with the first mate, who is half her age, while the captain falls in love with her. On one side of the stage is a backdrop resembling the deck of a ship; the other side is decorated to look like a madam's parlor in a brothel, complete with a gaudy chandelier and a fainting couch.

Westra Moltimmur (CG female Illuskan human **commoner** with Insight +2 and Performance +6), the play's leading lady, is one of Waterdeep's great treasures, and the cast and crew are very protective of her. Now in her seventies and having been married no fewer than seven times, she has a brisk sense of humor and a zest for life. She's also insightful enough to know that "Rongquan Mystere" isn't what he appears to be. She has seen the dark elves who watch over Rongquan and observed him using subtle hand gestures (Drow Sign Language) to communicate with them.

Speaking with Rongquan

Jarlaxle has instructed the stage managers to bring all visitors to him. In the guise of Rongquan, he claims to be a member of the Lords' Alliance who answers directly to Laeral Silverhand. He also seems to know all about the characters' meeting with Laeral (see encounter 1, "Alley") and says he can speak on her behalf. He asks about the *Stone of Golorr* and is disappointed if the characters don't have it. If they offer up the fake stone recovered in encounter 9, "Cellar Complex," Rongquan immediately realizes it's a fake.

If the characters aren't sure what to do next, Jarlaxle imparts the following information:

> "My friends, don't be discouraged. The wind is blowing in our direction! I've learned that Fenerus Stormcastle was arrested by the City Watch for theft and taken to a courthouse in the Castle Ward to face the judgment of a magister. No doubt he hid the stone before his capture. You must speak to him right away. You'll need to devise some sort of ruse to get close to Fenerus. I urge against violence, or you might find yourself locked up beside him."

If the characters ask why Laeral Silverhand doesn't question Fenerus herself or bail him out of jail, Jarlaxle laughs and says it would be politically unwise for the Open Lord to be seen negotiating with a man who has committed heinous crimes against the city.

Jarlaxle could speak to Fenerus himself, but he's not sure if the courthouse is warded against magic. He can't risk the exposure, so he sends the characters instead. If the characters refuse to work for Rongquan, he shrugs his broad shoulders and lets them leave unmolested, figuring they'll try to talk to Fenerus anyway.

If the characters attack him, Jarlaxle smiles, whistles for his drow bodyguards, and has at them. If the characters fall in combat, Jarlaxle and his guards stabilize dying party members before dragging all of them to a snowy alley and leaving them there with their gear. After the drow depart, a cold wind tears through the alley and awakens the unconscious characters.

Next Encounter

If the characters decide to speak with Fenerus, proceed with encounter 8, "Courthouse."

Theater: Winter

As this encounter opens, the characters follow a fleeing Zhent swashbuckler into a theater in the Trades Ward called the Brizzenbright. Named after Malkolm Brizzenbright, its dead owner, the establishment has struggled in recent years. It stays open in the winter for its own survival, but the theater is wickedly cold this time of year.

Brizzenbright's Ghost

Malkolm Brizzenbright, a **ghost**, greets all visitors in the lobby (area P1). Dressed in a suit, his hair unkempt, he floats in plain sight most of the time, waving his hands about in gestures of greeting and salutation. Locals are accustomed to his spectral form and his stock introduction: "Let not this harried visage diminish you, gentle-sirs and beautiful ladies, for I am but your friendly host. What fine art have we wrought for you this day? Buy your tickets and behold! You shan't be disappointed!"

The ghost can engage in light conversation. It is bound to the theater because Malkolm Brizzenbright's soul couldn't bear to leave the place. If the theater were to close down, the ghost would haunt it still, perhaps becoming more deranged over time. Only razing or burning the theater to the ground can force his spirit to depart forever.

Snakes in the House

After a harrowing rooftop chase, Vevette Blackwater (CE female Tethyrian human **swashbuckler**; see appendix B) has bought a ticket and slipped into the theater during a performance of *Blood Wedding*—a play about love, jealousy, and death. In the story, a young woman is brought to a castle by a count, only to fall in love with his younger brother, a man of faith. Her betrayal eats away at the jealous count. He murders his brother on his wedding day and pursues the bride, who hurls herself off the castle battlements in despair. The count is cursed by the gods and transformed into a creature of darkness, damned to live in his castle and feed on blood. A female cellist and two male violinists provide musical accompaniment.

The shivering audience includes thirty **commoners**. Also present is a Zhentarim spy named Agorn Fuoco (NE male Turami **bard**; see appendix B) and his companion, Amath Sercent (LE female Mulan **priest** of Bane). Agorn is swept up in the drama and fighting back tears while Amath pats his arm gently. Vevette takes a seat behind them and surreptitiously passes the *Stone of Golorr* to Agorn. Looking on from the back row is **Remallia Haventree** (see appendix B), a member of the Harpers who suspects Agorn of being a high-ranking Zhent. She has been watching him for a while now, hoping to identify other Zhentarim leaders in Waterdeep. Although Remallia appears to be alone, the two violinists (LG male Illuskan human **spies** with Performance +5) are Harpers under her command. Agorn and Amath are unaware that they're under surveillance.

Enter the Heroes

The characters are expected to buy tickets before entering the main theater. The house manager chases after them if they don't, threatening to summon the City Watch.

A character who makes a successful DC 14 Wisdom (Perception) check spots Vevette in the darkened theater. When this happens, Vevette springs from her chair and flees out the nearest door, planning to lead the characters on another merry chase. Remallia and her fellow Harpers watch with interest but don't get involved unless their lives or the lives of innocents are imperiled.

Next Encounter

If the characters take the bait, proceed with encounter 3, "Street Chase." Once Vevette's pursuers are out of sight, Agorn Fuoco and Amath Sercent use the distraction to slip away, exiting through the main doors and flagging down a hire-coach.

Encounter 7: Old Tower

The characters face enemies in a dilapidated tower built by some half-forgotten Waterdavian mage hundreds of years ago. It has the following features:

- All doors are unlocked except the one to area O5.
- The rooms have 15-foot-high ceilings, with 7-foot-high doorways connecting them.
- The tower is brightly lit by *continual flame* spells cast on wall sconces.

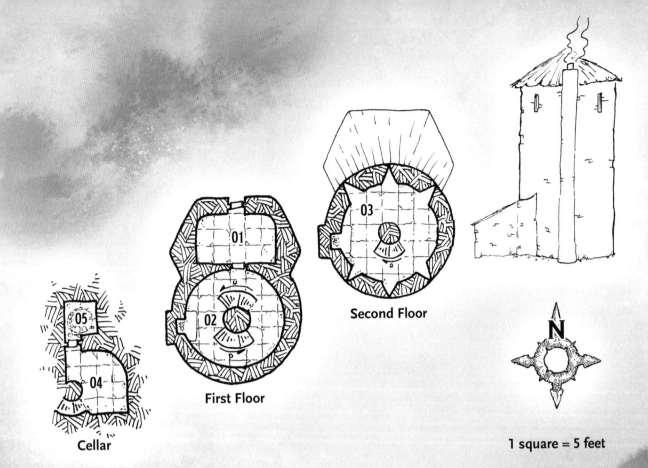

First Floor

Second Floor

Cellar

N

1 square = 5 feet

MAP 4.5: OLD TOWER

AREAS OF THE OLD TOWER

The following locations are keyed to map 4.5.

O1. VESTIBULE

The outer door has a tiny peephole with a closed iron shutter on the inside. Rotting tapestries adorn the walls, and mud and dirt have accumulated on the floor.

O2. GROUND LEVEL

Stone spiral stairs curl up into the tower and down into the cellar. Set into the west wall is a fireplace blackened with soot. A burned heap that used to be a padded leather chair lies near the fireplace.

O3. UPPER LEVEL

This room, formerly a wizard's laboratory, contains the following features:

- A soot-stained fireplace has a lidless iron cauldron hanging on an iron hook in its hearth and a wizard's portrait on the wall above the mantelpiece.
- The floor is littered with shards of broken glass, burned scraps of paper, twisted pieces of metal, and bird droppings.
- Other furnishings include a rocking chair, a trellis table, and the charred remains of a bookshelf, all shrouded in thick cobwebs.
- Arrow slits line the walls, and pigeons nest in the rafters.

Arrow Slits. Each arrow slit is 4 feet tall and 1 foot wide—big enough for a Small character or a slim Medium character to squeeze through.

Treasure. A thorough search of the room yields a random treasure, determined by rolling a d4 and consulting the Old Tower Treasure table.

OLD TOWER TREASURE

d4	Treasure
1	A charred *wand of magic missiles* (each time a charge is expended, there's a 50 percent chance that nothing happens and the charge is wasted)
2	A *potion of healing* mixed with a *potion of flying* (if this mixture is imbibed, roll on the Potion Miscibility table in chapter 7 of the *Dungeon Master's Guide* to determine the effect)
3	A cracked *driftglobe* that emits a flickering light but otherwise functions normally
4	A burned scroll tube containing two blank sheets of paper that are actually *paper birds* (see appendix A)

O4. CELLAR

This room contains the following features:

- A small, circular wooden table is surrounded by four stools made from empty barrels. A marked deck of playing cards is scattered atop the table, with a few stray cards lying on the floor.

- Three crates are stacked against the south wall. Each contains a twenty-day supply of edible rations.
- Set into the north wall is a sturdy oak door with iron fittings and a built-in lock.

Locked Door. The door to area O5 is locked. The lock can be picked by a character who uses thieves' tools and makes a successful DC 20 Dexterity check. The door can also be forced open with a successful DC 25 Strength (Athletics) check.

O5. TELEPORTATION CIRCLE

Arcane runes are inscribed in a circle on the floor of this otherwise empty chamber. The circle is a permanent teleportation circle (see the *teleportation circle* spell description in the *Player's Handbook*).

OLD TOWER: SPRING

The party's elusive quarry, a **kenku**, has taken refuge in an old tower. By the time the characters reach the entrance to the tower, the kenku has taken a hostage and fled to the upper level.

STREET URCHINS

Just prior to the kenku's arrival, three children entered the derelict tower on a dare. If this encounter occurs on or around Trolltide, the children are wearing troll masks. These noncombatants are named Nat, Jenks, and Squiddly (see "The Three Urchins," page 63).

The kenku has kidnapped Squiddly and taken him upstairs (area O3). The characters encounter Nat and Jenks in area O2; they beg the characters to save their young tiefling friend.

CONFRONTING THE KENKU

The kenku clutches the *Stone of Golorr* in one clawed hand and Squiddly the tiefling in the other. When cornered, the creature mimics the sound of a screaming child—its way of threatening to harm the boy unless the characters leave at once. The kenku doesn't respond to verbal threats or attempts at persuasion, but it can be bribed with coin, gemstones, or shiny baubles. It gives up both the stone and the boy in return for 100 gp worth of treasure.

If the characters and the kenku reach an impasse, Squiddly kicks the kenku in the shin, causing it to release him, and hides under some old furniture. This act initiates combat as the kenku draws its sword.

If he has a clear path to the stairs, Squiddly runs down them and rejoins his friends. The three children flee the tower together, disappearing into a nearby alley.

GAZER ATTACK

When the characters finally obtain the *Stone of Golorr*, three **gazers** (see appendix B) enter area O3 through the arrow slits and attack. They try to incapacitate whichever character has the stone and use their telekinetic rays to steal it. If successful, the gazers take the stone to a nearby alley.

NEXT ENCOUNTER

Whether the *Stone of Golorr* leaves the tower in the possession of the characters or the gazers, proceed with encounter 1, "Alley."

OLD TOWER: SUMMER

The old tower, formerly owned by a wizard, was recently bought by Esvele Rosznar, a young noblewoman with a fascinating alter ego (see "The Black Viper" in appendix B).

HOUSE ROSZNAR GUARDS

Esvele has brought four **guards** with her to the tower. They wear the livery of House Rosznar and stand guard in area O1.

BOUGHT AND PAID FOR

Through her network of spies, Esvele learned about Lord Neverember's friendship with the tower's previous owner. Not long thereafter, she found the entrance to the Vault of Dragons beneath the tower. Unfortunately for her, she doesn't know what keys are needed to enter it or what lies within. When the characters arrive, Esvele is in area O2, meeting with the following three guild representatives (**commoners**):

- Sembra Vashir (LN female Calishite human), of the Carpenters', Roofers', and Plaisterers' Guild
- Pynt Oomtrowl (CG female rock gnome), of the Cellarers' and Plumbers' Guild
- Jarbokken Frostbeard (LG male shield dwarf), of the Guild of Stonecutters, Masons, Potters, and Tile-makers

This meeting is a formality. As the new owner, Esvele is required by law to bring the building up to code. She is gathering cost estimates from the guilds involved but has no intention of proceeding with repairs. The arrival of the characters provides her with a welcome distraction.

Characters will have a tough time convincing Esvele that they have come for any reason other than to break into the Vault of Dragons. Esvele is willing to bring them on as business partners, allowing them access to the vault (preferably when there aren't guild representatives around) in exchange for an equal share of whatever treasure it might contain. She and the characters have each other over a barrel. She can't have them arrested for burglary without the authorities discovering the vault and seizing the tower. And they can't afford to deny the noblewoman what she wants, lest she divulge the vault's location to the authorities in exchange for a reward.

Esvele offers to help the characters obtain the keys needed to unlock the Vault of Dragons and insists on accompanying them during their first foray into the vault, claiming all the while that she's capable of looking after herself. However this business with the party unfolds, she tries to conceal her secret identity from the characters for as long as possible.

Esvele doesn't use a key to lock and unlock the door to area O5. She uses thieves' tools instead.

PATH TO THE VAULT

The entrance to the vault is hidden behind a secret door in the north wall of area O5. The secret door was crafted by skilled dwarf engineers and requires a successful DC 20 Wisdom (Perception) check to locate. Esvele has already disarmed a magic trap on the door, rendering it safe to open. Beyond it lies a dusty staircase that descends 90 feet to a 20-foot-wide corridor. The hall extends another 90 feet to the vault doors. To one side of the vault doors, a natural fissure in the wall once served as a grick's lair, but Esvele killed the grick and left its corpse on the floor.

OLD TOWER: AUTUMN

The characters come to this crumbling tower in the Dock Ward looking for the *Stone of Golorr*. Members of Bregan D'aerthe follow them invisibly. Superstitious locals think the tower is haunted, so they avoid it.

ANTIMAGIC FIELD

The interior of the tower is subject to a permanent *antimagic field* spell. Consequently, no magic functions inside the tower. This effect was left behind by the tower's previous occupant, a wizard hermit who dabbled in "wild magic" and could no longer control it. Because of the antimagic field, the magic lights that normally illuminate the tower have been suppressed. Only a *wish* spell or similar magic can end this antimagic effect.

TOWER SWORDS

Scattered on the floors throughout the tower are six longswords with no traces of rust or blood on them. These blades are **flying swords** rendered inert by the antimagic field. If a flying sword is taken from the tower, it animates and attacks.

WHERE'S THE STONE?

Fenerus hid the *Stone of Golorr* in the cauldron that hangs in the fireplace on the upper level (area O3). But it's not there anymore.

Before the characters reach area O3, three **drow gunslingers** (see appendix B) under the effect of *potions of invisibility* use their *levitate* spells to scale the outside of the tower and crawl through the arrow slits. While they are inside the tower, their *invisibility* spells are negated by the antimagic field. One of the drow quickly finds the stone and takes it before the characters show up.

Unless they were defeated earlier in the adventure, these drow are Jarlaxle's lieutenants: Fel'rekt Lafeen, Krebbyg Masq'il'yr, and Soluun Xibrindas. Replace any that were killed earlier in the adventure with other drow gunslingers, and roll initiative for each drow. Soluun (or his replacement) can't resist a good fight and attacks the characters, buying time for the other drow to escape. Once they're outside the tower, the fleeing drow become invisible again as they leap onto a nearby rooftop, but the potions wear off at the end of their next turns, enabling characters to chase after them.

NEXT ENCOUNTER

If the characters pursue the fleeing drow, proceed with encounter 5, "Rooftop Chase."

OLD TOWER: WINTER

The characters have learned that the *Stone of Golorr* is with Amath Sercent, a priest of Bane who is allied with Manshoon. She and her acolytes reside in Yellowspire, a Castle Ward tower so named because its bricks have a pale yellow tinge to them. Amath is in the midst of converting the tower into a temple of Bane. A teleportation circle in the basement allows for swift transport to and from Kolat Towers and Manshoon's extradimensional sanctum.

HOUSE OF TYRANNY

Amath Sercent (LE female Mulan **priest**) and her four followers (LE male and female **acolytes** of mixed ethnicities) dress in common clothing when outside the tower. Inside the structure, they wear fur-lined robes to stay warm. They refer to the tower as the House of Tyranny, and black prints of their right hands, with fingers and thumb held together, cover every interior surface. These handprints mimic the symbol of Bane.

Amath and her followers assemble here for worship but sleep elsewhere. When the characters first arrive, all five have gathered in prayer on the upper floor of the tower (area O3). Three black **flying snakes** nest in the rafters and join any battle here. During this ceremony, Amath and her acolytes hold candles and form a circle around a gagged and blindfolded broadsheet publisher named Shan Chien (N male Shou human **commoner**). The imperious, middle-aged man is shackled to the floor, and Amath carries the key to the shackles. The shackles can be broken by a creature that uses an action to make a successful DC 20 Strength (Athletics) check. Picking the shackles' lock requires thieves' tools and a successful DC 15 Dexterity check.

The Banites' ritual is designed to break Shan's will, making him subservient to Bane. Amath has been using this ritual to "turn" broadsheet publishers as part of a larger plot to control the flow of information in the city—a critical element of Manshoon's takeover. Shan was abducted by Amath's acolytes the night before while walking to his home in the Trades Ward. He publishes *The Targe*, a broadsheet that offers up vitriolic rants on all manner of local topics, including politics.

Amath has the *Stone of Golorr* in her pocket. She is expecting Manshoon or his simulacrum to arrive and retrieve it shortly.

OUTER SCAFFOLDING

The tower is encircled by wooden scaffolding covered with ice and snow. Despite its precarious appearance, the scaffolding is secure and safe to walk on, enabling creatures to scale the outside of the tower without having to make ability checks. The scaffolding rattles and creaks, however, and any creature that moves on it must succeed on a DC 16 Dexterity (Stealth) check or be heard by the tower's occupants.

SIMULACRUM

The characters must fight Amath and her acolytes to get the *Stone of Golorr*. When they finally obtain it, fate deals them an unkind hand as Manshoon's simulacrum (see "Manshoon" in appendix B) arrives by way of the

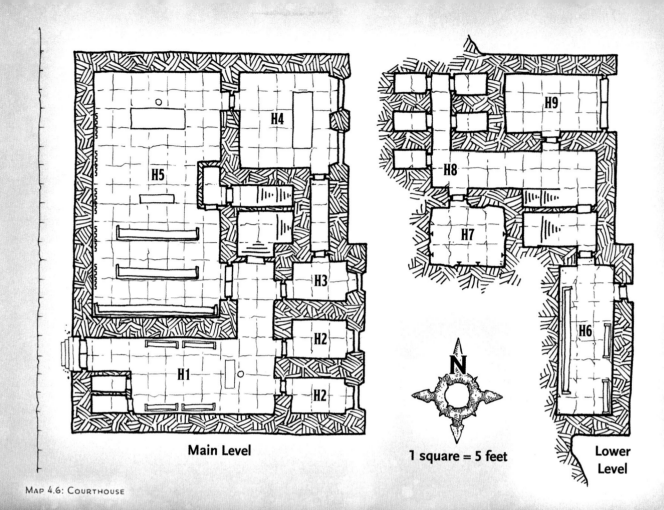

Main Level

1 square = 5 feet

Lower Level

MAP 4.6: COURTHOUSE

teleportation circle in area O5. If the characters had the opportunity and the foresight to destroy the circle prior to obtaining the stone, the simulacrum instead must travel to Yellowspire on foot, giving the characters ample time to get away before it arrives as long as they leave within 1 hour after obtaining the stone. The simulacrum tirelessly pursues the stone, and characters who flee would do themselves well not to leave tracks in the snow.

NEXT ENCOUNTER

If a character becomes attuned to the *Stone of Golorr*, it reveals the location of the Vault of Dragons, under the Brandath family mausoleum in the City of the Dead, and the three keys needed to enter it. When the characters are ready to visit the mausoleum, proceed with encounter 4, "Mausoleum."

ENCOUNTER 8: COURTHOUSE

People who are arrested by the City Watch are brought to a courthouse and detained until a magister can pass judgment on them. Each courthouse has the following features:

- Two **guards** stand outside each of the front and back doors (leading to areas H1 and H6) at all hours.
- Rooms have 10-foot-high ceilings, with 8-foot-high passages and 7-foot-high doorways connecting them.

- Windows are fitted with iron bars that require a successful DC 30 Strength (Athletics) check to bend.
- Doors are made of iron-bound oak and unlocked.
- All areas are brightly lit by *continual flame* spells cast on wall sconces.
- Cisterns on the roof collect rainwater, which is funneled by pipes down to the showers (area H7).

AREAS OF THE COURTHOUSE

The following locations are keyed to map 4.6.

H1. UPSTAIRS WAITING ROOM

This room has the following features:

- Two **guards** stand outside the doors to the records rooms (area H2) at all hours. Behind a desk sits a court clerk (**commoner**).
- Uncomfortable wood benches line the walls. A copper plaque mounted above each bench says, in Common, "Please have a seat. Someone will be with you shortly."
- Two privies are situated in a corner by the entrance.

Clerk. The clerk asks visitors what their business is and either directs them to the appropriate area of the courthouse or instructs them to wait. The clerk holds a key to the records rooms (area H2).

H2. RECORDS ROOMS

The doors to these rooms are locked. Inside, shelves lining every available inch of wall space hold boxes of papers dated by month and year. These papers are records of court proceedings and depositions.

H3. Clerks' Office

Two desks pushed together in the middle of the room hold quills, ink, and sheets of paper. Two court clerks (**commoners**) work here, supporting the magister on duty. Each clerk holds a key to the records rooms (area H2).

H4. Magister's Office

This grand office contains several plush armchairs and a large walnut desk. The seal of Waterdeep is emblazoned on the wood floor.

When not overseeing a trial, a magister on duty at the courthouse reviews cases and holds meetings here. If a magister is here, so is a **knight** who serves as a bodyguard.

H5. Courtroom

This room has the following features:

- Two **guards** are stationed here at all times.
- If court is in session, the magister is here along with a bodyguard (see area H4) and anyone else pertinent to the case being tried.
- A magister's cloth-draped desk faces a defendant's box and three rows of pews.
- Hanging on the west wall are tasseled banners depicting the coats of arms of the City of Waterdeep, the Waterdeep City Watch, and the Waterdeep City Guard, as well as the seal of the Lords of Waterdeep and the symbol of Tyr, god of justice.

H6. Downstairs Waiting Room

Nobles scheduled to testify in court and those waiting to visit prisoners are held here. The room contains the following features:

- Two **guards** are on duty in this room at all times.
- Mismatched couches line the walls.
- Old broadsheets rest in loose piles atop end tables.

H7. Showers

Dirty prisoners are stripped of their clothing and washed here before they are locked in cells. Protruding from the walls are iron nozzles that spew cold water when a chain next to the door is pulled. Drains in the stone-tiled floor keep the room from flooding.

H8. Cell Block

Two **guards** are stationed in this hall at all times.

Locked Cells. Five cells are spaced along this hall. The door to each cell is locked from the outside, and the guards stationed here hold the keys. A door's lock can't be picked from inside the cell.

H9. Watch Wagon

This room contains the following features:

- Two **veterans**, members of the City Watch, are here at all times.
- An armored carriage stands behind a pair of steel doors secured by an iron bar.

Armored Carriage. Two horses are needed to pull the carriage, which can hold up to eight Medium prisoners at a time. The back door to the carriage is secured with chains and two padlocks. Each veteran on duty has a key that opens one of the padlocks.

Barred Outer Doors. It takes two people to lift the bar that obstructs the doors to the outside. A successful DC 21 Strength (Athletics) check enables one person to do it alone.

Courthouse: Summer

After obtaining the *Stone of Golorr*, the characters are arrested by the City Watch soon after they emerge from the sewers.

Under Arrest

The arresting force consists of twelve **veterans**, a Watch sergeant and eleven constables. They demand that the characters surrender their weapons and come along quietly. For guidance on how to handle character arrests, see "Breaking the Law," page 10.

The characters are charged with disturbing the peace, a minor offense that carries a fine and results in an edict. The charge stems from their conduct in encounter 3, "Street Chase." Depending on how they comported themselves in previous encounters, the characters might be charged with additional crimes against the city or its citizens, possibly including brandishing weapons without due cause, robbery, assaulting a citizen, or murder. If they resist arrest, they are charged with hampering justice. See the Code Legal handout in appendix C for the penalties associated with such crimes.

Characters who give up their visible weapons without a fuss aren't searched, but those who give the Watch a hard time are searched for hidden weapons (and stripped of anything that could potentially cause harm). A character can conceal a Tiny object from the Watch with a successful DC 12 Dexterity (Sleight of Hand) check. If the *Stone of Golorr* is found during a search, the Watch sergeant inspects it, concludes that it's nothing of consequence, and returns it to its owner.

Dock Ward Courthouse

Arrested characters are brought to a courthouse in the Dock Ward and confined to cells (area H8) until their trial. Any items taken from them during their arrest are entrusted to the front desk clerk (area H1) pending the trial's outcome. A character can take a short rest while incarcerated and use that time to attune to the *Stone of Golorr*. After 1d6 hours, word comes down that the magister is prepared to hear the characters' testimony, whereupon the guards in area H8 unlock the characters' cells and escort them to the courtroom (area H5), where the magister is waiting.

False Captain

If Lord Cassalanter's **doppelganger** valet is still at large, it kills a Watch captain and uses the victim's uniform to impersonate another Watch captain the characters have met before. Then, in the guise of Hyustus Staget (see "The Watch Arrives," page 27), the doppelganger kills the guards in area H8 with its bare hands and uses their keys to open the characters' cells. "Hyustus" warns them that the magister is corrupt and suggests they flee the city before they're sentenced to death. "Hyustus" offers to deliver messages or items of import on their behalf while they make good their escape. The doppelganger is hoping that the characters will entrust the *Stone of Golorr* to it for safekeeping. Failing that, it hopes to wrest the stone from them during the chaos of the jailbreak.

If the characters refuse to play along, the doppelganger cries out in alarm, bringing the full weight of the courthouse garrison (ten **guards** and two **veterans**) down upon the characters, whom "Hyustus" accuses of beating the cell block guards to death. These reinforcements have no reason to believe that Captain Staget isn't who he appears to be, and they side with him in any conflict.

If the doppelganger obtains the *Stone of Golorr*, it promptly delivers it to Victoro Cassalanter. If the characters extricate themselves from the mess they're in, they can retrieve the stone from Cassalanter Villa (see chapter 6).

MEETING WITH THE MAGISTER

The presiding magister is Umbero Zastro, a handsome, eloquent, and fair-minded half-elf in his thirties. He's known for his finely honed sense of poetic justice and for meting out unconventional punishments.

Magister Umbero Zastro has the statistics of a **noble**, with these changes:

- He is lawful neutral.
- He is unarmed, unarmored (AC 11), and worth 0 XP.
- He has these racial traits: He has advantage on saving throws against being charmed, and magic can't put him to sleep. He has darkvision out to a range of 60 feet. He speaks Common and Elvish.

The magister has already heard the testimony of the arresting officers, as well as that of any eyewitnesses. The characters are given an hour to plead their case while he asks questions. A character who tries to deceive Zastro must make a Charisma (Deception) check contested by the magister's Wisdom (Insight) check. A character who loses this contest is found guilty of hampering justice, locked up for a tenday, and fined 200 gp, on top of any other punishments meted out for crimes committed against the city and its citizenry. Those who can't or won't pay the fine are sentenced to hard labor for a year in Amendsfarm, a City Guard-run labor camp among the farms of Undercliff.

If the characters committed one or more crimes, they are judged guilty and punished accordingly (see the Code Legal handout in appendix C). A character who pleads for leniency and succeeds on a DC 14 Charisma (Persuasion) check receives an alternate punishment for crimes that don't carry punishments of death or exile. This check is made with advantage if the character has renown in a respectable faction, such as Force Grey (the Gray Hands), the Emerald Enclave, the Harpers, the Lords' Alliance, or the Order of the Gauntlet. Alternate punishments for lesser crimes include the following:

- The character must make beds and clean bedsheets at local orphanages for a tenday, under guard supervision.
- The character must report to Morana Huldark, a dwarf member of the Guild of Watermen, and scrape barnacles off the docks for a tenday under her close supervision.
- The character must spend the next month delivering 30-pound casks of drinking water to the guards stationed atop the city walls.
- For a tenday, the character must stand on a particular street corner every afternoon from highsun to dusk and, like a broadcrier, shout out the crimes of which he or she has been found guilty while accepting the scoldings and verbal lashings of the citizenry.

Characters who are tricked into acting in accordance with the wishes of the doppelganger can be forgiven for crimes committed during the jailbreak, but only if the doppelganger is apprehended or killed. (It reverts to its true form when it dies.) *Speak with dead* spells can be cast on the cell block guards slain by the doppelganger to obtain testimony that clears the characters of the guards' murder.

NEXT ENCOUNTER

If a character becomes attuned to the *Stone of Golorr*, it reveals the location of the Vault of Dragons, beneath an old tower in the Sea Ward, and the three keys needed to enter it. When the characters are ready to visit the location, proceed with encounter 7, "Old Tower."

COURTHOUSE: AUTUMN

The characters have learned that Fenerus Stormcastle is in the custody of the City Watch at a courthouse in the Castle Ward. If they try to speak with him, they are met by the clerk at the front desk, who informs them that they must schedule a meeting with the magister first, because visitors need her written permission to see him. The clerk says the meeting with the magister can happen no sooner than highsun on the following day but can be persuaded to move up the time for a bribe of 10 gp or more.

There are alternatives to speaking with the magister, if the characters have sufficient renown in a politically influential faction—or a talent for deception:

- A character who has at least 4 renown in the Harpers can convince **Mirt** (see appendix B) to use his authority as a Lord of Waterdeep to secure Fenerus's release. Mirt has personally lost coin to the Blood Hawk Posse, so helping Fenerus squirm out of jail stings him deeply.
- A character who has at least 4 renown in the Lords' Alliance can arrange a meeting with **Laeral Silverhand** (see appendix B) at Piergeiron's Palace and convince her to give Fenerus what he wants in exchange for information on the stone's whereabouts. The safe return of Neverember's cache of dragons is more important to her than the fate of one brigand.
- The characters can purposely get themselves arrested in the Castle Ward. Even a minor crime can result in a brief period of incarceration until the magister has

time to render judgment. In the meantime, characters can try to speak to Fenerus.

- The characters can try to infiltrate the courthouse using mundane disguises or magic. Impersonating an official or using magic to influence one is a crime (see the Code Legal handout in appendix C), so they must be stealthy or skilled at deception.

MEETING WITH THE MAGISTER

The courthouse magister is Hester Barch (LG female Turami human **acolyte** with Insight +4), a petite woman in her seventies. Magister Barch is slow to anger and fond of sharing lengthy educational anecdotes and parables. Unknown to all but her closest aides, the magister has the innate psionic ability to cast the *detect thoughts* spell without somatic or material components. After using it once, the magister must finish a short or long rest before she can cast the spell again. Wisdom is her spellcasting ability (spell save DC 12).

The magister is disinclined to agree to any request for a private meeting with Fenerus, on the grounds that he's a shady, unrepentant person and a flight risk. The conditions under which she will permit a meeting are as follows:

- A character who has at least 3 renown in the Harpers or the Lords' Alliance, or a character who belongs to a Waterdavian noble family, makes a good argument and succeeds on a DC 15 Charisma (Persuasion) check.
- A character who is impersonating a noble or an official makes a good argument and succeeds on a DC 15 Charisma (Deception) check. If the check fails, Magister Barch sees through the ruse and uses her *detect thoughts* spell to verify that the character is in fact disguised as a noble or an official—a crime that carries a punishment of flogging followed by imprisonment for up to a tenday, plus a fine of up to 500 gp.
- A character tells the magister about the hidden cache of dragons and Fenerus's role in finding it.

TALKING TO FENERUS

Fenerus Stormcastle (N male Tethyrian **bandit captain**) is confined to a cell in area H8, waiting to stand trial. He is charged with multiple counts of theft (highway banditry) and assaults against Waterdavian citizens. Fenerus knew it was only a matter of time until someone tipped off the City Watch; he suspects that another member of the Blood Hawk Posse gave him up. The timing is unfortunate for him, since he was planning to earn a small fortune by turning over the *Stone of Golorr* to his Luskanite contact. Now, he plans to use the stone to escape imprisonment and wipe his criminal record clean.

If the characters can get close enough to speak with him, Fenerus refuses to divulge the stone's location until he is released and granted immunity for his past crimes. He knows that the presiding magister or a Lord of Waterdeep has the authority to give him what he wants.

The only condition under which Magister Barch will consider acquiescing to Fenerus's demands is if the characters convince her that such a decision is good for Waterdeep. To accomplish that, they either must use magic to beguile her (which is a crime and likely to result in the caster's arrest once the effect wears off), or they must tell her about the Vault of Dragons and the stolen gold. In either case, she insists on trying something before letting him off the hook: after taking a short rest, she has Fenerus brought to her courtroom and questions him about the stone. Surreptitiously, she uses her *detect thoughts* spell to scan his surface thoughts in an attempt to discern the stone's location. Given that the stone is foremost in Fenerus's mind, Magistrate Barch learns where it is hidden, shares the information with the characters, and returns Fenerus to his cell.

WHERE'S THE STONE?

Fenerus hid the *Stone of Golorr* on the top floor of an old tower in the Dock Ward—a tower warded against all forms of magic. If he is freed, he offers to lead the characters to the tower or provides directions so they can find it on his own.

NEXT ENCOUNTER

If the characters learn where Fenerus hid the stone and go after it, proceed with encounter 7, "Old Tower."

ENCOUNTER 9: CELLAR COMPLEX

Cellars and sewer tunnels intersect to create small dungeons under Waterdeep. These complexes have the following features:

- Ceilings and doorways are 7 feet high.
- There are no light sources.

AREAS OF THE CELLAR COMPLEX

The following locations are keyed to map 4.7. The complex has three distinct sections: the sewer tunnels (areas B1–B3), the southern cellars (areas B4–B9), and the northern cellars (areas B10–B11).

B1. SEWER ACCESS

This chamber has stone steps and a locked, iron-bound wooden door with a sign mounted on it that reads, in Common, "SEWER ACCESS: AUTHORIZED CITY OFFICIALS ONLY." The door to area B2 is locked. The lock can be picked by a character who makes a successful DC 17 Dexterity check using thieves' tools, or the door can be forced open with a successful DC 20 Strength (Athletics) check. City Watch captains hold keys to sewer access points that correspond with their assigned wards.

B2. SEWERS

Fresh sewage flows along a trough that runs parallel to a stone walkway. The sewage is 3 feet deep. Any creature immersed in it for 1 minute must succeed on a DC 11 Constitution saving throw or become infected with sewer plague (see "Diseases" in chapter 8 of the *Dungeon Master's Guide*).

Where the tunnel branches, a stone bridge spans the sewage pouring out of an eastern artery. There's no walkway in this arterial passage that leads to areas B3 and B4.

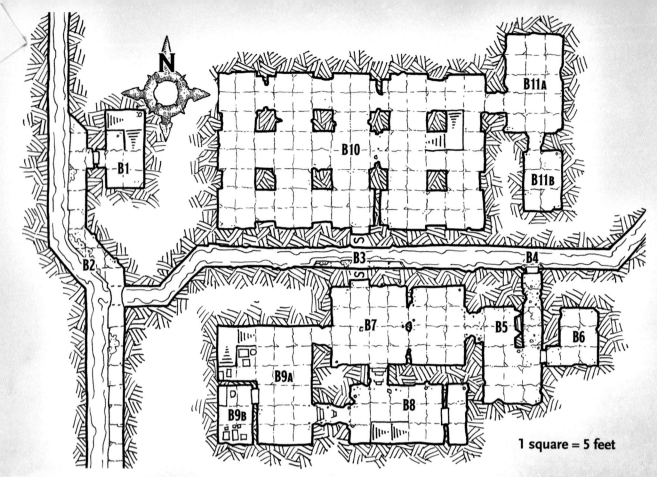

MAP 4.7: CELLAR COMPLEX

B3. SECRET DOORS

Secret doors blend with the surrounding stonework on opposite sides of this sewer tunnel. One door opens into area B7, the other into area B10. Characters who have a passive Perception score of 15 or higher spot both secret doors as they pass by. Otherwise, finding a secret door requires a search of the wall and a successful DC 15 Wisdom (Perception) check. The secret doors are set high enough that opening them doesn't cause sewage to flow into adjoining areas.

B4. RUSTY IRON DOOR

A door made of rusted iron is set into the wall above a dry, 1-foot-wide stone ledge. The door's lock corroded long ago, and the door squeals loudly on rusty hinges when opened.

B5. ARROW SLITS

A brick wall with arrow slits was added to this room at some point. The arrow slits are designed to allow archers to fire at intruders who come through the door at area B4. The arrow slits provide three-quarters cover.

B6. STORAGE ROOM

An unlocked wooden door closes off this empty room.

B7. RUBBLE-FILLED CELLAR

A wall has collapsed, creating a larger space out of two smaller rooms. The air is heavy with dust, and the floor is strewn with rubble, refuse, and rat droppings.

Secret Door. The secret door to area B3 is easily spotted from this side (no check required).

B8. SUNKEN CELLAR

This sunken cellar has these features:

- An unlocked iron door is set into the east wall.
- A crumbling stone staircase against the south wall climbs up to a landing, where a wooden door is held shut with a chain and a padlock.

Iron Door. The door opens into a small, empty storage room with hooks hanging from the ceiling.

Stairs Up. The lock can be picked with a successful DC 15 Dexterity check made using thieves' tools, or the door can be forced open with a successful DC 20 Strength (Athletics) check. It opens into an alley behind a boarded-up tenement.

B9. RAT-INFESTED CELLAR

These rooms are situated below a hostel (75 percent chance) or an orphanage (25 percent chance). Harmless **rats** crawl about, minding their own business.

B9a. Stone stairs climb 10 feet to a wooden door that opens into a street or alley. Crates and barrels stacked at the bottom of the stairs hold edible foodstuffs, but nothing else of value.

B9b. A plain wooden door opens into a room containing dusty furnishings in storage. The furniture includes a scratched wooden desk, several wobbly chairs, a coat rack, two small tables, and an empty wooden trunk. There's a 25 percent chance that one piece of furniture (determined randomly) is a **mimic** that usually feeds on rats but never passes up a bigger meal.

B10. Old Tavern Cellar

This spacious, empty cellar has the following features:

- Stone pillars and arches support the ceiling.
- Mismatched stonework on either side of a half-demolished wall indicates that this area was once two separate chambers.
- Stone stairs climb to a bricked-up doorway. (The door once led to an alley behind an old tavern.)

Secret Door. The secret door to area B3 is easily spotted from this side (no check required).

B11. Back Cellars

These rooms are extensions of area B10.

B11a. This room used to be a wine cellar. Its walls are lined with piles of rotting wood (storage racks) and broken bottles.

B11b. Once a cold storage room and root cellar, this empty chamber is choked with dust and cobwebs.

Cellar Complex: Spring

The characters have learned that a halfling necromancer named Losser Mirklav took the *Stone of Golorr*. He lives in a cellar complex under a powdered wig shop in the Trades Ward. The shop, Dandymops, is closed and locked with an iron gate. The lock can be picked by a character who makes a successful DC 15 Dexterity check using thieves' tools, or the gate can be forced open with a successful DC 25 Strength (Athletics) check. Since the shop is in a highly visible location, an attempt to break into it is 75 percent likely to be noticed by someone who alerts the City Watch. Two **veterans** of the City Watch arrive in 1d10 minutes to investigate the shop and talk to witnesses.

Xanathar's **gazer** (see appendix B) doesn't follow characters into the shop. It remains outside and waits for Xanathar Guild forces to arrive. If the characters destroyed the gazer in an earlier encounter, another one arrives with the Xanathar Guild forces.

Dungeon Entrance

Area B1 is the basement of the wig shop and the characters' point of entry into the cellar complex.

Misty Sewers

The dense fog from outside settles in the sewers, and areas B2, B3, and B4 are lightly obscured.

Necromancer

Losser Mirklav is a lightfoot halfling **mage**, with these changes:

- He is chaotic evil and has 31 (9d6) hit points.
- He has these racial traits: He is Small, and his walking speed is 25 feet. He can move through the space of a Medium or larger creature. He has advantage on saving throws against being frightened. He speaks Common and Halfling.
- He has the *animate dead* and *blight* spells prepared, instead of *counterspell* and *greater invisibility*. All his spell slots are currently expended.

Losser carries a spellbook bound in stitched flesh that contains all his prepared spells. He also has a key to

the padlocked door in area B8 and 4d10 gp in a pouch made of elf skin and cinched with a rope made of woven dwarf hair.

Losser has made several changes to the complex:

- Area B6 contains three beds—two sized for Losser's human apprentices and a smaller bed sized for him.
- Area B10 contains twelve **skeletons** that attack anyone other than Losser and his apprentices.
- Area B11 contains piles of human bones stolen from the City of the Dead. Losser hasn't gotten around to animating them yet.

Where's the Stone?

Before the characters reach Losser, kenku members of the Xanathar Guild break down the door leading into the cellar complex via area B8 and confront the necromancer. The characters find Losser cowering in one corner of area B7. Two **skeletons** stand between him and three **kenku**. The kenku aim to kill the halfling. Lying on the floor around them are four dead kenku and the remains of two destroyed (and previously animated) skeletons.

If the characters demand the *Stone of Golorr*, Losser tells them the truth: he surrendered it to the kenku, two of which fled south with it. In area B8, the characters see one **kenku** standing over the bodies of Losser's murdered human apprentices, Retchyn and Kreela. This kenku is joined by Xanathar's **gazer** (see appendix B). The kenku and the gazer try to hold off the characters for as long as possible, buying time for a second kenku to flee with the *Stone of Golorr*.

If the characters pursue the stone and leave Losser alive, he eventually slips away and retreats to area B11.

Next Encounter

Once the characters defeat Xanathar's forces in the cellar, they can chase after the fleeing kenku that has the *Stone of Golorr* in its clutches. Proceed with encounter 3, "Street Chase."

Cellar Complex: Summer

The characters are hot on the trail of three street urchins as the children scamper into the sewers under the Dock Ward.

Sickening Smell

The summer heat makes the sewer smell worse than usual, and characters become poisoned by the stench unless they cover their noses with perfumed scarves. The effect lasts until they leave the sewers. The street urchins and other creatures that live in the sewers are accustomed to the smell and aren't poisoned in this way.

Search for the Urchins

The characters approach the cellar complex from the east, eventually coming upon an iron door in the side of the sewer tunnel (area B4).

The street urchins took the *Stone of Golorr* to area B7 (which serves as their clubhouse), entering the room through a secret door (area B3). The eldest child, Nat, attuned to the stone, but contact with the aboleth so terrified her that she dropped it, screamed, and ran away.

The boys were panicked by her reaction and fled as well, leaving the stone in area B7. If the characters open the door at area B4, they startle the children on the other side, causing them to scream at the top of their lungs.

Communicating through the other children, Nat tells the characters where she dropped the stone and warns them that it's "alive." Neither she nor the boys are eager to see it again.

CHAIR TODAY, GONE TOMORROW

If the characters head to area B7, they see the *Stone of Golorr* underneath a wooden rocking chair. If the street urchins are present, one of them asks, "Where'd that rocking chair come from?"

The rocking chair is the **mimic** from area B9b. It heard the urchins' screams and investigated, hoping to snare an easy meal. It attacks anyone who harms it or reaches for the stone.

NEXT ENCOUNTER

Once the characters obtain the *Stone of Golorr*, they can leave the cellar complex. Proceed with encounter 8, "Courthouse."

CELLAR COMPLEX: AUTUMN

The characters have been encouraged to explore a Xanathar Guild hideout under the Southern Ward. They enter the location through area B1. The Xanathar Guild Roster table provides a summary of the forces stationed throughout the complex. The sections that follow describe some of the hideout's features.

XANATHAR GUILD ROSTER

Area	Creature(s)
B5	2 **goblins** behind arrow slits
B6	1 **half-ogre** that became poisoned after drinking six casks of cheap wine
B7	3 **duergar** and 1 **gazer** (see appendix B) standing guard while Thorvin Twinbeard (see appendix B) works on a mechanical beholder (see "Mechanical Beholder" below)
B8	Korgstrod Uxgulm, the **duergar** leader (40 hit points), seated in a stone chair and attended by 3 **kobolds** (see "Stone of Deception" below)
B10	7 **troglodytes** lurking in the shadows
B11a	1 **gibbering mouther** guarding a treasure chest in area B11b (see "Treasure Chest" below)

MECHANICAL BEHOLDER

A mechanical beholder built for the Day of Wonders parade lies on its side in area B7. Xanathar wants this mechanical version of itself to hover over the crowd, reminding the Lords of Waterdeep of the beholder's superiority, but no one can figure out how to make it fly. A character can use an action to try to activate the machine, doing so with a successful DC 10 Intelligence check. The activated beholder shoots dazzling lights from its eyestalks for 1 minute and then stops working.

If combat breaks out in the cellar complex, Thorvin Twinbeard flees up the stairs in area B8 and uses a key to unlock the door leading outside. He has no loyalty to the other creatures stationed here.

STONE OF DECEPTION

Korgstrod Uxgulm, the duergar leader, has what he believes to be the *Stone of Golorr*. He found it during a search of Fenerus's house in the Trades Ward. This stone is a clever imitation. It's gray and ovoid with streaks of black, but has no magical powers. Korgstrod has been unable to attune to it and assumes he's unworthy of it, not that the stone is fake.

Korgstrod plans to deliver the stone to Xanathar in due time and won't willingly part with it before then. He uses a whip to flog his kobold lackeys and keep them in line. The cowardly kobolds flee into the sewers if Korgstrod is attacked and cower in his presence otherwise.

TREASURE CHEST

An old, locked chest in the back of area B11b can be opened by someone who makes a successful DC 13 Dexterity check using thieves' tools. The chest contains 277 cp, 135 sp, a spherical gold beholder pendant with tiny gems for eyes (worth 250 gp), and a *spell scroll* of *darkvision*.

NEXT ENCOUNTER

Whether they find the fake stone or not, characters have little recourse but to consult with "Laeral" at the Seven Masks Theater in the Dock Ward. If they go there, proceed with encounter 6, "Theater."

ENCOUNTER 10: CONVERTED WINDMILL

This crumbling, two-story stone building was a windmill long before the city rose up around it. The following features apply unless an area description or encounter states otherwise:

- Rooms have 15-foot-high ceilings, with 10-foot-high passages and 7-foot-high doorways connecting them.
- Doors are wooden, closed, and unlocked.
- The walls are covered with graffiti, and the stone floors are strewn with garbage and detritus. Windows are empty lead frames without glass.
- There are no light sources.

AREAS OF THE CONVERTED WINDMILL

The following locations are keyed to map 4.8.

W1. STONE STAIRCASE

A curved set of stone stairs climbs 20 feet to the upper level. The stairs are covered with bird droppings, broken roof shingles, mud, and mold.

W2. SQUATTERS

During the spring, summer, and winter, each of these rooms is home to 1d6 + 1 squatters (**commoners**) who have made dens for themselves out of old furnishings and things salvaged from garbage piles. The squatters aren't looking for trouble.

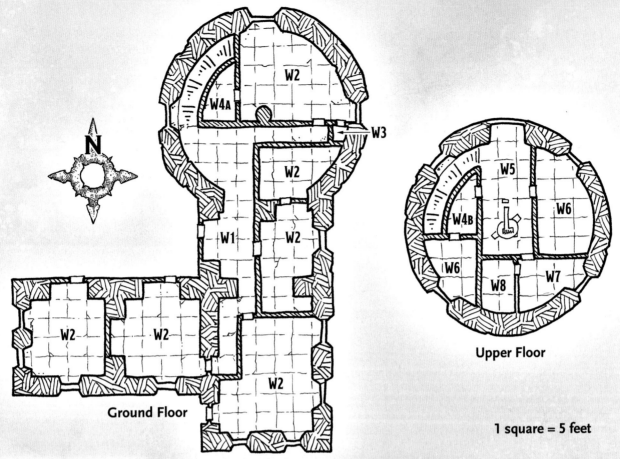

MAP 4.8: CONVERTED WINDMILL

Ground Floor

Upper Floor

1 square = 5 feet

For some food or coin, a squatter can direct or lead characters to the locked apartment on the upper level (area W7) and describe the apartment's inhabitants. A character can also secure a squatter's cooperation with a successful DC 10 Charisma (Intimidation) check.

W3. PRIVY
Beyond the door is nothing more than a hole in the floor from which rises a terrible stench.

W4. WEAK CEILING/FLOOR
Area W4a is directly underneath area W4b. The floor of the upper chamber collapses under the weight of the first Small or larger creature to walk across it. A character who has the Stonecunning trait or proficiency with mason's tools can tell that the floor is unsafe to walk on.

Any creature standing on the floor of area W4b when it collapses falls 20 feet, landing in area W4a. Any creature in area W4a when the ceiling falls in must make a DC 11 Dexterity saving throw, taking 4 (1d8) bludgeoning damage from falling debris on a failed save, or half as much damage on a successful one.

W5. ANCIENT MILLSTONE
An ancient millstone lies under a jumble of debris that includes machinery and pieces of the collapsed roof. Dust and cobwebs cover everything.

W6. PIGEON ROOSTS
Large sections of the roof have caved in above these rooms, leaving holes through which birds and precipita-

tion can enter. The floors are littered with broken shingles, bird droppings, wrecked furnishings, and other detritus, and scores of pigeons roost in the moldy rafters.

W7. SECURE APARTMENT
The north door to this room has been fitted with a shiny new lock that can be picked with a successful DC 15 Dexterity check using thieves' tools. The door can also be unlocked from inside the room, or forced open with a successful DC 20 Strength (Athletics) check.

This apartment is in good repair and contains the following features:

- A wood-framed, king-sized bed with clean mattresses stands against one wall. (Next to the bed, an unlocked door in the west wall leads to area W8.)
- The window was recently repaired and quietly swings open on oiled iron hinges.
- Across from the window, against the wall, stands a wooden armoire.

The armoire holds four clean sets of clothes, two gray cloaks, a heavy crossbow, and a wooden case containing twenty crossbow bolts.

W8. BACK ROOM
The section of conical roof directly above this chamber has mostly collapsed, filling the room with rubble. There's just enough space to open the door.

Converted Windmill: Spring

The key that the characters found in the mausoleum leads them to an old windmill in the Southern Ward. Volkarr Kibbens and Urlaster Ghann (NE male Illuskan human **commoners**) are hiding out in a secure apartment on the upper floor (area W7). In combat, they wield shovels that deal damage as clubs. Each carries 3d6 gp in a pouch.

Volkarr and Urlaster were recently hired by Losser Mirklav, a halfling necromancer, to help him break into mausoleums in the City of the Dead. They undertook the job because the pay was good, but they have no loyalty to the necromancer. If the characters confront them, Volkarr and Urlaster attack, but they surrender quickly if overwhelmed and share the following information in exchange for their lives and freedom:

- Losser Mirklav and his two human apprentices, Retchyn and Kreela, live in a cellar complex under the Trades Ward. The way to their lair is through Retchyn's powdered wig shop, which is called Dandymops.
- Losser is stealing bones from the City of the Dead to create an army of animated skeletons. (Neither Volkarr nor Urlaster knows why.)
- In the Garloth mausoleum, Losser killed a rat and took the small stone it was carrying. The rat vanished when it died, and Losser thinks the stone is magical.

Next Encounter
Once the characters set out to find the halfling necromancer, proceed with encounter 9, "Cellar Complex."

Converted Windmill: Summer

The characters head to a decrepit building in the Southern Ward that used to be a windmill. Therein, they expect to find the *Stone of Golorr* in the clutches of two treacherous **cult fanatics** named Arn Xalrondar (LE male Tethyrian human) and Seffia Naelryke (LE female Tethyrian human).

Cult Fanatics
Arn and Seffia are waiting in area W7, which they use as an apartment. They keep the door to the apartment locked at all times. They have cleared area W8 of debris and painted a pentagram in blood on the floor. At the points of the pentagram are five black globs of wax—the remains of burned candles.

Lord Cassalanter sent Arn and Seffia on a mission to retrieve the *Stone of Golorr* from his family's mausoleum. He also gave them secret orders to dispose of three other members of the cult whom he couldn't trust to keep quiet about the stone. Arn and Seffia would be horrified to learn that they failed in so simple a task; they try to correct their mistake by killing Vaelle Lurval if she's with the party (see "Mausoleum: Summer," page 70).

Devils' Arrival
As characters try to break into the cult fanatics' apartment, three **spined devils** arrive. The devils fly to the tower, knock on the apartment window, and are let inside by Seffia, whereupon Arn gives one of them the *Stone of Golorr*. When the characters enter, they see the devils fly off with the stone. The cult fanatics do everything in their power to enable the devils to escape.

Next Encounter
If the characters deal with the cult fanatics, they can chase after the fleeing spined devils by running across rooftops. Proceed with encounter 5, "Rooftop Chase."

Converted Windmill: Autumn

This old stone windmill was converted into a residence over a century ago and has fallen into disrepair. An eccentric Waterdavian artist lives here, and she hasn't been the same since her true love abandoned her. There are no squatters in the residence.

The outside doors are always locked. A lock can be picked with a successful DC 15 Dexterity check by a character using thieves' tools, or a door can be smashed open with a successful DC 15 Strength (Athletics) check. Any attempt to break into the tower is 75 percent likely to be seen or heard by one of Kalain's neighbors. Eight **veterans** of the City Watch arrive 10 minutes later to investigate the intrusion.

Let Me Paint You a Picture
Kalain, a famous Waterdavian painter, was commissioned to paint a portrait of Lord Dagult Neverember, then Waterdeep's Open Lord, in 1475 DR. Her meeting with Neverember marked the beginning of a torrid love affair that lasted over a year. One of the many gifts he lavished on her was an estate in the Sea Ward.

Their relationship faltered as Dagult's visits to Neverwinter became more frequent and extended. He made promises to Kalain that he failed to keep, and when she raised the subject of faithful commitment, he treated her poorly, for his true love was Neverwinter. Kalain became enraged after Dagult's rejection and turned to painting monsters that, in her mind, represented him. Her power to harness the Weave clings to the fabric of her works, giving her the ability to bring these monsters to life on command.

Ultimately, Neverember used his influence to ruin Kalain and divorce her from Waterdeep's high society. She was allowed to keep her home, but her works and her reputation were destroyed, slowly and methodically. Kalain's spirit was broken, leading to the onset of madness. Now she locks herself away, content to let time erode the last of her conscience. She always saw Dagult and Waterdeep as one and the same, and now they are both her mortal enemies.

Visiting the Residence
Kalain is unable to behave politely before strangers, for she believes they're all assassins sent by Dagult Neverember to murder her. The only person with whom she's civil is Vhaspar Holmdreg (LG male Illuskan human **priest**), who rents a room in the west wing of the residence and works in the North Ward at the Hospice of St. Laupsenn, a temple of Ilmater, god of suffering. Vhaspar is an old man in his seventies, half blind with cataracts, who brings her food twice a week, firewood three times

a week in the winter, and painting supplies every few months. Vhaspar has a key that unlocks the outer doors of Kalain's residence.

Displayed in every room except area W5 is one of Kalain's paintings. To determine the subject of any given painting, roll a d12 and consult the Painting Subjects table. It's possible for a subject to appear more than once. The residence is also crawling with rats. If Kalain is attacked, these vermin form six **swarms of rats** that defend her.

PAINTING SUBJECTS

d12	Subject	d12	Subject
1	Ankheg	7	Gibbering mouther
2	Carrion crawler	8	Hell hound
3	Displacer beast	9	Manticore
4	Ettercap	10	Minotaur
5	Gargoyle	11	Mummy
6	Ghast	12	Werewolf

KALAIN

Kalain spends most of her time in area W5, which serves as her studio. It contains moldy scraps of food, empty pots stained with colored paint, discarded brushes, and her easel, which is situated in front of a large, lead-paned window in the north wall. Upon the easel rests a fresh painting of a displacer beast. If the characters confront her, Kalain accuses them of being assassins, brings the **displacer beast** to life, and commands it to attack them.

Kalain is a half-elf **bard** (see appendix B), with these changes:

- She is chaotic evil.
- She has these racial traits: She has advantage on saving throws against being charmed, and magic can't put her to sleep. She has darkvision out to a range of 60 feet. She speaks Common and Elvish.
- Instead of the Song of Rest trait, she has the Art Imitates Life action option.

Art Imitates Life (3/Day). Kalain touches one of her paintings and causes its subject to spring forth, becoming a creature of that kind provided its CR is 3 or lower. The creature appears in an unoccupied space within 5 feet of the painting, which becomes blank. The creature is friendly toward Kalain and hostile toward all others. It rolls initiative to determine when it acts. It disappears after 1 minute, when it is reduced to 0 hit points, or when Kalain dies or falls unconscious.

PATH TO THE VAULT

A heavy stone trapdoor in the floor of area W4a can be found with a thorough search of the room and a successful DC 12 Wisdom (Perception) check. Pulling open the door reveals a stone staircase that descends 120 feet to a 20-foot-wide corridor, which extends for another 60 feet and ends before the doors to the Vault of Dragons. Kalain and Vhaspar know nothing of the vault or the trapdoor that leads to it.

CONVERTED WINDMILL: WINTER

An evil dragonborn named Thrakkus has converted an old, fire-scorched windmill in the Field Ward into a butcher's shop. A member of the Guild of Butchers, Thrakkus has a lucrative side business. Zhents loyal to Manshoon pay Thrakkus to chop up people they kill, and he sells the meat on the sly. As Deadwinter Day approaches, this meat is in high demand. The corpses are brought to him in the dead of night, most often delivered by Sidra Romeir (see chapter 8, area K2) in a covered cart pulled by a draft horse.

BUTCHERY

A red wooden sign carved to look like a butcher's cleaver hangs above the door of Thrakkus's butchery, which occupies the westernmost room of the west wing. The butchery is ice cold in the winter and reeks of meat and blood. A bloodstained chopping block dominates the room, and shelves of cut meat wrapped in bloody parchment line the walls. The floor is streaked with blood and covered with bits of gore.

Thrakkus padlocks the door at night. Picking the lock requires a successful DC 15 Dexterity check using thieves' tools. The door can also be forced open with a successful DC 18 Strength (Athletics) check.

LARDER

The chamber next to the butchery has been converted into a larder, the doors to which are padlocked at all hours. The locked doors are otherwise identical to the butchery door (see above). Like the butchery, the larder is frigid in the winter and smells of meat and blood. Six half-frozen humanoid carcasses are stacked under a 10-foot-square canvas tarpaulin near the western wall. Thrakkus hasn't gotten around to cutting them up yet.

SQUATTERS

The dragonborn allows squatters to dwell in his home. Those who can perform menial chores are spared and fed scraps of cooked meat; the rest end up on the chopping block. These homeless sods are too frightened of Thrakkus to speak ill of him, and the City Watch doesn't seem to care about crimes committed in the Field Ward.

THRAKKUS THE BUTCHER

The butcher has no time to suffer fools, and the characters are fools for meddling in his business. Thrakkus spends most of the day in the butchery. At dusk, he retires to his apartment, where he stays until dawn or until someone comes knocking with a body to dispose of. Thrakkus carries keys to the butchery, the larder, and his apartment (area W7).

Thrakkus is a dragonborn **berserker** of red dragon ancestry, with these changes:

- He is chaotic evil.
- He has these racial traits: He can use his action to exhale a 15-foot cone of fire (but can't do this again until he finishes a short or long rest); each creature in the cone must make a DC 13 Dexterity saving throw, taking 2d6 fire damage on a failed save, or half as much damage on a successful one. He has resistance to fire damage. He speaks Common and Draconic.

Where's the Stone?

Thrakkus hid the *Stone of Golorr* in a recent meat delivery to an alley in the Trades Ward. Thrakkus doesn't keep records of his illegal transactions, so the characters must interrogate him or one of the commoners that dwell in his residence.

Thrakkus is belligerent and not eager to give up his Zhent friends. A *charm person* spell or similar magic is needed to compel him to talk. His squatters are another matter; they roll over on Thrakkus quickly to save their own skins once the dragonborn butcher no longer becomes a factor in their well-being. Either approach yields the following information:

- Thrakkus's last shipment of meat was taken to a shop in the Trades Ward called Cuttle's Meat Pies. It's located in an alley.
- The meat was delivered by a member of the Guild of Butchers named Justyn Rassk. Thrakkus paid extra coin to see it delivered "quickly and quietly."
- Rassk has a blood-spattered horse-drawn cart that he uses to make deliveries outside the Field Ward.

The characters might know Justyn Rassk from their own dealings with the Guild of Butchers (see "Sample Guild Representatives," page 41).

Next Encounter

If the characters follow the trail of the meat delivery, proceed with encounter 1, "Alley."

Vault Keys

At the end of an encounter chain, a character who is attuned to the *Stone of Golorr* can learn the location of the Vault of Dragons and what three keys are needed to open its doors. The artifact also reveals that an adult gold dragon named Aurinax guards the vault.

The three keys needed to open the vault are chosen by you or determined randomly by rolling on the Vault Keys table. Illusory versions of keys don't open the door.

Every key can be found or procured in Waterdeep. If the characters don't already know the location of a key, they can gather information about it. To do this, a character must spend 1 day and 5 gp researching the location of a key. At the end of this day, the character makes a DC 15 Intelligence (Investigation) check, learning the location of the key on a success. If the check fails by 5 or more, the main villain learns of the search and sends lackeys to attack the characters and, if possible, wrest the *Stone of Golorr* from them:

- Xanathar sends either five **goblins** dressed up as children wearing Trolltide masks and a **bugbear** (70 percent chance), or four **wererats** in human form (30 percent chance).
- The Cassalanters send two **imps** in raven form, three human **cultists**, and either a human **cult fanatic** (70 percent chance), or four **spined devils** (30 percent chance).
- Jarlaxle Baenre sends Fel'rekt Lafeen and Krebbyg Masq'il'yr, or two other Bregan D'aerthe **drow gunslingers** (see appendix B), and six **drow**.
- Manshoon sends four Zhent **martial arts adepts** (see appendix B). There's a 50 percent chance that these Zhents are led by one of Manshoon's lieutenants, either Vevette Blackwater or Agorn Fuoco, if they're still alive (see chapter 8, area E8).

Key Descriptions

The keys listed in the Vault Keys table are further described below, in alphabetical order.

Adamantine Bar

The characters can purchase a 10-pound adamantine bar for 1,000 gp. The genasi smiths Embric and Avi (see chapter 2, area T3) can acquire one if the characters think to ask them.

Animated Construct

Any creature of the construct type works as this key, provided the creature hasn't been destroyed or rendered inoperable. If the characters have befriended Valetta, the dragonborn priest of Gond (see chapter 3), she happily releases Nim the nimblewright into their custody until they no longer have need of it.

An object animated by the *animate objects* spell also qualifies as this key.

Beardless Dwarf

Most female dwarves are beardless and thus meet the condition. A male dwarf NPC can be persuaded to shave his beard, either as a consequence of losing a bet or upon receiving some sort of recompense. The characters can also shave a male dwarf they have captured or against whom they have some sort of leverage.

Beholder Eyestalk

The eyestalk need not come from a true, living beholder. It can be plucked from a stuffed beholder (see "Old Xoblob Shop," page 23) or obtained from a lesser form of beholderkin, such as a gazer or a spectator. The eyestalk also need not be detached.

Vault Keys (roll three times, once for each key)

d6	First Key	Second Key	Third Key
1	Adamantine bar	Animated construct	Beardless dwarf
2	Beholder eyestalk	Bronze dragon scale	Cask of dwarven ale
3	Drunken elf	Gems worth at least 1,000 gp	Gift from a queen
4	Invisible creature	Painting of a dwarf miner	Pair of bugbear ears
5	Performance of "Your Beardy Face"	Severed drow hand	Shapechanger
6	Silvered warhammer	Sunlight	Unicorn

Xanathar (see appendix B) gladly accompanies characters to the vault if that's the way to guarantee getting its share of the treasure. Regardless of the arrangement it makes with the characters, "its share" equates to all the treasure. In other words, Xanathar turns on the party once the vault is unlocked, unless a powerful NPC (such as Laeral Silverhand or Vajra Safahr) is present to keep the mad beholder in check.

BRONZE DRAGON SCALE

Zelifarn, a **young bronze dragon**, has taken up residence in Deepwater Harbor. Many sailors and dock workers have seen the dragon, and Grinda Garloth (see "Encounter 2: Mistshore," page 65) owns an *apparatus of Kwalish* that characters can use to search for the dragon. Characters who go looking for Zelifarn find him lurking inside a shipwreck 120 feet underwater. As the characters approach the wreck, Zelifarn comes out and tries to scare them away. (He's not done searching the wreck for treasure.) He inflicts harm only in self-defense.

A successful DC 15 Charisma (Persuasion) check or an offer of treasure worth at least 1,000 gp convinces the dragon to talk with the characters and part with one of his scales. If the characters mention the contents of the Vault of Dragons, Zelifarn demands a promise of 10 percent of the gold before he gives them what they came for.

CASK OF DWARVEN ALE

A cask of dwarven ale is easily obtained at any market in Waterdeep for 5 gp. There is a 20 percent chance that the characters buy a knock-off brand that isn't made by dwarves. Any dwarf character can tell genuine dwarven ale from the fake stuff simply by having a taste.

DRUNKEN ELF

Any elf who is poisoned from drinking alcohol qualifies as this key.

GEMS WORTH AT LEAST 1,000 GP

One or more gemstones qualify as this key as long as their combined value is 1,000 gp or more. Such gems can be found during the adventure or bought in the markets of Waterdeep.

GIFT FROM A QUEEN

Laeral Silverhand, the Open Lord of Waterdeep, was once the queen of an ancient kingdom called Stornanter. The characters can recall this fact with a successful DC 20 Intelligence (History) check or learn it through information gathering. They can request an audience with Laeral through Jalester Silvermane or Mirt. Laeral gives them a gift—a feather quill given to her by the archmage Elminster himself—if they promise to return the stolen gold to Waterdeep's coffers.

INVISIBLE CREATURE

Any creature under the effect of an *invisibility* spell counts as this key, as do naturally invisible creatures.

A GOLD DRAGON GUARDS A PILE OF GOLDEN DRAGONS.

Painting of a Dwarf Miner

A painting of a dwarf miner priced at 5d10 gp can be found each day a character spends searching art shops. A character proficient with painter's supplies can create a painting that qualifies as this key. It takes 3d6 hours to finish the painting.

Pair of Bugbear Ears

The Xanathar Guild employs bugbears, and characters can chop the ears off any of them. A live bugbear also counts as this key.

Performance of "Your Beardy Face"

The dwarf love song, "Your Beardy Face," is a duet performed by bagpipers. The characters can obtain this music easily for 1 gp and hire two performers to play the piece for 10 gp each. A character who has proficiency with bagpipes can perform the song, though a successful DC 10 Charisma (Performance) check using bagpipes is required for the performance to count as this key. A glass jar in Cassalanter Villa (see chapter 6, area C3) plays this song when it is uncorked.

Severed Drow Hand

This ghastly key can be forcibly obtained from a member of Bregan D'aerthe or some other dark elf. If the characters have encountered no drow, they might hear rumors that Xanathar employs a drow advisor.

Shapechanger

Any living creature of the shapechanger subtype, such as a doppelganger or a wererat, serves as this key. Bonnie the doppelganger (see "Familiar Faces," page 20) can be persuaded to accompany the characters if she is friendly toward one or more of them. The characters can also reach out to the Shard Shunners, a local gang of halfling wererats. For an up-front payment of 500 gp, the wererats happily oblige.

Silvered Warhammer

The characters can buy a silvered warhammer for 115 gp, or they can give a silver bar to Embric and Avi (see chapter 2, area T3) and have the genasi smiths craft one.

Sunlight

Since the vault lies deep underground, natural sunlight is difficult to come by. Clever characters can buy twenty steel mirrors (5 gp each) and arrange them in places (and at the proper angles) so that sunlight from outside can be reflected underground and shone upon the vault entrance. Setting up these mirrors and getting their alignment just right takes 2d4 + 2 hours regardless of the number of characters involved.

Unicorn

Although conjuring up a real unicorn is likely beyond the abilities of the characters, they could ask Laeral Silverhand or Vajra Safahr to cast the *summon celestial* spell. The characters can gain an audience with Laeral or Vajra through Renaer Neverember or another well-connected NPC. If the characters tell Laeral or Vajra the truth about the Vault of Dragons and promise to turn the gold over to the authorities, either one agrees to accompany the characters to the vault and cast the spell.

The unicorn need not be a real unicorn to serve as this key. The Sea Maidens Faire (see chapter 7) uses a unicorn float in its parades, and a stuffed unicorn can be found in Cassalanter Villa (see chapter 6, area T18).

Vault of Dragons

Once the characters have the *Stone of Golorr*, they can use it to determine the location of the Vault of Dragons and the keys needed to enter it.

Vault Features

All areas of the vault have the following features:

- Any spell that tries to contact a creature in the vault fails, as does any spell that attempts to scry on the vault interior or any creatures within. Teleporting into the vault from outside is impossible.
- Walls are made of mortared stone. Doors are solid stone slabs with stone handles and hinges.
- Except in area V9, there are no light sources.

Areas of the Vault

The following locations are keyed to map 4.9.

V1. Vault Door

A 20-foot-high, 20-foot-wide stone corridor ends before an adamantine double door bearing Dwarvish runes. The doors have neither handles nor hinges. The writing on them reads, "THE THREE KEYS. BRING THEM FORTH."

The doors part, sliding back into the walls, when the three correct keys are brought with 5 feet of them. They remain open until Aurinax or someone else speaks the command word to close them ("Azaam"). The keys can open the doors from either side. The doors can't be forced open or damaged in any way, and attempts to circumvent them with magic fail automatically.

V2. Entrance Foyer

This vast chamber has the following features:

- Three age-worn columns support crumbling stone bridges 60 feet overhead, with the ceiling rising another 20 feet beyond that.
- Set into alcoves are twelve sets of double doors made of iron. Each door is 10 feet wide, 10 feet high, and embossed with images of dwarf warriors in plate armor.

Crumbling Bridges. The bridges connect area V4 to adamantine doors that seal off areas V6, V7, and V8. The eastern half of the northern bridge and the western half of the southern bridge are unstable. Either bridge collapses if more than 150 pounds of weight is applied to it. A creature standing on a section of bridge when it collapses must succeed on a DC 15 Dexterity saving throw or fall 60 feet to the floor below.

The middle bridge has a 15-foot-wide gap in it. A character can clear this gap with a running jump—but part of the bridge breaks away under the character's feet on

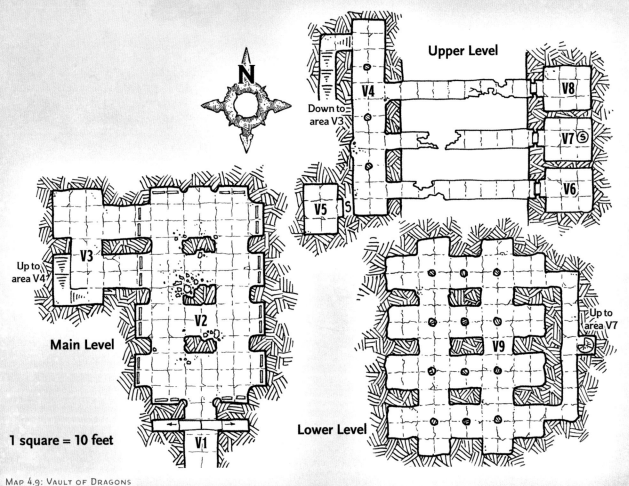

Map 4.9: Vault of Dragons

landing, forcing the character to succeed on a DC 15 Dexterity saving throw or fall to the floor below.

Iron Doors. Ten of the double doors are false and refuse to budge. The two sets of doors at the northern end of the west wall push open to reveal area V3 beyond.

V3. STAIRS AND FRESCO

This hall has the following features:

- At the south end of this chamber, expertly carved stairs climb 70 feet to area V4.
- The north wall bears a 20-foot-square fresco that depicts dwarves battling goblins.

Enthralling Fresco. A *detect magic* spell reveals an aura of enchantment magic on the fresco. Any creature within 30 feet of the fresco that can see it must succeed on a DC 12 Wisdom saving throw or be charmed by it for 24 hours. While charmed in this way, the creature can't willingly move out of sight of the fresco and defends it to the death. If forcibly moved away from the fresco, the creature tries to find its way back. The creature can't rest while under this effect. After 24 hours, the creature gains one level of exhaustion and can repeat the saving throw if it can still see the fresco, ending the effect on a success. A creature that succeeds on the saving throw is immune to the effect of the fresco for 24 hours. Destroying at least one 10-foot-square section of the fresco ends the effect for all creatures. Each 10-foot-square section has AC 17, 25 hit points, and immunity to poison and psychic damage.

V4. HALL OF MORADIN

This 20-foot-high hall has the following features:

- Three pillars running the length of the hall are carved to resemble warhammers, with their square heads pressed against the floor.
- The west wall bears a cracked mosaic that depicts a dwarf smith at a forge, crafting dwarves out of black metal and diamonds. (In the south end of the wall is a secret door.)
- Three archways in the east wall lead to crumbling bridges that span the entrance foyer (area V2) and end in front of adamantine doors (leading to areas V6, V7, and V8).

Black Pudding. A little more than halfway down the hall, a section of the western mural has broken off, forming a heap of shattered tile on the floor. A crack in the wall conceals a **black pudding** that gushes out and attacks characters who inspect the damage.

Secret Door. A character who searches the hall for secret doors and succeeds on a DC 17 Wisdom (Perception) check notices the outline of a secret door that leads to area V5. The door opens automatically when a dwarf (or a creature transformed into a dwarf with an *alter self* spell or similar magic) touches it; otherwise, a successful DC 17 Strength (Athletics) check is needed to push open the heavy door.

V5. Secret Room

This dust-filled room has lain untouched since the time of the Delzoun dwarves. Green copper urns on platforms overflow with coins, gems, and more.

Treasure. This room holds five copper urns (worth 25 gp each). Urn 1 contains five tourmalines (worth 100 gp each) mixed in with 200 cp. Urn 2 contains a *ring of warmth* mixed in with ten ordinary gold rings (worth 25 gp each) and 650 sp. Urn 3 is piled high with 250 gp. Urn 4 holds 33 blue quartz gemstones (worth 10 gp each). Urn 5 holds a 9-inch-tall silver statuette of a dwarf priest of Moradin with amethyst eyes (worth 250 gp and weighing 10 pounds).

V6. Hammer and Anvil

The adamantine door to this room has an *arcane lock* spell cast on it, but it swings open when a dwarf or a creature transformed into a dwarf touches it. Another creature can force it open with a successful DC 21 Strength (Athletics) check. A *knock* spell or similar magic also opens it. The door swings into the room on stiff adamantine hinges.

- The north, east, and south walls of this 20-foot-high room are adorned with dust-covered frescoes depicting dwarf smiths at work in their forges.
- An iron anvil sits atop a raised stone block in the middle of the floor. Both fixtures are draped in cobwebs.

Frescoes. A character who inspects the wall frescoes and succeeds on a DC 10 Wisdom (Perception) check notices that the stone hammer being wielded by the smith in the fresco on the south wall can be taken away from where it rests. When removed, it leaves a hammer-shaped indentation in the wall. Etched into the side of the hammer that was facing the wall is the following inscription in Dwarvish runes: "Let hearts be lifted and battles won." The hammer must be removed from its indentation for the inscription to be seen.

Iron Anvil. If the characters clear away the cobwebs, they see an inscription on the front of the stone block. Written in Dwarvish runes, it reads as follows: "Let the hammer fall and the anvil ring."

If the anvil is struck by the stone hammer that was taken from the wall, each creature in the room that can hear the anvil ring gains 10 temporary hit points that last for 24 hours. Once the anvil has bestowed this gift, it can't do so again for 24 hours.

V7. Dumathoin's Secret

This room is sealed by an adamantine door similar to the one in area V6. The room contains the following features:

- Four suits of rusted plate armor sans helmets, sized for a dwarf, stand in the corners of this 20-foot-high room. Each suit is draped in cobwebs.
- Dwarvish runes are carved into the far wall. The inscription reads, "A secret never before told will part Dumathoin's lips."

A successful DC 14 Intelligence (Religion) check identifies Dumathoin as the dwarven god of secrets. Any dwarf character automatically knows this.

Secret Stair. The engraving on the wall is a clue that this room holds a secret, specifically a trapdoor so well hidden that it can't be found by using magic or searching. But when any creature in the room speaks aloud a secret, the trapdoor flips open, giving access to a spiral stone staircase that descends 120 feet to area V9. The spoken admission must be true, and it must be something the character has not previously revealed.

V8. Ol' Fire Eyes

This room has the following features:

- A 10-foot-tall painted statue of an armored male dwarf wielding a battleaxe and wearing a mask stands at the back of this 20-foot-high room.
- Before the statue, set into the floor, is an adamantine trapdoor with a pull ring along one side.

Trap. A successful DC 17 Intelligence (Religion) check enables a character to recognize the statue as a depiction of Gorm Gulthyn, the dwarven god of vigilance also known as Fire Eyes. The statue melds seamlessly with the floor and can't be toppled. It also seems impervious to damage. A *detect magic* spell reveals an aura of evocation magic on the statue.

The trapdoor is false and can't be lifted. Anyone who touches the trapdoor or its pull ring must succeed on a DC 18 Dexterity saving throw or be struck by rays of magical fire that spring from the statue's eyes, dealing 22 (4d10) fire damage. The trap doesn't trigger if the target has total cover.

V9. Main Vault

When the characters arrive here for the first time, read:

> Although deep underground, this vault is lit by streams of sunlight that pour down from the ceiling, catching motes of dust in their luminous pools. Ornate columns support a thirty-foot-high vaulted ceiling, which is adorned with carvings of dwarves basking in the presence of their gods. Deep alcoves line the walls, and piled in one of them is a vast golden trove.
>
> Out of the dusty gloom steps an aged dwarf clutching a staff carved and painted to resemble a pair of entwined dragons—one red, one gold. Despite the dwarf's age, his eyes are steady and bright. "I wasn't expecting anyone," he says plainly. "As you can see, the place is a mess. Perhaps you should come back later, after I've tidied up a bit."

The dwarf, who calls himself Barok Clanghammer, is really the **adult gold dragon** Aurinax (see appendix B) in disguise. He guards the gold for Lord Dagult Neverember and holds the *dragonstaff of Ahghairon* (see appendix A) in exchange for his services. Dealing with the gold dragon presents an unusual challenge for the characters, and a peaceful resolution is more likely to benefit them than a violent one.

Aurinax is patient, wise, merciful, and vigilant. He remains in humanoid form until combat breaks out, since he can't easily carry the *dragonstaff of Ahghairon* in dragon form. The dragon attacks only in defense of itself, the staff, or the gold. The only individuals authorized to remove the gold under Aurinax's watch are Dagult Neverember and his appointed vassals, none of whom are currently in Waterdeep.

The characters can try to convince Aurinax that they have come on Neverember's behalf. Since he has never met them before or heard Neverember mention them by name, Aurinax is doubtful of their story. Fooling the dragon requires each character within his line of sight to succeed on a Charisma (Deception) check contested by the dragon's Wisdom (Insight) check. If even one character loses the contest, Aurinax senses that the group is lying to him. These checks are made with advantage if Renaer Neverember is with the party, since the dragon remembers meeting Renaer when he was but a child and can easily imagine a scenario in which Dagult Neverember might use his son as his vassal. (The dragon knows nothing of the animosity between Renaer and his father.)

The characters can try to convince the noble dragon that Lord Neverember embezzled the gold from the people of Waterdeep, and that it would be fair and just to see the coin safely returned to its rightful owners. Deep down, Aurinax knows where the gold came from, but the dragon has allowed his greed and his agreement with Lord Neverember to cloud his moral judgment. With a successful DC 18 Charisma (Persuasion) check, a character can talk the dragon into allowing the gold to be returned to the people to whom it rightfully belongs. The check is made with advantage if the characters brought a prominent city official with them, such as Mirt or Vajra Safahr, or if one of the characters professes to be a worshiper of Bahamut.

Any Charisma (Intimidation) check made to influence Aurinax automatically fails. After the first such attempt, all future Charisma checks made by the party to influence Aurinax have disadvantage.

Aurinax uses Legendary Resistance to avoid being charmed. If a character tries to charm him with a spell and fails, all future Charisma checks made by the party to influence Aurinax have disadvantage.

Treasure. Choose two alcoves in the vault. Piled in one alcove are 500,000 gp, the combined weight of which is 10,000 pounds. Scattered on the floor of the second alcove are sixty-five 100 gp gemstones—all that remains of Aurinax's current food supply.

Aurinax won't give up his gemstones or the *dragonstaff of Ahghairon* willingly, since they are his payment for guarding the gold. If need be, however, the dragon is willing to use the staff's power on behalf of the city in exchange for more gemstones.

LEAVING THE VAULT

As the characters leave the vault, with or without the gold, they are confronted by a hostile force sent by the main villain or villains. If the vault doors were left open, the characters encounter these antagonists in area V2; otherwise, they're lurking outside the vault, waiting for the characters to emerge:

- If Xanathar is the main villain, Noska Ur'gray (see appendix B) arrives with six **bugbears** and a **gazer** (see appendix B). If Noska is dead or otherwise indisposed, the beholder replaces him with Nar'l Xibrindas (see appendix B) and his **grell** bodyguard.
- If the Cassalanters are the villains, they send three **cult fanatics** and three **cultists**. Victoro's **doppelganger** manservant, Willifort Crowelle, leads the group in his tiefling guise unless the characters killed him or otherwise disposed of him earlier in this chapter or in chapter 6.
- If **Jarlaxle Baenre** (see appendix B) is the villain, he arrives with three **drow gunslingers** (see appendix B). Replace no-name drow gunslingers with Fel'rekt Lafeen, Krebbyg Masq'il'yr, and Soluun Xibrindas if they are alive and free.
- If Manshoon is the main villain, he sends his simulacrum (see appendix B) along with Agorn Fuoco (NE male Turami human **bard**; see appendix B), Vevette Blackwater (CE female Tethyrian human **swashbuckler**; see appendix B), and three Zhent **thugs**. If Agorn and Vevette were killed or otherwise disposed of earlier in this chapter or in chapter 8, replace each of them with one additional **thug**.

The forces sent by Xanathar, the Cassalanters, and Manshoon attack the characters on sight. Jarlaxle, on the other hand, congratulates characters for unlocking the Vault of Dragons and allows them to leave on the condition that they go empty-handed. He intends to see the gold safely returned to the city of Waterdeep but also demands the *dragonstaff of Ahghairon* for his trouble.

If Aurinax is alive, the characters can lure enemies to the dragon. Aurinax attacks any creature that attacks him or tries to steal his staff or the gold. He also defends the characters if he has made a deal with them.

FACTION REINFORCEMENTS

If the characters joined one or more factions in Waterdeep and kept them informed of their progress, you can have reinforcements arrive to help combat the villains or introduce a new element to the situation.

Bregan D'aerthe. If **Jarlaxle Baenre** (see appendix B) isn't the main villain, he arrives with his lieutenants, Fel'rekt Lafeen, Krebbyg Masq'il'yr, and Soluun Xibrindas, or three other **drow gunslingers** (see appendix B). Jarlaxle offers to help the characters if they agree to help him secure the gold for Waterdeep and the *dragonstaff of Ahghairon* for himself.

Harpers. **Mirt** (see appendix B) arrives with two female human **swashbucklers** (see appendix B). If he's still alive and not already with the characters, Renaer Neverember (see appendix B) replaces one of the swashbucklers.

Emerald Enclave. Jeryth Phaulkon sends three **swarms of rats** to assist the characters. Once the characters are no longer in peril, the rats disperse throughout the vault.

Force Grey. Vajra Safahr sends **Meloon Wardragon** (see appendix B) to help the characters secure the vault, unaware that Meloon has fallen under Xanathar's sway. If Xanathar is the main villain, Meloon helps the beholder's forces defeat the characters.

Lords' Alliance. Open Lord **Laeral Silverhand** (see appendix B) arrives with **Jalester Silvermane** (see appendix B) and six City Guard **veterans** to help characters secure the gold. Laeral's arrival forces Jarlaxle to be on his best behavior. After assuring Laeral of his good intentions, Jarlaxle cuts his losses and withdraws peacefully. If she is able to speak with Aurinax, Laeral convinces the dragon to relinquish the gold into her custody.

Order of the Gauntlet. **Hlam** (see appendix B) arrives and aids the characters as best he can. He and Aurinax met each other many years ago, and they are on fair speaking terms. Aurinax is fond of the monk, and characters who negotiate with the dragon in Hlam's presence gain advantage on their Charisma (Persuasion) checks.

Zhentarim. The Doom Raiders (see appendix B) arrive to help secure the vault, less any members who have been arrested or killed. If Manshoon is the main villain, Skeemo Weirdbottle betrays his fellow Doom Raiders and fights alongside Manshoon's simulacrum. If they and the characters emerge victorious, the surviving Doom Raiders propose to split the take evenly with the characters. If the characters refuse this offer and the Doom Raiders outnumber them, the Zhents turn against them, putting characters who are Zhentarim members in a predicament.

Adventure Conclusion

The adventure could play out in any of several ways, depending on who gets the gold and what's done with the treasure.

Dying in the Vault

If the characters die in the Vault of Dragons with the *Stone of Golorr* and the main villain doesn't know the vault's location, the secrets of the vault die with them. Though they succumbed in the process, they succeeded in keeping the gold out of the villain's clutches—a bittersweet victory, indeed.

Removing the Gold

If the characters recover Neverember's hoard and keep it for themselves, word gets out eventually.

Emissaries of the Harpers, the Lords' Alliance, and the Order of the Gauntlet come to the characters, asking that the gold be returned to Waterdeep. If the characters refuse to give it up, they are stripped of any memberships they might hold in these factions and quickly find themselves in political hot water. The Lords of Waterdeep charge them with the crime of robbery against the citizens of the city. The characters face up to 1 month of hard labor plus damages equal to the value of the stolen currency plus 500 gp. If they try to flee the city, the City Guard apprehends and imprisons them. If they somehow evade the local authorities, the Harpers and agents of the Lords' Alliance pursue them tirelessly.

Laeral Silverhand is prepared to let the characters keep one-tenth of the treasure (50,000 gp) for themselves. Even that much coin attracts unwanted attention, in the form of several people who beg loans or donations from them:

- Emmek Frewn (see "Business Rival: Emmek Frewn," page 42) needs 1,500 gp to pay off a loan with interest. If he doesn't repay the coin in a tenday, **Istrid Horn** (see appendix B) sends Zhentarim thugs to threaten, if not hurt, him. Emmek comes to the characters with hat in hand, preying on their generosity while denying any wrongdoing on his part.
- **Davil Starsong** (see appendix B) asks the characters for a donation of 5,000 gp to keep his branch of the Zhentarim afloat in Waterdeep. Recent altercations and legal issues have drained the Doom Raiders' coffers. If the characters refuse, the Doom Raiders are driven out of the city, yielding control of the Zhentarim in Waterdeep to Manshoon (if he's alive).
- Floon Blagmaar (see appendix B) asks the characters to give him 500 gp to cover a hefty gambling debt. If the characters refuse to give Floon the gold, he vanishes without a trace 1d10 days later.
- **Volothamp Geddarm** (see appendix B) asks the characters for 5,000 gp to fund an expedition that he hopes will inspire a future book, for which he'll give them special mention in said masterwork. If the characters seem hesitant, Volo reminds them that were it not for his starting them off on this adventure, they wouldn't have the gold in the first place.
- Jelenn Urmbrusk, a Masked Lord in debt to Manshoon, requests an interest-free loan of 10,000 gp, which she vows to repay within a year. In exchange, she promises to use her "considerable influence with the Lords of Waterdeep" to help them in the future. If the characters oblige, she makes good on her promise to pay them back and grants them a special favor (see "Marks of Prestige" in chapter 7 of the *Dungeon Master's Guide*). If they refuse, they will have made an enemy of the secret Masked Lord.
- Temples, charities, guilds, and down-on-their-luck strangers come knocking from time to time. What they ask for isn't much—a few gold here and there—but it all adds up.

Onward and Downward

The characters should be 5th level by the end of this adventure. In the weeks that follow, word of their deeds spreads to every corner of Waterdeep. Finally, a note is delivered to them that reads as follows:

> Undermountain beckons. See you at the Yawning Portal.

If the characters want to explore Undermountain, you can continue this campaign up through 20th level with the book *Waterdeep: Dungeon of the Mad Mage*.

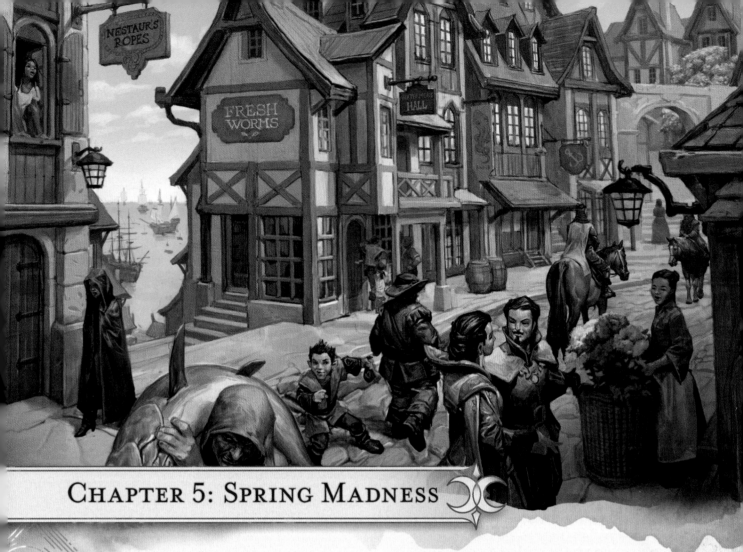

CHAPTER 5: SPRING MADNESS

ANATHAR HAS LET ITS PARANOIA GET THE better of it, and the beholder trusts no one. The *Stone of Golorr* disappeared from its lair while it was brokering a deal that would have merged the Xanathar Guild and the Zhentarim into a single criminal organization. Although the Zhents didn't steal the *Stone of Golorr*, Xanathar believes they did. Once content to merely possess the stone, the beholder is no longer confident of the gold's safety in the Vault of Dragons. Xanathar thinks that the gold would be safer under its watchful gaze, but without the *Stone of Golorr*, it can't remember where the gold is hidden.

Before running this chapter, review the "Beholders" section of the *Monster Manual*, particularly the section titled "A Beholder's Lair." Within its lair, Xanathar has access to lair actions, and characters might encounter the beholder's regional effects as well.

Characters who don't visit Xanathar's lair in the course of this adventure might have reason to do so in *Waterdeep: Dungeon of the Mad Mage*. In that adventure, the characters are most likely to approach the beholder's lair from Skullport (see area X4 for details).

As they explore Xanathar's lair, characters will see a recurring symbol that looks like a circle with ten equidistant spokes radiating out from its circumference. This symbol is Xanathar's personal rune as well as the symbol used to represent the Xanathar Guild.

FACING XANATHAR

Roll percentile dice to determine the beholder's location when the characters arrive, and consult the Xanathar's Location table.

XANATHAR'S LOCATION

d100	Location
01–50	Xanathar is talking to Sylgar, its pet fish, in area X19.
51–75	Xanathar is delivering a rambling sermon to minions in the audience chamber (area X18).
76–90	Xanathar is watching a fight in the Pit of Blood and Fortune (area X6).
91–00	Xanathar is contemplating its mortality in the crypt, amid the remains of past Xanathars (area X33).

If the characters attack the beholder, it destroys one character and tries to subjugate the rest. In exchange for their lives, the survivors must agree to help the beholder find the *Stone of Golorr*. If they refuse, the beholder destroys another character and repeats the offer. This process continues until the characters comply or none are left. Those who agree to the beholder's terms are permitted to leave with their lives.

If the characters give Xanathar the stone, it demands that they accompany it to the Vault of Dragons and help it defeat the vault's draconic guardian. Not fully trusting the characters to keep their part of the bargain, Xanathar brings along its majordomo, Ahmaergo, to keep an eye on them.

If Xanathar is reduced to half its maximum hit points, or if it believes its life to be in mortal danger, it activates its *ring of invisibility* and howls to Ahmaergo to "tear the usurpers limb from limb." While invisible, Xanathar flies to its sanctum (area X19) by the safest route.

Xanathar's greatest weakness is its insane love for its pet fish, Sylgar. A character who uses the fish for leverage can make a DC 16 Charisma (Intimidation) check. On a success, the fearsome beholder becomes a blubbering mess and acquiesces to almost any request the character makes. On a failure, Xanathar demands that the character release Sylgar at once or be disintegrated (and makes good on its threat).

FOILING XANATHAR'S OPERATION

Killing the beholder is probably beyond the characters' capabilities, but they can sabotage its operation in several ways, affecting either the beholder personally or the smooth functioning of the Xanathar Guild. They might even be able to marshal sufficient resources (including enough explosives) to bring down Xanathar's lair.

ENRAGE XANATHAR

Xanathar's mental state is precarious. Whenever it flies into a rage, the beholder tends to kill random minions.

ABDUCT OR KILL SYLGAR

Killing or stealing Xanathar's pet fish and preventing the fishkeeper, Ott Steeltoes, from replacing it causes Xanathar to become enraged.

DESTROY THE DREAM NULLIFIER

Xanathar's "dream nullifier" in area X20 gives it peace of mind and helps it sleep. Destroying this contraption makes the beholder unhappy.

TAKE ITS FOOD AWAY

Xanathar eats meals prepared by the kobold chefs in area X30. Killing these kobolds or otherwise preventing them from preparing meals makes Xanathar furious.

DISRUPT COMMAND

Even though the beholder is the supreme leader of the Xanathar Guild, its lieutenants manage the guild's day-to-day operations. The chain of command can be disrupted in any of the following ways.

ASSASSINATION

Killing one of Xanathar's most trusted underlings, such as Ahmaergo or Noska Ur'gray, throws the day-to-day operation of the guild into chaos for a tenday.

BLIND XANATHAR

Nar'l Xibrindas (see appendix B) has concocted a poison that can blind Xanathar and throw the guild into chaos.

> ## IMPORTANT UNDERLINGS
>
> Xanathar relies on underlings for advice, information, and day-to-day oversight of the Xanathar Guild. The following important underlings are described in appendix B:
>
> **Ahmaergo**, dwarf majordomo
> **Nar'l Xibrindas**, drow advisor
> **Nihiloor**, mind flayer
> **Noska Ur'gray**, dwarf enforcer
> **Ott Steeltoes**, dwarf fishkeeper
> **Thorvin Twinbeard**, dwarf engineer

SOW MISTRUST

If the beholder is tricked into believing there's a conspiracy to kill it or Sylgar, it disintegrates the suspected conspirators, leaving gaping holes in the chain of command.

DESTROY THE LAIR

Nar'l Xibrindas has smuggled *smokepowder* into the lair (see area X36) and, with Thorvin Twinbeard's help, identified areas that are structurally unstable. If these areas all suffer catastrophic damage, the lair collapses over the course of 1 hour. Characters can learn this information by speaking to Thorvin in area X13. The unstable areas are as follows:

Area X2, in the threshold of the secret door
Area X6, at the top of the stone buttresses
Area X17, at the base of any three pillars
Area X20, against the back wall
Area X22, between the columns
Area X30, anywhere in the kitchen
Area X33, anywhere in the crypt

As its lair collapses, Xanathar uses its Disintegration Ray to carve an escape tunnel and flees to safety with minor injuries. It uses its Telekinetic Ray to transport its pet fish, Sylgar, if it's within range. Underlings can flee with the beholder or through the tunnel to Skullport (area X4). Those who can't accomplish either of these things are killed in the collapse.

XANATHAR'S LAIR

Xanathar's lair is an ancient dungeon complex originally built by Netherese wizards and expanded by beholders over time. It connects to the subterranean town of Skullport by way of a long tunnel (area X4). A secret staircase (area X1) gives access to Waterdeep's sewers.

The lair has the following features, with exceptions noted in the text:

- Unless noted otherwise, rooms are 20 feet high and hallways are 15 feet high.
- Rooms and corridors are brightly lit by *continual flame* spells cast on wall sconces.
- Most doors are single, circular slabs of stone, 8 feet in diameter and 6 inches thick, with stone hinges on one side. Double doors are 16-foot-wide, 8-foot-high semicircles that split open down the middle. Doorknobs are set into stone fixtures shaped like Xanathar's symbol. (Xanathar can open or close an unlocked door using its Telekinetic Ray, or obliterate a locked one with its Disintegration Ray.)

Getting to the Lair

Very few members of the Xanathar Guild have access to the beholder's secret lair. If the characters want to get there, the following factions know where it is and can help them find it.

Bregan D'aerthe

Jarlaxle has a spy in the Xanathar Guild: the advisor Nar'l Xibrindas, who uses *sending* spells to transmit intelligence to his drow brethren. Bregan D'aerthe knows that the safest route to the beholder's lair is a secret staircase in the sewers of the Castle Ward. Any character who belongs to this faction can get this information from Jarlaxle or another source.

If the party includes at least one Bregan D'aerthe member with renown of 4 or more in the faction, four male **drow** are waiting for the party at the top of the staircase. Their names are Arannis Nur'zekk, Beldar Tlabbath, Rylvar Tlabbath, and Draknafein Uriss. Their orders are to help the characters complete their mission, whatever the cost. These drow also have secret orders to kill Nar'l Xibrindas, if he's still alive, and retrieve Jarlaxle's *bag of holding* (see area X35). If you're tracking experience points, each drow gets an equal share of the XP while a member of the adventuring party.

Harpers

Characters who belong to the Harpers can approach **Mirt** (see appendix B), who knows the location of Xanathar's lair. (He has dealt with the beholder many times as a Lord of Waterdeep.)

Mirt leads the characters to a secret staircase in the Castle Ward sewers (area X1). As the characters prepare to descend the stairs, Mirt tells them that Xanathar doesn't relate well to humanoids, doesn't trust them as a matter of course, and is prone to imagining conspiracies where none exist. He also tells the characters that Xanathar has a pet fish and is insanely protective of it.

Mirt won't accompany the adventurers, but he knows a secret that could be helpful: Thorvin Twinbeard, Xanathar's chief engineer, is a Harper informant. Mirt shares this secret with any character who has renown of 4 or higher in the Harper faction.

Lords' Alliance

Characters who are members of the Lords' Alliance can reach out to **Jalester Silvermane** (see appendix B). Jalester doesn't know the location of Xanathar's lair but can get the details from Laeral Silverhand.

With the information in hand, Jalester leads the party to a secret staircase in the Castle Ward sewers (area X1). As the characters prepare to descend the stairs, Jalester warns them to avoid confronting the paranoid and unpredictable beholder.

If one or more characters have renown of 4 or higher in the Lords' Alliance, Jalester offers to join the party on its mission into Xanathar's lair. If you're tracking experience points, Jalester gets an equal share of the XP while a member of the adventuring party.

EMERALD ENCLAVE

Characters who are members of the Emerald Enclave can learn the location of Xanathar's lair by speaking with Jeryth Phaulkon at Phaulkonmere. Jeryth tells them that she has been sending awakened rats into the sewers to find the beholder's lair, and that they recently discovered a secret staircase in the Castle Ward sewers leading down to it (area X1). She has one of the awakened rats lead them there. This **rat** has an Intelligence score of 10 and can speak Common.

ZHENTARIM

Characters who are members of the Zhentarim can approach Yagra Stonefist at the Yawning Portal (see "Familiar Faces," page 20). She recently learned about a "back door" to the beholder's lair from a drunken blabbermouth with ties to the Xanathar Guild. Yagra offers to lead them to a secret staircase in the sewers under the Castle Ward (area X1). "Trust me," she says, "it's safer than the route through Undermountain and Skullport."

Yagra will join their descent if the characters promise to pay her at least 1,000 gp. Otherwise, she wishes them well and heads back to the Yawning Portal. If you're tracking experience points, Yagra gets an equal share of the XP while a member of the adventuring party.

AREAS OF THE LAIR

The following areas correspond to the labels on map 5.1. This lair has two levels connected by staircases and secret doors.

X1. STAIRCASE OF EYES

Characters are most likely to enter Xanathar's lair by this route: a spiral staircase accessible from the Castle Ward's sewers and hidden behind a secret door. This staircase circumvents a more difficult route through Undermountain and Skullport, which is described in *Waterdeep: Dungeon of the Mad Mage*.

When the characters find the staircase, read:

> The walls of this narrow, spiraling staircase are carved with opened eyes that glow with a faint, magical light.

Characters feel as though they're being watched as they descend the stairs, and the feeling doesn't go away once they enter the beholder's lair. The dimly lit staircase descends for hundreds of feet, ending before a circular stone door that swings open into area X2.

X2. WATCHED HALL

This magically lit hall has the following features:

- The walls are carved with eyes of all shapes and sizes. Many of the orbs have stone eyelids that open and close at irregular intervals.
- Characters who succeed on a DC 14 Wisdom (Perception) check notice a ghostly eyestalk (scrying sensor) protruding from the ceiling directly in front of the double door to the south.
- A secret door is hidden in the west wall.

Blinking Eyes. The blinking eye carvings are slightly unnerving but harmless.

Scrying Sensor. The ghostly eyestalk is a magical sensor that allows one of the apprentice wizards in area X16 to monitor this hall. The eyestalk functions as an extra eye with darkvision out to a range of 60 feet. A character can ascertain the eyestalk's function with a successful DC 10 Intelligence (Arcana) check but can't determine who's peering through it, or from where. The eyestalk can't be damaged but is destroyed by a *dispel magic* spell. The sensor is suppressed within the area of an *antimagic field*.

Secret Door. The secret door can be found with a successful DC 15 Wisdom (Perception) check. To open it, one must press a nearby wall carving shaped like an eye. When this is done, the secret door swings inward, revealing a curved hallway (area X8) beyond.

X3. BEHOLDER ZOMBIE GUARD

A **beholder zombie** guards this magically lit room. Surrounding it are four **gas spores**, which look like immature beholders at first glance. All five creatures float in the middle of the room.

The beholder zombie is all that remains of a beholder that arose from the Underdark to challenge Xanathar's supremacy. After defeating its rival, Xanathar had the corpse animated and transformed into a lair guardian. The gas spores were added later.

The beholder zombie allows creatures that brandish the symbol of Xanathar to pass unmolested. Otherwise, it attacks. The gas spores don't attack but explode if they take any damage. The beholder zombie is immune to their Death Burst trait.

X4. TUNNEL TO SKULLPORT

This magically lit tunnel extends 300 feet eastward off the map. It ends at a staircase that climbs 20 feet to the Guts & Garters Inn, an establishment located in the subterranean town of Skullport, which is under Xanathar's control. See *Waterdeep: Dungeon of the Mad Mage* for more information on the inn and Skullport.

X5. HORROR'S ALCOVE

A suit of **animated armor** with Xanathar's symbol embossed on its breastplate stands in this alcove, appearing at a glance to be an ornate but inanimate suit of armor on display. It remains inert until it takes damage or is summoned to area X6 by Xanathar. (The beholder uses it to keep the spectators in the arena from getting too rowdy.)

X6. PIT OF BLOOD AND FORTUNE

Xanathar has turned this room into a gladiatorial arena. It also uses this location to dispose of underlings it no longer trusts in a manner that it considers entertaining.

This area has the following features:

- A magically lit, circular chamber has a thin layer of blood-soaked sand covering the floor and stone buttresses supporting its 40-foot-high domed ceiling.
- Ten-foot-high stone bleachers hug the northwest half of the room. Staircases lead from the bleachers to other areas of the lair, and a tunnel under the bleachers leads west to the monster cell block (area X7).

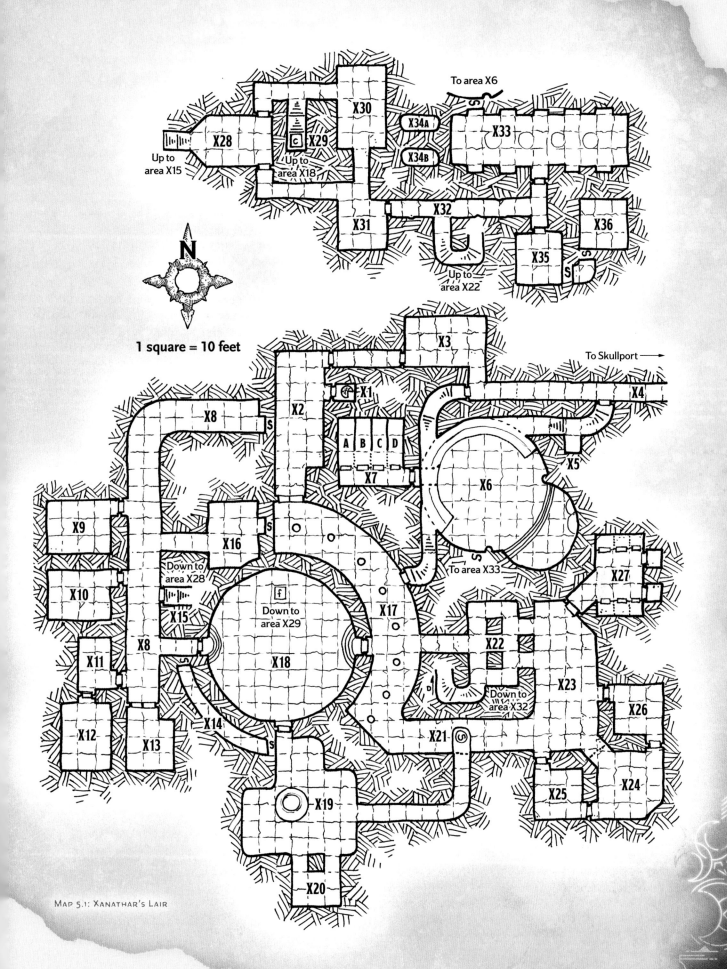

X28

Up to
area X15

X30

To area X6

X34A

X33

X29

Up to
area X18

X34B

X31

X32

X36

X35

Up to
area X22

N

1 square = 10 feet

X3

To Skullport →

X2

X1

X8

X4

A B C D

X5

X7

X6

X9

X16

X27

Down to
area X28

To area X33

X10

X15

X17

X8

X22

X11

X18

X23

Down to
area X32

X26

X12

X14

X13

X21

X24

X19

X25

X20

Map 5.1: Xanathar's Lair

- A semicircular recess in the southeast wall has steps leading up to it. Its floor is 5 feet higher than the arena floor, and the alcove is decorated with bouquets of Underdark fungi in stone vases and purple tapestries that bear Xanathar's symbol. Jutting from the curved roof of the alcove is a spectral eyestalk (scrying sensor).
- A secret door is hidden in the south wall.

If Xanathar is elsewhere, the arena is empty but under surveillance (see "Scrying Sensor" below).

If Xanathar is present, it hovers in the southeast alcove and uses its *ring of invisibility* to remain unseen. Standing on the steps of the alcove are two dwarves: Xanathar's majordomo, **Ahmaergo** (see appendix B), who presides over fight tournaments, and Xanathar's chief enforcer, Noska Ur'gray (see appendix B), who releases arena combatants from area X7. Ten human **bandits** and five **bugbears** (all members of the Xanathar Guild) guzzle ale and heckle combatants from the bleachers, while two **goblins** serve up salted rat intestines and stirge meat pies.

Joining a Tournament. If the characters enter during a tournament, they see a **minotaur** battling a scarred female halfling, Samara Strongbones (see area X7). The halfling doesn't want to die in a pointless battle and screams for help. If the characters intervene, the arena spectators turn violent and attack them. If the characters let the fight play out, Noska escorts the victor back to area X7 while Ahmaergo goads characters into joining the tournament. If the characters aren't willing to enter the tournament, Ahmaergo has them beaten unconscious and locked up while Xanathar watches silently.

Rules for running a tournament are described at the end of this chapter (see "Blood and Fortune," page 114). If a character joins the tournament and wins, or defeats its underlings, Xanathar is impressed enough to grant the party an audience, during which it tries to subjugate them (see "Facing Xanathar," page 99).

Scrying Sensor. The spectral eyestalk is a magical sensor, which allows an apprentice wizard in area X16 to monitor this room. See area X2 for more information.

Secret Door. The secret door in the south wall can be found with a successful DC 15 Wisdom (Perception) check. It pushes open to reveal area X33 beyond.

X7. CELL BLOCK

This area contains four cells separated by bars. The rectangular iron doors have locks built into them, and Noska Ur'gray carries the keys. Picking a lock requires a successful DC 15 Dexterity check using thieves' tools. Breaking down a cell door requires a successful DC 25 Strength (Athletics) check. The Cell Occupants table lists this area's prisoners.

CELL OCCUPANTS

Cell	Prisoners
A	A male **half-ogre** named Groz, a **minotaur** named Umpok, and a female **orog** named Charworl
B	Kidnapped Waterdavians: Xia Shung (NG female Shou human **bard**; see appendix B), Claudio Benzreck (LN male Tethyrian human **noble**), and Arthright Grayfalcon (CN male Illuskan **swashbuckler**; see appendix B)
C	A female **drow** named Raelyn Auvryndar, recently separated from her companion and subordinate, Zaibon Kyszalt (see area X24)
D	Samara Strongbones, a female lightfoot halfling, is a Zhentarim **spy** in league with Manshoon. She is chaotic evil and has these racial traits: She is Small, and her walking speed is 25 feet. She can move through the space of any Medium or larger creature. She has advantage on saving throws against being frightened. She speaks Common, Halfling, and Undercommon.

X8. HALL OF STATUES

This 20-foot-wide, magically lit hallway connects various areas controlled by the Xanathar Guild. It has the following features:

- Lifelike humanoid statues dot the hall.
- The first time the characters explore the hall, a **deep gnome** in clownish garb is dancing and cartwheeling up and down the hall, between the statues.

Gnome Clown. The garishly dressed deep gnome, Flutterfoot Zipswiggle, serves Xanathar as a jester. He carries a packet containing *dust of disappearance*. Unknown to Flutterfoot, the beholder has tired of the gnome and plans to turn him to stone when next they meet.

Flutterfoot knows the features and layout of Xanathar's lair, as well as the beholder's current whereabouts and the locations of secret doors, except the ones leading to area X36. He gleefully offers to serve as a guide if the characters correctly answer the following riddle:

> I come with a smile;
> In slaughter, I rest;
> I can be contagious,
> But my medicine is best.
> What am I?

The answer to Flutterfoot's riddle is "laughter." If the characters give the wrong answer, the gnome sprinkles himself with *dust of disappearance*, turns invisible, and flees.

Lifelike Statues. The statues are the petrified remains of intruders and Xanathar Guild members that were turned to stone by Xanathar. There are a dozen statues in all: four humans, three goblins, two drow, a dwarf, a halfling, and a tiefling.

Secret Door. The secret door to area X2 is clearly visible from this side. It is opened by turning a stone knob on the adjacent wall.

X9. GUILD BARRACKS

This magically lit room has the following features:

- The walls are covered with lewd graffiti written in Common, Dwarvish, Goblin, and Undercommon.
- In the front of the room is a ramshackle wooden table surrounded by empty barrels and casks that serve as stools. Drained tankards are strewn across the tabletop and the floor.
- A dozen moldy bunk beds are arranged in two rows at the back of the room.

Xanathar Guild Members. When they're not watching a tournament in the arena (area X6) or listening to Xanathar give a speech in the audience chamber (area X18), ten human **bandits**, members of the Xanathar Guild, sleep here. They're so drunk that, for the next few hours, they awaken only if they take damage. Also, they are poisoned while they remain intoxicated.

X10. Noska's Quarters

Xanathar's enforcer, Noska Ur'gray (see appendix B), resides in this magically lit room when he's not in the arena (area X6). The room contains the following features:

- A marble bathtub with clawed feet rests in the middle of the room, next to a large wooden cage containing a **rust monster**.
- Along the walls are piles of broken and rusted helmets, shields, and weapons.
- Hanging from hooks on the back wall are three mannequins made of straw and canvas, with a multitude of crossbow bolts sticking in them.

Noska keeps the rust monster as a pet and feeds it items from the piles of discarded helms, shields, and armaments. He uses the mannequins for target practice. The bathtub, which he has converted into a bed, is padded with straw and mangy furs.

Wooden Cage. A simple latch holds the cage door shut. The rust monster can't harm anyone while trapped inside.

Treasure. Hidden under a pile of rusty weapons is a wooden chest containing Noska's personal hoard: 37 gp, 151 sp, 360 cp, and four bloodstones (worth 50 gp each).

X11. Ahmaergo's Collection

Xanathar's majordomo fetishizes minotaurs and has decorated this magically lit room accordingly:

- A stuffed, glowering minotaur stands at the north end of the room. A large greataxe rests on a wooden rack in front of it.
- In the middle of the room is a 10-foot-long, 5-foot-wide, 3-foot-high rectangular slab of stone with a hand-carved, miniature model of a stone maze atop it.

Stone Maze. A *detect magic* spell reveals an aura of conjuration magic around the model maze. A creature that touches the maze becomes the target of a *maze* spell (save DC 15). Once the effect triggers, it can't do so again until the next dawn.

Stuffed Minotaur. When someone other than Ahmaergo opens the southern door, the skeleton of the stuffed minotaur erupts out of its skin, becoming an animated **minotaur skeleton**, and arms itself with the greataxe. It attacks all intruders, pursuing any who flee into area X8 or X12. The minotaur skeleton obeys Ahmaergo's commands.

X12. Ahmaergo's Quarters

The magical lights in this room have been dispelled, rendering the chamber dark. Characters who have a light source or darkvision can discern the following features:

- The room has been converted into a maze, its walls made of stacked crates nailed together with boards. The walls rise to meet the 20-foot-high ceiling.
- Humanoid bones litter the floor. (Ahmaergo gathered the bones from Undermountain and put them here as grisly decorations.)

The maze fills the entire room but for a 10-foot-square area in the southwest corner, where Ahmaergo keeps a wooden chest and a bed made from the skulls, bones, hide, and fur of minotaurs.

Getting through the maze takes time but isn't difficult, except that Ahmaergo has rigged a tripwire halfway through. A character in the lead who is searching for traps spots the tripwire with a successful DC 12 Wisdom (Perception) check. Once spotted, it can easily be avoided or disarmed. If the trap is triggered, the walls of the maze come crashing down. Every creature in the collapsing maze is hit by debris and must make a DC 12 Dexterity saving throw, taking 10 (3d6) bludgeoning damage on a failed saving throw, or half as much damage on a successful one.

Treasure. Ahmaergo's chest contains 121 gp in a sack made of stitched flesh, a carved malachite figurine of a minotaur (worth 250 gp), and a *potion of healing*.

X13. Thorvin's Workshop

Double doors swing open into a magically lit chamber containing the following:

- Thorvin Twinbeard (see appendix B), Xanathar's engineer, is building a large contraption in the middle of the room. Floating nearby is an albino **gazer** (see appendix B).
- Tools cover stone tables throughout the room. (There are enough tools here to assemble two sets of mason's tools, one set of smith's tools, and two sets of tinker's tools.)
- Other furnishings include a cot and a stack of wooden casks filled with Wyrmwizz Ale (a Skullport brew).

Albino Gazer. Xanathar dreamed this gazer into existence and sent it to spy on Thorvin, whose loyalty the beholder is beginning to question. The gazer is itself disloyal. A wizard character can befriend it with a successful DC 11 Charisma (Persuasion) check and turn it into their familiar with a *find familiar* ritual. When the gazer becomes a familiar, its alignment changes to match that of its new master.

Thorvin Twinbeard. When it is finished, Thorvin's contraption will enable Xanathar to pulverize creatures that it petrifies, turning them into a fine powder that can be used to make plaster. The pulverizer consists mainly of a tall stone bin with grinding gears at the bottom, and a chute where the powdered stone pours out.

The pulverizer is a pet project of Thorvin's that allows him to hang around Xanathar's lair and gather information, which he sells to the Harpers. (Thorvin puts the coin he earns from the faction in a bank, far from the beholder's prying eyes.) If one or more characters approach him and claim to be Harpers, Thorvin is upset that they would risk exposing him as a spy, pointing to the albino gazer. If the characters befriend the gazer and promise to go away, Thorvin truthfully answers as

many as three questions. He's never seen Ahmaergo's chambers (areas X11 and X12) but knows the rest of the lair well.

If the characters are looking for a way to mess with Xanathar's operation, Thorvin suggests they coerce Nar'l Xibrindas, the beholder's advisor (see area X18), into giving them the large supply of *smokepowder* that he smuggled into the dungeon. Thorvin also tells them where to plant the *smokepowder* to cause the most damage (see "Destroy the Lair," page 100).

X14. Secret Hallway

This magically lit hall is concealed behind secret doors. It circumvents the audience chamber (area X18) and gently slopes down toward the east. Finding either secret door requires a successful DC 15 Wisdom (Perception) check.

X15. Stairs to the Maze

Characters at the top of these magically lit stairs can hear loud music and raucous laughter boiling up from below. The staircase descends 20 feet to area X28.

X16. Panopticus Guard Station

This room contains the following features:

- Five bald shield dwarves, their heads covered with purple eye tattoos, sit around the edge of a glowing circle on the floor. Their eyes are scrunched shut, but they are aware of their surroundings.

- Protruding from the ceiling, directly above the circle, is a large, flaring bronze "bell" similar in shape to the mouth of a tuba.
- Set into the back of a recessed wall is a secret door that leads to area X17.

Dwarves. The five tattooed dwarves operate Xanathar's "panopticus" magical surveillance system. They fight only in self-defense. They are **apprentice wizards** (see appendix B), with these changes:

- They are neutral.
- They have these racial traits: Their walking speed is 25 feet. They have advantage on saving throws against poison and resistance to poison damage. They have darkvision out to a range of 60 feet. They speak Common and Dwarvish.
- Nihiloor the mind flayer has psychically and surgically altered the dwarves so that they sleep with one eye open and half their brains asleep at any time.

Amplification Bell. The bronze bell is connected to a tube that runs through the stone and into the nearby audience chamber (area X18). The bell amplifies sounds underneath it and transmits those sounds to the audience chamber.

Scrying Circle. A *detect magic* spell reveals an aura of divination magic around the circle, which the dwarves use to scry on various other locations within the dungeon: the entrance hall (area X2), the arena (area X6), the antechamber of madness (area X23), the recreation hall (area X28), and the downstairs hall (area X32). One dwarf watches each location and communicates what it sees via the bronze bell. The scrying circle functions for no one else. It is suppressed within an *antimagic field* and can also be dispelled (DC 17). When the circle ceases to exist, the ghostly eyestalk sensors in the above-mentioned locations disappear as well.

Secret Door. The secret door can be spotted with a successful DC 15 Wisdom (Perception) check. A pedal hidden in the floor, when stepped on, causes the door to swing inward.

X17. Promenade

Pillars carved with eyes follow the curvature of the hall, and these eyes seem to track creatures as they pass by. This isn't a magical effect but an optical illusion.

Majordomo. If he's not with Xanathar in the arena (area X6), **Ahmaergo** (see appendix B) is conducting a routine inspection of the dungeon. The characters can hear the dwarf's echoing footfalls as he approaches their location. If he sees intruders and is outnumbered, Ahmaergo retreats to area X22, heads downstairs to gather reinforcements from area X28, and leads a search party to capture the interlopers. If he sees only one intruder, he draws his axe and attacks.

Secret Door. The northernmost end of this hallway displays a fresco of a leafless tree that has lidless eyes embedded in its branches. Pressing a specific eye causes a door-shaped section of the wall to swing open into area X16. Characters can find the secret door and the switch with a successful DC 15 Wisdom (Perception) check.

X18. Audience Chamber

Xanathar greets visitors and makes speeches to its minions in this 40-foot-high domed chamber. Characters who were seen by the scrying sensors anywhere in the dungeon complex can't surprise the creatures here. The magically lit room contains the following features:

- The circular floor is tiled in black marble and bears a gold mosaic of Xanathar's symbol.
- Jutting from the ceiling is a bronze, bell-shaped protuberance. (This fixture is the other end of the sound amplifier described in area X16.)
- Displayed against the curved walls are a dozen lifelike statues (the remains of humans, drow, dwarves, goblinoids, and kobolds who defied the beholder).
- Hidden in the floor is a secret trapdoor.

While in this room, Xanathar uses its *ring of invisibility* to remain unseen and can use a bonus action to activate or deactivate a psychedelic display of magical lights, each one the size of a human eyeball. The lights fill a 10-foot cube in the middle of the room, and the beholder can throw its voice so that it seems to emanate from the same area. Any character who succeeds on a DC 13 Wisdom (Insight) check can tell that the display isn't the source of the voice.

If the beholder is here, it's using the psychedelic light display to deliver an incoherent, self-aggrandizing speech to a group of sycophantic underlings consisting of ten human **bandits** and two **duergar** who have never seen Xanathar's true form. These minions clutch tankards of Wyrmwizz Ale (a cheap Skullport brew)

and toast Xanathar whenever the beholder commends itself. Xanathar's treacherous **drow mage** advisor, Nar'l Xibrindas (see appendix B), stands in front of the open door to area X19, clapping weakly at the speech. Floating next to Nar'l is his **grell** bodyguard. If Xanathar has been warned that the characters are near, it wraps up its speech and grants them an audience; see "Facing Xanathar," page 99, for more information.

If Xanathar is elsewhere, this room contains only Nar'l and the grell. Nar'l tries to lure adventurers into a showdown with the beholder. If he is wounded, he flees through the trapdoor in the floor and retreats to area X35 while the grell covers his escape.

If the party includes members of Bregan D'aerthe and Nar'l recognizes them as such, he gives them his vial of eyescratch poison so they can blind Xanathar with it. This act of treachery, witnessed by the grell, turns the creature against him.

Secret Trapdoor. A hidden trapdoor in the floor can be found with a successful DC 15 Wisdom (Perception) check. It can be lifted with a successful DC 12 Strength (Athletics) check, revealing a wooden ladder that leads down to area X29.

X19. Xanathar's Sanctum

This magically lit room has a flat, 30-foot-high ceiling and contains several features:

- Luminous violet particles drift through the air like mist. A successful DC 12 Intelligence (Nature) check reveals that these are Underdark spores.
- A 20-foot-diameter fishbowl dominates the room. Filled with water, it also contains a small coral reef, a miniature shipwreck, and a sunken treasure chest.
- A smaller fishbowl, 3 feet in diameter, rests on a pedestal next to the larger bowl. A dwarf wearing a skullcap adorned with eyestalks feeds a trout-sized fish that swims in circles in this smaller bowl.
- A 10-foot-diameter silver mirror is embedded in the western wall. Letters are engraved into its frame.
- The eastern tunnel starts 10 feet above the floor and gently slopes upward to area X21. (Xanathar uses this passage as an escape route.)

If Xanathar (see appendix B) is here, it's invisible and speaking affectionately to the fish while the dwarf, Ott Steeltoes, feeds it.

Dwarf Fishkeeper. Ott Steeltoes (see appendix B) is Xanathar's fishkeeper. If he sees intruders and the beholder isn't present, Ott draws his dagger and stammers, "You shouldn't be here! Stay back, or I'll call the boss!" Ott can't telepathically communicate with Xanathar, but he thinks he can. He closes his eyes and frantically asks for Xanathar to return to its sanctum and disintegrate the intruders.

Fishbowls. Xanathar's pet fish, Sylgar, is the only creature that the beholder loves as much as itself. In fact, there have been many Sylgars over the years, but Ott is skilled at acquiring a replacement before Xanathar realizes its beloved pet has died.

Sylgar's large fishbowl weighs about 6,000 pounds, and the treasure chest at the bottom is real (see "Treasure" below). The small fishbowl weighs 60 pounds

NAT, JENKS, AND SQUIDDLY HAVE
A TROLLTIDE SCARE.

and is used primarily for feedings. Xanathar uses its telekinesis ray to transfer Sylgar from one fishbowl to another.

Mirror. Carved into the mirror's frame is the word "Xoblob." A *detect magic* spell reveals an aura of divination magic around the mirror. Speaking the word "Xoblob" within 10 feet of the mirror causes its reflective surface to become a scrying sensor, showing the Old Xoblob Shop and the street in front of it, as seen through the eyes of the stuffed beholder that hangs in the shop's display window (see "Old Xoblob Shop," page 23).

Spores. The purple spores are infused with *faerzress*, a magical radiation found in the Underdark. A creature that ends its turn in the room must succeed on a DC 13 Constitution saving throw or suffer a random form of short-term madness, determined by rolling on the Short-Term Madness table in chapter 8 of the *Dungeon Master's Guide*. A creature doesn't need to inhale the spores to be affected by them. Once the madness ends, the creature becomes immune to the spores in this room.

Treasure. The treasure chest is unlocked and contains thirty 100 gp gemstones. If Xanathar has retrieved the *Stone of Golorr*, the artifact is also here.

X20. DREAM NULLIFIER

This side chamber contains the following features:

- A 6-foot-diameter bowl made of crystal lattice pulsates with multicolored light as it floats 10 feet off the floor.
- A mangy straw pallet lies on the floor under the bowl. (The fishkeeper, Ott Steeltoes, uses the pallet as a bed.)

Dream Nullifier. Xanathar hired a wizard to construct a device that would prevent it from accidentally dreaming another beholder into existence. The bowl-shaped "dream nullifier" magically wakes Xanathar when it starts to dream about other beholders. If the bowl is engulfed by an *antimagic field* or targeted by a *dispel magic* spell or similar effect, it crashes to the floor and shatters into a million pieces.

X21. BEHOLDER ESCAPE ROUTE

Set into the floor at the north end of a tunnel that gently slopes down to area X19 is a circular stone plug that opens in the ceiling of the hallway below. Xanathar can

---

> ### REPLACING THE MIND FLAYER
>
> Nihiloor the mind flayer has carved out its own lair within Xanathar's lair (areas X23 through X26). If Nihiloor is killed earlier in the adventure, replace it with a mind flayer named Qrr'zarq.
>
> Qrr'zarq comes from a colony of mind flayers in Undermountain that wants to implant Xanathar with an illithid tadpole and, through a magical process called ceremorphosis, turn the beholder into a thrall. Qrr'zarq is waiting for an opportunity to implant the tadpole while Xanathar is alone and asleep. The mind flayer doesn't want adventurers to complicate or ruin its brilliant plan, which it keeps to itself. It offers to help characters who agree not to harm it or the beholder.

lift the plug with its telekinesis ray, creating an opening just large enough for it to float through. A character can lift the stone plug with a successful DC 19 Strength (Athletics) check.

X22. ARRIVAL POINT

Any creature holding the correct key that steps through the magical portal in area Q11 of the Xanathar Guild hideout (see chapter 1) appears here, between the columns of rock.

A curling staircase in the southwest corner descends 20 feet to area X32.

X23. ANTECHAMBER OF MADNESS

This great hall has the following features:

- A **kuo-toa whip** and six **kuo-toa** guard the hall. They gather in front of an iron portcullis in the southeast corner and tear bits of flesh off the bones of a recently slain dwarf.
- A ghostly eyestalk protrudes from the ceiling in the middle of the hall.
- The floor is littered with bones and covered with a thin layer of sticky, translucent slime.

Kuo-toa. These insane creatures are under the control of the mind flayer in area X24 and obey its telepathic commands to the best of their ability. When they detect intruders, they cry out, "Ooop! Ooop!" to alert their illithid master, then charge into battle.

Portcullis. The portcullis between this area and area X24 can be raised with a successful DC 22 Strength (Athletics) check, or with a *knock* spell or similar magic. The lever to raise the portcullis is in area X24.

Scrying Sensor. The ghostly eyestalk is a magical sensor that allows one of the apprentice wizards in area X16 to monitor this room. See area X2 for more information.

Sticky Slime. The slime-covered floor is difficult terrain for all creatures except kuo-toa, other creatures that have the Slippery trait, and creatures that fly.

X24. EXTRACTION CHAMBER

A portcullis separates this room from area X23, and the lever to raise and lower it is set into the north wall. Characters who peer through the bars of the portcullis can see the room's contents:

- In the middle of the room, a blood-spattered chair made of carved stone stands atop a 10-foot-square, 1-foot-high stone slab. Iron manacles are bolted to the chair's armrests.
- Trapped in the chair is a stunned and weaponless male **drow** in a chain shirt. He is trying to free himself of his bonds but is making no progress.

Drow Captive. The drow, Zaibon Kyszalt, was captured in Skullport and brought here for interrogation. His superior, Raelyn Auvryndar, was also captured and is confined in area X7. Zaibon wants to free her and escape into Undermountain, where House Auvryndar has outposts.

Nihiloor has a key that unlocks the chair's shackles. A character can unlock each shackle with a successful DC

15 Dexterity check using thieves' tools, and a creature shackled to the chair can slip free of these bonds with a successful DC 25 Dexterity (Sleight of Hand) check.

The mind flayer has telepathically interrogated Zaibon and learned about a House Auvryndar plot to conquer Skullport, as well as mounting tensions between the drow houses of Auvryndar and Freth. The mind flayer is getting ready to implant an intellect devourer in Zaibon's skull, then use him to undermine the drow plot and foment war between the drow houses. (Were Zaibon less useful, the mind flayer would have extracted his brain and turned it into an intellect devourer instead.) Zaibon knows nothing of the fate that awaits him.

Mind Flayer. If the characters haven't already dealt with Nihiloor, the mind flayer interrupts as they interact with Zaibon, entering from area X26 with an **intellect devourer** in its hands. If Zaibon is free of the chair, he tries to get as far away from the mind flayer and its "pet" as he can. Nihiloor doesn't pursue anyone who flees, trusting that they won't get far.

X25. Food for Thought

This magically lit room contains these features:

- The room reeks of death and carnage.
- Three wooden tables are arranged corner to corner, forming a triangle, in the middle of the room. The floor around them is stained with blood.
- Atop two of the tables, held down with leather straps, are two humans (**commoners**) dressed like homeless men. One looks dead, and the other gibbers like a madman. The third table is bare except for an area of sticky blood at one end.

Unhappy Meals. The Xanathar Guild captures homeless Waterdavians and brings them here for Nihiloor to feed on. After devouring their brains, the mind flayer gives their corpses to his kuo-toa thralls to eat.

The two men, a locksmith named Skarn Zarphoul and a broadcrier named Holvan Ebberek, recently heard a dwarf getting his brain sucked out. Skarn is stunned and catatonic from the shock of it, and Holvan is a gibbering lunatic. A *greater restoration* spell or similar magic restores either man's sanity. The men were hooded and brought here separately, so they know nothing of the dungeon's layout or occupants (other than the mind flayer). If their sanity is restored, they are eager to return to their families in Waterdeep.

X26. Devourer Spawning Pool

This room has the following features:

- In the middle of the area is a 10-foot-diameter, 2-foot-deep circular pool containing luminous green brine. Swimming in the brine are four **intellect devourers**.
- If it has not been encountered and defeated elsewhere, Nihiloor the **mind flayer** (see appendix B) is standing in the pool with the intellect devourers.
- Rusty manacles are bolted to the walls. (Hosts for the intellect devourers are chained in these locations.)

The brine is a magical substance that radiates an aura of transmutation magic under the scrutiny of a *detect magic* spell. Nihiloor uses it to transform humanoid brains into intellect devourers. The process is far from

perfect. A full 90 percent of the brains left in the brine rot and die, while the remaining 10 percent transform after marinating for 1d4 + 1 days.

Nihiloor and the intellect devourers make their stand here. If the characters flee, the mind flayer sends the intellect devourers after them and stays behind.

X27. Prison

Nihiloor the mind flayer uses this prison to confine potential hosts for his brood of intellect devourers. Captured characters might find themselves incarcerated here until they can be made into hosts. The area contains the following features:

- Eight locked iron doors lead to cells, some of which have bars separating them.
- Three **kuo-toa whips** stand guard here and attack any creature other than Nihiloor that enters, including other kuo-toa. One of the whips carries the keys to the cell doors on a ring.
- A 1-foot-tall figurine of an otherworldly creature rests atop a slime-covered alabaster pedestal against the east wall, between two cell doors.

Cells. A character outside a cell can pick its lock with a successful DC 20 Dexterity check using thieves' tools. Each cell contains a reeking chamber pot and no other furnishings.

Imprisoned in the westernmost cell along the north wall is Hyustus Staget, a captain of the City Watch whom the characters have met (see "The Watch Arrives," page 27). He was kidnapped while off duty and is without his armor and weapons. If Hyustus has died for whatever reason, replace him with a female human Watch officer named Cressa Galavarco (LG female Tethyrian **veteran** with no armor or weapons). Whoever is here has a date with an intellect devourer.

God Figurine. The figurine on the pedestal is crudely fashioned out of clay. It has the head of a hammerhead shark, the upper torso of a bare-chested male, dragon wings sprouting from its shoulders, and octopus tentacles where its legs should be. The kuo-toa modeled it after an imaginary god they call Garshoogah.

X28. Guild Recreation Hall

Deafeningly loud music and chatter fill this magically lit room, which is decorated like a tavern:

- Ten human **bandits** (members of the Xanathar Guild) sit around two trellis tables, drinking Wyrmwizz Ale, smoking pipes, clapping their hands, and stomping their feet while two **goblins** wearing chamber pots on their heads dance and sing atop a third table.
- If he's not with Xanathar in the arena (area X6), Noska Ur'gray (see appendix B) is here, drinking with the others.
- A wooden rack along the east wall holds five large ale barrels with spigots punched into them. Protruding from the ceiling above the barrels is a ghostly eyestalk (scrying sensor).

Xanathar Guild Members. These villains are celebrating the capture of an off-duty City Watch captain (see area X27). Characters who eavesdrop on the chatter hear one guild member say, "We caught ourselves a

Watch captain! Ahmaergo says the boss is happier than a pink flumph, whatever that is. Today, free ale! Tomorrow, gold and glory!" This proclamation is followed by loud cheers.

Goblins. The goblins, Lulz and Vellix, are servers who have allowed themselves to get swept up in the reverie. If a fight breaks out, they hide under a table and throw themselves at the mercy of the party if the characters emerge victorious.

Scrying Sensor. The ghostly eyestalk is a magical sensor that allows one of the apprentice wizards in area X16 to monitor this room. See area X2 for more information.

X29. TRAPDOOR

At the top of a staircase is a landing with a ladder leading up to a stone trapdoor that requires a successful DC 12 Strength (Athletics) check to be lifted. The trapdoor opens into area X18 above.

X30. XANATHAR'S GOURMET KITCHEN

A delightful aroma wafts down the hall from this kitchen, blending the scents of rare spices, savory meats, and fresh herbs. The room contains the following features:

- Seven **kobolds** wearing white toque hats dash between stout tables, frantically preparing meals for Xanathar and arranging the food on silver platters.
- Two **gazers** (see appendix B) dreamed into reality by Xanathar oversee the kobolds and use their telekinesis rays to hoist and deliver food platters.
- Two iron stoves stand against the east wall, with a slender spice rack nestled between them.

When it comes to meals, Xanathar prefers the finest Sword Coast cuisine, including a healthy diet of mushrooms, as opposed to uncooked meat. All the meals prepared here are for the consumption of Xanathar alone.

The gazers attack intruders on sight, while the kobolds flee by the easiest route.

Spice Rack. The rack contains thirty bottles of rare spices worth 10 gp each.

X31. THE OTHER KITCHEN

Black smoke follows the stench of burned meat and bread down the hallway. This magically lit kitchen has the following features:

- A haggard male halfling frantically tries to cook meat, knead dough, simmer sauce, and mix spices all at once.
- An iron stove stands against the south wall, and cooking utensils hang from hooks just beyond the halfling's reach.

Halfling Cook. When the halfling spots the characters, a relieved smile crosses his face. "Finally!" he says excitedly. "I haven't had a break in half a tenday. Make sure you stir the sauce once every five minutes." He then hands the characters his apron, mistaking them for the actual kitchen staff.

Bepis Honeymaker is a honey merchant who was kidnapped from his Trades Ward home a month ago. The Xanathar Guild tried to ransom him back, but seemingly his relatives either couldn't pay or decided not to. (In truth, his rotten in-laws destroyed the ransom notes and told Bepis's wife and children that he ran away with another family.) Ahmaergo has put him to work as a cook but threatens to give him over to the mind flayer Nihiloor every so often.

Bepis is a strongheart halfling **commoner**, with these changes:

- Bepis is lawful good.
- He is Small and has 3 (1d6) hit points.
- He has these racial traits: His walking speed is 25 feet. He can move through the space of a Medium or larger creature. He has advantage on saving throws against being frightened. He speaks Common and Halfling.

X32. STAIRS AND SCRYING SENSOR

A staircase curls up to area X22, and a ghostly eyestalk sprouts from the hallway ceiling. The eyestalk is a magical sensor that allows one of the apprentice wizards in area X16 to monitor this corridor (see area X2 for more information).

X33. CRYPT OF XANATHARS PAST

This room contains the following features:

- Suspended in floor-to-ceiling crystal cylinders are four dead beholders preserved in embalming fluid. Magical lights illuminate the cylinders from within.
- Nine shallow alcoves have murals of beholders painted on their walls. Standing in each alcove is a beholder-shaped copper urn atop a green marble pedestal. The lid of each urn is molded with ten eyestalks. (At the back of the westernmost alcove in the north wall is a secret door.)
- The western wall is carved to display a scowling beholder flanked by two hooded wizards. Beneath each wizard's cowl, one glaring eye is visible.

Xanathar (see appendix B), if present, is gazing somberly at the tombs of past Xanathars.

Beholder Urns. The copper urns contain the dust of disintegrated beholders. If the dust from an urn is poured out, it coalesces into the vague shape of a floating beholder for a few seconds, makes a growling noise, then loses cohesion and falls to the floor.

Crystal Crypts. Each crystal cylinder has AC 10, 15 hit points, resistance to slashing and piercing damage, and vulnerability to bludgeoning damage. If a cylinder is shattered, the fluid within it washes across the floor as the dead beholder lands with a wet plop and expels 1d4 baby **gas spores** that grow to full size in 30 days. Any character infected by these gas spores gains the following flaw until the disease is cured: "I hate other beholders. If I see a beholder, I must try to destroy it."

Secret Door. The secret door can be found with a successful DC 15 Wisdom (Perception) check. It pulls open to reveal area X6 beyond.

Wall Carvings. Any character who studies the carvings on the west wall and succeeds on a DC 12 Wisdom (Perception) check notices that each wizard's eye is a button that can be pushed. If a character pushes either button, or uses an object or spell to do so, the beholder carving on the wall discharges a green ray that the character can dodge with a successful DC 16 Dexterity saving throw. If the ray hits, the character appears to be disintegrated but is actually teleported to area X34a or X34b, depending on which button was pushed. Once a button is pushed, it locks in place for 1 hour and can't be pushed again until that time elapses. A character can forcibly reset a button by making a successful DC 20 Dexterity check using thieves' tools.

X34. Wizard Tombs

These crypts were built to hold the remains of two wizards who lived in this dungeon complex long before Xanathar took it over. Only one wizard is entombed here, however. The fate of the other wizard is unknown. Both chambers are encased in solid stone and brightly lit by *continual flame* spells cast on wall sconces.

X34a. In the middle of this tomb rests a gold marble sarcophagus, its lid carved in the likeness of a long-haired human wizard who wears a robe adorned with closed eyes. The sarcophagus can't be pried open or damaged, but if a spell is cast within the tomb, the eyes of the robe open all at once—an eerie yet harmless effect—and the lid slowly levitates into the air, revealing the contents of the sarcophagus: a shriveled, inanimate mummy wearing *eyes of charming*. After 1 minute, the eyes on the lid close as it slowly sinks back down, resealing the sarcophagus until another spell is cast within the tomb.

A character who dons the *eyes of charming* can see, through its blue lenses, a blue metal tile shaped like a four-pointed star on the west wall. The tile is invisible otherwise, but can be found with a tactile search and a successful DC 17 Wisdom (Perception) check. When a creature touches the tile, all creatures in the tomb are instantly teleported to the arena (area X6).

X34b. This tomb is empty except for an invisible, blue metal tile on the west wall. It functions identically to the one in area X34a.

X35. Nar'l Xibrindas's Office

The *continual flame* spells that once lit this room have been dispelled. Characters need light sources or darkvision to see here. The room contains the following features:

- Two open crates rest against the north wall.
- A stone desk in the southwest corner is completely free of papers. The chair behind it is carved with a spider motif.
- Bare stone bookshelves stand against the east wall.

Crates. One crate contains fifty stuffed beholder dolls. The other contains thirty onyx trophies (worth 25 gp each) depicting a smiling beholder being caressed by hands. The dolls and trophies are among the prizes given to winners of Xanathar's combat tournaments.

Desk. The chair behind the desk has a secret compartment under its left armrest that can be found and opened with a successful DC 15 Wisdom (Perception) check. This tiny compartment contains a small black key that unlocks both of the desk drawers. A character

can pick each lock with a successful DC 17 Dexterity check using thieves' tools.

The first drawer holds Nar'l's spellbook, a sturdy tome bound in black leather and wrapped in webbing. It contains all the spells that Nar'l has prepared, plus the *sending* spell.

The second drawer contains a *bag of holding* that belongs to Jarlaxle Baenre. Nar'l borrowed this magic item and used it to smuggle kegs of *smokepowder* into Xanathar's lair (see area X36).

Secret Doors. A stone bookshelf in the southeast corner of this room rotates into the wall, revealing a secret passage that curves north. A character can find this secret door with a successful DC 15 Wisdom (Perception) check, or simply by pushing on the bookshelf.

A second secret door at the end of the curved hall can be found without an ability check; it pulls open to reveal a dark and dusty chamber (area X36) beyond.

X36. Secret Room

This room has the following features:

- The room is unlit and choked with dust and cobwebs.
- Twenty kegs of *smokepowder* are neatly stacked in the middle of the room. Each keg has a paper label, written on which are the words "SMOKEPOWDER! DO NOT OPEN!" in Common and Elvish.

Neither Xanathar nor its loyal underlings know this room exists. When Nar'l found it, he asked to have the

adjoining room (area X35) turned into his office so that he could keep this room secret. The only other individual who knows about this room is Thorvin Twinbeard, Xanathar's chief engineer, but he's not inclined to tell the beholder about it.

Kegs. Each keg comes with a fuse and holds 5 pounds of *smokepowder* (see appendix A). To collapse Xanathar's lair, at least two kegs must be placed at each weak point (see "Destroy the Lair," page 100).

SPECIAL EVENTS

You can use one or both of the following special events as the characters make their way through Xanathar's lair, or as they try to thwart Xanathar's agents in Waterdeep.

BLOOD AND FORTUNE

The beholder holds gladiatorial tournaments whenever it needs a little violence to brighten its day. The winners of a tournament receive trophies, and wagers are made on the sly.

A single tournament has twelve combatants and consists of three fights with short rests in between. Failure to heed the following rules result in a combatant's disqualification:

- All tournament combatants must wait in area X7 until they're called to area X6 to fight.
- During a fight event, no combatant can leave the arena or attack anyone who isn't a combatant in that event.

TOURNAMENT STRUCTURE

Noska Ur'gray takes the twelve combatants and assembles them in four teams of three. To keep the fights interesting, Noska tries to even out the teams as much as possible. A team might have all player characters, all NPCs, or a combination of the two.

The first fight pits team 1 against team 2. The second fight pits team 3 against team 4. The third and final fight pits the winning teams of the previous two fights against one another. A fight ends when all combatants on one team are incapacitated, killed, or disqualified.

WINNING THE TOURNAMENT

Each member of the winning team who survives the third fight receives a stuffed Xanathar doll with a pocket in its mouth that holds a 100 gp gemstone, and an onyx trophy carved to look like a smiling beholder being caressed by hands (worth 25 gp).

TOURNAMENT WAGERS

Spectators like to place side bets on their favorite teams. The maximum wager is 10 gp. A character who places a wager on the team that wins the tournament receives winnings equal to five times the wager.

TROLLTIDE SLAUGHTER

Trolltide is a fun springtime holiday for most Waterdeep denizens, including Xanathar, but the beholder has planned a cruel twist on the holiday this year.

The Xanathar Guild recently captured some trolls in Undermountain. The trolls are fitted with eyeless helms and ball-and-chain shackles around their ankles. They are then set loose in different wards of the city during Trolltide. When the characters happen upon such a scene, read:

> Children in troll masks run through the fog and drizzle, knocking on doors and stopping adults in the streets. Those who aren't placated with candied apples, sticks of salted meat, and other treats perpetrate all manner of tricks. A grumpy old woman has a rat thrown in her face. A burly dwarf has his pipe pilfered.
>
> A small crowd of onlookers is gathered around a ten-foot-tall wicker effigy of a troll, stamping their feet as two young men struggle to set the likeness ablaze with sputtering torches.
>
> Suddenly a white-haired man bolts toward the crowd, his face a mask of terror. Behind him lurches a massive, green-skinned giant dragging a ball and chain across the cobbled street. A blind helm covers the troll's eyes, but its mouth is a veritable cavern of sharp teeth. It flails its arms, slashing at the fog around it, and lets out a horrible wail of frustration. The crowd panics at the sight of it and flees into the mist and rain. Meanwhile, two members of the City Watch sneak up behind the blind troll, hoping to strike a mortal blow.

The white-haired man is a Waterdavian noble of no real accomplishments named Bromas Sultlue. When he sees the characters, he shouts, "It's a troll! Do something!" If the characters intervene, the two City Watch **veterans** fight alongside them. These constables act on the same initiative count. On their initiative count each round, there's a noncumulative 20 percent chance that another **veteran** arrives and joins the fray.

The **troll** is blinded while wearing the eyeless helm, and the ball-and-chain shackles clamped around its ankles reduce its walking speed to 20 feet. In this state, its challenge rating is 4 (1,100 XP). As the characters battle the troll, children in troll masks bravely pelt the creature with candied apples.

DEVELOPMENT

If the characters contribute to the defeat of the troll, the City Watch is grateful. Bromas Sultlue congratulates them and spends the next tenday recounting every detail of the battle to friends and family members. The story of the characters' heroism spreads, and they gain many new patrons at their tavern. For the next six tendays, when determining the tavern's profitability, add 20 to rolls on the Running a Business table (see "Tavern Keeping Expenses," page 41). Thereafter, add 10 to such rolls to represent Waterdeep's lingering fondness for the "Trollslayers of Trollskull Alley."

CHAPTER 6: HELL OF A SUMMER

Victoro and Ammalia Cassalanter struck a deal with Asmodeus, Lord of the Nine Hells. Three years ago, they traded away the souls of their children to escape financial ruin. The soul of their eldest son, Osvaldo, was taken immediately. What was left behind was transformed into a chain devil, which the Cassalanters confined to their attic. Their two youngest children, Terenzio and Elzerina, are doomed to lose their souls when they turn nine years old a mere ten days after Founders' Day, a midsummer festival that celebrates Waterdeep's founding.

After the deal was struck, the Cassalanters enjoyed a miraculous comeback. Their banking and money-lending business thrived while their competition suffered. The disappearance of their eldest son (and heir apparent) earned them sympathy. Their philanthropic endeavors bought them legitimacy and new friends. They became the envy of Waterdavian nobility in short order. Seemingly blessed, the Cassalanters attracted new followers to their cult of devil worship, which was Asmodeus's plan all along.

Reneging on a contract with Asmodeus is a luxury no mortal can afford, but there is a way for Lord and Lady Cassalanter to save the souls of Terenzio and Elzerina. A clause in the contract allows them to preserve their remaining (and future) children's lives by instead paying "one shy of a million gold coins, and the sacrifice of one shy of one hundred unfortunate souls." The Cassalanters have most of the coin they need, but they require the gold from the Vault of Dragons to buy their children's salvation without bankrupting themselves.

Victoro is in charge of locating the Vault of Dragons and securing the gold within it. Ammalia, for her part, plans to sacrifice ninety-nine souls in one fell swoop by throwing a feast on Founders' Day featuring poisoned food. Both the souls and the gold must be paid to Asmodeus at the same time. Foiling either one of these schemes spells doom for the Cassalanters' plot and their youngest children.

CULT OF ASMODEUS

Lord and Lady Cassalanter are the heads of a secretive cult of Asmodeus. The cult convenes at midnight once every tenday in the temple of Asmodeus beneath Cassalanter Villa. During rituals of worship, members of the cult, including Lord and Lady Cassalanter, wear crimson robes, golden masks, and golden sacrificial daggers. The masks and daggers are worth 75 gp each for the gold alone.

MEET THE CASSALANTERS

Each member of the Cassalanter family relaxes in different parts of the house and reacts separately to the discovery of characters intruding in their home. Lord and Lady Cassalanter are often out of the house on business, especially as Founders' Day draws near; they return home an hour before dinner.

LADY AMMALIA CASSALANTER

Lady Cassalanter reacts with surprise to the sight of uninvited guests, but quickly conceals her feelings with a welcoming smile. She attempts to gain the intruders' confidence by pretending to believe that they are guests of Victoro's and saying that she simply was not told of their presence. With this pretense established, she tries to learn the characters' true intentions, casting *charm person* on the party using a 5th-level spell slot (affecting up to five creatures within 30 feet) if necessary. Using magic in this way is illegal, but Ammalia has a lot of goodwill banked in Waterdeep—enough to curry favor with a magistrate.

During the hours when Ammalia is home and awake, her location in the villa can be determined randomly:

d100	Ammalia's Location
01–70	She's tending to her butterfly garden (area C25).
71–90	She's smoking on the balcony (area C25a).
91–00	She's weeping before Osvaldo in the attic (area C24).

LORD VICTORO CASSALANTER

Victoro Cassalanter reacts with fiery rage to the sight of uninvited guests. He demands to know their names and calls for the butler, Willifort Crowelle, to show them out. If he has the chance, he subtly casts *dominate person* on one of the characters using an 8th-level spell slot (extending its duration to 8 hours) to plant a spy among their ranks. As soon as the intruders are gone, he retires to his office (area C6) and uses his action to take total control of the dominated character. The dominated character reports to the City Watch that the party broke into Cassalanter Villa and must be arrested for their crime.

During the hours when Victoro is home and awake, his location in the villa can be determined randomly:

d100	Victoro's Location
01–70	He's in his office (area C6).
71–90	He's in the reading room (area C4).
91–00	He's with Ammalia at one of the three locations mentioned above.

CASSALANTER LORE

A successful DC 15 Intelligence (History) check reveals the following information about Cassalanter Villa and its inhabitants:

- The Cassalanters fell on hard times a few years back, but they have since reversed their fortunes and restored their lucrative banking and money-lending business.
- Victoro and Ammalia's eldest son disappeared three years ago when the family was on the verge of bankruptcy. They have two surviving children, young twins named Terenzio and Elzerina.
- Lord Victoro Cassalanter is the only living heir of the late Caladorn Cassalanter, a former Masked Lord and a hero of the North.
- Over the years, the Cassalanters have founded a number of philanthropic societies and made generous donations to temples dedicated to good-aligned deities. They are known to worship Siamorphe, a demigod whose ethos is the nobility's right and responsibility to rule.

TERENZIO AND ELZERINA

The Cassalanter twins aren't members of their parents' cult and have no other friends, since they are privately tutored and rarely allowed to leave the estate. Around strangers, Terenzio becomes suspicious and meek, while Elzerina seems brash and outgoing. Both children are incredibly excited to meet friendly strangers and treat their "new friends" to a trip around the house. They help the characters sneak through the villa, since the children know they aren't supposed to have guests.

During the hours when the children are awake, their location in the villa can be determined randomly:

d100	Terenzio and Elzerina's Location
01–50	They're playing in their room (area C18).
51–75	They're in the library (area C3).
76–00	They're chasing butterflies in the garden (area C25).

Terenzio and Elzerina have places in the house that their parents have forbade them from visiting—and that they are excited to explore, now that they have friends to accompany them. These locations are as follows:

- Their father's office (area C6)
- The attic (area C24)
- The wine cellar area (C28)

If asked about their parents, Terenzio and Elzerina report that their parents are searching for some missing dragons. (What their parents plan to do with a bunch of scary, winged reptiles is beyond them, and Terenzio and Elzerina are too scared to ask.) If befriended, they reveal that their father keeps a journal in his office (area C6).

If asked about their older brother, Osvaldo, Terenzio and Elzerina repeat what their parents have told them: he's attending school in a faraway city (they don't recall which one). Neither knows the cruel fate that has befallen Osvaldo (see area C24) or suspects that a similar fate awaits them.

HEAD SERVANTS

The head servants of Cassalanter Villa are members of the cult. These four servants are described below. All appear to be tieflings, though one is not. The following changes apply to the tieflings' stat blocks:

- The tieflings are lawful evil.
- They have these racial traits: They know the *thaumaturgy* cantrip, and Charisma is their spellcasting ability for this spell. They have resistance to fire damage. They have darkvision out to a range of 60 feet. They speak Common and Infernal.

WILLIFORT CROWELLE

Willifort dresses in a sharp black suit and wears thin-rimmed spectacles. He's a **doppelganger** that usually takes the form of an aging male tiefling, and he greets all guests in the entrance hall (area C1).

As the Cassalanters' chief butler and Lord Victoro's personal attendant, Willifort Crowelle makes a point of knowing everything that transpires within the villa. If the Cassalanters have guests, he escorts them during their entire visit, using stealth if necessary. He ushers nosy guests away from areas or objects that might link the Cassalanters with the Asmodeus-worshiping cult.

TISSINA KHYRET

Madame Khyret is the personal attendant to Ammalia Cassalanter and is the family's chief housemaid.

Madame Khyret dresses in a long black gown and wears a headdress with black tassels. She is an aging tiefling **cult fanatic**, and she spends most of her time in the master sitting room (area C19).

LAIBA "NANA" ROSSE

Laiba Rosse, better known as "Nana," is the caretaker and private tutor for Terenzio and Elzerina, and she does her best to keep track of their every move. Even so, the two often sneak away from her watchful eye.

Nana dresses in flowing red robes. She is a female tiefling **cult fanatic** who relaxes in the twins' playroom (area C17) when she's not with the children.

JANDAR CHERGOBA

As the head chef of Cassalanter Villa, Jandar determines each day's menu and oversees all activity in the kitchen.

Jandar is a male tiefling **cult fanatic**. He is often in the kitchen (area C10).

FACING THE CASSALANTERS

Lord and Lady Cassalanter are formidable spellcasters and devoted to one another. If one is assailed within Cassalanter Villa, the other arrives as quickly as possible.

A direct confrontation with the Cassalanters will likely result in defeat for the characters, or—if the characters and the Cassalanters both escape with their lives—their arrest for assaulting nobility. The Cassalanters have no desire to kill the characters, even in self-defense. They take great pains to divide and subdue the party with their magic while not inflicting grievous harm.

If the characters reduce Ammalia to 30 hit points or fewer and Victoro is with her, he banishes her to safety for a few brief moments while he continues fighting. If either Victoro or Ammalia is reduced to 30 hit points or fewer and the other Cassalanter isn't present, they try to negotiate with or bribe their assailants.

The Cassalanters don't fear being arrested, since they have faith that their wealth, reputations, and contacts will keep them out of prison. They do fear the ticking clock of Founders' Day. They plead for the characters to allow them to carry out their plan, if only to save Terenzio's and Elzerina's lives.

DISRUPTING THE CASSALANTERS' OPERATION

Killing or injuring the Cassalanters carries grave legal consequences, but the characters can hinder the Cassalanters by destroying or stealing Ammalia's stash of midnight tears poison (area C22), destroying the statue of Asmodeus in the temple (area A7), or keeping Lord Neverember's gold out of their clutches.

GATHERING INFORMATION

If the Cassalanters are the main villains, the characters might come to their villa if their search for the *Stone of Golorr* or the Vault of Dragons hits a dead end. Victoro Cassalanter keeps information related to his own search for the stone and the Vault of Dragons in his office (area C6).

CASSALANTER VILLA

When the characters first come near the gates of Cassalanter Villa, read or paraphrase the following:

> Cassalanter Villa's stark white walls and gleaming crimson roof and turrets stand out even among the other opulent estates of the Sea Ward. A three-story mansion lies in the midst of picturesque green gardens dappled with hedges and water features. The estate is surrounded by a tall white brick wall, with a single wrought-iron gate as an entrance. The Cassalanter family crest—a green Y overlapping a stylized goose being fed—is emblazoned on the gate, and armored guards stand at attention on either side.

Cassalanter Villa is an extravagant manse with dozens of lavish chambers for the masters of the house and their guests—but its splendor belies the terrible secret it holds. The temple of Siamorphe that once lay beneath the estate has been desecrated by Victoro and Ammalia's devil-worship. Now, this great chapel is dedicated to the Lord of the Nine Hells.

APPROACHING CASSALANTER VILLA

The grounds of the Cassalanters' estate are patrolled by hired **guards**. Two of them stand outside the gate of the estate, two more stand outside the front door of the house, and a total of six patrol the grounds at any time. These guards are humans and are outfitted in livery that bears the crest of House Cassalanter.

The house is surrounded by a well-manicured lawn. A cobblestone path leads from the estate's exterior gate to both the front entrance (area C1) and the entrance to the coach house (area CH1). The villa's grounds feature numerous deciduous trees and meticulously tended gardens.

SPOTTED BY THE GUARDS

Characters who try to infiltrate Cassalanter Villa are more likely to be arrested than to be killed. The security detail around Cassalanter Villa is meant to raise an alarm and deter petty thieves, not to stop determined adventurers. If the guards spot an intruder, they do the sensible thing: call the authorities.

The City Watch has small, single-person "watch boxes" set up on nearly every street corner in the Sea Ward, including the intersection just outside the gates of Cassalanter Villa. If a guard sounds the alarm, the Watch member on duty fetches a force of forty City Watch **veterans** to cordon off the property.

REINFORCEMENTS

If the City Watch gets involved, Lord and Lady Cassalanter become worried that someone has caught onto their plot. The number of guards patrolling the grounds doubles, and Victoro dispenses with all human guards inside the house. Whenever a guard is mentioned in an interior area, that guard is now a **bearded devil** disguised as a human. A disguised devil looks like a muscular, bearded male human in house livery. A creature that observes one closely can, with a successful DC 15 Wisdom (Perception) check, notice its "beard" writhing.

DENIZENS OF CASSALANTER VILLA

Cassalanter Villa is home to no one but Lord and Lady Cassalanter, their children, their personal attendants, and their guards. All the other servants who work at the villa live in dingy homes in the Dock Ward or the Field Ward and travel across the city in the wee hours of the morning to arrive before the Cassalanters awake.

With the exception of their personal attendants, the Cassalanters replenish their servants regularly. Most move on to other jobs, but occasionally a servant discovers the secret vault (area C29), visits the forbidden attic (area C24), or otherwise learns too much. Such folk are fated to become sacrifices to Asmodeus.

VILLA FEATURES

The following features are found throughout the villa:

- Ceilings in rooms are 25 feet high, with 7-foot-high corridors and doorways connecting them.
- Doors are made of exotic hardwood. If a door is locked, the lock can be picked by a character who makes a successful DC 15 Dexterity check using thieves' tools, or the door can be forced open by a character who makes a successful DC 20 Strength (Athletics) check. Victoro, Ammalia, and the head butler, Willifort, hold keys to every room in the house.
- Floors are made of wood and covered with soft woolen carpets. Creatures walking in carpeted rooms have advantage on Dexterity (Stealth) checks.
- All areas are well lit by oil lamps, lanterns, or chandeliers.
- The Cassalanters keep no silver objects (with the exception of coins) in their house, since silver is harmful to devils.

AREAS OF THE VILLA

The following areas correspond to the labels on map 6.1. The villa connects to the temple of Asmodeus through a secret door in area C28.

If the occupants or features of a location change during the Founders' Day party, the text includes a "Founders' Day" section describing those changes.

GUEST HOUSE

The Cassalanters host guests in this stately guest house.

CG1. Mud Room. Guests can remove and store dirty cloaks and boots here.

CG2. Storage. Guests can store their traveling gear here.

CG3. Dining Room. This room is furnished with two dining tables, each surrounded by six chairs.

CG4. Kitchen. Guests are expected to dine with the Cassalanters in the manor but can prepare their own breakfast here.

CG5. Parlor. This room is furnished with a billiard table, a card table, and four luxurious armchairs.

CG6. Sitting Room. This room features an upright piano and four luxurious armchairs.

CG7. Bedrooms. Each room contains a bed for two, a pair of wardrobes, a small vanity with matching stool, and a storage trunk for valuables.

CG8. Master Bedroom. This room has a balcony and contains a large canopied bed, a standing mirror in a gilded frame, a writing desk and matching chair, a dresser, a tall wardrobe, and an owlbear throw rug draped over a padded chair with matching ottoman.

COACH HOUSE

The Cassalanters own three carriages—one for their banking business, one for public appearances, and one for private use. They also own six horses: four **draft horses** to pull carriages and two **riding horses**. The horses are kept in stalls that are cleaned every morning just before dawn. Tack, bridles, feed, and other necessities for the horses are stored in the coach house as well.

C1. ENTRANCE HALL

This hall has the following features:

- A magnificent harpsichord sits in the hall.
- A crimson carpet runs down the hall toward an open door to the foyer.
- Light from a crystal chandelier reflects off more than three dozen holy symbols of Siamorphe perched on wall shelves, each in the form of a silver chalice with a golden sun etched on its outside.

If the characters are expected guests, Willifort Crowelle (see "Head Servants," page 116) awaits them here and guides them to the smoking room (area C12) to meet with Lord Cassalanter. He allows them to explore the house while they wait but follows them doggedly.

Founders' Day. The hall is filled with chatty guests holding flutes of sparkling wine. One is playing the harpsichord.

C2. GARDEN MUDROOM

This room has the following features:

- A **guard** dressed in House Cassalanter livery sits idly on a crate, watching the outside door.
- The floor is caked with mud. Several rows of muddy boots and gardening gloves are strewn about the floor.

Founders' Day. Esvele Rosznar, the **Black Viper** (see appendix B), is hiding in an alcove and putting on her Black Viper mask and hood. She is wearing a sleek black leather suit, and a frilly ball gown lies at her feet. Esvele has slipped away from her overbearing parents, Rolteme and Azalea Rosznar, and is preparing to sneak through the villa and rob the Cassalanters blind.

The characters can convince the Black Viper to help them as they scour Cassalanter Villa by succeeding on a DC 14 Charisma (Intimidation or Persuasion) check. If Esvele decides to help the characters, she fights alongside them and discovers treasure and secret doors automatically.

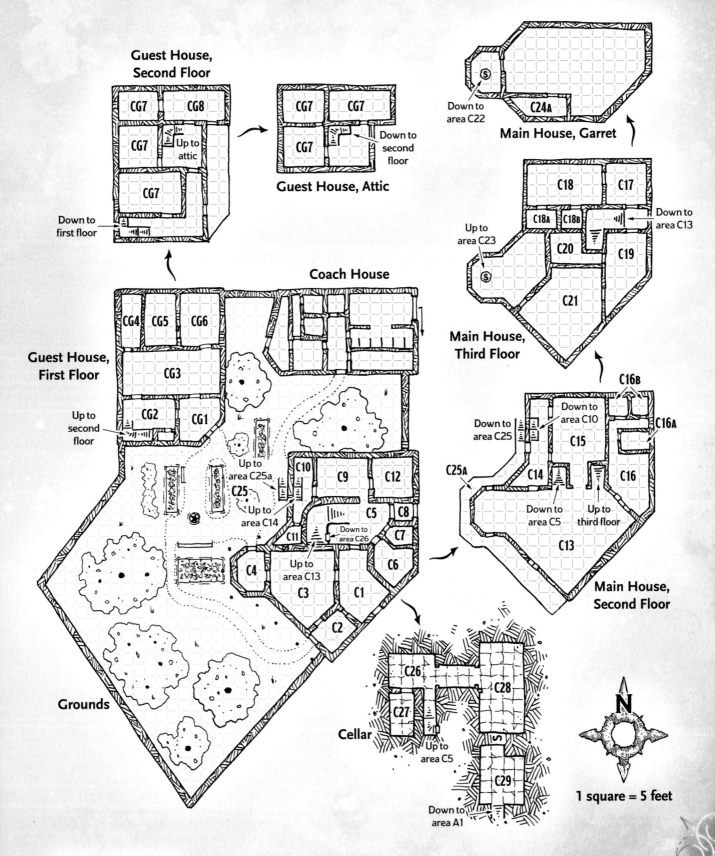

Guest House, Second Floor

CG7 CG8 CG7 Up to attic CG7

Down to first floor

Guest House, Attic

CG7 CG7 CG7

Down to second floor

Main House, Garret

C24A

Down to area C22

Coach House

Guest House, First Floor

CG4 CG5 CG6

CG3

Up to second floor

CG2 CG1

Up to area C25a

C25

C10

Up to area C14

C25

C9

C12

C5 C8

C11

Down to area C26

Up to area C13

C7

C4

C3

C6

C1

C2

Grounds

Main House, Third Floor

C18 C17

Up to area C23

C18A C18B

Down to area C13

C20 C19

C21

Main House, Second Floor

C16B

Down to area C25

Down to area C10

C16A

Down to area C25

C15

C25A

C14

Down to area C5

C16

Up to third floor

C13

Cellar

C26

C28

C27

C29

Up to area C5

Down to area A1

N

1 square = 5 feet

MAP 6.1: CASSALANTER VILLA

C3. Library

This is the Cassalanters' private library. It contains the following features:

- The scent of old parchment hangs thick in the air.
- The walls are lined with tall shelves packed with colorful, leather-bound books. Each bookshelf is outfitted with a ladder on a rolling track to enable people to reach the highest books.
- Shelves that take up the entire southwest wall hold not books but eighty wide-necked glass bottles filled with swirling mist and sealed with corks.
- Hanging on the north wall between two bookshelves is a 7-foot-tall portrait of Lord and Lady Cassalanter holding two infant children and standing beside their teenage son, Osvaldo. (This portrait conceals a secret door.)

If Terenzio and Elzerina are here, they're playing on the sliding ladders.

Books. None of the books are magical.

Jars of Mist. The glass bottles on the southwest shelf contain magically captured sounds, including songs, operas, and recorded lectures. Uncorking a bottle temporarily releases its auditory contents into the library, after which the sound returns to its bottle. Breaking a bottle releases the sound, but the sound dissipates after it plays once. All the bottles are labeled. Sample contents include the following:

- "Ahghairon's Dragonward," a lecture given by Khelben Arunsun about the dragonward that protects Waterdeep (see "Ahghairon's Dragonward," page 6).
- "Canticle of the Silver Chalice," a hymn to the demigod Siamorphe.
- *Wulfgar and the Crystal Shard*, an epic opera detailing the adventures of a barbarian, a dwarf, and a drow in Icewind Dale.
- "Your Beardy Face," a traditional dwarven love song popular in the Moonsea region.

Secret Door. The Cassalanter family portrait hides a secret door. Tilting the painting causes the door to swing outward on hidden hinges, revealing the pantry (area C11) beyond. A character can notice a slight gap beneath the secret door with a successful DC 18 Wisdom (Perception) check.

C4. Reading Room

This reading nook has the following features:

- Light pours into this room through four tall bay windows that look out on the butterfly garden (area C25).
- Furnishings include a luxurious armchair and a small side table where an empty wine glass sits atop a small book.
- A door in the northern wall has a butterfly-shaped, stained-glass peephole.

If **Victoro Cassalanter** (see appendix B) is here, he's reading a historical text titled *The Rise and Fall of Hellgate Keep* and taking notes in his journal.

Journal. The small book on the side table is a journal that Victoro Cassalanter uses to take notes while reading. It mostly contains dry observations on atlases of Faerûn and history books. A character who flips through the journal and succeeds on a DC 15 Intelligence (Investigation) check can pick out a few notes made by Victoro that are unrelated to his reading:

- "Neverember's dragons are an answer to our prayers."
- "The Cassalanter mausoleum. Inform Y. G." (The initials refer to Lady Yalah Gralhund.)
- "Golorr is an aboleth. Now it all makes sense."

If the characters are still searching for the *Stone of Golorr* in chapter 4, you can include in this journal a clue regarding the stone's location. (If the Cassalanters have the stone, it's hidden in area C6 when it's not in use.)

C5. Foyer

Two **guards** in House Cassalanter livery are stationed in this marble-floored foyer at all hours. It has seven exits:

- A door to the entrance hall (area C1)
- An open arch that leads to a spacious dining room (area C9)
- Three unmarked doors on the east wall (to areas C6, C7, and C8)
- A grand staircase that ascends to the second floor (area C13)
- An unassuming door under the stairs that leads to the cellar (area C26)

Founders' Day. The foyer is filled with lavish bouquets in ceramic floor vases and wealthy guests chatting loudly and drinking sparkling wine, while the gentle music of a string quartet drifts down from upstairs.

C6. Victoro's Office

The door to this room is locked. The room contains the following features:

- Tall stacks of legal tomes and financial ledgers rest atop a solid mahogany desk.
- A freestanding suit of bronze armor (complete with helm, gauntlets, and greatsword) stands just inside the door.

If **Victoro Cassalanter** (see appendix B) is here, he's seated behind the desk with fingers steepled, deep in thought.

Armor. The suit of armor standing by the door is a **helmed horror**. It obeys Victoro's commands. When Victoro isn't present, it attacks anyone who opens the door without a key or anyone not of Cassalanter blood who opens Victoro's desk. The Cassalanter children know about this construct and warn friendly characters about it.

Desk. Victoro's desk is locked and can be opened with Victoro's golden key. A character can pick the lock by succeeding on a DC 18 Dexterity check using thieves' tools. The desk drawer contains thirteen sealed scroll tubes, a signed contract inside each one. These contracts outline the terms of loans made by Victoro to various nobles, merchants, and guilds. The drawer also has a secret compartment that characters can find with a successful DC 18 Wisdom (Perception) check. It holds a holy symbol of Asmodeus crafted from solid gold (worth 250 gp).

Stone of Golorr. If the Cassalanters have the artifact and aren't using it, it is also hidden in the desk's secret compartment.

C7. Cloakroom

This walk-in cloakroom contains the Cassalanter family's expensive coats and cloaks, and it also has room for the garments of up to one hundred guests.

C8. Covered Porch

This covered porch is the entryway typically used by the Cassalanters' servants. Ten servants (human **commoners**) eat here at mealtimes.

C9. Family Dining Room

This room holds the following noteworthy features:

- A dozen chairs surround a beautifully carved dining table in the middle of the room.
- The table is set with golden plates, utensils, goblets, and candlesticks. Silk napkins add to the display.

The Cassalanters dine here as a family, sometimes inviting a guest or two to join them.

Founders' Day. During the party, the dining table is converted into a card table. Ten wealthy nobles are playing a high-stakes game of Three Dragon Ante. A character can play a round by betting 5 gp and making a DC 15 Intelligence check, adding a proficiency bonus if the character is proficient with gaming sets. On a successful check, the character wins 10 gp. On a failed check, the character loses the stake.

Treasure. The gold table settings and candlesticks are worth 2,500 gp in total.

C10. Kitchen

From sunrise until an hour after sundown, this kitchen is a hive of activity:

- A half dozen chefs run to and fro, seasoning meat, mixing batter, and otherwise preparing an impressive variety of food.
- A rotund, red-faced man in a tall white hat barks orders at his underlings, brandishing a sharp knife with every instruction.

Stairs in this room lead to the banquet kitchen on the second floor (area C14).

The head chef, Jandar Chergoba (see "Head Servants," page 116), oversees six chefs (human **commoners**). If Jandar believes the characters are a threat, he shouts "For'zaal," causing ten knives to magically rise from the counters and attack. These knives are **flying swords** that deal 4 (1d6 + 1) piercing damage on a hit.

Founders' Day. Jandar isn't here. Instead, he's preparing Ammalia's poisoned feast in a cooking pavilion out on the estate's sprawling lawn.

C11. Pantry

This room contains the following features:

- Casks of ale, fresh water, and cooking oil are stacked in the middle of the room.
- Shelves of foodstuffs and ingredients line the walls.

- The back wall of the pantry is one large wine rack that contains a variety of splendid bottled wines. (This wine rack conceals a secret door.)

Locked Iron Box. Jandar Chergoba, the head chef, keeps his golden sacrificial dagger, golden mask, and crimson robes (see "Cult of Asmodeus," page 115) in a locked iron box underneath a sack of potatoes. The box can be unlocked with Jandar's golden key, or by a character who makes a successful DC 15 Dexterity check using thieves' tools. A character can also pry it open with a successful DC 25 Strength (Athletics) check.

Secret Door. The secret door to the library (area C3) can be detected by a character who makes a successful DC 18 Wisdom (Perception) check. The character discovers that lifting a bottle of Baldur's Gate pinot noir from the rack unlocks the door and allows it to be pushed open.

C12. Smoking Room

This room contains the following features:

- One **guard** in House Cassalanter livery stands here, absentmindedly examining the regal portraits that adorn the walls and rest on fancy easels in various spots.
- Fine armchairs arranged throughout the room smell faintly of pipeweed; the scent is almost obscured by incense and delicate perfume.

If Lord Cassalanter has invited the characters to his home for any reason, he meets them here. If the conversation turns to business, he has Willifort bring his guests glasses of fine brandy and pipes filled with pipeweed.

Portraits. The portraits on the walls depict several generations of Cassalanters. The ones on the easels, more recently painted, include the following:

- A somber young Victoro with his beaming human father
- A wedding portrait, showing Victoro and Ammalia smiling and carefree
- Twelve-year-old Osvaldo holding a ceremonial rapier
- Ammalia sitting with baby Terenzio and Elzerina in her lap while Victoro reads them a fairy tale

C13. Ballroom

This elegant ballroom contains the following noteworthy features:

- In the center stands an eerie, human-sized wood-and-cloth mannequin with a painted face. It is dressed like a ballroom dancer.
- The polished marble floor is a dazzling mosaic that depicts a silver chalice with the image of a golden sun on its outside. Characters who succeed on a DC 10 Intelligence (Religion) check recognize it as the holy symbol of Siamorphe, demigod of nobility.
- Gilded mirrors and handsome tapestries festoon the walls. Along the west wall, windows with crimson drapes stretch from the floor to the ceiling.

Despite its grandeur, this ballroom seems strangely dismal without anyone dancing in it. Stairs lead down to the foyer (area C5) and up to a hallway outside areas C17 and C19.

Dancing Construct. The dressed "mannequin" is a magical construct that serves as a dance partner. It has the statistics of a **nimblewright** (see appendix B) but has no effective attacks and is worth 0 XP. When a humanoid bows or curtsies before the construct, it makes the other gesture while a *magic mouth* spell plays a recorded message in Common: "Which dance would you like? Galliard? Pavane? Waltz?" The construct follows its partner's lead until the dance ends, when it becomes still again.

Founders' Day. During the party, dozens of wealthy masked guests dance to a lively waltz played by a string quartet.

C14. Banquet Kitchen

The banquet kitchen is an additional cooking space used in conjunction with the main kitchen during social functions. It is otherwise empty, and its doors are locked.

Founders' Day. The kitchen is bustling with activity as four chefs (human **commoners**) prepare an array of pies for the noble guests.

C15. Banquet Hall

The only piece of furniture in this expansive hall is a long wooden dining table that happens to be a giant mimic in disguise. It has the statistics of a normal **mimic**, with these changes:

- The mimic is Large and has 75 (10d10 + 20) hit points.
- As an action, it can make three attacks: two with its pseudopods and one with its bite.
- It has a challenge rating of 3 (700 XP).

The mimic is well treated by the Cassalanters and won't harm any member of the household. It obeys only Lord and Lady Cassalanter.

Founders' Day. The room is outfitted with dozens of chairs, and the table is filled with food. Two dozen party guests are gorging themselves here at any time. Four **doppelgangers** from the Yawning Portal have slipped into the party disguised as nobles. Their leader, Bonnie (see "Familiar Faces," page 20), poses as a minor noblewoman going by the name Lymeria Lhaurilstar; she was hoping to have a fun night at the party, but she's willing to help the characters if they need aid.

C16. Piano Room

A gleaming grand piano is pushed against the wall of this dusty room. Behind it are several unmarked closets.

This room is generally empty unless a social event is taking place or Nana Rosse is giving the Cassalanter children a piano lesson.

Founders' Day. Wealthy guests are chatting here and using the powder rooms (area C16b).

C16a. Storage Closet

This closet holds crates filled with winter blankets, mops, and other household necessities.

C16b. Powder Rooms

These rooms are locked. They contain mirrors and are largely unused except during social functions.

Founders' Day. Fancy nobles are waiting in line to freshen up.

C17. Playroom

This room contains the following features:

- Strewn about on the floor are giant stuffed toys, jack-in-the-boxes, dolls, and a rocking horse shaped like a warhorse.
- A large mobile in the form of a butterfly hangs from the ceiling, turning listlessly.

If she hasn't been dealt with elsewhere, the twins' nanny, Laiba Rosse (see "Head Servants," page 116), sits here and crochets dolls for the children.

C18. Twins' Bedroom

The twins' bedroom contains the following features:

- Two four-poster beds take up the bulk of this room.
- At night, the room is cluttered with dozens of toys. In the morning, the toys are returned to their toy boxes by a housemaid.
- A life-sized stuffed unicorn stands in one corner.

If Terenzio and Elzerina are here, Terenzio is dressed in a crude dragon costume and is being chased around the room by his sister, who is wearing a knight's helm and swinging a wooden sword.

Stuffed Unicorn. This inanimate object counts as an actual unicorn for the purpose of opening the Vault of Dragons (see "Vault Keys," page 90).

C18a–C18b. Closets

These closets are filled with stuffed animals and spare blankets.

C19. Master Sitting Room

Lady Cassalanter's attendant, Tissina Khyret (see "Head Servants," page 116), spends most of her time here when she's not with her mistress. The room is furnished for comfort and includes overstuffed chairs, fainting couches, and a wine bar.

C20. Linen Closet

This closet is packed with folded bedsheets and other assorted linens. Two of the downy duvets stacked in this room are **rugs of smothering** that attack any creature that isn't a Cassalanter or one of their servants. Any combat in this room draws the attention of both Laiba Rosse (area C17) and Tissina Khyret (area C19).

Lockbox. Willifort Crowelle and Tissina Khyret keep their cult regalia (see "Cult of Asmodeus," page 115) in a gold-embellished lockbox hidden under a stack of quilts bearing images of flying devils. The box can be unlocked with either Willifort's or Tissina's golden key, or by a character who succeeds on a DC 14 Dexterity check using thieves' tools. It can also be pried open with a successful DC 16 Strength (Athletics) check.

C21. Master Bedroom

The door to this room is locked. The room contains the following noteworthy features:

- The walls are adorned with nine friezes, each one depicting a layer of the Nine Hells.
- A four-poster bed draped in deep red curtains and tipped with gold spires stands before an ornate door carved from dark hardwood with a gold latch. (This door is locked and leads to area C22.)

A search of the room reveals a golden lockbox tucked under the bed.

Golden Lockbox. Both Victoro and Ammalia keep their cult regalia (see "Cult of Asmodeus," page 115) in a solid gold lockbox (worth 750 gp) hidden under their bed. The box can be unlocked with either Victoro's or Ammalia's golden key, or by a character who makes a successful DC 14 Dexterity check using thieves' tools. It can also be pried open with a successful DC 16 Strength (Athletics) check.

If the box is opened by any means other than a golden key, poison gas sprays out from holes in the underside of the lid, filling a 15-foot-radius sphere centered on the box. This trap can't be disarmed. Any creature in its area must make a DC 13 Constitution saving throw, taking 22 (4d10) poison damage on a failed save, or half as much damage on a successful one. The gas dissipates quickly.

C22. Ammalia's Private Study

The door to this room is locked. The room contains the following features:

- The walls are lined with bookshelves packed with thick tomes.
- A grimoire with a red leather cover sits on a desk carved from dark oak.
- A ladder leads up to a trapdoor in the ceiling.

Bookshelves. The books on the shelves include works of fiction and nonfiction.

Desk. Aside from the grimoire (described below), the desk holds an ornate golden candlestick (worth 125 gp), a golden inkwell (worth 25 gp), and a feathered quill pen (worth 15 gp). The desk drawer contains a wax seal bearing the Cassalanter crest, Ammalia Cassalanter's spellbook (which contains all the spells she has prepared), and ten vials of jet-black poison known as midnight tears (see "Poisons" in chapter 8 of the *Dungeon Master's Guide*). Ammalia plans to taint the Founders' Day feast with the poison (see "Special Events").

Red Grimoire. The tome on the desk, bound in crimson leather, details a diabolical ritual that Ammalia and Victoro enacted to first contact the archdevil Asmodeus. Opening it reveals nothing but blank pages with a few drops of dry blood on them. If a drop of humanoid blood is spilled on any page, Infernal text on that page becomes legible, remaining so until the book is closed. The blood remains even after the text vanishes.

Any character with the Ritual Casting feature (or the Ritual Caster feat) who spends 24 hours reading the book can master the ritual described within. The ritual takes 11 minutes to cast and requires incense and a vial of unholy water (which are consumed during the performance of the ritual). At the end of the ritual, a proxy of Asmodeus appears and grants its summoner the benefit of a *commune* spell. The proxy is formed of incense smoke and resembles a pit fiend. A character must finish a long rest before performing the ritual again.

Trapdoor. The trapdoor in the ceiling is the entrance to the attic.

C23. Attic Landing

A thick scent of sulfur pervades the attic. The only illumination is a beam of light that shines feebly through a shuttered window at the west end of the room.

This attic is soundproof as long as no doors are open. Osvaldo's howling can be heard outside the attic only if the trapdoor between this room and area C22 and the door between this room and area C24 are both open at the same time. Additionally, creatures that have telepathy can't communicate telepathically with creatures outside the attic unless the doors are open.

Terenzio and Elzerina have heard howling coming from the attic two or three times in their lives and are curious about what lurks there.

C24. Osvaldo's Prison

If **Ammalia Cassalanter** or **Victoro Cassalanter** (see appendix B) or both are present, the door to this room

is unlocked but closed. Otherwise, it's locked shut, and Victoro and Ammalia carry the only keys. When the characters first open the door, read:

> You are greeted with a wave of incoherent howling, as if opening the door broke down a dam that had been holding back a madman's screams.

Osvaldo Cassalanter (see appendix B) shrieks and moans at all hours of the day. He is trying desperately to get someone to hear him and come to his rescue. If one or both of his parents are here, he spits curses at them as they weep before him.

Guarding the room are two **imps** in spider form. They answer to Lord Cassalanter, and their job is to kill birds, rats, and other vermin that find their way into the attic. They attack anyone who tries to free Osvaldo or threatens other family members present.

The Cassalanter heir apparent is a soulless abomination thanks to his parents' thoughtless greed. His empty shell of a body has been transformed into a **chain devil** that his parents have imprisoned using his own chains. A 10-foot-diameter pentagram has been burned into the floor around him. A *detect magic* spell reveals a powerful aura of abjuration magic emanating from the symbol.

Osvaldo's chains are wrapped around the beams and timbers that frame the room. He can't damage the house, nor can he break his own chains. He can only howl impotently at the misery being inflicted on him. He is thoroughly insane and can't be reasoned with.

A successful DC 15 Intelligence (Arcana) check reveals that the pentagram prevents Osvaldo from manipulating his chains, and that the effect ends if another creature enters the area encompassed by the pentagram. The magic of the pentagram can also be dispelled (DC 15). If he is freed, Osvaldo regains control of his chains and attacks indiscriminately. If he is reduced to 0 hit points, the chain devil cries out for his mother before melting into a pool of sickening black ichor.

C24a. Attic Storage

This room contains derelict furnishings draped in black linens: chairs, coat racks, freestanding mirrors, dress mannequins, and the like. These draped objects take on a sinister countenance in the gloom but are harmless.

C25. Butterfly Garden

In the spring, Ammalia Cassalanter's gardens attract caterpillars, which transform into butterflies come summer. Lady Cassalanter's butterfly garden is the envy of her peers. The sweet scent of flowers and herbs filters up from the planters and rose bushes.

If Terenzio and Elzerina are here, they are frolicking in the garden. If **Ammalia Cassalanter** (see appendix B) is here, she's watching the children or tending to her garden. Six **imps** in raven form hang around the butterfly garden and occasionally prey on Ammalia's prized pets when their mistress isn't looking. Despite their insolence, Ammalia uses these imps as spies. She sends them on missions throughout the city. They also warn Ammalia of trespassers and attack anyone who threatens a member of her family.

Founders' Day. During the party, two young, hot-blooded nobles have accidentally offended one another. They have changed into dueling garb and are fighting with rapiers to resolve their differences while onlookers drink wine and cheer them on.

C25a. Garden Balcony

This balcony overlooks the grounds of the Cassalanter estate and even offers a view of the Sea of Swords beyond the outer wall of the Sea Ward.

If **Ammalia Cassalanter** (see appendix B) is here, she's smoking and either staring dismally out toward the ocean or watching her children in the garden below (area C25).

C26. Cellar

This cellar is kept free of dust and cobwebs by servants. It is unsettlingly cold, no matter the time of year. It contains spare furniture, a laundry tub, and trunks full of old clothing.

C27. False Vault

The door to this vault is made of solid iron and sports three different locks. Victoro and Ammalia each have a set of keys for them. Opening the door without the keys requires a character to succeed on three consecutive DC 20 Dexterity checks using thieves' tools. On a failed check, all three locks reset. The door has AC 19, a damage threshold of 10, 90 hit points, and immunity to poison and psychic damage. A creature can break it down with a successful DC 27 Strength (Athletics) check.

The vault is empty.

Cold Trap. If a creature enters the vault without first saying "Gold is my shield," an intense blast of magical cold fills the room. All creatures in the vault at that time must make a DC 16 Constitution saving throw, taking 36 (8d8) cold damage on a failed save, or half as much damage on a successful one.

A *detect magic* spell reveals the secret to disabling the trap: a tiny magical glyph is inscribed in the middle of the ceiling. If this glyph is dispelled with a successful casting of *dispel magic* (DC 16), the trap ceases to function.

C28. Wine Cellar

This cellar contains the following features:

- The east wall is lined with nearly thirty casks of wine.
- A faint draft comes from the south end of the wine cellar. The draft betrays the location of a secret door.

The servants rarely spend much time here, since the cellar is unlit and cold. Characters feel a strange sense of foreboding here.

Secret Door. A faded holy symbol of Siamorphe, a silver chalice bearing a golden sun symbol, is painted on the south wall. If the sun symbol is pushed, the wall grinds open, revealing area C29 beyond. A character who searches the wall automatically detects the secret door and can, with a successful DC 10 Wisdom (Perception) check, figure out how to open it.

C29. Secret Vault

Most of the Cassalanters' wealth is tied up in investments, but the family keeps a stack of twenty 5-pound silver trade bars (worth 25 gp each) here for emergencies. At the back of the vault is a dark staircase that descends 30 feet to the temple of Asmodeus (area A1).

Founders' Day. In addition to the treasure noted above, the vault contains five hundred sacks containing 1,000 gp each (liquidated family assets). If the Cassalanters were successful in looting the Vault of Dragons, the vault contains an additional five hundred sacks (the sum total of the treasure taken from the vault), for a total of 1,000,000 gp. The gold remains here until it's taken down to the temple (see "Special Events," page 130).

Temple of Asmodeus

Beneath Cassalanter Villa lies a secret temple where Victoro leads a cult that worships Asmodeus. Cult members include evil-minded nobles as well as deluded commoners lured by the prospect of wealth and status. The entire cult gathers in the temple at midnight on the first day of every tenday for a dark mass. During these ceremonies, they pledge their devotion to the Lord of the Nine Hells, call out the names of their enemies, and beseech Asmodeus to visit ruin upon their foes. They also drink wine, share gossip, and offer the occasional sacrifice. For the Cassalanters, these events are opportunities to flaunt their power and impose their will on their lessers.

JENKS CATCHES SIGHT OF LADY CASSALANTER IN THE SUMMER STREET.

Temple Features

The following general features apply to the temple:

- Rooms are dimly lit by flickering candles placed in tall, slender, wrought-iron candlesticks.
- Ceilings in rooms are 10 feet high unless noted otherwise. Passages are 8 feet tall, with 7-foot-tall doorways.
- Doors are made of iron-banded wood.
- Cultists who aren't members of the nobility wear cheap red robes, devil masks, and wooden amulets that bear the symbol of Asmodeus.

Areas of the Temple

The following areas correspond to the labels on map 6.2. The temple is connected to Cassalanter Villa by a staircase that connects with area A1. Also, an underground stream (area A9) leads away from the temple's lower level and eventually lets out in the Mud Flats northwest of Waterdeep.

Changes to the temple that occur during cult gatherings are noted in the "Cult Gathering" sections.

A1. Hall of the Damned

The features of this hall are readily apparent:

- In the middle of the hall, a spiral staircase descends 20 feet to the lower level (area A3).
- The faint sound of chanting is audible coming from a corridor to the northwest.
- To the south are three cells with iron-banded wooden doors. A small, barred window is embedded in each door at the height of a human's eye. The cell doors face a stone pillar. Hanging from a hook on the pillar is a ring of keys.

Cells. When the Cassalanters decide to sacrifice humans in their rituals, they lure homeless Waterdavians to their estate and confine them in these cells. The keys to unlock the doors hang from the stone pillar. A lock can be picked by a character who makes a successful DC 15 Dexterity check using thieves' tools. All three cells are currently empty.

Chanting. The sound is that of a prayer to Asmodeus being recited by the cultists in area A7.

A2. Balconies

Two crumbling balconies with stone railings overlook the temple's ceremonial hall (area A7). The distance to the floor below is 20 feet.

Collapsing Floor. The balcony floors have weakened with age. Any Medium or larger creature that steps onto a 5-foot-square marked C on the map must make a DC 15 Dexterity saving throw as the floor crumbles and falls away, leaving a gaping hole. On a failed save, the creature falls 20 feet and lands prone on the floor below (area A7) amid stone debris. On a success, the creature avoids the fall by leaping to an adjacent, unoccupied space. The sound of the collapsing floor can be heard throughout the temple.

A3. Anterior Vestibule

The spiral staircase from area A1 ends at this chamber.

Asmodeus Portrait. Mounted on the back wall of an alcove to the north is an 18-foot-high, 9-foot-wide portrait in a gilded frame. The picture depicts a strikingly handsome and impeccably dressed bearded man with small horns protruding from his forehead. He carries a ruby-tipped cane. Any character who succeeds on a DC 10 Intelligence (Religion) check recognizes the figure as Asmodeus.

Cult Gathering. During cult gatherings, a **bearded devil** guards each of the doors leading to area A7.

A4. Family Crypt

Twelve stone sarcophagi are packed into deep recesses in the walls. The plaster lid of each sarcophagus is carved in the likeness of a noble clutching a chalice that bears a symbol of the sun. The sarcophagi contain nothing but dust and bones.

The spirits of several dead members of the Cassalanter family are bound to this crypt. They manifest as three dark, vaporous **specters** plus a **ghost** that looks like the insubstantial image of a handsome, clean-shaven man of knightly bearing clad in plate armor. These undead attack any living creatures but can't leave the crypt or approach within 5 feet of any creature that wears a holy symbol of Asmodeus.

The ghost is all that remains of Caladorn Cassalanter, a former Masked Lord and hero of Waterdeep. The ghost halts its attack and calls off the specters if a character wears or presents a holy symbol of Siamorphe. After it is shown such a symbol, the ghost guides characters to its personal crypt (area A4a).

A4a. Caladorn's Crypt

A dusty stone sarcophagus occupies this crypt, its plaster lid carved in the likeness of a handsome, clean-shaven nobleman clutching a chalice engraved with the symbol of the sun. The likeness resembles the ghost of Caladorn Cassalanter (see above).

Treasure. Caladorn's bones have turned to dust, but his suit of *+1 plate armor* remains. Also lying in the dust is a *mace of disruption*. If Caladorn's ghost is present when one or both magic items are removed from the sarcophagus, it asks, "Do you vow to use these items to defeat the forces of darkness?" An answer in the affirmative is sufficient to lay the ghost to rest. Before vanishing for good, it says, "Use the mace to destroy the effigy of evil incarnate. End the corruption to restore my family's honor." (The "effigy" is the statue of Asmodeus in area A7.)

A4b. Empty Crypt

This crypt contains nothing but dust and cobwebs.

A5. Cultists' Chamber

This room has the following features:

- Six wooden cots stand against the north and south walls.
- The west wall is carved with four bas-reliefs of pit fiends.

Tired cultists sleep here after ceremonies, particularly if they drank too much wine.

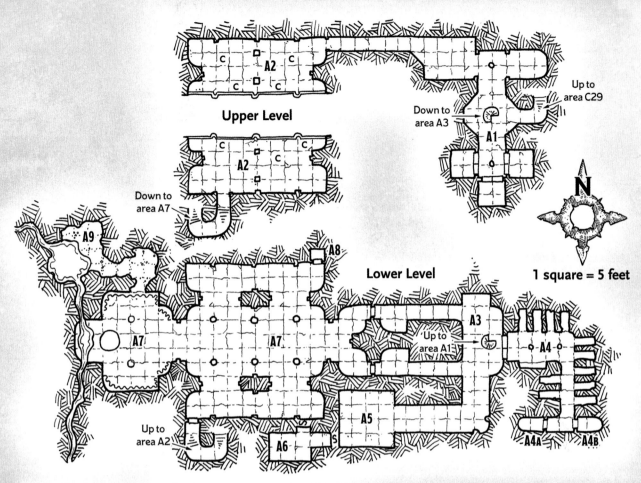

Upper Level

Up to area C29

Down to area A3

A1

A2

Down to area A7

Lower Level

1 square = 5 feet

A9

A8

A7

A7

A3

Up to area A1

A4

Up to area A2

A5

A6

A4A

A4B

MAP 6.2: TEMPLE OF ASMODEUS

Secret Door. Behind one of the bas-reliefs is a secret door, which can be detected with a successful DC 13 Wisdom (Perception) check. Pushing against the sculpture causes a secret door to swing open into area A6.

A6. SECRET VESTRY

This room is hidden behind two secret doors that aren't disguised on the inside, where a stone knob on each door allows it to be pulled open with ease. The room contains the following features:

- Against the south wall stand two black wardrobes with nine-pointed stars carved into their doors.
- A pair of tall, slender mirrors are mounted on the west wall, their stone frames carved with serpents.
- Stacked in the middle of the room are six casks of wine used for cult celebrations.

Each wardrobe contains five complete outfits of cult regalia sized for adult humans: red robes, devil masks, and wooden amulets shaped in the symbol of Asmodeus.

Cult Gathering. An hour before a cult gathering, five human **cultists** are here donning their regalia.

A7. CEREMONIAL HALL

This hall has a 30-foot-high vaulted ceiling and a pair of 20-foot-high balconies (see area A2) overlooking it. Its other features as follows:

- Rows of flickering candles in iron candlesticks form a pathway to a 30-foot-tall stone statue at the west end

of the hall. The statue depicts a smiling, bearded man of diabolical bent, with small horns protruding from his brow and cloven hooves instead of feet. At the base of the statue, clutched in a stone claw erupting from the floor, is a 3-foot-deep, 9-foot-diameter stone bowl filled with crackling flames.

- Three human **cultists** wearing red robes, devil masks, and wooden holy symbols of Asmodeus kneel before the statue, feverishly chanting an infernal hymn. (During a cult gathering, the number of cultists present increases dramatically.)
- The walls around the statue are covered by large tapestries that depict scenes of human debauchery. (Behind the north tapestry is a rough-hewn passage that leads to area A9.)

The Cassalanters' ritual to save Terenzio and Elzerina plays out here (see "Special Events," page 130).

Cult Gathering. If the cult is here in force, thirty human **cultists** stand in neat rows before the statue, chanting to Asmodeus with wooden goblets in hand while their leader, **Victoro Cassalanter** (see appendix B), tosses offerings into the bowl. Roughly half of the cultists are members of the nobility; the rest are Waterdavian rabble brought into the cult to fill out the ranks. Standing around the perimeter are Willifort Crowelle, Tissina Khyret, Laiba Rosse, and Jandar Chergoba (see "Head Servants," page 116). Their job is to make sure the other cultists behave themselves while **Ammalia**

Cassalanter (see appendix B) walks gracefully through the crowd with a golden decanter, ceremonially pouring wine into the cultists' goblets for toasting to the Lord of the Nine Hells. Lady Cassalanter's six **imps** (see area C25) are perched invisibly on the statue.

Devil Statue and Sacrificial Bowl. The statue once depicted Siamorphe, but the Cassalanters used *stone shape* spells to recast it into an image of their dread lord, Asmodeus. The massive bowl at the foot of the statue was also fashioned with *stone shape* spells; it radiates a strong aura of conjuration magic when subjected to a *detect magic* spell or similar magic. Magical flames erupt from the bowl as long as it remains intact. Any creature that enters the flames or starts its turn in them takes 4d10 fire damage. A creature reduced to 0 hit points by this damage turns to ashes. Nonmagical objects tossed into the flames are destroyed.

If the statue is struck by a *mace of disruption*, it cracks and falls to pieces, shattering the bowl as it tumbles down. Any member of the cult who witnesses the destruction of the statue takes 11 (2d10) psychic damage.

Secret Door. The secret door leading to area A6 can be found with a successful DC 13 Wisdom (Perception) check. Pushing on that section of wall causes it to swing open.

Stream. Flowing behind the statue is a stream that enters and exits through 1-foot-high, 2-foot-wide arched culverts.

A8. Storage Closet

Against the back wall of this closet stands an unlocked cabinet with a black rug laid out before it. The cabinet contains a golden decanter (worth 125 gp) and shelves holding wooden wine goblets.

Cult Gathering. The cabinet is empty, as the decanter and goblets are being put to use in area A7.

A9. Stream and Pool

An underground stream flows through the west side of the temple and into a 5-foot-deep pool here before meandering northwest and emerging in the Mud Flats.

Special Events

If the Cassalanters fail to obtain the *Stone of Golorr*, the following events don't come to pass. As a consequence, Terenzio and Elzerina are transformed into **lemures** as their souls are forfeit ten days after Founders' Day. Shattered by their failure and their loss, Victoro and Ammalia Cassalanter vow to destroy those who thwarted them.

Getting the Gold

This event can occur only on Founders' Day or sooner.

Armed with the *Stone of Golorr* and the keys to unlock the Vault of Dragons, Victoro Cassalanter enters the vault, uses a *disguise self* spell to appear as Lord Dagult Neverember, and tricks Aurinax the gold dragon into relinquishing the gold. A dozen House Cassalanter **guards** disguised as members of the City Guard stuff the gold into sacks while a dozen more haul the sacks

to a pair of waiting carriages for safe transport back to Cassalanter Villa. Each sack holds 1,000 gp, and each carriage can hold fifty sacks (50,000 gp) at a time. Getting the gold from the Vault of Dragons to Cassalanter Villa takes ten round trips (five per carriage) and the better part of a day. Three invisible **imps** accompany each carriage, which is driven by a **bearded devil** wearing a hat and a high-collared cape to conceal its true nature. Upon arrival at Cassalanter Villa, each carriage is met by a dozen **guards** in House Cassalanter livery, who unload the sacks of gold and place them in area C29.

Day of the Damned

This event occurs only if the Cassalanters obtain the gold from the Vault of Dragons.

Ammalia Cassalanter hosts a grand party on Founders' Day that begins in the early afternoon and ends at midnight. Wealthy guests begin to arrive in the late afternoon and gather inside the villa, away from the sun and heat, while one hundred of Waterdeep's poorest residents—most brought from the Field Ward—gather under pavilions set up on the lawn. Hired actors dressed as Waterdeep's founders parade around, and bards play lively tunes. No one suspects that the food in the pavilion tents has been laced with midnight tears—a poison that will slay the impoverished guests at the stroke of midnight. Ammalia is immune to poison and thus partakes freely of the delicious food. Wealthy guests who remain holed up in Cassalanter Villa eat and drink at separate tables and are spared a grisly end.

An hour before midnight, the entertainers disperse as Ammalia begins making toasts to her wealthy guests, turning them into unwitting accomplices by virtue of their presence and thus ensuring their silence. Meanwhile, house guards prevent any of the rabble from leaving, forcibly detaining anyone who tries to flee. Unless the characters prevent the poor folk from eating the tainted food, those attendees consume the poison and perish at the stroke of midnight.

While Ammalia plays host, Victoro instructs his cultists to remove the sacks of gold from House Cassalanter's vault (area C29) and hurl them into the sacrificial bowl (area A7). They finish shortly before midnight. At the stroke of midnight, as the poison does its work, Ammalia keeps an eye on her wealthy guests and orders Tessina Khyret to notify Victoro that the deed is done. Standing before the statue of Asmodeus in the temple, Victoro summons a **barbed devil** and informs it that payment has been made in full. The devil declares (in Infernal) that the payment is "satisfactory" and informs Victoro that the souls of Terenzio and Elzerina will not be taken to the Nine Hells. It then disappears whence it came, leaving the Cassalanters to bask in their triumph.

After the party, in the dark hours of morning, the corpses of the dead are cast into the fiery bowl in area A7, leaving no evidence of foul play. In the days and months that follow, Victoro and Ammalia use threats of diabolical retribution to silence witnesses and wield their political clout to quash criminal investigations.

CHAPTER 7: MAESTRO'S FALL

ARLAXLE, THE LEADER OF BREGAN D'AERTHE, sees membership in the Lords' Alliance as his path to power beyond Luskan. As the secret lord of a city with an unsavory reputation, he has had a hard time getting a seat at the table with other cities of the North when it comes to trade and defense of the region. Thus, he plans to use the stolen gold to bargain with Laeral Silverhand for inclusion in the alliance, and to oust Neverwinter and its lord Dagult Neverember—Jarlaxle's fiercest political opponent—from the group.

FACING JARLAXLE

As the characters investigate the Sea Maidens Faire, they could run into Jarlaxle, especially if they take a kick-in-the-door approach and storm the vessels of the traveling carnival. When Jarlaxle learns that the characters are aboard one of his ships, he arranges to meet with them in the guise of Zardoz Zord. If they refuse, Jarlaxle orders his crew to cast the characters overboard—or takes care of the job himself if he must.

If he thinks the adventurers can be trusted, Jarlaxle proposes that they join his search for the Vault of Dragons. He intends to return the gold to Laeral Silverhand, less 5,000 gp for the characters in exchange for their help. He offers another 5,000 gp for their help in recovering the *dragonstaff of Ahghairon*. If the characters accept, Jarlaxle upholds his end of the agreement. Once the gold is secure, he gives the characters their cut.

If the characters don't agree to Jarlaxle's terms, or if they assault him, he tries to knock them unconscious and leave them without clothes or equipment in a gutter in the Dock Ward. He stores their equipment in area J16 aboard the *Eyecatcher*, with the exception of any magic items. Those he stashes in area U4 aboard the *Scarlet Marpenoth*, his secret submarine.

In the unlikely event that Jarlaxle is killed, Bregan D'aerthe raises him from the dead within a tenday. Once he's back in action, he tries to recover any gear that was stolen from him.

DISRUPTING JARLAXLE'S OPERATION

Characters can hinder Jarlaxle in the ways described in the following two subsections.

DESTROY THE FIGUREHEADS

The figureheads on Jarlaxle's ships (area J8) create illusions around drow crew members, making them appear human. If a figurehead is destroyed, the drow on that ship remain belowdecks to ensure that they don't draw unwanted attention.

SINK OR STEAL A VESSEL

If the characters sink or steal one of his sailing ships or the *Scarlet Marpenoth*, Jarlaxle tasks his crew members with finding out what went wrong. In the case of a sunken ship, such wanton destruction could also involve the City Watch, especially if the act results in people drowning.

Sea Maidens Faire

Jarlaxle Baenre's seafaring carnival travels up and down the Sword Coast in three ships. The *Eyecatcher*, Jarlaxle's flagship, is ostentatious. Mounted underneath it is the *Scarlet Marpenoth*, a submarine of Lantanese design. The second ship, the *Heartbreaker*, is primarily used to transport performers, strange creatures, and wagons. The third ship, the *Hellraiser*, transports musicians and decorative floats. The *Heartbreaker* and the *Hellraiser* are presently docked, while the *Eyecatcher* is anchored in the harbor.

All three ships are crewed by drow who are magically disguised to appear human. Despite their disguises, the drow still have the Sunlight Sensitivity trait.

Approaching the Ships

The *Heartbreaker* and the *Hellraiser* are docked across from each other at the same pier in the Dock Ward. The characters need only walk up a ramp from the pier to area J1 on either ship. The pier is so busy that no one takes notice of the characters until they are on a vessel.

Jarlaxle's flagship is anchored in Deepwater Harbor, a mile away from his other ships. To reach the *Eyecatcher*, the characters must travel there by using another vessel, by swimming, or by flying. If the characters approach in a vessel known to the crew, such as a rowboat from another of Jarlaxle's ships, the characters arouse no suspicion until they are seen on deck. The crew of the *Eyecatcher* crew sends word to Jarlaxle immediately if the characters approach in an unknown vessel.

If the characters approach the *Eyecatcher* in an underwater vehicle, such as Grinda Garloth's *apparatus of Kwalish* (see chapter 4), the character piloting must succeed on a DC 12 Dexterity (Stealth) check to keep the vehicle from being spotted by the crew of the *Scarlet Marpenoth*. If the characters approach by swimming, each of them must succeed on a DC 10 Dexterity (Stealth) check to avoid being spotted by the crew of the *Eyecatcher*.

Crews

The characters can learn valuable information by interrogating crew members and carnival performers.

Ship Captains

Although Zardoz Zord (Jarlaxle Baenre) commands the fleet, each ship has its own captain: a Bregan D'aerthe **drow mage** disguised as a slender, well-dressed human. These captains know of Jarlaxle's plans. They communicate with each other and with Jarlaxle by way of *sending* spells, which they prepare instead of *fly*.

Velgos Ephezzrin captains the *Hellraiser* in the guise of a human named Fergus Crabwater. He enjoys wine a little too much, and characters have advantage on Charisma checks made to interact with him during a meal.

Tylan Ilueph captains the *Heartbreaker* as a human named Klarr Besham. He's a humorless taskmaster whose tarantula familiar is always on his shoulder.

Llorath Pharn captains the *Eyecatcher* as a human named Tarwind Arryhook. He loves games of chance and can't resist a good wager.

A successful DC 15 Charisma (Deception or Persuasion) check and the mention of Zardoz Zord's name is enough to gain an audience with a ship captain. If the characters capture one of the captains and succeed on a DC 15 Charisma (Intimidation) check, they learn the following information by asking the right questions:

- "The Sea Maidens Faire and all its ships are under the command of Captain Zardoz Zord of Luskan." (A ship captain won't divulge Zord's true identity unless magically compelled to do so.)
- "Zord has a cabin aboard the *Eyecatcher* and spends a lot of time there with Margo Verida and Khafeyta Murzan, two of the Faire's star performers."
- "A year ago, the Sea Maidens Faire visited the island nation of Lantan, where Zord acquired a submarine called the *Scarlet Marpenoth*. The submarine is mounted underneath the *Eyecatcher*."
- "Zord has operatives searching for an artifact called the *Stone of Golorr*, which leads to a place called the Vault of Dragons." (For security, the captains aren't kept informed as to the mission's progress.)
- "Zord has drow spies in Waterdeep—Fel'rekt Lafeen, Krebbyg Masq'il'yr, and Soluun Xibrindas. All carry Lantanese firearms."
- "Our disguises are powered by a magical figurehead fixed to the fore of each ship."

Sailors

The *Eyecatcher*, the *Heartbreaker*, and the *Hellraiser* are crewed by twenty sailors each: three **drow elite warriors** (mates) and seventeen **drow**, all magically disguised as slender humans while aboard their vessel. All are loyal members of Bregan D'aerthe, and all know that Zardoz Zord is Jarlaxle Baenre in disguise. They know nothing about the *Scarlet Marpenoth* or Jarlaxle's plans.

The crew has orders not to fraternize with strangers or guests. Characters who question crew members can learn the following:

- "Zardoz Zord is master of the Sea Maidens Faire. If you want to meet him, talk to a ship captain." (A sailor won't divulge Zord's true identity unless magically compelled to do so.)
- "The Sea Maidens Faire is based out of Luskan."

Carnies

Most of the carnival performers and workers are human **commoners** trained to perform a handful of tasks or stunts. (Performers have proficiency in the Performance skill.) They're kept in the dark about most things, but they're not oblivious. With a successful DC 10 Charisma check, a character can cajole or trick a carny into revealing one of the following pieces of information:

- "Zardoz Zord uses magic to get from the *Eyecatcher* to the other boats. I've never seen him in a rowboat."
- "The sailors communicate with each other using odd hand signals." (Members of Bregan D'aerthe use Drow Sign Language.)
- "All the sailors have an aversion to sunlight."
- "Have you noticed the sailors have the slightest hint of an Elvish accent?"
- "All the crew members are men. Very odd."

DISCOVERING THE DROW

Any character who spends 1 hour observing a ship's crew can make a DC 15 Wisdom (Perception) check. With a successful check, the character notices that most crew members speak Common with an Elvish accent and exchange hand signals when they think no one is looking. A drow character recognizes the hand signals as Drow Sign Language.

The changes wrought by the magic of the ships' figureheads (see area J8) fail to hold up to physical inspection, meaning that characters who interact with crew members have a chance to notice the illusion. For example, a character who grabs one of the sailors by the ear would quickly realize by touch that the ear is pointed, not rounded as it appears. Additionally, any drow character who boards one of these ships instantly takes on the illusory form of a human of the same gender, height, and weight, because of the magic of the ship's figurehead.

SHIP FEATURES

Each ship has the statistics of a sailing ship (see the Airborne and Waterborne Vehicles table in chapter 5 of the *Dungeon Master's Guide*) as well as the features described in the following subsections.

ALARMS

If intruders are detected or a fight breaks out on one of the ships, the entire crew (one **drow mage** captain, three **drow elite warriors**, and seventeen **drow**) mo-

bilizes to combat the threat. The drow prefer to take captives or render enemies unconscious rather than kill them. Captives are thrown in the brig (area J15) until Jarlaxle decides what to do with them, and their gear is stowed in the armory (area J16).

CEILINGS

Cabins, holds, and passageways have 8-foot-high ceilings with 6-foot-high doorways connecting them.

DOORS

Unless otherwise noted, doors are made of wood. A door's lock can be picked by a character who makes a successful DC 15 Dexterity check using thieves' tools, or a door can be forced open by a character who makes a successful DC 15 Strength (Athletics) check. A ship's captain has keys to all locked doors aboard his vessel.

ELEVATOR PLATFORMS

Each ship is equipped with an elevator platform that can be lowered and raised with a lever to make loading and unloading cargo easier. When not in use, this platform stays in the lowest cargo hold of each ship. See the descriptions of the cargo holds for more information.

LIGHTING

Areas belowdecks are brightly lit by hanging lanterns.

RIGGING

Rigging can be climbed without an ability check.

Areas of the Ships

The *Eyecatcher*, the *Heartbreaker*, and the *Hellraiser* have the same general configuration and occupants, corresponding to map 7.1. Exceptions are noted in an area's description and on the map.

J1. Main Deck

Three sailors (**drow**) and a mate (**drow elite warrior**) are on deck at all times. If the characters board the ship and ask to speak with the captain, the mate asks their business before even thinking about disturbing him.

Jolly Boats. Four rowboats are stacked on top of each other on this deck. Ropes and pulleys are used to hoist these boats in and out of the water.

J2. Storage

The smell of tar permeates this cluttered cabin, which contains the following features:

- Barrels of tar are secured with nets to the starboard wall below mounted tools.
- Against the port wall, tight rolls of white canvas are stacked on top of each other and secured with rope.

J3. Mates' Cabin

This cabin has the following features:

- Twin hammocks hang perpendicular to one another. Two off-duty mates (**drow elite warriors**) relax in the hammocks.
- Three walnut chests sit under the hammocks. The chests are unlocked.

Treasure. Each chest holds two sets of common clothes, a waterskin filled with wine, and a pouch containing 3d6 gp and 4d10 sp.

J4. Crew Cabins

Each of these cabins holds four hammocks. One off-duty sailor (**drow**) rests in each cabin.

J5. Galley

Heat and savory scents burst from this cramped cabin, which contains the following features:

- A busy cook (**commoner**) works a frying pan with one hand and stirs a pot with the other over a small stove.
- Dirty dishes are stacked in a washbasin.
- A table holds foods in various states of preparation.

The cook is too busy to speak with characters, and is quick to holler in alarm if attacked, drawing the attention of the crew.

J6. Pantry

Secured to the walls are racks of cooking ingredients, including jars of spices, sacks of flour, and casks of lard.

J7. Dining Cabin

The crew dines here throughout the day. At any given time, the cabin contains the following:

- Six sailors (**drow**) are enjoying a meal.
- Aboard the *Heartbreaker* or the *Hellraiser*, the sailors are joined by 1d4 carnies (**commoners**).
- Furnishings include a table, ten stools, and two oak cabinets containing dishes, tankards, and utensils.

J8. Forecastle

The forecastle is within sight of the sailors on the main deck (area J1), the aft castle lower deck (area J9), and the aft castle upper deck (area J11).

Figurehead. A gilded wooden figurehead of a female elf with flowing hair sticks out from the ship's prow, reaching forth with both hands. Since the figurehead is unpainted, there's no way to tell that it depicts a drow, but a character who inspects the figurehead closely and succeeds on a DC 13 Wisdom (Perception) check notices a tiny embossed spider on its forehead.

A *detect magic* spell or similar magic reveals an aura of illusion magic around the figurehead—the effect that makes every drow aboard the ship appear as a human. A drow's gender, height, and weight are unchanged; the illusion affects only appearance, not voice or mannerisms. Casting *dispel magic* on a disguised drow causes the illusion around it to wink out only for a moment. An *antimagic field* suppresses the figurehead's magic within the field's area. Destroying the figurehead ends the effect throughout the ship. A figurehead has AC 15, 50 hit points, and immunity to poison and psychic damage.

J9. Aft Castle Lower Deck

This deck has the following features:

- Two sailors (**drow**) are here at all times.
- Stairs to port and starboard climb to the aft castle upper deck (area J11) and the captain's wheel.

Anchor. The ship's anchor is accessed from this deck. It can be raised or lowered by one creature in 10 rounds (1 minute), by two creatures in 5 rounds, by three creatures in 3 rounds, or by four creatures in 1 round.

J10. Captain's Cabin

Regardless of which ship the characters are on, this opulent cabin contains the following features:

- Stylish purple drapes cover the large windows that look out over the harbor.
- To one side of a central pillar rests a comfortable bed, its oak headboard carved to resemble a kraken. An oak dining table surrounded by six high-backed chairs rests on the opposite side of the central pillar.
- Other furnishings include a glass-doored cabinet containing shelves of books, a wooden trunk sealed with a padlock, and a small writing desk.

Captain. Each ship's captain (**drow mage**) can usually be found here, with a **nimblewright** (see appendix B) acting as an attendant and bodyguard.

A captain is happy to meet with characters who ask to speak with him, mostly to gauge whether they pose a threat. If the characters are polite, the captain invites them to join him for a meal. If the characters grow tiresome or threatening, he commands them to leave the ship at once, sounding an alarm if they refuse.

Fastened to each captain's belt is a ring holding a number of keys. One key unlocks the trunk in this cabin; other keys unlock any locked doors on the captain's ship.

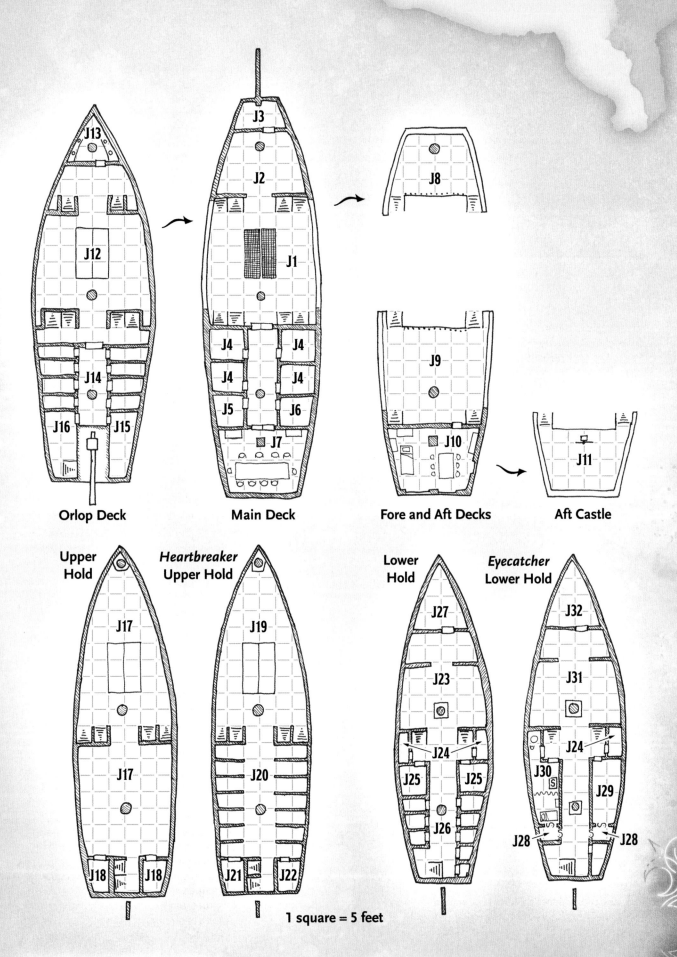

Orlop Deck

Main Deck

Fore and Aft Decks

Aft Castle

Upper Hold

Heartbreaker Upper Hold

Lower Hold

Eyecatcher Lower Hold

1 square = 5 feet

Book Cabinet. Each captain keeps a modest collection of mundane books. Each hides his spellbook in a secret space under the bottom shelf, which can be found with a successful DC 14 Wisdom (Perception) check. The spellbook contains the following spells: *cone of cold, control water, counterspell, detect magic, fireball, fly, greater invisibility, ice storm, mage armor, magic missile, misty step, Rary's telepathic bond, sending, shield, suggestion, thunderwave, water breathing,* and *web.*

Locked Trunk. A successful DC 20 Dexterity check by a character using thieves' tools opens the padlock, or it can be broken off with a successful DC 20 Strength (Athletics) check. The trunk contains folded clothes, 250 gp in a sack, 1d6 pearls (worth 100 gp each) in a silk pouch, a *potion of water breathing,* and a bottle of excellent wine (worth 25 gp), bearing a label in the shape of an eye patch and the name "One-Eyed Jax" in Common.

J11. Aft Castle Upper Deck

This highest deck of the ship is within sight of the forecastle (area J8), the main deck (area J1), and the aft castle lower deck (area J9). It has the following features:

- The ship's wheel stands atop the deck.
- Two sailors (**drow**) are stationed here at all times.

Wheel. If the ship is sailing with a full crew, a character who has proficiency with water vehicles can stand at the wheel and steer the vessel.

J12. Upper Cargo Hold

This hold contains the following features:

- Large grilled doors in the ceiling open to allow goods to be moved to and from this hold using the cargo elevator. A 15-foot-by-10-foot section of floor opens to reveal the lower cargo hold (area J17 aboard the *Eyecatcher* or the *Hellraiser*; area J19 aboard the *Heartbreaker*).
- Crates and barrels stacked to the ceiling are tied down to ensure that they don't move. These containers hold food and water for the crew and the carnies.

Cargo Elevator. To activate an elevator platform, a creature must stand on the platform and use an action to pull a lever up or down. The platform can't be raised higher than the main deck (area J1) or lowered deeper than a ship's lowest cargo hold.

The trapdoor in the floor opens when the cargo elevator is raised. If the platform is raised to area J1, the trapdoor remains open until the elevator platform returns to this area or area J17 (J19 on the *Heartbreaker*).

J13. Head

The reek of urine fills the cramped head. Privies—each little more than a bench seat with a hole open to the water below—are this room's only features.

J14. Carnies' Cabins

Eight narrow cabins are fitted with hammocks, each of which holds a resting carnival performer or worker (**commoner**). Carnies call for help when they are confronted by intruders and fight only in self-defense.

J15. Brig

A door made of crisscrossing iron bars and fitted with a sturdy lock seals off this cabin, whose only feature is a chamber pot. The captain carries the key to the door. The lock can be picked by a character who makes a successful DC 17 Dexterity check using thieves' tools (made with disadvantage from inside the cell). A successful DC 23 Strength (Athletics) check forces the door open. The door has AC 19, a damage threshold of 10, 27 hit points, and immunity to poison and psychic damage.

Jailed Sailor. There's a 25 percent chance that a sailor (**drow**) is being held in the brig after punching a crewmate during an argument.

J16. Armory

The drow store their weapons and armor here while the ship is at sea. If the characters are captured and stripped of their equipment, their nonmagical belongings are stowed here. The cabin has the following features:

- Empty weapon racks and armor hooks line the walls.
- Stairs lead down into the ship's belly.

Safe (Eyecatcher Only). The armory aboard the *Eyecatcher* also features a 750-pound cast iron safe with a combination lock. Jarlaxle and his lieutenants (Fel'rekt Lafeen, Krebbyg Masq'il'yr, and Soluun Xibrindas) know the combination: 1–20–59. A character can pick the lock with a successful DC 25 Dexterity (Investigation) check using thieves' tools. Each attempt takes 1 minute. A *knock* spell or similar magic also opens the safe, which contains three pistols, twelve leather packets of *smokepowder,* three leather pouches containing twenty bullets each, and 250 gp in a sack.

Stairs. The stairs lead to area J17 on the *Eyecatcher* or the *Hellraiser,* or to area J20 on the *Heartbreaker.*

J17. Lower Cargo Hold
Eyecatcher and Hellraiser only

The fantastical floats of the Sea Maidens Faire are broken down and kept in the lower cargo hold of the *Hellraiser,* while the *Eyecatcher* holds pieces of broken and experimental floats. (See area J19 for a description of the *Heartbreaker*'s lower cargo hold.)

Cargo Elevator. If the cargo elevator platform is lowered to this area while creatures are in the 15-foot-by-10-foot space where the platform lands, each of those creatures must succeed on a DC 10 Dexterity saving throw or take 11 (2d10) bludgeoning damage and be knocked prone and restrained until the platform is raised. A creature that succeeds on its saving throw moves to a space of its choice next to the elevator platform without provoking opportunity attacks.

Hellraiser's Hold. The hold of the *Hellraiser* is mostly cleared out on days when parades are scheduled, except for empty storage trunks. On other days, it contains the following paraphernalia:

- Various trunks filled with musician, dancer, acrobat, and clown costumes
- Casks holding confetti, glitter, and body paint
- Bundles of wooden stilts (4 and 8 feet high)
- Papier-mâché beholders mounted atop 10-foot poles

- A float topped by a life-size mechanical unicorn ridden by a mechanical drow ranger waving two scimitars (when a lever under the float is pulled, the unicorn farts a 15-foot cone of confetti, which it can do twice before needing to be refilled)
- A float topped with two mechanical goblins that repeatedly punch each other when wound up
- A float bearing a mechanical armored knight battling a mechanical pit fiend (when wound up, the knight cleaves with its sword while the devil flaps its wings)
- Deflated black, blue, green, red, and white dragon balloons (they float magically when filled with air, and their size is Huge while inflated)
- An enormous tarrasque puppet for five puppeteers
- Wagon covers decorated with tassels and painted with colorful patterns and creatures
- Horse and ox harnesses, all brightly decorated

Eyecatcher's Hold. The aft section of the hold of the *Eyecatcher* is guarded by four **giant spiders** painted in bright colors. These arachnids have been trained by Jarlaxle since they were hatchlings, and they can pass themselves off as inanimate float decorations by remaining perfectly still until they attack. They aren't hostile toward drow, whose true nature they sense despite the ship's illusion magic. Characters who have a passive Wisdom (Perception) score of 17 or higher realize that the spiders are a threat before the creatures attack.

All sorts of damaged and unfinished attractions are stored here, including the following:

- A number of broken clockwork monsters
- Half-completed or broken wagon covers and puppets
- A deflated balloon of an oversized flumph that has a small gash in it (a *mending* cantrip can repair the damage)
- An undecorated float, topped with an unpainted mechanical gold dragon made of canvas stretched over a wooden frame

Rigged with a glass canister of flammable gas, the mechanical gold dragon is designed to breathe fire when a lever is pulled. Pulling the lever cracks the canister and sets the dragon on fire. If the fire breaks out here and isn't extinguished promptly, it spreads to other parts of the hold after 1 minute. Crew members in other parts of the ship detect smoke 5 minutes later, by which time the hold is a raging inferno. Crew members will focus on saving the submarine (if it's still attached) before abandoning ship.

J18. Craft Supplies
Eyecatcher and Hellraiser only

Each of these cabins contains materials used to decorate floats:

- Glitter, feathers, fabric, paper, scissors, sewing needles, spools of colored thread, and flasks of glue are strewn over small tables.
- Schematics for parade floats are tacked to the walls alongside various tools.

J19. Lower Cargo Hold
Heartbreaker only

Beastly odors fill the hold of the *Heartbreaker*, becoming stronger as the characters get closer to the creature pens (area J20). The hold is mostly empty on parade days. On other days, it contains disassembled wagons (axles, wheels, and cages) that are used to pull exotic creatures through crowded streets. Tools needed to assemble and repair the wagons hang from hooks on the walls.

Cargo Elevator. If the cargo elevator platform is lowered to this area while creatures are in the 15-foot-by-10-foot space where the platform lands, each of those creatures must succeed on a DC 10 Dexterity saving throw or take 11 (2d10) bludgeoning damage and be knocked prone and restrained until the platform is raised. A creature that succeeds on its saving throw moves to a space of its choice next to the elevator platform without provoking opportunity attacks.

J20. Creature Pens
Heartbreaker only

This section of the hold reeks of animal musk and waste. When they're not being paraded through city streets in cage-wagons, the monstrous attractions of the Sea Maidens Faire growl, chortle, stamp, snort, and roar in closed stalls. Two handlers (**commoners** with proficiency in Animal Handling) walk from stall to stall, carrying buckets of food and speaking softly to the creatures.

Each pen is effectively a cell equipped with a sliding door that can be double-latched from the outside. A wagon assembled in area J19 can be backed up to any pen. With the pen door open, a successful DC 15 Wisdom (Animal Handling) check then coaxes a caged creature into the back of a wagon. This check is made with advantage if food is given to the creature. If this check fails by 5 or more, the creature escapes, panics, and begins attacking indiscriminately as it tries to win its freedom. Any such ruckus alerts the animal handlers or other crew members if they are nearby.

The following creatures are kept in the twelve pens:

Two **apes**	Four **giant fire beetles**
One **rhinoceros**	One **hippogriff**
One **tiger**	One **axe beak**
One **allosaurus**	Two **death dogs**
Two **panthers**	One **giant vulture**
One **owlbear**	One **polar bear**

The death dogs and the giant vulture are evil, and the giant vulture can understand Common (though it can't speak). They seize any chance to escape and revel in the suffering of other creatures.

J21. Handlers' Cabin
Heartbreaker only

This cabin contains hammocks for the two handlers who work in area J20. If the creatures have been taken on parade, the handlers are asleep in their hammocks.

NAT, JENKS, AND SQUIDDLY ENJOY A WINDY AUTUMN DAY ON THE DOCKS.

J22. Beast Supplies
Heartbreaker only

Supplies and food for the creatures in area J20 are stored here:

- Haunches of meat hanging from the ceiling give this cabin a sickly sweet scent.
- Shovels, ropes, chains, buckets, bales of hay, and several large crates are pushed against the walls.

The crates hold a variety of lichens, mosses, and fungi that are fed to the herbivorous creatures. A successful DC 20 Intelligence (Nature) check identifies the vegetation as native to the Underdark, and the haunches of animal meat as deep rothé—an ox-like creature raised for its meat by drow in the Underdark.

J23. Gunslingers' Hold
Heartbreaker and Hellraiser only

No one is allowed down here without the captain's permission, and the guards have orders to kill trespassers on sight. This area contains the following features:

- Two **drow gunslingers** (see appendix B) stand guard outside area J27.
- The hold is filled with barrels containing ale and fresh water. The barrels are held down by cargo nets hooked to the floor.

Drow Gunslingers. The drow take cover behind the walls that divide this area as they shoot. They fight to the death to keep intruders from reaching area J27.

J24. Cleaning Supplies

These closets hold mops, brushes, buckets, and soap used for scrubbing the decks.

J25. Gunslingers' Cabins
Heartbreaker and Hellraiser only

These two cabins are the quarters of the drow gunslingers in area J23. Each contains the following features:

- A hammock hangs on the wall opposite the door.
- A wooden mannequin and a walnut chest rest against the wall by the door.

The mannequins double as armor racks, though no armor currently adorns them.

Treasure. Each chest holds two sets of common clothes, a water skin filled with wine, and a pouch containing 3d6 gp and 4d10 sp.

J26. Lockers
Heartbreaker and Hellraiser only

Lining this hall are eight closets used as storage lockers by the workers and performers of the Sea Maidens Faire. They contain traveling clothes and outerwear hanging on hooks, as well as boots and shoes.

J27. Smokepowder Storage
Heartbreaker and Hellraiser only

The locked door to this forward cabin has a wooden sign nailed to the outside that reads, in Common and Elvish, "RESTRICTED AREA. DO NOT ENTER." The room contains the following features:

- Twenty wooden kegs are secured to the walls with ropes. Each keg has a paper label, written on which are the words "SMOKEPOWDER! EXPLOSIVE!" in Common and Elvish.
- A shelf above the kegs is lined with wooden boxes.

Boxes. Ten wooden boxes on the shelf each contain one hundred pistol bullets.

Kegs. Each keg holds five pounds of *smokepowder* (see appendix A). When one keg explodes, all other kegs within the area of effect explode as well. If half the kegs explode at once, the blast blows a hole in the forward hull large enough to sink the ship. If all twenty kegs explode at once, the blast blows half the ship to smithereens, shatters windows throughout the Dock Ward, and can be heard as far away as the Field Ward.

J28. Walk-in Closets
Eyecatcher only

The doors to these closets are locked from the outside.

Port Closet. This closet abuts Jarlaxle's cabin (area J30) and contains tailored outfits and cloaks for every season and occasion, as well as towels. Against the back wall stands a wooden mannequin wearing an eye patch. A secret door along one wall can be detected with a successful DC 15 Wisdom (Perception) check.

Starboard Closet. This closet abuts the guest cabin (area J29) and contains a half-dozen gowns and two soft fur cloaks on hangers, ladies' hats on hooks, and fancy towels and shoes on shelves. A secret door along one wall can be detected with a successful DC 15 Wisdom (Perception) check.

J29. Guest Cabin
Eyecatcher only

This richly appointed cabin is set aside for special guests. It contains a large bed, a wooden chest, a freestanding mirror, and a dresser with a lyre atop it. Empty wine bottles roll back and forth across the floor as the ship moves. The bed holds three giggling figures:

- **Jarlaxle Baenre** (see appendix B), in the guise of Zardoz Zord (absent if he's marshalling the Day of Wonders parade; see "Special Events," page 145)
- Margo Verida, a female Amnian human **bard** (see appendix B)
- Khafeyta Murzan, a female Mulhorandi human **swashbuckler** (see appendix B)

Margo and Khafeyta both joined the Sea Maidens Faire within the past year—Margo as a lyrist, Khafeyta as an acrobat. Jarlaxle has taken a romantic interest in both women, who are also in love with each other.

Margo and Khafeyta are polite but terse. Both are neutral good. If attacked, they grab their weapons and other belongings and flee through a secret door (see below).

If separated from Jarlaxle and compelled to divulge information about their host, Margo and Khafeyta reveal some or all of the following facts:

- Zardoz Zord is a drow named Jarlaxle in disguise.
- Each ship in the Sea Maidens Faire is crewed by drow. The ships' figureheads cast illusions on the drow, making them appear human.

- Jarlaxle wants the Lords' Alliance to recognize his city, Luskan, as a new member, and he wants to push Neverwinter out of the alliance.
- A year ago, the Sea Maidens Faire visited the island nation of Lantan, where Jarlaxle obtained a Lantanese submarine and several clockwork servants.

Secret Door. A secret door leading to a walk-in closet (area J28) can be found with a successful DC 15 Wisdom (Perception) check.

Treasure. Margo's lyre is worth 30 gp. An unlocked chest at the foot of the bed holds four sets of costume clothing and a jewelry box containing six gold bracelets (worth 25 gp each), two diamond rings (worth 250 gp each), and a pearl necklace (worth 500 gp).

J30. Zardoz Zord's Cabin
Eyecatcher only

The doors to this cabin are locked. If anyone other than Jarlaxle turns the handle of either door, a *magic mouth* spell activates and shouts, "By Lolth's teeth, have you no manners?" The sound is loud enough to be heard by Jarlaxle (if he is in area J29), and he comes to investigate. The room contains the following features:

- The sweet smell of lavender permeates the cabin. (The scent is created by magic and can be dispelled.)
- A **nimblewright** (see appendix B) stands in a small alcove next to a chess table. An empty wine bottle on the table is labeled "One-Eyed Jax" in Common.
- Behind a purple curtain, a bed is covered by a soft blue blanket and matching pillows. Next to the bed is a wooden chest with clawed feet.

Nimblewright. The nimblewright serves Jarlaxle as a servant, and it obeys its master's commands without question. Absent orders, it attacks anyone who discovers the trapdoor in the floor (see below).

Secret Doors. Any character who searches the cabin and succeeds on a DC 15 Wisdom (Perception) check finds a secret door leading to a walk-in closet (area J28) and a secret trapdoor in the floor.

The trapdoor has an *arcane lock* spell cast on it, but rapping on it three times suppresses the spell for 1 minute. Alternatively, the trapdoor can be forced open with a successful DC 25 Strength (Athletics) check.

Below the trapdoor, a metal ladder descends to the bottom of a 10-foot-long, 3-foot-diameter steel tube with a circular metal hatch at the bottom. The hatch is opened by turning its valve wheel, which grants access to area U1 on the *Scarlet Marpenoth*. This area is magically pressurized to keep water from entering the ship if the hatch is opened while the submarine isn't docked.

Treasure. The chess set features jade pieces shaped like drow and is worth 2,500 gp.

J31. Training Area
Eyecatcher only

Jarlaxle trains here regularly. The space contains the following features:

- Ropes are strung throughout the area like webs.
- Four rapiers hang from a wooden rack attached to the mast.

- Five beat-up mannequins made of wood, straw, and canvas stand about the room. Each holds a wooden sword and a wooden shield.
- A dartboard mounted on one wall has a shiny dagger sticking into it.

Attack Mannequins. As a bonus action, Jarlaxle can command the five magic mannequins to animate and attack a single target of his choice. Each mannequin has the statistics of **animated armor**. Mannequins that take damage become inanimate until Jarlaxle uses another bonus action to reanimate them. A mannequin targeted by a *mending* cantrip regains 1 hit point.

Dagger. The dagger in the dartboard is a *+1 dagger*.

Ropes. The ropes make all parts of this area difficult terrain. As part of its movement, a creature can maneuver around the ropes with a successful DC 15 Dexterity (Acrobatics) check, negating the ropes' effect for that creature until the end of its turn.

J32. Jarlaxle's Sauna
Eyecatcher only

The door to this room is closed with an exterior hook latch. When the door is opened, clouds of steam billow out from the area beyond. This steam is created magically and can be dispelled with a successful casting of *dispel magic* (DC 14). The room holds only a wooden bench.

Steam. The steam has no adverse effect for the first hour. For each additional hour spent in this room, a creature must succeed on a DC 11 Constitution saving throw or gain one level of exhaustion. Creatures immune to fire damage automatically succeed on this save.

Scarlet Marpenoth

Jarlaxle's submarine, the *Scarlet Marpenoth*, is mounted underneath the *Eyecatcher* and can be seen only by creatures under the water. Jarlaxle retreats here if the *Eyecatcher* comes under attack.

Drow Crew

The magic that conceals the true appearance of drow aboard Jarlaxle's ships doesn't extend to the *Scarlet Marpenoth*. Characters who encounter drow while sneaking around the submarine are questioned. If the drow don't get the answers they want, they attack. Any nearby drow who hear a fight break out will investigate and team up to repel boarders.

Gnome Engineers

Rock gnome engineers maintain and operate the *Scarlet Marpenoth*. These gnomes are **apprentice wizards** (see appendix B), with these changes:

- The gnomes are neutral good.
- They are Small and have 7 (2d6) hit points each.
- They have these racial traits: They have advantage on all Intelligence, Wisdom, and Charisma saving throws against magic. Their walking speed is 25 feet. They have darkvision out to a range of 60 feet. They speak Common and Gnomish.

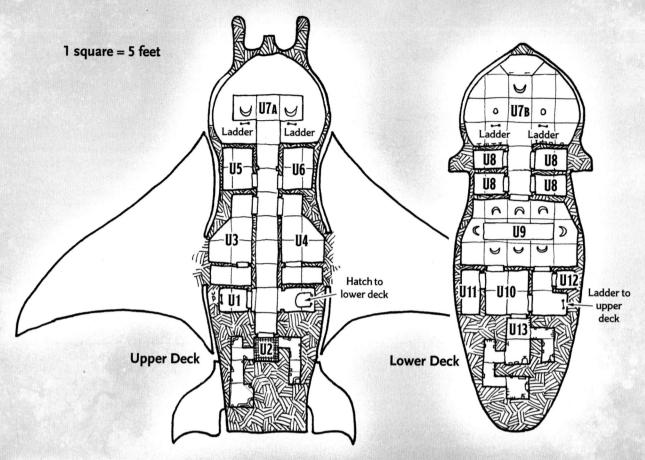

1 square = 5 feet

Ladder · U7A · Ladder

U5 · U6

U3 · U4

Hatch to lower deck

U1

U2

Upper Deck

U7B

Ladder · Ladder

U8 · U8

U8 · U8

U9

U11 · U10 · U12

Ladder to upper deck

U13

Lower Deck

MAP 7.2: SCARLET MARPENOTH

The gnomes know a great deal about submarines and very little about everything else. They are treated well by Jarlaxle, but a successful DC 15 Charisma (Intimidation) check or a bribe of 100 gp or more can convince a gnome to surrender its master keys, tamper with the engine, or pilot the submarine as the characters direct.

SUBMARINE FEATURES

The *Scarlet Marpenoth* has AC 20, 300 hit points, a damage threshold of 15, and immunity to poison and psychic damage. The submarine's structural integrity fails when the vessel drops to 0 hit points, whereupon it floods and sinks. The submarine is worth 15,000 gp intact and requires at least one pilot and one engineer to operate. It has a maximum speed of 2 miles per hour and can hold up to 10 passengers plus 2 tons of cargo.

The submarine has the following general features:

- Interior spaces are unlit. (The drow and the gnomes rely on darkvision to see.)
- All furnishings and features are bolted down.
- Chambers are 8 feet high, with 6-foot-high passages and doorways connecting them.
- Air magically circulates through a complex ventilation system and small metal grills set into the floors.
- Doors are made of steel and have AC 19, 27 hit points, a damage threshold of 10, and immunity to poison and psychic damage. A door's lock can be picked by a character who makes a successful DC 18 Dexterity check using thieves' tools. A door can be forced open by a character who succeeds on a DC 25 Strength (Athlet-

ics) check. Jarlaxle and the gnomes aboard the *Scarlet Marpenoth* have keys to all locked doors. All doors are airtight while closed.

AREAS OF THE SCARLET MARPENOTH

The following locations are keyed to map 7.2.

U1. ENTRANCE HATCH

Characters descending from Zardoz Zord's cabin on the *Eyecatcher* (area J30) arrive in this chamber. From this side, the circular metal hatch is opened by turning its valve wheel. This area is magically pressurized to keep water from entering the *Scarlet Marpenoth* if the hatch is opened while the submarine isn't docked to the *Eyecatcher*. But if both the outer hatch and the inner door are opened underwater, the submarine will flood.

U2. ENGINE ROOM

The door to this area is locked. A plaque on the door reads "ENGINE ROOM" in Common and Gnomish. The room has the following features:

- The engine room is filled with machines that hiss, whir, and clatter constantly. A rock gnome named Breena Bafflestone monitors the machinery at all times. Nearby is a copper speaking tube, which enables her to communicate with the control room command center (area U7b).
- Drawers in the walls contain screwdrivers, wrenches, and other tools.

- To port and starboard, 3-foot-high, 2½-foot-wide passageways lead deeper into the machinery. Medium creatures must squeeze to move through these passages.

Machinery. The engine is a quasi-magical machine that controls the submarine's propulsion and depth and powers the fins and rudder that control direction. A *detect magic* spell or similar magic reveals an aura of transmutation magic throughout the area.

A character who has proficiency with tinker's tools can use the tools to disable the engine with a successful DC 15 Intelligence check. The same check reactivates the disabled engine. Whether it succeeds or fails, each check represents 10 minutes of work. The engine can also be destroyed. It has AC 16, 50 hit points, and immunity to poison and psychic damage.

U3. Soluun's Stateroom

If he has not been encountered and disposed of elsewhere, a **drow gunslinger** named Soluun Xibrindas (see appendix B) is here, worshiping before a shrine of Lolth. His stateroom has the following features:

- The port alcove contains a net hammock and a steel footlocker.
- A black metal shrine of Lolth covered in tiny spider statuettes stands against one wall. At its top is a sculpture of the demon goddess, with the head and upper body of a female drow and the lower body of a spider.
- A Lantanese diving suit hangs in the closet to the south.

Diving Suit. This experimental device consists of a pressure-resistant padded suit, made of canvas with iron fittings and iron gauntlets. A fishbowl helmet attaches to the suit's collar and functions as a *cap of water breathing*.

Treasure. The shrine weighs 50 pounds and is worth 125 gp as an art object. The footlocker contains a pouch holding 50 gp and a *potion of healing*. The potion's crystal flask, shaped like a spider, is worth 25 gp.

U4. Jarlaxle's Stateroom

The door to this tidy cabin is locked. The cabin contains the following features:

- The scent of lavender magically permeates the cabin. (The scent is created by magic and can be dispelled.)
- A hammock is suspended in the starboard alcove. A *detect magic* spell or similar magic reveals that the wall behind the hammock radiates an aura of transmutation magic.
- Other furnishings include a tall harp with a stool nearby, a harpsichord with a matching bench, a free-standing mirror, and a large wooden trunk.

Closet. The locked closet aft of the cabin contains a wooden rack stocked with sixty bottles of wine. Each one is a rare vintage worth 25 gp.

Magic Window. Touching the wall behind the hammock renders the wall transparent from this side, and touching it again makes this "window" go away. When the wall is transparent, creatures in the cabin can see out, but creatures outside the submarine can't see in.

Wooden Trunk. The trunk isn't locked. Lifting the lid causes panels in the front and sides to open, releasing a swarm of mechanical spiders that attacks anyone other than Jarlaxle. This swarm has the statistics of a **swarm of insects (spiders)**, with these changes:

- The swarm is made up of Tiny constructs.
- It doesn't require air, food, drink, or sleep.
- The swarm has vulnerability to lightning damage, is immune to exhaustion, and can't be charmed, frightened, paralyzed, petrified, knocked prone, or poisoned.

The chest has a secret compartment in the bottom that can be detected and opened with a successful DC 13 Wisdom (Perception) check. If Jarlaxle has the *Stone of Golorr*, he keeps it in the secret compartment, along with any magic items he might have claimed from the characters. The compartment is otherwise empty.

U5. Fel'rekt's Stateroom

If he has not been encountered and defeated elsewhere, a **drow gunslinger** named Fel'rekt Lafeen (see appendix B) is here, cleaning his pistol. His stateroom contains a net hammock and a steel footlocker.

Treasure. Fel'rekt's footlocker contains 65 gp in a pouch, a comb carved from dragon bone (worth 5 gp), and a pair of obsidian dice (worth 25 gp).

U6. Krebbyg's Stateroom

If he has not been encountered and defeated elsewhere, a **drow gunslinger** named Krebbyg Masq'il'yr (see appendix B) is here, sharpening his sword. His stateroom contains a net hammock and nothing else.

U7. Control Room

The control room has two levels: an observation deck (U7a) and a command center (U7b), with two ladders running between levels. Two circular soundproof windows are embedded in the port and starboard bulkheads. The window panes are made of glassteel, a resilient metal magically rendered transparent. Curious **merfolk** who live in Deepwater Harbor investigate the submarine from time to time, and might be seen peering through the windows.

U7a. Observation Deck. If **Jarlaxle Baenre** (see appendix B) is forced to retreat to the submarine, he is here when the characters first arrive. The observation deck is an elevated, 10-foot-high metal platform with a grilled floor, supported by two metal columns. Two padded swivel chairs are bolted to the deck, which is enclosed by a thin steel railing. The height of each chair can be adjusted to accommodate a Small or Medium creature. Between the two chairs is a bronze periscope that can be raised or lowered whenever the submarine is detached from the *Eyecatcher*.

U7b. Command Center. Three rock gnome engineers named Lorella Middenpump, Tervaround Waggletop, and Anverth Leffery are on duty here, along with two **drow elite warriors** named Karabal L'enz and Marro Qaz'arrt. The drow guard the control room and keep the gnomes on task.

Lorella sits in the pilot's swivel chair, which is bolted to the floor and can be lowered or raised to

accommodate a Small or Medium creature. The chair is situated before a panel of dials, levers, and buttons. Tervaround and Anverth stand by the back wall, monitoring gauges and performing system checks. A copper speaking tube enables them to communicate with Breena Bafflestone in the engine room (area U2).

The gnomes can pilot the *Scarlet Marpenoth* without needing to make a check. Any other creature must succeed on a DC 20 Intelligence check to figure out the controls. From the control panel, the pilot can detach the submarine from the *Eyecatcher*, as well as control its speed, direction, and depth. The pilot can electrify the outer hull for 1 minute, after which the system requires 1 hour to recharge. Any creature that comes into contact with or starts its turn in contact with the outer hull when it's electrified must make a DC 15 Dexterity check, taking 22 (4d10) lightning damage on a failed save, or half as much damage on a successful one. A creature wearing metal armor has disadvantage on this saving throw.

U8. Engineers' Staterooms
Each of these four compartments contains an off-duty rock gnome engineer sleeping in a small hammock, beneath which are two steel footlockers. The four rock gnomes are named Cockaby Fapplestamp, Ellywick Fiddlefen, Gerbo Reese, and Zaffrab Horcusporcus.

Footlockers. Each footlocker belongs to a particular gnome engineer stationed aboard the *Scarlet Marpenoth*. Both contain folded clothes sized for a gnome. One of them also holds a set of grease-stained overalls and a set of tinker's tools that belong to the gnome asleep in the bunk. There is a 25 percent chance that a footlocker also contains a clockwork toy, a fire starter, or a music box (as described in the "Rock Gnome" section in chapter 2 of the *Player's Handbook*).

U9. Dining Room
This room has the following features:

- A walnut dining table is surrounded by eight padded swivel chairs. The height of each chair can be adjusted to accommodate a Small or Medium creature.
- Soft, ambient music fills the room, created by magic.

U10. Galley
This room has the following features:

- An iron stove sits in one corner.
- In the opposite corner stands a steel food preparation table with utensils dangling above it. Built into the table is a lidded steel box attached to a pedal on the floor below. When the pedal is pumped, water and moving brushes scrub dishes and utensils that have been placed into the box.
- A cart holds cutlery and dishes.

U11. Pantry
Metal shelves lining the walls hold fresh fruit, vegetables, casks of wine, and meat. Two steel barrels (one containing ale, the other drinking water) stand beneath the shelves.

U12. Privy

This privy has a toilet and a washbasin, both attached to pipes. Above the basin is a hinged mirror, behind which is a compartment containing soap and towels.

U13. Air System

The door to this area is locked. A plaque on this door reads "AIR SYSTEM" in Common and Gnomish. The room has the following features:

- The area is filled with machines that hiss, whir, and clatter constantly.
- Drawers in the walls contain screwdrivers, wrenches, and other tools.
- To port and starboard, 3-foot-high, 2½-foot-wide passageways lead deeper into the machinery. Creatures that are Medium or larger must squeeze to move through these passages.

Machinery. The quasi-magical machinery in this area generates and circulates fresh air throughout the submarine. A *detect magic* spell or similar magic reveals an aura of conjuration magic throughout the area.

A character who has proficiency with tinker's tools can use them to disable the machinery with a successful DC 15 Intelligence check. The same check reactivates the disabled machinery. Whether it succeeds or fails, each check represents 10 minutes of work. The machinery can also be destroyed. It has AC 16, 50 hit points, and immunity to poison and psychic damage.

When this machinery shuts down, air stops pumping throughout the vessel. Unless the air system is reactivated, creatures trapped in the submarine that need oxygen to breathe will begin to suffocate after two days (see "Suffocating" in chapter 8 of the *Player's Handbook*).

SPECIAL EVENTS

You can use one or more of the following events if the characters take an interest in the Sea Maidens Faire.

THE FRIENDLY DRAGON

This encounter can be used as the characters approach the *Eyecatcher*. Read:

> In the water ahead, a large shape speeds toward you. As it gets closer, you recognize it as a dragon with bronze-colored scales. Slewing to a stop, the creature gives a toothy grin, then raises a claw in a small wave. "Well met!" it chirps.

Zelifarn, a **young bronze dragon**, recently moved into Deepwater Harbor. He has spent the past several months scouring wrecks at the bottom of the harbor for treasure and stashing precious baubles in a hidden underwater cave. Recently, he noticed a strange craft mounted on the underside of the *Eyecatcher*. His attempts to treat with the crew have met with no success, but he's curious to know more. Since the characters appear to be headed toward a rendezvous with the *Eyecatcher*, Zelifarn would like them to find out all they can

about the underwater vessel without raising suspicion. The dragon promises to meet them again after they have completed their mission. In exchange for information, he offers to give the party a barnacle-covered chest that he found recently. He hasn't opened it yet, so its contents are unknown to him, but he can smell gold inside.

TREASURE

Zelifarn approaches the characters again as they leave the *Eyecatcher*. If they tell him more about the contents of the submarine and he believes that they're being truthful, he gives them the promised reward: an old chest with a rusted lock that can be busted or pried open with a successful DC 13 Strength (Athletics) check. It contains 300 sp plus a golden amulet shaped like an octopus with amethyst eyes (worth 250 gp).

A secret compartment in the chest's lid can be found with a successful DC 11 Wisdom (Perception) check. It contains a stoppered wooden scroll tube that holds a *spell scroll* of *revivify*.

A NIGHT TO REMEMBER

If the characters stake out the ships of the Sea Maidens Faire, they observe strange activity on the pier during their first night of surveillance:

> A thick fog unexpectedly rises along the water, engulfing vessels and docks alike. As the gray miasma thickens, the creaking sound of shifting ships becomes increasingly haunting. Suddenly, you spot three shadows gliding through the gloom like elves slipping through a forest. Where they came from and where they're going, you don't know.

The shadowy figures are the three **drow gunslingers** Fel'rekt Lafeen, Krebbyg Masq'il'yr, and Soluun Xibrindas (see appendix B). If any of these drow are dead or otherwise indisposed, replace them with **drow elite warriors**. The drow used the cover of the fog to come ashore in one of the *Eyecatcher*'s rowboats. The boat is tied off at the end of the pier between the *Heartbreaker* and the *Hellraiser*.

These Bregan D'aerthe spies are on their way to a secret meeting with **Laeral Silverhand** (see appendix B). The Open Lord is waiting for them in an alley in the Dock Ward, under the cloak of an *invisibility* spell. She remains invisible for the entire meeting.

Harper spies in Luskan recently warned Laeral that Jarlaxle might be in Waterdeep. She reached out to him with a *sending* spell to arrange this meeting, in the hope of finding out his plans. The characters can follow the drow spies to the rendezvous. If the drow realize they're being followed, they make no effort to shake their pursuers. If they're attacked, they scatter and try to complete their mission before heading back to the *Eyecatcher*.

If a battle erupts and escape appears impossible, the drow fight to the death. A City Watch patrol consisting of six **veterans** arrives 1d4 minutes later to make arrests.

JARLAXLE'S LETTER

One of the Bregan D'aerthe spies carries a letter for Laeral. It bears the wax seal of Luskan and is written in Jarlaxle's elegant hand, in Elvish. It reads as follows:

> To Her Ageless Majesty, Laeral Silverhand, the Witch-Queen of Stornanter, Lady of the North, She of the Seven Sisters, Chosen of Mystra, and Open Lord of Waterdeep:
>
> Your spies are to be commended! Rest assured, my presence in your fair city is purely recreational—though if fortune smiles upon me, this visit could benefit us both.
>
> Your predecessor left the City of Splendors in a sorry state, but you have done wonders to lift the spirit of the citizenry during your short time in office. I know how politics offends you, so forgive me for taking this opportunity to point out the obvious. We can make both our cities stronger and strike back at he who robbed Waterdavians of their wealth and dignity. I'm speaking, of course, of that dirty sack of rats, Dagult Neverember. That's the phrase you used to describe him yesterday to the emissary from Mirabar, is it not? Evidently, my spies are also to be commended!
>
> Why let Neverember get away with his crimes against Luskan and Waterdeep? Can we be allies, if not friends? These are the questions that haunt my dreams, as surely as I haunt yours.
>
> Sincerely,
>
> J

Laeral isn't surprised that Jarlaxle lacks the courage to meet her in person. She thanks the drow messengers for delivering the letter, cautions them to mind the City Watch and the City Guard, and heads back to the Palace of Waterdeep. The drow spies return whence they came.

CONVERSATION WITH LAERAL

If Laeral becomes aware of the characters, she appears before them and asks what business they have with Bregan D'aerthe. If the characters have not met the Open Lord before, she might impress them with her plain-spoken manner and lack of pretense. Alone and outside the political maelstrom, she acts more like an adventurer than a city official.

If the characters inquire about the letter, she shows it to them and asks their opinions on Luskan's joining the Lords' Alliance. In her mind, Luskan is a greedy pirate state that can't be trusted under any circumstances. If the characters feel similarly, she trusts them enough to ask for their help in finding and securing Lord Neverember's hidden cache of dragons. In exchange, she promises them a 5,000 gp reward and Waterdeep's gratitude.

DAY OF WONDERS PARADE

The Day of Wonders is the grandest parade of the fall season, and Jarlaxle wants the Sea Maidens Faire to be a part of it. In the guise of Zardoz Zord, he pays a visit the day before the holiday to the House of Inspired Hands, Waterdeep's temple of Gond, to coordinate with the acolytes in charge of organizing the parade. He presents a detailed plan that commingles the attractions of the Sea Maidens Faire with the bizarre inventions of the temple—a plan that is well received.

The evening before the Day of Wonders, workers begin assembling the wagons and floats of the Sea Maidens Faire on the pier. Early the following morning, the docks are a hive of activity as performers practice their routines and caged creatures are offloaded one by one. An hour before highsun on this crisp and windy autumn day, the Sea Maidens Faire makes its way to the House of Inspired Hands to meet up with the Gond worshipers and their contraptions. From there, the parade strikes out in earnest, marching through Waterdeep's streets to the cheers of the local folk. Zardoz Zord serves as grand marshal, leading the parade on the back of a rainbow-feathered diatryma summoned using his *feather of diatryma summoning* (see appendix A). For Jarlaxle, the parade is a chance to show off and be cheered; he has no ulterior motive for participating in the event.

WHILE THE BOSS IS AWAY

As the Sea Maidens Faire parades through Waterdeep, the characters can slip aboard one or more of Jarlaxle's ships. If things turns violent aboard a ship, its captain uses a *sending* spell to contact Jarlaxle. Jarlaxle is supremely confident that his crews can overcome any threat, so he doesn't rush to their defense at the first sign of trouble. Only if the characters do considerable damage will he treat their attack as a setback.

If the characters escape a confrontation on the ships but leave behind witnesses who can identify them, it takes Bregan D'aerthe several days to track them down (assuming Jarlaxle hasn't already met them). Although killing the characters would be easy at that point, Jarlaxle would rather put them to work for him. He has them watched but doesn't provoke hostilities until such time as the reward clearly outweighs the risks.

ESCAPED BEAR

The Sea Maidens Faire parade ends where it started—at the docks. As the attractions are being loaded back onto their ships, the Faire's **polar bear** gets loose, fleeing into the Dock Ward before its handlers can corner it. News of the escaped bear spreads quickly, and sightings are frequent. If the characters impressed one of the drow ship captains, he contacts them by way of a *sending* spell and asks for help. He wants the bear retrieved before the City Guard finds and kills it, offering a reward of either 250 gp or a *potion of water breathing*.

The characters can track and corner the polar bear with a successful DC 16 Intelligence (Investigation) or Wisdom (Survival) check. Whether a check succeeds or fails, each attempt represents 1 hour of searching. If the characters find the bear within 4 hours, it can be lured back to the Sea Maidens Faire with food or a successful DC 14 Wisdom (Animal Handling) check. The captain then makes good on the promised reward. If the characters don't find the bear, members of the City Guard get to it first and kill it.

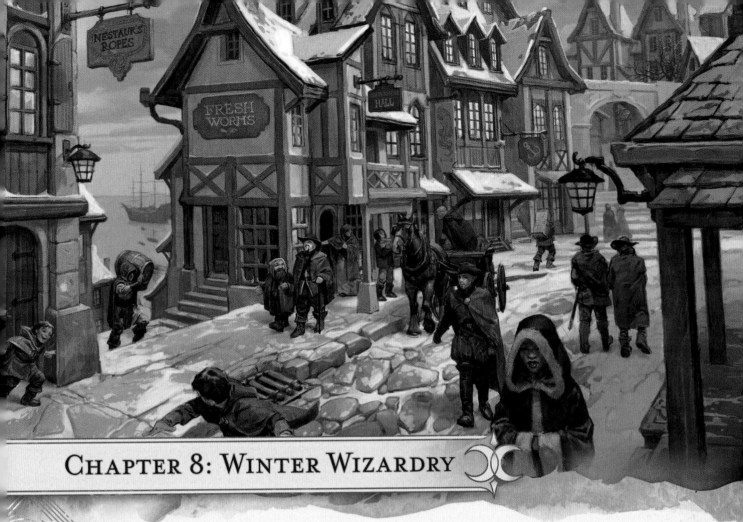

CHAPTER 8: WINTER WIZARDRY

ANSHOON YEARS TO RULE WATERDEEP as a tyrant, take over the Zhentarim, and use both seats of power to plunder and control the Sword Coast. He needs the gold in the Vault of Dragons to pay off Masked Lords and Zhentarim leaders whose support will be instrumental when the time comes to oust Lady Laeral Silverhand as Open Lord. Manshoon has a long list of powerful enemies, among them the Harpers, Elminster of Shadowdale, Halaster Blackcloak of Undermountain, and the Blackstaff of Waterdeep. These enemies would quickly move against Manshoon if they learned he was hiding in Waterdeep. For his evil plans to succeed, Manshoon must operate in the shadows for the time being.

FACING MANSHOON

A head-on battle with Manshoon isn't likely to go well for the characters. That said, the wizard's greatest weakness is that he has powerful enemies in Waterdeep. The risk of exposure keeps him hidden, and the characters can thwart him by furnishing his enemies with proof that he's alive (after a fashion) and operating in Waterdeep. When it comes to Manshoon clones, deciding to "let the city deal with it" is a wise course of action.

If the characters find themselves at the evil wizard's mercy, Manshoon will gladly trade their pitiful lives for the *Stone of Golorr* and the keys to unlock the Vault of Dragons. In exchange for helping him get the gold, he

promises the characters 10 percent of the trove (50,000 gp). Manshoon has no intention of honoring this agreement, but it can help buy the characters some time.

If the characters manage to kill Manshoon and the local authorities are made aware of the act, no murder charges are filed. Rather, the characters' actions are celebrated. Laeral Silverhand summons them to the Palace of Waterdeep to thank them officially, in her capacity as Open Lord. Sometime later, Vajra Safahr invites them to Blackstaff Tower to thank them for their service and offer them membership in Force Grey.

DISRUPTING MANSHOON'S OPERATION

Characters can hinder Manshoon in the following ways.

RELEASE THE BARLGURA
If the characters free the barlgura demon in area K15 and allow it to roam Kolat Towers, Manshoon loses many followers to the demon's rampage.

REPORT MANSHOON
Delivering proof that Manshoon is hiding in Waterdeep to Laeral Silverhand, Mirt, the Harpers, Force Grey, the Blackstaff, the Lords' Alliance, the Order of the Gauntlet, the City Watch, or the Watchful Order of Magists and Protectors triggers a far-reaching effort to oust him from the city. Such proof can be obtained from any of Manshoon's lieutenants, who can be captured and

turned over for interrogation. These lieutenants include Sidra Romeir (area K2), Manafret Cherryport (area K3), Urstul Floxin (area E5), Vevette Blackwater and Agorn Fuoco (area E8), and Havia Quickknife and Mookie Plush (area E10).

The ledger in area E13 also contains proof of Manshoon's malfeasance. Giving it to Laeral Silverhand, Vajra Safahr, Mirt, or a magister provides enough evidence for them to act on.

Once Manshoon's whereabouts are established, the City Guard cordons off and surrounds Kolat Towers. The Blackstaff and the Watchful Order assist as needed. If the characters deactivated the force field, the siege is brief and Manshoon's forces are routed. If the force field remains in place, the Watchful Order can deactivate it.

When all is said and done, Manshoon is forced to retreat to his extradimensional sanctum. From there, he continues his search for the Vault of Dragons while fending off attackers.

STEAL MANSHOON'S SPELLBOOK

Stealing the spellbook from area E13 causes Manshoon to slow his search for the Vault of Dragons while he either tries to replace it or sends a simulacrum (see appendix B) and other forces to retrieve it.

KOLAT TOWERS

This dilapidated, two-towered edifice stands tall in the Southern Ward. Its neighbors are aware of the magical force field that surrounds it, and they can see light from *continual flame* spells spilling out of the windows,

Despite these persistent magical effects, most folk believe the structure is abandoned. Others think it's haunted by the ghosts of the Kolat brothers. They're wrong, of course.

Manshoon posts no visible guards outside Kolat Towers, since he wants others to believe the site is abandoned. The evil wizard and his underlings come and go using teleportation circles inside the towers.

FORCE FIELD

An invisible field of magical force surrounds and covers Kolat Towers. The field is paper-thin and stands just outside the outer wall of the estate, extending upward to contain the buildings in their entirety. Nothing can pass through the barrier, including air, fog, rain, and snow. Creatures that don't realize the field is there bounce off it, with birds especially prone to striking it. The ground outside the field is regularly littered with the tiny corpses of birds that broke their necks hitting it, and street cleaners come by every morning to sweep them up.

DIGGING UNDER THE FORCE FIELD

There are no openings in the force field, which extends 1 foot underground. It takes 1 hour for a character with a shovel to dig a hole deep enough for a Medium creature to squeeze through, going under the field to the other side of the towers' outer wall. Since Kolat Towers is surrounded by other buildings, there's a 75 percent chance that any digging attracts 2d6 members of the City Watch (**veterans**), who put a stop to it.

USING MAGIC TO BYPASS THE FORCE FIELD

Characters can use magic such as a *dimension door* or *misty step* spell to teleport from one side of the force field to the other. A *disintegrate* spell or a successful *dispel magic* (DC 19) spell cast at the field creates a 10-foot-square opening that lasts for 1 minute.

DESTROYING THE FORCE FIELD

A magic rune in area K18 generates the force field. Destroying that rune ends the effect.

KOLAT TOWERS FEATURES

The following general features apply to Kolat Towers:

- Kolat Towers is a multistory structure, with each level standing 20 feet higher than the one below it. Its rooms have 15-foot-high ceilings, with 7-foot-high doorways connecting them.
- Climbing the outside walls without equipment requires a successful DC 15 Strength (Athletics) check.
- Each of the doors in the towers, as well as the door in the outer wall, is made of iron-bound oak and has AC 16, 27 hit points, and immunity to poison and psychic damage. If a door is locked, it can be picked by a character who makes a successful DC 15 Dexterity check using thieves' tools, or it can be forced open with a successful DC 20 Strength (Athletics) check. Manshoon, Manafret Cherryport, and Havia Quickknife have keys to the locked doors.
- Windows have leaded frames and dirty glass panes. They are latched from within and swing inward on iron hinges. A successful DC 11 Dexterity check using thieves' tools opens a window from the outside.
- Unless otherwise noted, all areas are brightly lit by *continual flame* spells cast on wall sconces.
- Some of the staircases in Kolat Towers are invisible. They are revealed by a *see invisibility* spell or similar magic. A creature traversing stairs it can't see can move on the steps at half speed without any problem. A creature that moves any faster than half speed must succeed on a DC 10 Dexterity (Acrobatics) check or slip, tumble down the stairs, and fall prone at the bottom of them.

AREAS OF KOLAT TOWERS

The following encounter locations are keyed to map 8.1.

K1. STOREROOM

The outer door is locked from the inside, and the room has neither heat nor light sources. Crates stacked around the room are packed with meat, and bear the seal of the Fellowship of Salters, Packers, and Joiners.

K2. DINING ROOM

This room contains the following features:

- Three Zhents in black armor sit around a stone dining table, playing Three-Dragon Ante (a card game). The table is set with silver.
- Eight moth-eaten banners hang from the walls. Each bears an arcane sigil that represents a different one of the eight schools of magic.

Zhents. The card players are Sidra Romeir (LE female Calishite human **veteran**) and two subordinates (LE male Tethyrian human **thugs**). Since the force field around Kolat Towers keeps out riffraff, Sidra assumes the characters are guests of Manshoon arriving for a clandestine meeting. If the characters give her no reason to believe otherwise, she and her thugs escort them wherever they ask to go. If it becomes clear that the characters don't belong in the towers, Sidra and her thugs attack. Combat in this area draws the attention of Manafret Cherryport in area K3, who investigates.

Sidra wears a *teleporter ring* (see "Teleporter Rings," page 157).

Treasure. Silverware on the table is worth 100 gp.

K3. KITCHEN

Mouthwatering scents fill this room, which contains the following features:

- If he hasn't already been drawn elsewhere, a portly halfling stands atop a stool and cooks at an iron stove.
- A green, ghostly hand floats above a trellis table, holding a knife and cutting carrots and celery.
- A staircase curves up one wall, leading to area K7.

Zhent Cook. The halfling, Manafret Cherryport, is one of Manshoon's lieutenants. He loves to cook, and uses his *mage hand* cantrip to cut vegetables. He assumes the characters are intruders unless convinced otherwise. Any ability check to do so is made with disadvantage, since Manafret knows that Manshoon would have informed him if guests were expected. If the mage suspects the characters are intruders, he surreptitiously pours a vial of assassin's blood (see "Poisons" in chapter 8 of the *Dungeon Master's Guide*) into the stew before asking them to taste it and give him an honest critique. He then cries out to the guards in area K2 and attacks. Combat in this area draws the attention of the Zhents in areas K2 and K7, who investigate.

Manafret is a lightfoot halfling **mage**, with these changes:

- Manafret is neutral evil and has 31 (9d6) hit points.
- He has these racial traits: He is Small, and his walking speed is 25 feet. He can move through the space of a Medium or larger creature. He has advantage on saving throws against being frightened. He speaks Common and Halfling.

> ### KOLAT TOWERS LORE
>
> With a successful DC 15 Intelligence (History) check, a character can recall the following information about Kolat Towers. An NPC familiar with Waterdeep's history, such as Mirt or Volo, can also provide this information.
>
> - Kolat Towers once belonged to two eccentric brothers, Duhlark and Alcedor Kolat. Both were wizards.
> - Over time, the brothers discovered new ways to harness magic, but Duhlark became paranoid that others might steal their secrets. He encased Kolat Towers in a magical force field.
> - Duhlark's paranoia continued to grow, until he suspected Alcedor of selling their secrets. Alcedor left the towers, never to be heard from again, and Duhlark became a recluse who died in his own fortress.

Manafret wears a *teleporter ring* (see "Teleporter Rings," page 157).

Treasure. A cupboard holds a dozen jars of herbs and spices. Among them is a flask labeled "Assassin's Blood," which contains six doses of the poison.

K4. Musty Library

This musty room is situated at the bottom of the main tower, and it has no door on level 1. It contains the following features:

- A suit of dented plate armor stands in the center of the room.
- Tomes are packed into built-in stone bookshelves, with a tall alcove above each shelf holding a gargoyle. (Two of these sculptures are living **gargoyles**.)
- An in-progress game of Dragonchess sits on a marble table in a reading nook.
- A stone staircase spirals up to area K6.

Gargoyles. The two real gargoyles are indistinguishable from the inanimate gargoyle statues in the high alcoves. When intruders start poking around the room, the gargoyles swoop down and attack.

Tomes. Any character who spends an hour searching the bookshelves finds a fat tome titled *Flumph Mating Rituals*, with an embossed image of two flumphs on the cover, their tendrils entwined. The cover is a false one, wrapping around a tome bound in dragon hide—a disguised spellbook that contains the following wizard spells: *arcane lock, burning hands, comprehend languages, counterspell, darkvision, dimension door, find familiar, levitate, sending,* and *unseen servant.* (You can replace any of these spells with a spell of the same level.)

Treasure. The Dragonchess set is made of hand-carved ivory and is worth 500 gp.

K5. Garbage-Filled Room

This room is on level 1 of the outermost tower but isn't accessible from that floor. It reeks of garbage and has the following features:

- Ankle-deep refuse fills the chamber.
- Black scorch marks stretch from floor to ceiling along the walls and the stairs, which lead up to area K10.

Manshoon's servants throw their garbage here. The Kolat brothers created some magic items in this room, and an experiment gone awry caused the scorch marks.

K6. Main Tower Landing and Ledge

Level 2 of the main tower has the following features:

- A stone landing with no railings has a door leading to area K7 and a stone spiral staircase descending to area K4. An invisible staircase with no railings (see "Kolat Towers Features," page 149) hugs the wall as it climbs from the landing to area K11.
- Across from the landing, a wide stone ledge protrudes from the northeast wall beneath a window. A pair of identical wooden chests sits atop the ledge. (One chest is real. The other is a **mimic**.)

Ledge. There's no easy way to access the ledge, which is 8 feet away from the landing and at the same height.

Characters can try to jump onto the ledge, or they can hook a rope onto the railing on the level above (area K11) and swing across the gap. They can also use magic to cross. Anyone who falls off the landing or the ledge lands in area K4, 20 feet below.

Mimic. A character who touches the mimic becomes adhered to it. The mimic attacks if disturbed or when a character inspects the real chest next to it.

Treasure. The genuine chest is unlocked and contains thirteen items, each of which can be used as an arcane focus: two crystals (worth 10 gp each), an orb (worth 20 gp), four rods (worth 10 gp each), and six wands (worth 10 gp each).

K7. Reading Room

This room contains the following features:

- A burly half-orc clad in black leather armor sits in an overstuffed chair in the northernmost corner of the room, reading a book.
- Large framed pictures of cities and landscapes hang on the walls, and a worn, blood-spattered rug covers the floor. Other furnishings include a pair of rocking chairs, a couch, and an ottoman.
- Mouthwatering scents rise from a staircase that curves down to the kitchen (area K3).

Zhent. Yorn the Terror is reading a copy of *Volo's Guide to Monsters*, autographed on the title page by the author with an added note that reads, in Common: "For Yorn. I hope you find the orc chapter illuminating!"

Yorn is a half-orc **thug**, with these changes:

- Yorn is neutral evil.
- He has these racial traits: When reduced to 0 hit points, he drops to 1 hit point instead (but can't do this again until he finishes a long rest). He has darkvision out to a range of 60 feet. He speaks Common and Orc.

Yorn values his own well-being above all else. He is initially indifferent toward intruders. If Yorn believes the characters aren't a threat, he's happy to chat with them about the inhabitants and the layout of Kolat Towers. He has never visited Manshoon's extraplanar sanctum, but he does know that the teleportation circle in area K22 is the way to get there.

Combat in this area draws the attention of Manafret Cherryport in area K3, who investigates.

Treasure. Yorn carries 36 cp, 20 sp, 12 gp, 8 taols, and a gem-studded ivory toothpick (worth 25 gp) in a pouch.

K8. Apprentice Bedroom

This narrow room contains the following features:

- Three single beds are bunched less than an arm's length apart beneath a staircase that leads up to area K12.
- At the foot of each bed is a wooden chest.

The Kolat brothers once took on apprentices, who slept here. Manshoon now allows his own apprentices—Ered Payno, Havi Termock, and Savara Firethorn—to do the same. All three can be found in area K15.

Treasure. Inside each chest is a set of common clothes, a spare spell component pouch, candles, ink,

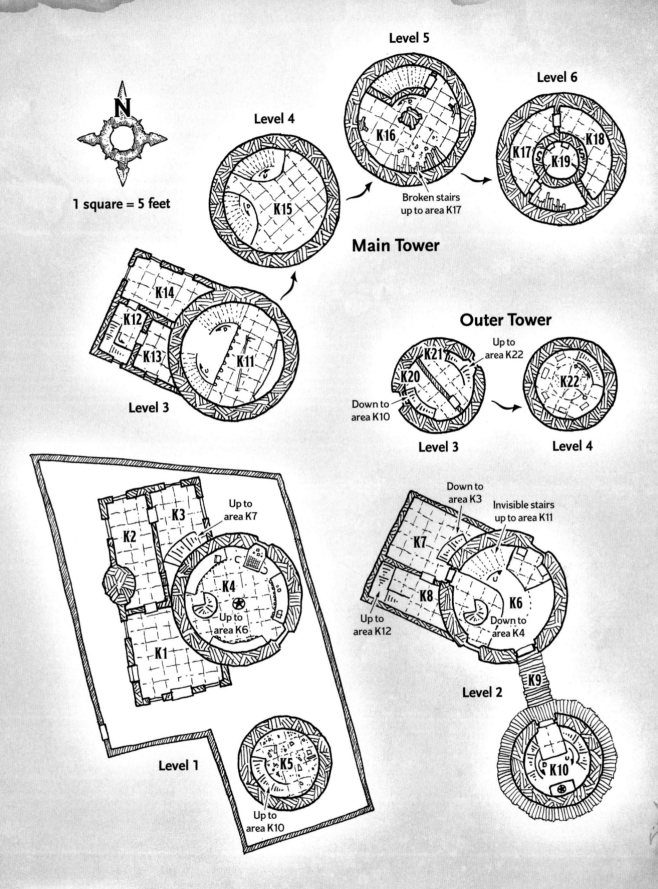

Level 5

Level 6

Level 4

Main Tower

K16

K17 K18
K19

Broken stairs
up to area K17

K15

Outer Tower

1 square = 5 feet

Up to
area K22

K14

K12

K13

K21
K20

K11

Down to
area K10

Level 3

Level 3

K22

Level 4

Down to
area K3

Invisible stairs
up to area K11

Up to
area K7

K7

K3

K2

K8

K6

K4

Up to
area K12

Down to
area K4

Up to
area K6

K1

K9

Level 2

K5

K10

Level 1

Up to
area K10

MAP 8.1: KOLAT TOWERS

pens, paper, and 3d6 gp. Each chest also holds a spell-book that contains all the spells its owner has prepared. In addition, Ered's spellbook contains *burning hands*, *knock*, and *lightning bolt*; Havi's spellbook contains *charm person*, *detect thoughts*, and *major image*; and Savara's spellbook contains *comprehend languages*, *phantasmal force*, and *phantom steed*.

K9. Bridge and Walkway

A wooden bridge connects the two towers 20 feet above the ground, and a walkway attached to the bridge encircles the outside of the outer tower. The bridge and the tower walkway lack railings. Their planks and stones groan and crack underfoot but are safe to walk on.

K10. Wizard Statue

This level of the outer tower consists of a landing and a narrow ledge with the following features:

- The landing is 10 feet square and is met by two staircases. One descends 20 feet to area K5, and one ascends 20 feet to area K20.
- The narrow ledge built into the southeast wall has a life-size statue of a bearded human wizard standing atop it. The wizard looks angry and is leveling a stone wand at the door to area K9.

Statue. The statue depicts Duhlark Kolat, and a *detect magic* spell or similar magic reveals an aura of transmutation magic around it. The first time a character steps onto the landing, the statue levitates 1 foot above the ledge and intones the following warning in Common:

> "I am Duhlark Kolat, the great wizard and master of this tower! How dare you invade my home! Leave at once or be destroyed by magic beyond your comprehension!"

The threat is empty, but the statue continues to levitate for 1 minute before sinking back down to the ledge. The magic resets after 1 hour. While it is levitating, the statue can be easily pushed or pulled around.

Casting *dispel magic* on the statue while it's floating causes it to fall, topple off the ledge, and shatter in area K5 below. Anyone in that area when the statue falls must succeed on a DC 10 Dexterity saving throw or take 22 (4d10) bludgeoning damage.

K11. Laboratory

This room consists of a ledge connected to the levels above and below by invisible staircases (see "Kolat Towers Features," page 149). One staircase descends 20 feet to area K6, and the other climbs 20 feet to area K15. The area contains the following features:

- Shattered glass covers the floor, and a large wooden trellis table has been knocked on its side.
- A large empty cabinet dominates the back wall.

This laboratory has been picked clean by Manshoon and contains nothing of value.

K12. Staff Display

This room contains the following features:

- A half-dozen staffs of various styles are hung proudly on the walls at the top of the landing.
- A staircase descends to area K8.

Staffs. Each staff is different in construction and style: a twisted birch branch, a sturdy oak dowel, a glittering haft of stone, a steel pole carved with blue runes, a dimpled copper staff topped with a copper crescent moon, and a blown-glass cane capped with a black marble orb.

All six staffs animate and attack interlopers who enter the area without being escorted by Manshoon or one of his lieutenants. The staffs have the same statistics as **flying swords**, except they deal bludgeoning damage on a hit. If a fight breaks out in this area, the creatures in area K14 come to investigate.

K13. Holding Cell

The door to this room has a narrow, barred window set into it. The door is locked and trapped (see below). As the characters approach the door, read:

> A raspy voice calls out from beyond the door. "If you be good, let us rid these towers of evil's stench. If you be evil, open the door so we may battle, and my eternal boredom can end." Beyond the door's barred window, a gargoyle lurks in a stone cell, challenging you in a low growl. "Come on, then!"

Trapped Door. A *glyph of warding* spell has been cast on the door, set to trigger when it is opened by anyone other than Manshoon. The glyph, which resembles an ornate letter M, can be found with a successful DC 18 Intelligence (Investigation) check. The glyph targets the creature that opens the door with a *blindness/deafness* spell (save DC 18).

Lady Gondafrey. Duhlark Kolat long ago trapped a magical experiment in this cell: a **gargoyle** that has been imbued with the personality of a human knight of Tyr (god of justice) named Lady Gondafrey. This gargoyle has an Intelligence score of 10 and an alignment of lawful good. It speaks Common, and its face looks more humanoid than gargoyle. Manshoon is amused by the creature, so he keeps it alive but locked in the cell.

If the characters free Lady Gondafrey, she offers to fight alongside them; however, she quickly turns against any character who exhibits cruel or unlawful behavior. She can offer helpful information about Kolat Towers, and she is familiar with both the layout of the towers and the current occupants of the place. She knows that Manshoon resides in an extraplanar sanctum accessible through a teleportation circle that his lieutenants can activate using special rings. The gargoyle doesn't know where the teleportation circle is located, nor does she know why Duhlark transferred her consciousness into her present form.

The gargoyle retains fragmented memories of the life of Lady Gondafrey, a native Waterdavian who served in the City Watch. After identifying Duhlark Kolat as a suspect in several local disappearances, she darkened his doorstep in 1379 DR, the Year of the Lost Keep. Annoyed by this invasion of his privacy and not in his right mind, Duhlark captured Lady Gondafrey, used a spell to meld her form with that of a gargoyle, and imprisoned her.

If the gargoyle travels with the party, roll a d10 each day at dawn. On a roll of 1, Lady Gondafrey's alignment becomes chaotic evil for 24 hours as the gargoyle's innate demeanor exerts itself. In this state, the creature tries to orchestrate the characters' deaths, going so far as to attack lone characters.

K14. Servants' Quarters

This room contains the following features:

- Furnishings include four beds, a small table with four chairs, and tattered window curtains.
- Four Zhent **thugs** relax here—one trying to rest, two others playing cards, and the fourth sitting on the edge of a bed, re-stringing a heavy crossbow.

The thugs work for Manshoon and leap up to attack anyone they don't recognize as one of their own. A successful DC 17 Charisma (Deception) check convinces these Zhents that the characters are their allies.

Treasure. Resting in small piles and neat stacks on the table are 74 cp, 52 sp, 19 gp, and 4 taols.

K15. Summoning Chamber

This room is connected to the levels above and below by invisible staircases (see "Kolat Towers Features," page 149), one descending 20 feet to area K11 and the other climbing 20 feet to area K16. This area contains the following features:

- A 10-foot-diameter circle of runes has been drawn on the floor in blood that is now dried. Smoke billows from four iron braziers placed around the circle.
- Three **apprentice wizards** (see appendix B) stand outside the circle, chanting an incantation. A **barlgura** is slumped motionless within the circle.

The three wizards here are Manshoon's apprentices—Ered Payno (LE male Damaran human), Havi Termock (CE female Chondathan human), and Savara Firethorn (NE female Tethyrian human). Each wears a *teleporter ring* (see "Teleporter Rings," page 157). The magical incantation that the three are reciting has quelled the barlgura and rendered it unconscious. If any of them stop chanting, the demon awakes and becomes enraged, though it remains bound within the circle. Whenever it takes damage, the barlgura can attempt a DC 10 Charisma check. On a successful check, it breaks out of the circle and attacks any creature it can reach.

Freeing the barlgura disrupts Manshoon's operation, forcing the wizard to spend time and resources defeating the fiend and replacing slain underlings.

K16. Construct Workshop

The invisible staircase from area K15 ends in front of a closed door. The door is unlocked and opens into the room, which contains the following:

- Bits of clay, stone, bone, and metal litter the floor and cover a wooden table in the middle of the room.

- The floor creaks and tilts slightly when stepped on, and it can be seen to be detached from the walls. Two oversized iron clamps on opposite sides of the room hold the floor in place. Each of these rusty mechanisms is attached to an iron lever.
- A wooden staircase once climbed 20 feet to the next level, but it has partially collapsed.

The Kolat brothers once crafted constructs in this workshop. The magical clamped floor was built as a precaution in case one of the experiments went berserk.

When a creature that doesn't work for Manshoon's Zhentarim enters this room without being escorted, the metal scraps on the floor fly together, forming a suit of **animated armor** that attacks. When the armor is reduced to 10 hit points or fewer, it tries to pull one of the levers on its next turn.

Floor Clamps. Pulling a lever is an action that causes both clamps to release the floor, which is then magically driven upward into the ceiling. Creatures standing on the floor are knocked prone and must make a DC 20 Dexterity saving throw as they slam into the ceiling, taking 22 (4d10) bludgeoning damage on a failed save, or half as much damage on a successful one. The floor then settles a few feet below the ceiling, cutting off access to the stairs down to area K15 but leaving characters free to climb up the collapsed staircase to area K17. (The magical floor was designed to prevent a berserk golem from reaching the lower chambers of the towers, and potentially the city beyond, while the Kolat brothers dealt with it.) After 10 minutes, the floor descends to its normal level and the clamps lock it down again.

Partially Collapsed Stairs. A creature can climb the stairs to area K17 with a successful DC 10 Dexterity (Acrobatics) check. If the check fails, the creature falls 10 feet.

K17. Flesh Golem

This unlit hallway contains the following features:

- Any character who inspects the hall for traps and succeeds on a DC 17 Wisdom (Perception) check notices 1-inch-diameter holes drilled into the walls at ankle height, set at regular intervals along the length of the passage.
- A **flesh golem** stands in front of the door to area K18.
- A one-way secret door is set into the innermost wall.

Golem Trap. The flesh golem was created by Duhlark Kolat. Manshoon chose to leave it here and instructed his lieutenants not to disturb it. It moves to attack anyone other than Duhlark who approaches within 10 feet of it. A character disguised as Duhlark (using the statue in area K10 as a model) can fool the golem with a successful DC 10 Charisma (Deception) check.

The golem stands on a pressure plate. When it steps off the plate to attack someone out of its reach, the weight on the plate is lifted, causing poison gas to erupt from the holes in the walls. When the trap triggers, each creature in the hall must make a DC 12 Constitution saving throw, taking 10 (3d6) poison damage on a failed saving throw, or half as much damage on a successful one. The gas lingers for 1 minute unless dispersed with a *gust of wind* spell or similar magic. While the gas

NAT, JENKS, AND SQUIDDLY MAKE THE BEST OF WATERDEEP'S HARSH WINTER.

persists, a creature in the hall must repeat the saving throw at the start of each of its turns. The golem is immune to the poison gas.

One-Way Secret Door. A character who makes a successful DC 15 Wisdom (Perception) check notices the secret door that leads to area K19. This door opens normally only from inside area K19, and only a *knock* spell or similar magic can force it open from this side.

K18. ARCANE RUNE

This unlit hall is choked with dust and cobwebs. It contains the following features:

- An elaborate rune is inscribed on the back wall at the southernmost end of the hall. (The rune isn't visible from the doorway to area K17.)
- A secret door is set into the innermost wall.

Arcane Rune. A *detect magic* spell or similar magic reveals a powerful aura of conjuration magic around the rune. A successful DC 15 Intelligence (Arcana) check confirms that this rune sustains the force field around Kolat Towers, and that the rune can be destroyed. It has AC 10, 22 hit points, and immunity to poison and psychic damage. The rune can't be dispelled normally, but each successful *dispel magic* cast on it (DC 19) deals 16 (3d10) force damage to it.

The first time damage is dealt to the rune, a **red slaad** magically springs forth from it and attacks all creatures in the hallway.

When the rune is destroyed, the force field around Kolat Towers disappears.

Secret Door. A character who makes a successful DC 15 Wisdom (Perception) check notices the secret door that leads to area K19.

K19. DUHLARK'S BEDROOM

This room is accessible through either of the secret doors that lead to areas K17 and K18. It contains the following features:

- A **flameskull** bobs in the middle of the room, which is choked with dust and cobwebs.
- An oval canopy bed veiled in cobwebs sits across from two narrow bookshelves.
- The room smells like a tomb.

Manshoon found Duhlark Kolat's skeletal remains in the bed and transformed his skull into a flameskull. He left the rest of the bones alone, hidden behind cobwebs. The flameskull attacks anyone other than Manshoon who confronts it, shouting, "Get out of my house!" between casting spells and throwing off fire rays.

Bookshelves. Manshoon removed any tomes of value from the bedroom, leaving noticeable gaps on the shelves between mundane books on a variety of esoteric subjects.

Among the volumes on one shelf is a false book titled *The Man from Damara*—a wooden block painted to resemble a book, which is wired to a secret compartment in the base of the shelf. A character can detect the shelf and discern how to open it with a successful DC 15 Wisdom (Perception) check. Tugging on the book causes the

compartment to pop open, revealing Duhlark's *wand of binding* hidden inside.

K20. ALCEDOR'S PRIVATE LIBRARY

This room has the following features:

- A tall oak bookshelf contains a few scattered books (all mundane and worthless), but is mostly bare. Above the bookshelf hangs a beautifully crafted sign that reads "Alcedor" in Common.
- A staircase descends 20 feet to area K10.

K21. DUHLARK'S PRIVATE LIBRARY

This room has the following features:

- A tall oak bookshelf holds a few dozen books. Above the bookshelf hangs a beautifully crafted sign that reads "Duhlark" in Common.
- A staircase ascends 20 feet to area K22.

Bookshelf. The bookshelf holds thirty books in total. If any of them are disturbed, they fly off the shelves and form a swarm that attacks all creatures in the room. The book collection has the statistics of a **swarm of bats**, with these changes:

- The books lack the Echolocation and Keen Hearing traits.
- Replace the swarm's Bites attack option with a Slam attack option that deals the same amount of bludgeoning damage.

If there are no creatures to attack on its turn, the book collection returns to the bookshelf. The books are otherwise nonmagical and cover a wide array of subjects.

K22. TELEPORTATION CIRCLE

A staircase rising from area K21 leads to this highest chamber of the outer tower. It contains the following features:

- A **spectator** floats in the middle of the room, and four **flying snakes** flutter above the rafters.
- Runes inscribed on the floor form a large, faintly glowing circle.
- Five wooden treasure chests with sturdy padlocks rest against the walls.

Guardians. The spectator guards the treasure chests and attacks intruders who aren't being escorted by Manshoon or one of his lieutenants. The flying snakes join the battle, fighting as allies of the spectator.

Teleportation Circle. The teleportation circle functions as described under the spell of the same name in the *Player's Handbook*. Additionally, a creature wearing a *teleporter ring* (see "Teleporter Rings," page 157) can use this circle to access the teleportation circle in Manshoon's sanctum (area E1). A *teleporter ring* that is brought within 5 feet of the circle begins to hum softly.

Treasure Chests. The padlocks on the chests are illusory but feel real to the touch. A *detect magic* spell or similar magic reveals an aura of illusion magic around each one. Attempts to pick or break the locks fail, but a *knock* spell or similar magic causes a lock to open.

Chest 1 has the image of an anvil carved into its lid. It contains a set of smith's tools (worth 20 gp).

Chest 2 has iron bands and contains a set of painter's supplies (worth 10 gp), as well as three small pots of colored paint (blue, red, and yellow).

Chest 3 has tiny clawed feet and contains six blank spellbooks with leather covers (worth 50 gp each).

Chest 4 has a flat lid with a city scene painted on it. It contains a scholar's pack (worth 40 gp) and a book of Dwarvish phrases. A character who doesn't speak Dwarvish can use the book to communicate on a rudimentary level with friendly dwarves.

Chest 5 is inlaid with silver and topped with a silver statuette of a rearing hippogriff (worth 25 gp). Inside is a wooden rack that holds eight glass vials—six containing *potions of healing* and two containing individual doses of essence of ether (see "Poisons" in chapter 8 of the *Dungeon Master's Guide*). The poison can be identified with a successful DC 13 Intelligence (Nature) check.

EXTRADIMENSIONAL SANCTUM

Manshoon's extradimensional sanctum exists in a finite demiplane. Created by the original Manshoon, it is known to the wizard's clones, and it currently serves as the lair of the clone described in this adventure.

Outside Manshoon's sanctum, the demiplane is a vast void filled with swirling purple mist. Any creature that enters this mist is teleported to area E1 and must make a DC 18 Constitution saving throw, taking 22 (4d10) force damage on a failed save, or half as much damage on a successful one.

There are no cardinal directions in this extradimensional space; compasses spin futilely in the absence of north, south, east, and west.

SANCTUM FEATURES

These features apply to all areas in the extradimensional sanctum:

- Rooms have 10-foot-high ceilings, with 8-foot-high passages and 7-foot-high doorways connecting them. The walls, floors, and ceilings throughout are made of seamless alabaster.
- Doors are made of iron and have AC 19, 27 hit points, and immunity to poison and psychic damage. A locked door can be picked by someone who makes a successful DC 17 Dexterity check using thieves' tools, or can be forced open with a successful DC 25 Strength (Athletics) check. As an action, Manshoon or his simulacrum can lock or unlock any door in the sanctum by touch.
- Except where noted, areas of the sanctum are brightly lit by *continual flame* spells cast on wall sconces.

AREAS OF THE SANCTUM

The following locations are keyed to map 8.2.

E1. ARRIVAL POINT

This room is the extradimensional sanctum's anchor to the Material Plane, and one can teleport to this chamber

---

> **TELEPORTER RINGS**
>
> To access Manshoon's extraplanar sanctum, one needs a *teleporter ring*: a brass signet ring bearing a stylized M, and which emanates an aura of conjuration magic when targeted by a *detect magic* spell or similar magic. Manshoon gives these rings to his most trusted servants.
>
> As an action, a creature wearing a *teleporter ring* can activate the teleportation circle either in area K22 or area E1, teleporting itself and up to six other willing creatures from one circle to the other.

from other places on the Material Plane. The room has the following features:

- A teleportation circle is inscribed on the alabaster floor here. Characters teleported to this area from area K22 appear within the circle.
- The ceiling and three of the walls are made of 6-inch-thick sheets of transparent glass, through which the swirling purple mist that fills the demiplane can be seen. The fourth wall is made of alabaster and has a locked iron door set into it (leading to area E2).
- A black-robed female human with a bald, scarred head watches this room through a glass window set into the wall of another room (area E3).

Dreadful Host. The figure watching through the window is Kaevja Cynavern (see area E3), and she can see through the purple mist between the two rooms easily enough. She uses a *sending* spell to contact Manshoon as soon as the characters arrive. Manshoon sends his simulacrum (see appendix B) to unlock the door to area E2 and greet the new arrivals. It takes 1 minute for the simulacrum to arrive (from area E7), during which time Kaevja uses another *sending* spell to inform a random character that "Your gracious host is on the way, and looks forward to meeting you."

When the simulacrum arrives, it passes itself off as Manshoon as it welcomes the characters to its extradimensional sanctum. It offers a guided tour, gesturing for the characters to enter area E2 ahead of it. If they comply, it triggers the alarm in area E2 and attacks.

Glass Walls. Each 5-foot section of glass wall has AC 13, 30 hit points, and immunity to acid, poison, and psychic damage. The purple mist that fills the demiplane doesn't enter this area even if the glass is shattered.

Teleportation Circle. The teleportation circle functions as described under the spell of the same name in the *Player's Handbook*. Additionally, a creature wearing a *teleporter ring* (see "Teleporter Rings," page 157) can use this circle to access the teleportation circle in Kolat Towers (area K22). A *teleporter ring* that is brought within 5 feet of the circle begins to hum softly.

E2. FOYER

The door to area E1 is locked. All other doors leading from this room are unlocked. This foyer has the following features:

- Set into the alabaster floor is a large symbol in black marble, depicting a winged snake biting a coin. Characters recognize this as the symbol of the Zhentarim. (The coin conceals an alarm mechanism.)

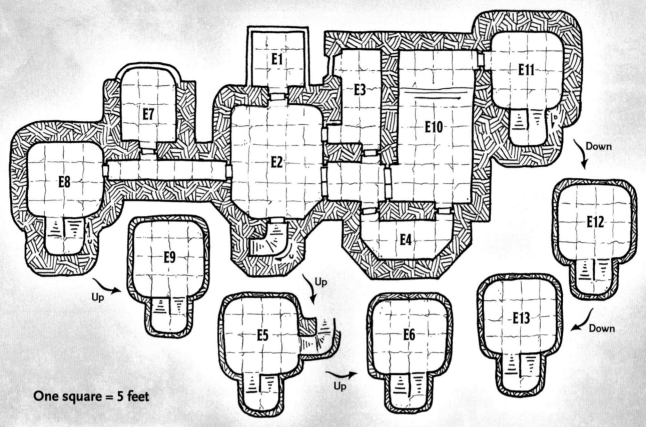

One square = 5 feet

Map 8.2: Extradimensional Sanctum

- Hanging on the walls are twelve metal masks bearing human-like visages.

Alarm Mechanism. The 1-foot-diameter, disk-shaped tile that serves as the coin in the Zhentarim symbol is actually a pressure plate. When pressed or stepped on, it sounds a magic gong that can be heard throughout the sanctum. The alarm can be disabled by someone who makes a successful DC 20 Dexterity check using thieves' tools, but it triggers accidentally if the check fails by 5 or more. The alarm brings the following defenders, who attack all intruders in the room:

- Kaevja Cynavern (see area E3)
- The Manshoon simulacrum (see area E7)
- Vevette Blackwater and Agorn Fuoco (see area E8)
- Havia Quickknife and Mookie Plush (see area E10)

If the characters manage to overcome all these foes, they are free to explore the sanctum. Manshoon awaits them in area E12.

Characters who are reduced to 0 hit points by Manshoon's defenders are knocked unconscious. If the entire party is defeated, the unconscious characters are stripped of their spellbooks and magic items (including any *teleporter rings* they obtained in Kolat Towers). They then awaken in a back alley of Waterdeep with 1 hit point each. If the characters return to Kolat Towers, they find the place cleared out and the teleportation circle in area K22 permanently dispelled.

Masks of Manshoon. The masks belong to Manshoon and have been worn by him in the past. A *detect magic* spell or similar magic reveals an aura of evocation magic around each one. Any creature that dons a mask takes 9 (2d8) lightning damage. Once this effect triggers, the mask becomes nonmagical and harmless.

E3. Guard Station

A 5-foot-square window in this area looks out toward area E1. Unless she has been drawn elsewhere, Kaevja Cynavern stands watch in front of the window.

Kaevja was a Red Wizard of Thay until she saw an opportunity to study magic under Manshoon. Before he accepted her, Manshoon forced her to remove her distinctive Thayan head tattoos and to trade in her Red Wizard robes for black ones.

Kaevja Cynavern is a female Mulan human **mage**, with these changes:

- Kaevja is lawful evil. She knows Common, Draconic, Dwarvish, and Elvish.
- She has the *sending* spell prepared instead of the *fly* spell, and she carries a yellow *elemental gem*.

In battle, Kaevja breaks the *elemental gem*, summoning an **earth elemental** and commanding it to attack her enemies.

E4. Pantry

This room contains the following features:

- Floor-to-ceiling shelves are stuffed with breads, cheeses, dried meats, nuts, and a few baskets of fresh produce.

- Two barrels labeled "WATER" and two labeled "ALE" are crammed into a corner.

E5. LABORATORY

This room contains the following features:

- Beakers, bottles, and test tubes are set on a marble table in the middle of this room, next to a basin of water.
- One staircase descends 10 feet to area E2, and another ascends 10 feet to area E6.

Urstul Floxin. If he survived earlier encounters with the characters, Urstul Floxin (see appendix B) stands at the table, dourly scrubbing lab equipment. He is being punished for allowing the *Stone of Golorr* to slip through his fingers (during the events of chapter 3). Nevertheless, he remains loyal to Manshoon. If he is confronted, Urstul feigns anger toward the wizard and offers to help the characters defeat him, but this ruse can be seen through by someone who makes a successful DC 14 Wisdom (Insight) check. Given the chance, Urstul leads the characters to Manshoon, then attacks them to prove his unwavering loyalty in front of his master.

If the characters fall for Urstul's ruse but nevertheless demand that he relinquish his weapons in order to accompany them, the Zhent assassin laughs at them and attacks.

E6. BINDING CHAMBER

A circle inscribed with runes is carved into the alabaster floor of this room. It radiates an aura of abjuration magic when targeted by a *detect magic* spell or similar magic.

Manshoon uses the circle to bind extraplanar creatures. When a celestial, an elemental, a fey, or a fiend is summoned inside the circle, it can't voluntarily leave that area until its summoner uses an action to suppress the circle's magic for 1 minute. The magic is also suppressed if any part of the circle falls within an *antimagic field*, or if *dispel magic* (DC 17) is successfully cast on it.

E7. MANSHOON'S SIMULACRUM

This room is extremely cold and contains the following features:

- Frigid air blows into the room through small vents in the floor. In the middle of the room is an open sarcophagus carved from ice, which contains a humanoid figure made of snow.
- The back wall is made of 5-inch-thick curved glass. Frost covers the glass, partially blotting out the swirling purple mist of the demiplane beyond.

Simulacrum. If it hasn't been summoned elsewhere, Manshoon's simulacrum (see appendix B) is standing before the glass wall with its back to the door. The simulacrum resembles a robed wizard with long black hair, pale skin, and an articulated metal left hand and forearm. Its face is concealed behind a steel mask that bears a smiling visage. The simulacrum attacks anyone it doesn't recognize.

Extreme Cold. The rules for extreme cold (see chapter 5 of the *Dungeon Master's Guide*) apply in this room.

Glass Wall. Each 5-foot section of glass wall has AC 13, 30 hit points, and immunity to acid, poison, and psy-

chic damage. The purple mist that fills the demiplane doesn't enter this room even if the glass is shattered.

Simulacrum Sarcophagus. This ice-carved container weighs 1,000 pounds and begins to melt if taken out of the room. The snow figure in the sarcophagus is part of the material component of a *simulacrum* spell. Manshoon can use it to create a new simulacrum if his current one is destroyed.

E8. READING ROOM

This room contains the following features:

- Delightful warmth radiates from a brazier of green flame encircled by eight cushioned chairs.
- Unless they've been drawn elsewhere, two of Manshoon's lieutenants are here: Vevette Blackwater (CE female Tethyrian human **swashbuckler**; see appendix B) and Agorn Fuoco (NE male Turami human **bard**; see appendix B). Vevette is relaxing in a chair, while Agorn strums a lyre.
- An alabaster staircase ascends 10 feet to area E9.

Zhents. Vevette and Agorn are two of Manshoon's most trusted followers. Vevette commands the wizard's forces against the Xanathar Guild, while Agorn commands those who oppose the Zhents that aren't loyal to Manshoon. At the moment, they are resting in the sanctum while awaiting orders from Manshoon.

Green Flame Brazier. A *detect magic* spell or similar magic reveals an aura of evocation magic around the brazier. The brazier casts a *fireball* spell (save DC 15) centered on itself whenever a creature in the room speaks the words "green flame" aloud. Once the brazier has cast this spell, it can't do so again for another 24 hours. Agorn knows this feature of the brazier, and he uses it in combat if the situation is desperate.

E9. LIBRARY

Alabaster shelves line every wall and jut out into the center of this room, all of them packed with books that deal with subjects of interest to wizards. Manshoon has amassed a sizable collection, including ten rare volumes he removed from Duhlark Kolat's collection.

Treasure. Each rare book is worth 50 gp, and the entire collection is worth 5,000 gp.

E10. AUDIENCE CHAMBER

High-ranking Zhents who desire an audience with Manshoon come here. The room contains the following features:

- The area is split into two levels, with alabaster steps climbing 3 feet to a smaller raised platform overlooking the larger area. The platform is bare except for three golden banners hanging on the back wall, each displaying the symbol of the Zhentarim—a black, winged snake biting a coin.
- The lower part of the room contains a black marble table surrounded by high-backed wooden chairs. The table stands out in stark contrast against the alabaster walls and floor.
- If they haven't been drawn elsewhere, two of Manshoon's followers are sparring and engaged in mock fisticuffs atop the table.

Zhents. Two female lightfoot halflings—Havia Quick-knife and Mookie Plush—believe that Manshoon is the rightful leader of the Zhentarim. They serve him fearlessly, and will sacrifice themselves to ensure that his plans come to fruition. They are **martial arts adepts** (see appendix B), with these changes:

- Havia and Mookie are lawful evil.
- They have 49 (11d6 + 11) hit points each.
- They have these racial traits: They are Small, and their walking speed is 25 feet. They can move through the space of a Medium or larger creature. They have advantage on saving throws against being frightened. They speak Common and Halfling.

Havia and Mookie each wear a *teleporter ring* (see "Teleporter Rings," page 157).

E11. ZHENT QUARTERS

This room contains the following features:

- Pressed against the walls of this room are five wooden beds (three sized for humans, two for halflings).
- Next to each bed is a wooden chest.
- An alabaster staircase descends to area E12.

Kaevja Cynavern, Vevette Blackwater, Agorn Fuoco, Havia Quickknife, and Mookie Plush all sleep here.

Treasure. In addition to folded clothes and worthless personal effects, each of the chests holds treasure.

Kaevja's chest contains a gold amulet inset with a red crystal rune (worth 250 gp). A successful DC 15 Intelligence (Arcana) check reveals that the rune is a symbol of evocation, though the amulet is nonmagical.

Vevette's chest has three *potions of healing*.

Agorn's chest contains a bundle of love letters from someone named Tamzyn. Hidden in one of the envelopes is an elegant platinum necklace (worth 250 gp), featuring a tiny cameo containing a sketched portrait of a beautiful Turami woman.

In Havia's chest is a golden comb shaped like a stylized dragon with tiny rubies for eyes (worth 250 gp).

Mookie's chest contains a tiny halfling doll. Stuffed inside the doll is a pouch that holds five 100 gp pearls.

E12. MANSHOON'S QUARTERS

No one aside from Manshoon is allowed down here. The alabaster stairs that lead to this room descend 10 feet farther to area E13.

This room contains the following features:

- Across from the stairs stands a large bed with purple sheets. Sitting on the edge of the bed is a handsome young male human in elegant robes. Long black hair partially conceals his angelic face as he attaches a metal appendage to the withered stump of his left arm.
- The only other piece of furniture is a table with legs carved to resemble winged serpents. Displayed on the table is a metal mask with an intimidating, tyrannical visage.

The handsome young figure is **Manshoon** (see appendix B), who is much older than he looks.

This version of Manshoon isn't spoiling for a fight. He commends the characters for making it this far and shows no concern for the Zhents they defeated to reach him, since he considers all his followers expendable. The characters' best chance of survival is to convince Manshoon that they can be cowed or bribed into working for him. Weary of his conflict with the Xanathar Guild, Manshoon suggests that the characters prove their usefulness to him by hunting down and killing Xanathar in its lair (see chapter 5). Manshoon also demands that they keep his presence in Waterdeep a secret for now, saying that he will reward them for their discretion "when the time comes." In exchange, he allows the characters to return to Waterdeep and promises them positions of power in his organization once Xanathar's death is confirmed. He has no intention of making good on this promise, but refusing to work for him puts the characters in a tight spot, since the evil archwizard can't risk exposure.

If a fight breaks out, Manshoon grabs his *staff of power* (which he hides under the bed) and holds his ground. For more information on how to play Manshoon, see "Facing Manshoon" at the beginning of this chapter.

Tyrant's Mask. The mask on the table is nonmagical, but Manshoon likes to put it on before meeting with his followers.

E13. MANSHOON'S STUDY

The alabaster stairs end here. The room contains the following features:

- A plush lavender carpet covers the floor.
- In one far corner of the room, a low table is set between two purple couches. The table has a thin drawer built into it.
- In the other far corner, Manshoon's spellbook rests atop a black marble lectern protected by an invisible **helmed horror**. The construct attacks anyone other than Manshoon who disturbs the book (becoming visible as it does so). It obeys Manshoon's commands if he is present, and it fights until destroyed.

Table. The table's drawer has an *arcane lock* spell cast on it. The spell can be bypassed by someone who makes a successful DC 25 Dexterity check using thieves' tools, or with a *knock* spell or similar magic. The drawer can also be forced open with a successful DC 21 Strength (Athletics) check. Inside is a leather-bound ledger that provides a paper trail implicating Manshoon in two blackmail schemes. An hour spent studying the ledger uncovers the following information:

- Corylus Thann, a racist Waterdavian noble, is paying the Zhentarim not to reveal that he hired Zhent thugs to assault nonhumans.
- Jelenn Urmbrusk, a Waterdavian noble, receives regular payments from the Zhentarim to offset monies he loses in bad investments.

The ledger doesn't reveal that Corylus Thann and Jelenn Urmbrusk are Masked Lords, or that Manshoon's blackmail of them also forces them to use their influence to cover up or dismiss crimes perpetrated by Manshoon's forces in Waterdeep. If the authorities obtain the ledger, they round up anyone suspected of having ties to Manshoon or the Zhentarim, which disrupts the wizard's operation (see "Disrupting Manshoon's Operation," page 147). Surprisingly, neither Corylus nor Jelenn is arrested or even questioned.

Slipped into the ledger is a piece of paper with a list of names in Manshoon's handwriting. Manshoon keeps this list of Masked Lords whose identities he knows, with check marks indicating the ones he's blackmailing:

Mirt
Corylus Thann √
Thardouk Starbuckler
Jelenn Urmbrusk √
Dorgar Adarbrent

Manshoon's Spellbook. This spellbook weighs 20 pounds and is covered in beholder hide. It contains all the spells Manshoon has prepared (see appendix B) plus the following spells: *alarm, alter self, animate dead, antimagic field, arcane lock, blight, dispel magic, dominate monster, dream, etherealness, Evard's black tentacles, feather fall, fireball, fly, gaseous form, geas, gentle repose, glyph of warding, hold monster, major image, mass suggestion, phantom steed, protection from evil and good, scrying, symbol, telekinesis, teleport, teleportation circle, Tenser's floating disk, tongues, true seeing, vampiric touch, wall of fire,* and *wish.* Stealing or destroying this spellbook disrupts Manshoon's operation (see "Disrupting Manshoon's Operation," page 147), since he must devote time and resources to retrieving or replacing it.

If Laeral Silverhand has the opportunity to trade for Manshoon's spellbook, she offers the characters a sailing ship and a set of *bracers of archery* for it. Vajra Safahr offers the characters membership in Force Grey, a *cape of the mountebank,* and a *wand of lightning bolts* for the book.

Stone of Golorr. If Manshoon has the *Stone of Golorr,* he keeps it in the drawer of the table along with his ledger.

SPECIAL EVENTS

You can use one or more of the following special events before or after the characters explore Kolat Towers and Manshoon's extradimensional sanctum.

BLACKMAILED LORDS

The events described in this section might occur if the characters obtain the ledger from area E13 and use the information in it to confront either Corylus Thann or Jelenn Urmbrusk about their suspicious dealings with Manshoon. The Thann and Umbrusk families have walled estates in the Sea Ward.

CORYLUS THANN

The Thanns are Waterdeep's most prominent vintners and have deep roots in the city. Corylus (LE male Tethyrian human **noble**) is happy to let other members

of his family manage the wine business while he focuses on his duties as a Masked Lord. Unfortunately, he lacks the principles and sound judgment that have led to House Thann's success in the past. He also places the welfare of humans above nonhumans. In the past, he has used Zhentarim thugs to inflict harm on nonhumans who sought positions of political power in the city. Now the Zhents are blackmailing Corylus, threatening to expose his bigotry unless he uses his influence as a Masked Lord to cover up their illegal activities.

The characters are most likely to encounter Corylus as he travels through the city by coach, accompanied by six human **guards** who watch his back and keep the rabble at bay. Corylus refuses to speak with the party. If the characters become an annoyance, he has eight crooked members of the City Watch (human **veterans**) crack down on them, then uses his position as Masked Lord to clear any charges leveled against these Watch members. Corylus refuses to be indebted to anyone, so any attempt by the characters to curry favor with him is met with suspicion, if not outright hostility. Even if they dispose of Manshoon, Corylus refuses to acknowledge that he owes them anything.

Jelenn Urmbrusk

Jelenn (N female Tethyrian human **noble**) is a proud woman in her fifties who desperately wants to get out of debt. Several bad investments ruined her money-lending business, and most of her reliable customers have turned to other providers such as the Cassalanters. Jelenn could have borrowed money from any of a number of nobles in the city or sold off some of the property her family owns in Waterdeep, but doing so would have turned her private financial woes into local gossip. Fear of that exposure led her to borrow money from the Zhentarim instead—a decision she has come to regret. The Zhents working for Manshoon promise to keep their relationship secret on the condition that she do everything in her power to further the group's welfare in Waterdeep.

When not dealing with her slimy creditors, Jelenn is occupied with Masked Lord business. She has no time for a face-to-face meeting with anyone she doesn't know. Characters can confront her as she comes or goes to and from her villa, but she never travels without sixteen **guards** who form a protective wall around her. If the characters brazenly mention Manshoon or the Zhentarim by name to her, Jelenn demands that they leave her alone or face dire consequences. Jelenn's threat is mostly bluster, since she's not eager to make enemies.

If the characters free Jelenn from the yoke of the Black Network by defeating Manshoon, her debt is effectively canceled. In her delight, she grants them a special favor (see "Special Favors" in chapter 7 of the *Dungeon Master's Guide*). On the other hand, if they threaten to go to the press with Manshoon's ledger in an attempt to blackmail or discredit her, she pretends to go along with them while secretly using her influence as a Masked Lord to make their lives difficult.

Deadwinter Day Feast

The Fellowship of Innkeepers—in conjunction with the Bakers' Guild, the Guild of Butchers, and the Vintners', Distillers', and Brewers' Guild—decides to hold a Deadwinter Day feast for the residents of Trollskull Alley. Broxley Fairkettle (see "Sample Guild Representatives," page 41) asks the characters if they would be willing to host the feast in their tavern. He believes the gesture would be appreciated by their neighbors, in light of the recent deaths in the area (see chapter 3).

If the characters offer up their tavern for the feast, guild representatives arrive to stock and decorate it for the event. During the three days before the holiday, the tavern is bustling with activity and excitement. Hundreds show up on the day of the feast to partake—not only residents of Trollskull Alley, but also folk from neighboring streets. There's plenty of food to go around, but the tavern practically groans under the weight of the crowd, and additional tables are set up outside to handle the overflow. People don't appear to mind, even as heavy snow begins to fall. Members of the City Watch are on hand to make sure everyone behaves.

Nothing violent happens during the Deadwinter Day feast, but the tavern suffers damage as a result of the crowds. The Carpenters', Roofers', and Plaisterers' Guild offers to make repairs for free, but the characters must close the establishment for a tenday to facilitate the work. The closure has no effect on business in the long term, however, since the feast fosters such goodwill that clients return in force when the tavern reopens.

The feast is a great opportunity for characters to hobnob with neighbors, guild members, and City Watch constables, as well as to gather information on local happenings.

Secret Simulacrum

If the characters make an enemy of Manshoon, he tries to capture one of them and replace that character with a magical duplicate created using the *simulacrum* spell. If one of the players is absent for a game session and circumstances allow it, Manshoon targets that character for replacement while the rest of the party is distracted by other matters. You don't need to roleplay the character's capture; just assume it happens. To create a simulacrum of the character, Manshoon needs some hair, fingernail clippings, or other piece of the character's body. Once he obtains the necessary components from the captured character, he creates the simulacrum and sends it to the party with instructions to spy on the group and undermine it from within.

If Manshoon embeds a simulacrum within the party, talk privately to the player whose character has been replaced. Then have that player run the simulacrum until it is destroyed or the character it replaced is reintroduced. The simulacrum has the same statistics as the character, but it has only half the character's hit point maximum and can't gain levels.

Volo's Waterdeep Enchiridion

A Visitor's Guide to the City's Splendors

By Volothamp Geddarm
Under the generous patronage of the Lords Melshimber

Published by Tym Waterdeep Limited in association with the
Fellowship of Innkeepers and the Fellowship of Carters and Coachmen

I, Volothamp Geddarm, verily attest to the veracity of the words
printed herein. "Set your course by the truth and you shall never be
lost, no matter how far you wander." I coined this well-worn
adage myself years ago, and it has served me well in all my travels.*

*Consider any antinomy, jactitation, mendacity, obloquy, pasquinade,
parapraxis, traducement, or similar found in this document to be corrigendum.
Address all claims of such to:

Abricade Fellswop, Solicitor
17 Mulgomir's Way, Castle Ward
Waterdeep

ELCOME, TRAVELER! YOU HAVE IN YOUR hands the foremost and most up-to-date guide to the city—smiled over by none other than its Open Lord, Lady Laeral Silverhand. This chapbook will serve you well until my seminal work on the subject, *Volo's Guide to Waterdeep*—sadly long out of print, but now a tome prized by collectors—can be updated and printed anew. Ask any broadsheet seller, innkeeper, shopkeeper, tavern owner, or bookseller if they'll soon have copies of the new edition for sale!

ENTERING WATERDEEP

Likely you have already arrived in Waterdeep and borne witness to some of its many wonders. But in case this pamphlet has found its way beneath your worthy eyes in anticipation of your visit, due to the commendable efforts of some friend or family member who loves you dearly, I shall explain briefly the circumstances of entry.

You will have traveled through lands claimed and controlled by the Lords of Waterdeep long before you see its walls. If you've come from the south by the Trade Way, you'll have met the City Guard at their post at Zundbridge. From the north by way of the Long Road, you'll have passed under their watchful eyes at the town of Rassalantar. And whether by land or sea, you'll likely also have been spotted by the Griffon Cavalry—even if you have not spotted them.

Worry not. Waterdeep is a welcoming city, and you have nothing to fear from these guardians unless you lead a rampaging army of orcs, a horde of gnolls, or similar. They don't even require a toll be paid. (Beware any City Guard who demands a toll, and report the incident to a magister of Waterdeep at your earliest convenience.)

If you travel in a large caravan or on a ship, you will be required to register with a magister at the gate at which you arrived or with the harbor magister. Magisters can easily be recognized by the black robes they wear (and, in fact, are commonly called "black robes" as a result) and the City Guard force that always accompanies them. Be aware that magisters can pass a sentence without a trial. It behooves you to treat them with proper respect.

If you travel overland in a small party or alone, you aren't required to register with a magister unless your stay extends beyond a tenday. At that point, you must register with a magister either at the harbor, the gates, or the city courts. Discovery of your failure to do so can result in a fine or forced labor. Of course, registration subjects you to monthly taxation. But as a truculent old acquaintance from the Dales once told me, "The sheep gives the shepherd its fleece or there'll be mutton for dinner." That is, the magisters will get you either way, so you might as well register up front.

That said, many canny visitors with business for a month or a season betimes avail themselves of the hospitality of inns in Undercliff, the pleasant farmland east of the city proper. The less well-off often find accommodation in the Field Ward. Because neither are official wards of the city, they aren't subject to taxation. Note, however, that because both these areas have yet to be formally accepted as wards of the city, they don't benefit from the securities of Guild Law or the protection of the Watch. If you choose to follow this path, be on your guard. Fools rush in where auditors fear to tread.

Regardless of what size party you arrive with or by what means, if you arrive by night or in winter, expect to register. In winter and at night the gates are shut. Ships aren't expected at night or as a regular occurrence after the first frost of the coming season, and are often met at docking by a magister—or by a contingent of the Guard who will hold travelers aboard until a magister can be summoned.

None of these rules apply to the city's least used gate, the West Gate. This smaller gate opens onto the Mud Flats—a mucky beach used by clam diggers, shore fishers, and those brave enough to bathe in the cold waves. Those who make a living through fishing with nets or traps also use this gate, keeping their small boats on the beach to avoid docking fees. Locals register with the Guard as they exit and as they enter. No magister is stationed at the gate, but no new arrivals to Waterdeep are accepted here.

If you approach by air, expect a vigorous pursuit by and confrontation with the Griffon Cavalry. Only specially licensed individuals and mounts can fly over Waterdeep. It is best to land well outside the city and approach on foot.

YOUR ARRIVAL IN THE CITY

The splendors that await you in Waterdeep are legendary. Each of the city's wards is detailed in this work, telling you what to expect depending on where you are, as well as what thrilling things you might see and do. Before that, however, there are the small matters of knowing something of the history of the place you visit, and of understanding how to comport yourself in the Sword Coast's grandest metropolis.

A LONG HISTORY (IN BRIEF)

"There shall come a time when our city and its deepwater bay shall grow in fame and fortune across many realms and many worlds. Folk shall know of Waterdeep, our City of Splendors, and sing its praises. I have seen it thus, and I endeavor to make it true."

—Ahghairon, the first Open Lord of Waterdeep,
circa 1032 DR

People have inhabited the plateau upon which Waterdeep stands for longer than human histories record. But as is the way across the dangerous North, civilization at the foot of Mount Waterdeep has crested and ebbed in great waves. Elf scholars assure me that it was once the site of Aelinthaldaar, the capital of their ancient empire of Illefarn. So it was already a glorious place when a dwarf prospector named Melair discovered mithral beneath the mountain. In agreement with the Illefarni, Melair called kith and kin to mine under the mountain and in the plateau, and thus Clan Melairkyn came to rule below as the Illefarni did above.

THE SEA MAIDENS FAIRE PARADE

But this fruitful alliance lasted less than the lifetime of a dwarf, for the emperor of the elves—what they call a "coronal"—commanded that all leave in the Retreat, that great exodus of elves from Faerûn to their mystical isle of Evermeet. Not all elves agreed with this edict, and many were determined to stay. Well, what emperor has ever willingly allowed another to sit in his throne? The coronal had all of Aelinthaldaar razed by magic, and the remaining elves splintered into separate kingdoms. The Melairkyn, of course, saw this as a breaking of their bargain, and never again did they deal with elves. Instead, they tunneled ever deeper under the mountain, never to be heard from again.

So it was that the humans who came to the deepwater harbor found it empty and suitable for their own purposes. For more than a thousand years, folk lived and traded at the site of what would become Waterdeep, but their identities remain a mystery—with a curious exception. We know that at some point during this period, the wizard Halaster Blackcloak built his tower at the base of Mount Waterdeep and came to rule the lands around—until he, like the Melairkyn, vanished under the mountain.

Various warlords later claimed the plateau's harbor as their own, but it was one known as Nimoar who is best remembered. *A History of Waterdeep: Age One, The Rise of the Warlord* records how Nimoar raised a wooden stockade to protect the settlement around the harbor, claiming rule over the town that by then was being called "Nimoar's Hold, the Town of Waters Deep."

War between orcs and elves in lands farther north drove hordes of trolls south to claw at the fledgling city, and amid this danger, Nimoar died of old age. Many bloody struggles unfolded between local folk and trolls, until the magic of a youth named Ahghairon turned the fortunes of war against the "everlasting ones," which were destroyed or scattered. Ahghairon improved slowly in skill and power with the passage of the years, until he became a great mage. He is said to have discovered a supply of *potions of longevity*, or learned the art of making such, for he lived on and on, still physically in his prime for decade after decade.

A History of Waterdeep: Age Two, The Lords' Rule Begins records that in the year 1032 DR, Ahghairon (then in his 112th winter) argued with Raurlor, who was then Warlord of Waterdeep. Raurlor wanted to use Waterdeep's acquired wealth and strength of arms to create a northern empire. Ahghairon defied him before all the people, and Raurlor ordered the mage to be chained. But when Ahghairon magically turned aside all who sought to lay hands on him, Raurlor struck at the mage with his own sword. Ahghairon then rose into the air, just out of reach, and used his magic to transmute Raurlor's blade into a hissing serpent. When the serpent struck Raurlor, he died in full view of his shocked followers.

Ahghairon then gathered the leaders of Waterdeep's armies and powerful families. While runners sought to bring them to the castle, flames roared and crackled in the empty warlord's throne at Ahghairon's bidding, so

that none could sit there. Then, when the gathered host of worthies met in the audience chamber, the wizard seated himself on the flaming throne. Immediately the fires died away, leaving both the throne and Ahghairon unharmed.

From this seat—the very one on which the Open Lord sits to this day—Ahghairon decreed how the city would be governed. While he would sit as lord openly, a council of other lords of nearly equal power would rule with him. But the identity of those other lords would be hidden even from each other, thus preventing any of them from being approached and influenced by bribe or threat. So it was that Ahghairon established Waterdeep's system of governance.

Ahghairon was instrumental in establishing many of Waterdeep's other institutions, such as its black-robed magisters, its Griffon Cavalry, and the city's many guilds. The first Open Lord ruled wisely for over two centuries before the magic sustaining his health failed. He now lies entombed in his tower, which you can still see standing in the courtyard of the Palace of Waterdeep. Beware that you don't approach too close, however, lest you stumble into the invisible barrier—a "force cage," I am told—that surrounds the tower.

Within that barrier lie additional protective wards, as demonstrated by the floating bones of the last person who tried to defy them. The name of this poor soul has been lost to time, but the miscreant was likely a wizard who sought to steal the magic treasures that had been entombed with their former owner. Now they hang in

the air beyond the invisible force cage in rough semblance of their natural position, occasionally displaced temporarily by strong winds or mischievous children with long sticks.

Ahghairon's wise rule is celebrated on the first day of Eleasis, which has come to be known as Ahghairon's Day. For more about this day, see "City Celebrations."

Many significant events stand out in Waterdeep's history. But none have had so great an effect on daily life than the three apocalyptic periods known as the Time of Troubles, the Spellplague, and the Sundering—the most recent (and hopefully final). On all these occasions, the actions of gods at war with one another led to the loss or the twisting of magic in the world. During the Time of Troubles, Waterdeep stood at the center of events. But the effects of the more recent crises can still be seen in the city today, even though they occurred a great distance from where Waterdeep stands.

When the gods walked among mortals during the Time of Troubles, they were cast down to the world by the mysterious Overgod Ao in 1358 DR. Until then, none but the gods had known of Ao's existence, and since then, we have learned little more. As all know, the crisis began with the theft of the *Tablets of Fate* by the vile and ambitious gods Bane and Myrkul, later joined by Bhaal. These mystic artifacts supposedly determine the extent of the gods' power, and dictate how they use that power. As punishment for this affront, Ao cast down the gods (or the ones that humans worshiped, at any rate) and then demanded that they return the tablets to him.

But Ao was not omniscient, it seems, nor overly wise. The gods didn't seek out the tablets, and thus it was left to mortal heroes to sort out the mess. They did so, their efforts culminating in Waterdeep. It was on the slopes of Mount Waterdeep that Ao was last seen, when he granted godhood to the human heroes Kelemvor, Midnight (who became Mystra), and Cyric.

It is no surprise, then, that Waterdeep has since attracted a steady stream of pilgrims who worship Midnight at Mystra's temple and pay homage to Kelemvor in the City of the Dead. It might surprise you, though, to learn that Waterdavians had a short-lived penchant for worshiping Ao. The Cynosure—that great marble-pillared structure on the edge of the Market, now rented out for private and public events—was built as a temple to Ao. But his worship fell from favor when all prayers to him went unanswered, and folk realized they had no idea what he stood for or who he was. You can visit the Cynosure to see sculptures and paintings of all the major participants and events in the Time of Troubles. Entrance is free to the public on any day when no event (such as a meeting of guilds, a noble's coming-of-age ball, or some such) is scheduled.

In the Year of Blue Fire (1385 DR), the Spellplague gripped the world. None knew it at the time, but it has since been divined that Cyric's long hatred for Mystra boiled over and led to his murder of the goddess of magic. I was absent from the world at this time—indisposed by the force of an *imprisonment* spell. Elminster has since explained the events to me, but I must confess that much of what he said made little sense. It was a long lecture having something to do with stars, "crystal spheres," and "demiplanar reality mirrors." Suffice it to say, parts of our world switched with parts of another one, and magic was again disrupted.

During this period, the powerful magical fields that protect and affect Waterdeep became unstable. This led to the disastrous activation of most of Waterdeep's amazing walking statues during an earthquake. In the years before, the walking statues were often hidden on the Ethereal Plane, to be called forth only in times of great peril. Many in the city doubted that such massive, sapient constructs were even real, let alone that they guarded the city invisibly. The Spellplague confirmed their existence for all to see, though, and each carved a swath of destruction through Waterdeep before it was stopped. Now the walking statues stand about the city in various states of readiness or disarray—one of the most obvious of Waterdeep's so-called splendors.

After the Spellplague came the Sundering. Elf scholars insist on calling it the Second Sundering, asserting that the creation of Evermeet thousands of years ago was a similar happening. Regardless of the name you give it, the event that unfolded beginning in 1482 DR was the result of another world—called Abeir, I am told—passing again into our own. The gods were once more cast into the mortal realm, this time embodied in mortal beings known as Chosen. The old troublemaker Ao seems to be the cause of it all, though why he chose to cast down the gods was a matter of dispute even among those entities while they were with us.

Apparently, all of this was foreseen by Waterdeep's legendary wizard Khelben Arunsun, and it was only through his wisdom and the efforts of Elminster, Laeral Silverhand—now the Open Lord of Waterdeep—and a handful of others that the world was saved. According to Elminster, Ao remade the *Tablets of Fate* as a result, restoring the divine order and separating Abeir from Toril. But take that as you may. According to that roguish longbeard, he saves the world without anyone noticing every other month or so.

SURVIVING IN THE CITY

Waterdeep is, by and large, the most civilized city on the Sword Coast. Yet civilized doesn't mean safe, nor does it mean easy to navigate. Many day-to-day elements of life in Waterdeep that residents take for granted are, to new arrivals, a bevy of wonders and dangers not seen in any other settlement within a thousand miles. Here's what you need to know to survive your first few hours in the city. Mark this section for frequent reference!

THE CODE LEGAL

Waterdeep is no village led by hidebound hierarchs or petty fiefdom ruled by the whim of a warlord. It is a city of laws molded by Tyr's spirit of justice. As a rule, you can trust members of the City Watch to do their duty diligently, and you can expect that the city's magisters will be fair. If you have cause to come before the Masked Lords or the Open Lord herself, rest assured that if your cause be just, justice will be done. If, however, you find yourself in the wrong, know that though it might take time to weigh that wrong on Tyr's scales, his hammer will fall—and it will be wielded by Waterdeep with a vengeance.

Unlike in less civilized settlements, punishment for crimes in Waterdeep isn't typically used as public entertainment. Scheduled executions occur behind the high walls of Castle Waterdeep, and floggings are carried out in the watch post nearest the sentencing. The Watch makes every effort to take individuals into custody quietly, so as not to disrupt other citizens. Those bystanders generally return the favor by giving altercations between criminals and the Watch a wide berth.

Waterdeep has a complex library of law and custom set by precedent, the main body of which can be read in the Code Legal. This document is available in multiple languages at the Palace of Waterdeep, and (in the Common tongue) provided on request by the magisters at the gates and in the harbor. Be aware that the Code Legal provides only an outline of typical sentences for various offenses, and magisters have broad discretion when meting out justice as they see fit. Any Masked Lord can overturn a magister's ruling, but there's rarely a Masked Lord around when you need one.

ARMS, ARMOR, AND COMBAT

Individuals accustomed to the rough-and-tumble life in much of the North are often surprised by the fact that Waterdavians go about unarmed and unarmored. Yet Waterdeep doesn't have any law that forbids carrying weapons or armor. Instead, it has a culture of civility that makes such behavior unnecessary.

Dueling has long been illegal in Waterdeep, as has any sort of act involving assault. Individuals caught brawling by the Watch will all be arrested and judged regardless of who started the fracas, or why. (The tavern brawls that typically break out under the influence of too much drink will often be overlooked by the Watch, as long as the proprietor doesn't seek payment for damages and no one is significantly injured.) Sport fighting, such as boxing or wrestling, is legal only if it occurs in a location registered with the city for that purpose. Additionally, any blade more than one foot in length is subject to an extra tax whenever it is sold, which helps to explain why Waterdavians prefer to carry knives and knuckledusters for self-defense.

Businesses and individuals do employ armed guards, but except for nobles or foreign envoys, few people travel about the city with such protection. As such, the sight of armed and armored individuals walking the streets who aren't in the livery of the city or one of its noble houses inspires caution in most Waterdavians. Folk assume that you wouldn't bother lugging around such equipment unless you either intend violence or expect that it might soon be visited upon you.

CITY WATCH

The first soldiers you see in service to the city will be the members of the City Guard who patrol the roads leading to Waterdeep, watch the walls, guard civic structures, and protect magisters. Waterdeep's streets, however, are policed by an altogether different force: the City Watch. The similarity of their names often confuses newcomers, so I offer this handy mnemonic: "The Guard guards the walls while the Watch watches all."

You can recognize any member of the City Watch by the uniform: a green-and-goldenrod doublet and a tall steel helmet. Each typically carries a long truncheon, a dagger, and a buckler. Because most citizens in Waterdeep don't bear weapons, these tools prove a more than ample deterrent to criminal activity. Members of the Watch typically don't carry crossbows or other weapons to attack at range, but running from the Watch—though it may be a time-honored tradition for local miscreants—rarely works out for newcomers to the city. I guarantee that all members of the Watch know the streets they patrol and that area's residents better than you do, even if you stay in Waterdeep for ten seasons.

WATCH TALK

Members of the City Watch employ a sort of slang in dealing with the public. As a visitor, it behooves you to know what they mean.

"What befalls?" means "Someone tell me what's going on here."

"Hold!" means "Don't move a muscle."

"Down arms!" means "Drop your weapons."

"Talk truth!" means "Answer me" or "Tell the whole story."

"Robes" references the black robes—in other words, one of the magisters. "Do we need robes here?" or something similar should be taken as a threat.

The City Watch has watch posts throughout the city. These stations are often off the main thoroughfares, tucked away in small courtyards or at cross streets. A watch post can be recognized by the green-and-gold lantern outside it, lit even during the day with a *continual flame* spell. A watch post serves as an organizational headquarters and armory. Anyone who wishes to report a crime may do so at a watch post in the event a Watch constable can't be found elsewhere. A watch post typically contains a few holding cells where people arrested for crimes can be detained until they're marched to a courthouse jail before standing trial.

Small squads head out from the watch posts on daily and nightly rounds of the city streets, or on special assignments involving protection or investigation. A mere pair of Watch operatives might discreetly patrol in the Castle Ward; in contrast, squads of eight walk the Dock Ward, increasing to as many as a dozen at night. If Watch members spot trouble they can't handle, they blow shrill tin whistles to summon more of their members—an act that alerts nearby citizens as well.

City Watch members follow a strict code of conduct that makes them one of the most trusted police forces aside from paladin-patrolled Elturgard. As long as you don't engage in unlawful behavior, you can expect to be left untroubled by the Watch.

THE WATCHFUL ORDER OF MAGISTS AND PROTECTORS

Expect to be questioned at the gate, or when you register with a magister, regarding your ability to cast arcane magic. Wizards, sorcerers, and other arcane spellcasters who intend to stay in Waterdeep for any length of time are required to register with the city, and will be strongly encouraged to join the Watchful Order of Magists and Protectors, headed by the Blackstaff.

Members of the Watchful Order are expected to render service to the city when called upon, acting as temporary members of the City Watch or City Guard. Their expertise often helps investigators determine whether magic was used to commit a crime in the city. Members can also expect to be tapped for assistance during and after fires, natural events that cause multiple casualties, or other nonmagical disasters.

Members of the Watchful Order form a more or less sociable association in the city, working together to keep an eye on any spellcasters who opt not to join their guild. Any havoc caused by a spellcaster in Waterdeep risks drawing the wrath of the Lords of Waterdeep—so it behooves the Watchful Order to watch all its members.

COINAGE

As should be expected of any city of standing, Waterdeep mints its own coins. All taxes, fines, and guild fees must be paid either in Waterdavian coin or the currency of any member settlement of the Lords' Alliance. Though no law requires you to pay for goods or services in Waterdavian coin, the drudgery of weighing foreign currency and checking its purity prompts many retailers and operators of swift-exchange businesses—including drays and hire-coaches—not to accept anything but coins minted in Waterdeep.

Though you can trade your coinage for Waterdeep currency with anyone willing to do so, the exchequers at the Palace of Waterdeep make exchanges with no associated fee. The queue there can be quite long, necessitating that you make an appointment—often a day or more in advance. For a swifter transaction, I recommend any member of the Guild of Trusted Pewterers and Casters, or of the Jewelers' Guild. Both have the most reliable scales and abide by guild-wide rates of exchange.

Be sure to exchange taols and harbor moons before leaving the city, as their value greatly diminishes elsewhere!

TAXES AND FEES

As established in the first year of the reign of the previous Open Lord, Dagult Neverember, Waterdeep collects a monthly tax from all who live within its official wards. The tax is 1 shard per person above the age of ten years, and is collected door-to-door by patrols of the City Guard on the last day of each month.

Individuals who so desire can pay a single dragon in tax and receive a writ exempting them for twelve months, but the writ must be produced every month when the Guard calls, or a new payment is required. If the Guard knocks at a door and receives no answer, a notice of lien with an estimation of tax is affixed to the door. The debt must be dealt with before the next month ends, with payment to be made to any magister.

Those who have no fixed residence can still be taxed if they are confronted in any building, be it an inn or an outhouse. So if you're out and around on the last day of the month, you'll no doubt experience "taxing traffic" as the streets become clogged with people trying to avoid the collectors.

Waterdeep also raises revenue by charging other fees, such as the following:

1 nib per day for rental of a stall in the Market
1 shard (above and beyond any fines imposed) from anyone convicted by a magister, per conviction
1 dragon per conveyance leaving the city, empty or full
5 dragons per ship that touches dock in Waterdeep (except for city ships and diplomatic vessels), collected from the captain and covering a stay of up to fourteen days (a ship that leaves the harbor and returns during that time pays the tax upon reentry)

In times of trouble, direct taxes can also be imposed:

A **fire tax** (usually 1 dragon per household), levied whenever a fire destroys a large portion of the city
A **wall tax** or harbor tax (usually 1 dragon per household) raised to directly pay for needed repairs or expansions
A **lance tax** raised to provide a payroll for mercenaries hired by the city when required (usually 1 shard per household each tenday until the Lords repeal the tax)

COINS OF WATERDEEP
HERE ARE IMAGES OF THE CITY'S COINS, WHICH AREN'T TO SCALE.

NIB
COPPER COIN ABOUT THE SIZE OF A THUMBNAIL (1 NIB = 1 COMMON COPPER COIN)

SHARD
SILVER COIN, SLIGHTLY SMALLER THAN THE NIB (1 SHARD = 10 NIBS)

TAOL
BRASS COIN, ABOUT TWO INCHES SQUARE WITH A HOLE LARGE ENOUGH FOR A NIB TO FIT IN (1 TAOL = 200 NIBS)

DRAGON
GOLD COIN, HALF AGAIN AS LARGE AS A NIB (1 DRAGON = 100 NIBS)

SUN
PLATINUM COIN, TWICE AS LARGE AS A NIB (1 SUN = 1,000 NIBS)

HARBOR MOON
PLATINUM CRESCENT INSET WITH ELECTRUM, ABOUT THREE INCHES LONG WITH A HOLE LARGE ENOUGH FOR A NIB TO FIT IN (1 HARBOR MOON = 5,000 NIBS)

Getting About

Perambulating is the superior manner of experiencing the city and all its splendors. But if you've come with your own conveyance, the weather is inclement, or some other reason drives you to use the roads, the following are facts you need to know.

Traffic and Travel

Waterdeep is a city of broad boulevards that thrum with traffic. All day and well into the night, a bewildering melee of wagons, carts, horse and pony riders, carriages, buggies, hire-coaches, and Waterdeep's signature towering drays (further discussed below) surges through its major thoroughfares. Fortunately, most roads are flanked by paved sidewalks that give pedestrians plenty of space, and most of the widest roads have raised dividers that allow an individual crossing a street a safe space to step out of the fray and wait for traffic to pass.

The city's centuries-old layout dictates its traffic patterns today. Waterdeep lies on a plateau adjacent to a long mountain that shields much of it from the sea. In the southern third of the city, where the land slopes up from the harbor, the High Road and the Way of the Dragon are the two main south–north roads. These converge both at the Waymoot near the southern gate, and in the heart of the Trades Ward where the city is at its narrowest—bounded by Castle Waterdeep, high on a spur of the mountain, and the walls of the City of the Dead. The conjoined boulevard then splits to the north, continuing as the High Road, and to the west as a boulevard called Waterdeep Way, heading toward the Palace of Waterdeep (not to be confused with Waterdeep Castle, which it passes hard by). In the middle of the city, six boulevards run north from Waterdeep Way, where they meet the road that encircles the Market. On the other side of the Market, five boulevards continue north.

The aforementioned boulevards, along with the Street of the Singing Dolphin in the Sea Ward, are the major arteries of the city. Hire-coaches and drays can be most frequently found on those streets, and traffic is at its most hectic there. Most other roads in the city run east to west, but regardless of their direction, traffic elsewhere is generally less hectic and thus safer to cross.

Street Signs

Thanks to the Scriveners', Scribes', and Clerks' Guild, Waterdeep has a remarkable custom of labeling its streets, and even many of its alleyways and courts. The method of identification varies by ward and neighborhood (including brass plates, carvings in stone, and stencil-painted wooden signs), but street names are typically displayed on the corners of buildings at intersections, roughly a dozen feet above ground. The name of the road you travel on will be on the wall nearest, while the name of the crossing road will be around the corner. Simply ingenious!

Landmarks

Proud Mount Waterdeep provides a useful landmark for general orientation. It stands stark across the skyline to the west, its far slopes dropping right into the sea. A spur of the mountain juts inland, and atop the easternmost point of this spur stands Castle Waterdeep. If you can see these landmarks, it's relatively easy to orient yourself. The mountain peak looms over the southern third of the city near the port in the south. The City of the Dead lies opposite the northern ridge of Mount Waterdeep, which descends down to the Field of Triumph, the city's great coliseum.

One of Waterdeep's titanic walking statues, no longer mobile, offers another way to orient yourself on a local scale. At nine stories tall, twice the height of any buildings nearby, the Honorable Knight stands guard in a block of buildings between Snail Street and the Way of the Dragon. Positioned as it is nigh the place where four wards meet, you can use it to judge where you stand. If it is south and west of your position, you are in the Trades Ward. North and west? The Southern Ward. South and east? The Castle Ward. North and east? You're in the Dock Ward.

TRAFFIC WARDENS

During particularly heavy traffic and at congested areas such as the great oval road around the Market, you might see a member of the City Watch serving as a traffic warden. Traffic wardens signal with small blue hand flags for traffic to proceed, and with yellow flags for traffic to hold. A traffic warden can often be heard blowing a whistle. When you hear it, look to the warden to see if you are being signaled. Failure to take care might result not only in accident but also arrest.

DRAYS

These towering vehicles are, I believe, unique to Waterdeep. Invented by exiles from Lantan in the last century, a dray is a long, glassed-in carriage with bench seating that provides additional open-air bench seating on its roof. The driver sits at the level of the roof seating, providing a vantage point to see over other traffic and make eye contact with other dray drivers. You can enter this contraption through the back whenever it stops or slows down enough to make mounting the rear step safe.

A fare taker stands at the back of the lower seating area to take your coin (typically 2 to 4 nibs). You can choose to ride inside or ascend the spiral stairway at the rear to ride atop the vehicle. Most drays run on the main north–south boulevards, but some circle the Market, and a few run along the smaller east–west roads in rough areas. Be warned that when the demand for drays is high—during rain or snow, or to get to or from an event at the Field of Triumph—conditions become crowded and perfect for pickpockets.

HIRE-COACHES

If you desire to travel in relative comfort and be the master of your destination, simply give a spirited wave and shout to any hire-coach driver who has no passengers. Each of these handsome, two-wheeled black coaches comfortably seats two travelers (perhaps four if you're quite slim and very well acquainted), who ride facing the road ahead. The hire-coach's driver sits high and to the rear of the carriage, manipulating the horses by means of long reins and a short whip on a rod. The fare must

THE UNFLAPPABLE WATERDAVIAN

Natives of the City of Splendors are notoriously slow to take offense. A Waterdavian plainly states their feelings as a warning, so that one is apt to hear "I don't find that amusing, friend," said pleasantly before real anger is shown. Some visitors misinterpret such behavior as cowardice or ignorance ("He was too stupid to realize I insulted him!"). For those who act on such misjudgments, however, surprise and regret are the usual results.

Most Waterdavians are also slow to take fright unless facing magic or monsters. A swaggering warrior threatening them is quite likely to be stared at calmly, or even sneered at. "The only mortals that Waterdavians fear are a few unstable wizards and the Lords," Durnan often says to those who are surprised by the nonchalance of the Yawning Portal's regulars concerning the open entrance to Undermountain in their midst. "And only when they've incurred the wrath of said persons themselves."

be agreed upon and paid before the journey, but only rarely will the cost exceed a half-dozen shards.

CARRIAGES

The well-to-do—or those who want to ride in luxury during a day out—can hire a full carriage, many of which are as finely outfitted as those owned by the nobility. Up to eight can take such a ride in silken comfort. Prices and services vary, but generally you agree to rent the carriage, the services of the driver, and any attendant servants or guards for a full day.

TRAVEL IN WINTER

The folk of Waterdeep often remain indoors in the colder months, particularly when it rains or snows. The flow of trade and travelers into the city slows to a trickle during winter, and as a result, traffic diminishes and drays and hire-coaches become more scarce. Fortunately, the Fellowship of Carters and Coachmen works with the Wheelwrights' Guild and the Wagon-makers' and Coach Builders' Guild to convert the drays and hire-coaches that do operate into sledges, so that some are available even in the worst weather.

NOBILITY

While you might encounter dwarf diplomats from Gauntlgrym, satraps of Amn, duchesses of Tethyr, or thanes of the Northlanders in Waterdeep, the nobles you really need to know about are the city's own. Seventy-eight noble family lines are found here, many of which can trace their lineage back to the city's founding. Books have been written about individual families—histories of their accomplishments and how they fit into the webs of wealth and patronage that govern nobles' activities—so it is beyond the scope of a pamphlet this size to attempt to describe their particulars. I can, however, endeavor to equip you with the tools to recognize nobility and to interact with the higher class.

SPOTTING A NOBLE

Nobility in Waterdeep are granted the right to bear arms. In the legal code of the city, this means not merely the ability to carry a weapon, but the right to retain up to seventy equipped soldiers. These soldiers always wear a house's colors and the house's "arms of grace"—a heraldic device often borne on a shield, worn as a cloak pin, or affixed to a helmet. Others throughout the city, even foreign dignitaries, are permitted to retain only up to sixteen armed warriors, and laws against impersonating those in the employ of the nobility mean that other mercenaries and bodyguards most often dress plainly, so as not to be mistaken for the retinue of a noble. So your first clue that you might be in the company of a noble is the sight of a large number of armed and uniformed soldiers.

Many nobles, particularly younger ones seeking entertainment, travel without an entourage of guards or only in the company of other nobles. In this case, you'll know you're in the presence of nobility because of the deference others give them. Follow suit, and you should be fine.

Above all, be polite. Always address a known noble as "Lord" or "Lady." A short bow or a nod of the head to acknowledge a noble upon each meeting and parting is customary. Obsequiousness and servility is something all Waterdavians scorn, but you should also beware of acting in an overly familiar, boastful, or disrespectful way when in the presence of any noble. Though this sort of behavior isn't a crime, and laws against dueling prevent a noble from initiating a direct armed confrontation, the noble families of Waterdeep have immense power in the city, often in unexpected quarters. Many have influence in nations as distant as Calimshan and Cormyr. Be assured that any slighting of a noble will not be forgotten or easily forgiven.

If you're not certain whether someone is a noble, address the gentleman as "Saer" or the gentlewoman as "Goodwoman." Neither will give offense, and generally a noble will politely correct you as to their actual title.

NOBLES AND PATRONAGE

Nobles in Waterdeep are patrons of and investors in all manner of businesses in the city and abroad, as well as the many expressions of the arts. They spend coin to fund celebrations, contests at the Field of Triumph, upkeep at the city's temples and shrines, civic projects, guild events, and charitable actions such as burial of the unknown dead. Their motives are manifold, but their actions—no matter the reason—earn them loyalty and high regard from those who benefit from their largesse.

Seeking patronage from a noble without having been introduced to that person is considered an insult, so you must first befriend someone in a noble's employ or circle of influence. Doing so is no guarantee of ultimate success; much time and coin can be wasted trying to curry favor with an acquaintance of a noble who turns out to be unscrupulous or of little help for some other reason. My advice is to do something deserving of attention, whatever your vocation, and someone from the noble families of Waterdeep will eventually show an interest.

KNOW A NOBLE'S BUSINESS

In the words of that quarrelsome acquaintance of mine from the Dales, "Before you strut your stuff in the chickens' preening circle, get to know the other cocks first." This colorful aphorism applies well to the affairs of nobility, because when you have interaction with a noble, you are at the same time dealing with one's entire family—as well as a network of business associates and allies. That situation can put you in a troublesome spot if you are unaware of the noble's connections.

GUILDS AND GUILD LAW

No aspect of life in Waterdeep goes untouched by at least one of its more than forty guilds. Virtually every profession has an associated guild, and there's hardly a citizen of the city who doesn't belong to one or more guilds, or doesn't work for someone who does. As a visitor to Waterdeep, you need to know this, lest you run afoul of "Guild Law." Guild Law isn't technically in the legal code of Waterdeep, but guilds are mentioned in the oldest surviving legal documents—penned by Ahghairon himself—and the rules of Guild Law are respected by wise city folk.

A WONDROUS PEOPLE

Whenever you find yourself in a bustling city, you're likely to spot a wonderful variety of folk. You hear words in languages utterly foreign to you, and you smell dishes both delectable and strange. Waterdeep is the ultimate city of such delights, and before long, the alien thing becomes familiar to you, and the stranger becomes your friend.

The people of Waterdeep are among the greatest of its splendors. Fashion, comportment, love—these things are practiced with an art and a zest in the city uncommon elsewhere. Visit a festhall or festival and see for yourself! And don't miss the cross-dressing performers who regale audiences with humor and song. Fabulous—that word doesn't begin to describe it, especially when they enhance the merriment with magic.

The city is also a haven for those who define for themselves what it means to be a man or a woman, those who transcend gender as the gods do, and those who redefine entirely who they are. What confidence! I never tire of witnessing it. I have seen folk in Waterdeep whose lives are more magical than the marvels possible with spells.

Guilds take their laws seriously, as do members of the City Watch and the magisters. If you flout a guild's traditions, you can expect not only public scorn but also a visit from enforcers of the law. In addition, many guilds have their own codes of accusation, trial, and punishment, such as:

- A member of the Bakers' Guild who sells bread baked in the wrong shape will be drenched with water and coated in his own flour.
- Heckling a member of the Jesters' Guild will result in the offending party being jeered at in public by no less than four guild members for a period of four days.
- Any ship that unloads its cargo without due observance or aid by the Guild of Watermen shall have its cargo seized or thrown into the harbor.

Many guilds have codes that entwine each other, complicating matters even more for the outsider. In Neverwinter, if you want to construct a building, you simply purchase the land and hire workers to build it. In Waterdeep, the Surveyors', Map-, and Chart-makers' Guild must first be consulted upon designation of the plat, then brought in to draw or approve the construction plan. The Cellarers' and Plumbers' Guild must then clear and prepare the site, only after which will you be able to hire members of the Carpenters', Roofers', and Plaisterers' Guild to erect the structure.

Moreover, the work will not be complete until members of the Guild of Fine Carvers and the Guild of Stone-cutters, Masons, Potters, and Tile-makers design and craft any decorative elements of wood, stone, or ceramics, and after the Most Careful Order of Skilled Smiths and Metalforgers has manufactured and installed any door hinges. If the building is to be connected to the sewers or a city water supply, the Cellarers' and Plumbers' Guild must be called upon again to do that work. Want glazed windows installed? For that, you need to hire members of the Guild of Glassblowers, Glaziers, and Spectacle-makers.

If you do business in the city as anything other than a purchaser of goods and services, I strongly advise you to seek out a local solicitor and pay to be guided through the process. No guild of solicitors exists, so be sure your choice comes highly recommended by individuals you can trust. To learn the peculiarities of any guild's rules, consult someone on duty at the guild headquarters or ask a senior guild member.

All that said, working at a guild-related profession without being a member of that guild isn't illegal. Guild members have no lawful recourse to interfere in the business of someone who chooses to not join the organization. But if you practice a trade or operate a business without becoming a member of the appropriate guild, word spreads, and you'll find that your coin isn't good for purchasing the goods or services of anyone who is a guild member. Since that group includes virtually everyone who sells the necessities of life or offers shelter for a fee, the benefits of joining a guild swiftly become apparent to those who procrastinate in this regard.

THE WARDS OF WATERDEEP

Newcomers to the city of Waterdeep are often confused by the importance that Waterdavians give to wards. In other cities, such as Baldur's Gate and Neverwinter, districts are bounded by rivers or walls. But in Waterdeep, one can traverse from ward to ward by crossing a street—a fact that offers the drivers of hire-coaches some amusement when an ignorant tourist requests a ride to an adjacent ward.

Each ward has its own history, legends, and traditions based around who lived there in the past, famous or infamous events, and the uncanny things that continue to occur. For example, children (and even some adults) hop on one foot when crossing Asmagh's Alley in the Castle Ward. Why? Well, Asmagh was an apothecary who poisoned many patients, then buried them upright beneath the alley under cover of night. He was discovered, and some say that as many as eighty bodies were subsequently pulled up from holes under the alley's wide flagstones. Though this happened over a century ago, children passing through the alley still sing a song: "Hop for the hollows, hop for the dead, hop on the flagstones, hop on their heads." As you stroll down Warrior's Way or the Street of Silver, listen for the children's delighted screams and go give it a try.

These shared stories and traditions impart to each ward a different culture, just as much as distinctions of class and wealth. Yet nothing drives residents to identify with their wards as much as festivals and sport. Nearly every race and parade in the city features a competition between wards as part of the festivities. On such days, homes and businesses fly the colors of their wards, trot out their mascots, and sing rousing songs that celebrate where they live. If you stay in the city for even a month, you're sure to see some version of this display of civic spirit.

SEA WARD

The Sea Ward stands proud on the high ground above Mount Waterdeep's sunset shadow. The rich and the powerful (or those who wish you to think such of them, and can afford the rent) reside or run their businesses here. When the warlords and pirates of early Waters Deep gained enough gold, they built fortresses on what used to be fields of grass tousled by sea wind. You can still see the remains of some of those old castles incorporated into the palatial homes of the noble families that dwell in the Sea Ward. For the best all-around view of the glittering homes enshrouded by garden walls, go to where Diamond Street and Delzorin Street cross, nigh to Mystra's House of Wonder, and simply spin in a circle.

Blue and gold are the Sea Ward's colors in competitions, and the ward's mascot is the sea lion—a fanciful combination of fish and feline. There's a persistent but patently false legend that the famous Lion Gate at the Field of Triumph is the gaping maw of a sea lion. The architectural designs for the gates show this to be false, however, and they can be viewed in the Map House—the guildhall of the Surveyors', Map-, and Chart-makers' Guild in the Castle Ward.

Must-see locations in the Sea Ward begin, of course, with the Field of Triumph, but just across the street is the no less remarkable House of Heroes—the largest temple in the city. Dedicated to Tempus, its many grand halls celebrate the city's champions of both battle and sport. The winners of ward competitions are paraded here after their victories, often carried on shoulders or passed from hand to hand over the heads of a crowd. It is a sight you shouldn't miss.

You should also visit the House of Wonder. This is surely the most splendid temple dedicated to the gods of magic—with Mystra foremost among them, of course—in all the world. Although your eye will be drawn to its ornate towers, brilliant mosaics, and magical displays, look also for the humble violets growing amid the ostentation. These delicate flowers were Ahghairon's favorite, and they are planted about the temple in memory of him.

SPEAK LIKE A NATIVE

The many idioms and slang expressions of Waterdavians would take a whole book to explore, but here I explain a few that might otherwise mystify.

"Dabbler but no master" and "No mastery blazing forth"
These idioms trace their origin to Ahghairon, who early on in his studies of magic humbly said, "I am no wizard. I am a dabbler but no master of magic; it seems no mastery burns within me." Both now serve as expressions of false modesty applied to any skill or craft, not just magic use.

"Sharpjaws," "fastfists," "bullyblades," and "alleyblades"
Those who boast of martial skill but who shrink from violence or lack real ability are "sharpjaws." In sharp contrast are Waterdeep's "fastfists" (any lout easily provoked to violence), "bullyblades" (battle-hardened mercenaries hired as muscle), and "alleyblades" (muggers and thieves).

"Longride" and "Last ride"
To a caravan merchant, a drover, or a farmer from the lands around Waterdeep, as well as any Waterdavian who rides for sport, recreation, hunting, or falconry, the late afternoon is "longride," and dusk is "last ride."

"Which the greater thief?"
Tuezaera Hallowhand was a famous "lone cat" thief of Waterdeep in the 1200s DR, who disappeared suddenly and is thought to have come to a violent end. She once robbed a wizard and wrote this on his wall with a fingertip dipped in his favorite red wine: "I take things. You take freedom with your spells. Which of us is the greater thief?" Waterdavians now use this phrase in argument with one another over all kinds of matters when comparing wrongs done.

"Doth thy mirror crack?" or "Hurl but think not?" or "Take but not count cost? Be nothing, then!"
Laeral Silverhand, then the Lady Mage of Waterdeep when she was married to Khelben "Blackstaff" Arunsun, once publicly rebuked an overambitious wizard of the Watchful Order of Magists and Protectors thusly: "If I hurl spells but think not of consequences, I am nothing. If I take lives but count not the cost, I am nothing. If I steal in the night and see not the faces of the devastated come the next morning, I am nothing. If I make decrees like a ruler but undertake none of the other responsibilities of the throne, I am nothing. And if I do all these things in the name of the Watchful Order, I am less than nothing. Doth thy mirror crack?"

These scornful words are remembered and used almost daily in Waterdeep even a century later.

SWIFT JUSTICE

Two other temples in the ward are as impressive, but in different ways. The beauteous House of the Moon has the tallest tower of any temple in the city, rising some seventy-five feet above the street. At its top, priests of Selûne bask in the light of the moon in all seasons. The House of Inspired Hands, dedicated to Gond, presents an altogether less peaceful experience. Here, all the great innovative minds of the city invent and experiment, attempting to create everything from flying machines to stronger door hinges. But don't expect a museum of marvels such as can be found in Baldur's Gate. At this site, "worship is work," as anyone at the temple is liable to tell you.

If you're looking for some good fortune, you should surely visit the Tower of Luck, a temple complex dedicated to Tymora. The "tower" in question is actually a many-pillared atrium ingeniously roofed over with glass. Beneath the roof, a bronze sculpture of a diminutive Tymora, depicted as a laughing young girl, appears to be leaping from the very top of an astounding fountain. To pay your respects and make a wish, you come around to the fountain on a walkway and toss your coin to Tymora. Managing to land it in her outstretched hand is a sure sign of her favor.

If you need to refresh yourself during your travels, or perhaps to primp before an important meeting or a night out, visit Sune's faithful at the Temple of Beauty. Its marbled public baths and mirrored salons are open from before dawn to after dusk. There's no fee for these services, or for the advice and aid of the temple's many pleasant attendants, but donations are encouraged.

Two parks in the Sea Ward might also be worth your time. The Shrines to Nature, just a block away from the Tower of Luck, are resplendent gardens dedicated to nature gods like Mielikki and Silvanus. The park is closed to all except residents of the Sea Ward. Yet from beyond the iron fence that surrounds it, you can catch glimpses of the superb shrines, statues, and fountains within. The Heroes' Garden is the only green space in the city that is open to the public besides the City of the Dead, but it is tucked away so far to the north in the Sea Ward that it gets few visitors—which is a pity, since the fine statuary in this lush garden portrays many of the figures important to the city's history.

I hesitate to mention a last location in the Sea Ward, and I will not reveal where to find it, for reasons that will soon become apparent. There is a house in the Sea Ward without windows or doors. You can't see it from the street, and those who live near it will not speak of it to others. You'll know you are near it when you see blue tiles on the streets and walls leading into an alley that passes under the surrounding buildings. At night, these tiles glimmer dimly with the blue light of foxfire. More than one route leads into the Blue Alley, as this place is known, but there are precious few ways out. Most who enter don't come back. If you see blue tiles, turn around and walk away before it is too late.

NORTH WARD

Nobles aplenty live in the North Ward, but the character of this ward is more peaceful than that of the Sea Ward. Though it has taverns and shops to suit a variety of tastes, the tenor of the area tends toward reserved and polite. Most streets are lined with row houses inhabited by the families of prosperous people of business, investing, and civic service. They are each wealthy enough to employ a servant or two, or they endeavor to appear as such.

For the best experience in the North Ward, go there just before dawn, buy a broadsheet, and settle in at a café with a view of the street. Watch as the ward comes quietly to life around you. At first, it will be so silent that you'll be able to hear the resident a street over who opens her sash for fresh air and clears her throat. Then the birdsong will begin, and shortly thereafter, you'll hear and then see the drays arriving with servants. These aren't the live-in staff used by noble houses, but people hired to come and work for a day. Most of them come from less affluent parts of the city, arriving with the tools of their trade and outfitted in their customary garb: launderers and cooks in white, chimney sweeps and housecleaners in black, valets and child-minders in gray, gardeners in green, and tutors in blue.

As these servants spread out to knock on doors and begin their work, the residents of the ward take their exits, parting fondly with spouses and children, their footsteps tramping along the sidewalks or taking them into rattling hire-coaches. In the span of just an hour, the North Ward comes to noisy life and then settles again into quiescence, until later in the day when the process reverses itself, as residents return from work and servants leave.

The liveliest, and perhaps the loveliest, part of the ward is the Cliffwatch. Here, the plateau upon which Waterdeep sits features cliffs so steep and high that the city wall is interrupted to either side of them. Some of the most lavish residences and most luxurious taverns and inns of Waterdeep stand along this space, boasting terraces and balconies that allow one to take in the beautiful sight of the countryside to the east. Yet you need not pay their high prices, for a public walkway along the cliff's edge offers pedestrians ample opportunity to enjoy the view.

The North Ward's colors are green and orange, and its mascot is the gentle white dove, depicted in flight. Many North Ward homes have dovecotes on their roofs, and the great flocks of the birds that circle over the city at dawn and dusk are a delight to behold.

CASTLE WARD

The Castle Ward is the heart and mind of Waterdeep, if not its soul. It houses the city's military forces, courts, government, and the Market—the largest market square of any city in the North. It encompasses the City Navy's docks in the Great Harbor and all of Mount Waterdeep, and it is home to six walking statues, numerous temples, and many other landmarks.

Castle Waterdeep stands above the city on a great bluff that extends out from the mountain, its towers soaring hundreds of feet into the sky. It surprises many to learn that this isn't where Waterdeep's rulers reside, nor from where the city is governed. The castle was and is a redoubt of last defense should the city be attacked, but for well over a century, the ruler of Waterdeep has occupied the Palace of Waterdeep—also known as Piergeiron's Palace, and still called that by elderly and long-lived citizens (including many elves).

Though not quite as large as the castle, the palace is far more comfortable and lavishly decorated, with many halls used by government officials, guildmasters, and nobles for meetings and court proceedings. If you have reason to be invited (not compelled, I should hope!) to meet with the Masked Lords or the Open Lord of Waterdeep, it will likely take place in the audience chamber of the palace. There, you can witness the ancient and humble throne that Ahghairon first sat upon so long ago.

Many other buildings in the ward are given over to city business, including several courts for magisters and the barracks of the City Guard. So many of the ward's structures are offices and meeting halls for business owners, solicitors, publishers, and the like that the Castle Ward has the smallest resident population of all the wards.

Many landmarks of interest are found in this ward aside from the six walking statues (discussed later in this chapbook). You could hardly see them all in a day, but the following are highly recommended.

Blackstaff Tower is a squat black blot in the otherwise pretty ward. Humble though the edifice might be, looking at the place for too long can give you a queasy feeling and the sense that you are being watched—almost as if the tower itself has turned an unseen and wrathful eye upon you. Perhaps you think this fanciful. Well, go and try it yourself!

On the opposite end of the mountain, close to the Naval Harbor, stands Mirt's Mansion. Once a fortress-like and glowering tower, it has been upgraded with more delicate fashions of architecture since the return of its long-absent owner.

MAJOR TEMPLES OF WATERDEEP

Deity or Deities	Temple Name	Location
All deities	Holyhands House	North Ward
All elven deities	Temple of the Seldarine	Castle Ward
Gond	House of Inspired Hands	Sea Ward
Helm	Helm's Hall	Southern Ward
Ilmater	Hospice of St. Laupsenn	North Ward
Lathander	Spires of the Morning	Castle Ward
Mielikki, Silvanus	Shrines of Nature	Sea Ward
Mystra	House of Wonder	Sea Ward
Oghma	Font of Knowledge	Castle Ward
Selûne	Tower of the Moon	Sea Ward
Sune	Temple of Beauty	Sea Ward
Tempus	House of Heroes	Sea Ward
Tymora	Tower of Luck	Castle Ward
Tyr	Halls of Justice	Castle Ward
Umberlee	The Queenspire	Beach

Mirt has quite a history with Durnan, the proprietor of the Yawning Portal. Together they descended into "the Well," as the entrance to Undermountain was known in olden days. Waterdeep used to throw criminals in the Well, leaving them to die horribly in Undermountain's dungeons. Durnan and Mirt entered the dungeons of their own free will—and not only that, but returned laden with treasures. Both used magic to extend their lives, but they eventually parted ways. Mirt kept on with a life of adventure, while Durnan built the tavern called the Yawning Portal over the Well and now, almost two centuries later, charges coin to descend into it. Not a bad way to part fools from their money!

The glorious Spires of the Morning, dedicated to Lathander, is one of Waterdeep's most beautiful temples. But it is rivaled in this ward by the Temple of the Seldarine, dedicated to all the elf gods. The journey through Mount Melody Walk, a tunnel cut through Mount Waterdeep, to New Olamn's academy of music and other arts is a wondrous daytime excursion. The Market offers a wild array of sights, smells, and sounds in which folk might lose themselves for a tenday. The Font of Knowledge is a temple to Oghma, yes, but also the city's largest public library. Titles written throughout the ages can be viewed here—under the watchful eyes of the temple's priests. In short (if I can claim this section of the enchiridion to be such), the Castle Ward offers far too many splendors to list them all here.

The Castle Ward's colors are blue and purple, and its mascot is a griffon, typically depicted in gold. These borrow colors from the city's flag and reference the Griffon Cavalry, of course. Champions for the ward often come from among the ranks of the Guard, the Navy, or the Cavalry. Although such competitors have often have the advantage in races and competitions, their crowds of rabidly cheering fans are naturally much smaller than those of other wards.

TRADES WARD

Shopping, shopping, shopping galore! Or eating, eating, eating! Or drinking, drinking, drinking! Or lavish accommodations, or fine art, or legendary parties! The Market in the Castle Ward is the largest market square in the city, but the Trades Ward is like a market town in itself—and is easily thrice the Market's size.

This ward bustles day and night with activity, both on the street and on balcony walkways that run the length of blocks and are sometimes layered five stories high. Shop signs appear to leap out from buildings, whose sides are plastered with advertisements all vying for the attention of the eye. Glove shops, shoe shops, jewelry stores, perfumeries, flower shops, cake shops, taverns, cafés, tea shops, inns, row houses, boarding schools, offices, dance academies, grocers, pottery stores, armor vendors—as long as it's not illegal, you can find it in the Trades Ward. But if you are looking for something illegal, the Trades Ward is likely the place to get that too.

THE STATELY, CLEAN, AND WELL-DEFENDED CASTLE WARD

Do not do so too loudly, though. The City Watch has a heavy presence in this ward, in the form of both open patrols and officers working out of uniform.

As befits a place of so much business, many guilds have their halls in this ward. Of particular note is the House of Light, the hall of the Guild of Chandlers and Lamplighters. Outside the building, a wagon-sized mound of wax with hundreds of wicks is kept lit day and night, while being continually built up with adhered candles. Inside, the best works of the guild are put on display and sold, including not just candles of various colors, lamps, and chandeliers, but elaborate waxwork constructions that depict all sorts of subjects from personages of note, to dragons, to complex and abstract lattices—all represented as fantastical candles.

Magic users should be wary in the Court of the White Bull. Long ago, this plaza was a grazing area for livestock, including an albino calf that was born here. The calf's owner built the White Bull Tavern, which thrived on the spot for years and gave the area its name. You'll not find the tavern now, though. It vanished, utterly destroyed during an infamous spell battle between the archmage Thongalar the Mighty and the evil mage Shile Rauretilar and his apprentices. In the storm of magic that touched down here, Shile and his apprentices all perished and the fabric of the Weave was rent, such that Azuth, god of wizards, was forced to appear and set things right. He is said to have stitched reality and the Weave back together, but a wrinkle in the fabric remains. To this day, magic brought to bear in the Court of the White Bull sometimes goes awry, and the use of magic items and spells is forbidden in the area.

The Trades Ward uses green and purple as its colors, and its mascot is the mimic. This tradition supposedly arose because when mascots were first chosen, the Trades Ward took a chest of gold as its own—and was roundly mocked by citizens of other wards for not picking a creature. Now, every four years, the ward reveals a new object for its mascot, declaring it to be the mimic. The nature of the object is subject to much speculation and rumor until its unveiling. For months afterward, the object becomes the source of practical jokes in Waterdeep. Rock gnomes and wizards cause illusory mouths to lunge from real versions of the object, artisans craft beautiful fakes out of cake or paper that are easily crushed when assumed to be real, and so on. As of the writing of this enchiridion, the current mimic is a tankard.

SOUTHERN WARD

It is called the Southern Ward, not the South Ward. Waterdavians are peculiar about this, and if you insist on referring to it as the South Ward, expect to be corrected or thought a fool. The name derives not merely from its southerly location in the city, but from the southerners who settled in this district as the city grew. Today, the ward still hosts most of the traveling merchants who visit the city, and is made up of many enclaves, blocks, and streets primarily occupied by citizens who trace their ancestry to other realms.

One can indulge in the finest halfling food here, enjoy the best singers of Calishite music, and examine the most stunning works of dwarven crafting—but the first challenge is finding where these treats are housed. The Southern Ward has long been a district of laborers catering to travelers, so its folk have adopted the architectural custom of building homes and businesses above stables or around inn yards, near to where wagon trains are housed.

Residents of the Southern Ward take pride in their legacy as overland travelers and hardworking folk, so it should be no surprise that the ward's mascot is the mule. On their competition flags, a pugnacious mule in rampant pose stands on a field of red and white—colors said to represent the blood and tears the people of the Southern Ward have shed during their labors.

Not a landmark as such, but surely a sight that must be seen, is the Moon Sphere. This isn't a structure but an event that occurs during every full moon, when a glowing, spherical field of blue light appears in the square known as the Dancing Court. Any creatures that enter the sphere find that they can fly about inside it just by willing themselves to do so. For centuries, Waterdavians have used these supernatural events to develop a unique flying style of dance—but amateur enthusiasts aren't welcome, except on certain daylight appearances of the full moon.

Even when the full moon isn't out, the Dancing Court is worth visiting because of the adjacent festhall, the Jade Dancer. During appearances of the Moon Sphere, people sometimes daringly leap into the field of magic from the balconies of this three-story tavern, dance hall, and inn. But the festhall takes its name from a peculiar dancer within it rather than those in the court outside. The "Jade Dancer" is an eight-foot-tall jade statue of a woman that magically animates and dances for patrons—and on occasion serves as a bouncer. Elminster has informed me that despite its dexterity and seemingly fragile beauty, the Jade Dancer is as puissant as a stone golem. So enjoy the show, but don't get too rowdy.

DOCK WARD

The Dock Ward was long considered the most dangerous district in the city, but the Field Ward has since taken that title. I don't doubt the residents of the Dock Ward are glad of it, for in some respects this area has never truly deserved its bad reputation.

Yes, aside from the Field Ward, this is the area where most of Waterdeep's poor reside. Yes, it is home to some of the least literate people in the city. Yes, most of its taverns are inhabited by habitual drinkers, and far too many inns charge by the hour. But all must concede this: the residents of the Dock Ward often work the hardest while living under the harshest conditions.

Warehouses, poorhouses, and tenements dominate much of the area. Streets are steep throughout, and few have space alongside for pedestrians. Wandering through the ward can be a bewildering journey without a guide. Except in the immediate vicinity of the piers, shop signs and advertising of any kind are rare, and warehouses and other businesses often have no sign at all. You either know where you are going and have reason to be there—or you are lost, and a likely mark for pickpockets or worse.

CITY OF THE DEAD

Streetlamps don't fare well in the Dock Ward. Their candles, oils, and glass are too regularly stolen or smashed. The Guild of Chandlers and Lamplighters makes a halfhearted attempt to repair the streetlamps at the start of each season, but for most of the year, locals are forced to carry their own light when traveling these streets at night.

The colors of the Dock Ward are burgundy and orange, and its mascot is a swordfish that has always been depicted as green for reasons lost to time. The folk of the Dock Ward take competition seriously, and they frequently draft their champions from the rough-and-tumble sailors who come to the city. (Some say they draft pirates, but that is pure slander.) Frequent complaints arise that these women and men are more citizens of the sea than of the Dock Ward itself. But if they register with a magister and pay taxes, they are as welcome to compete as any long-term resident of Waterdeep.

CITY OF THE DEAD

I could write a book about the City of the Dead. It is such a fascinating place, filled with so much history and so many stories. But alas, there would be few buyers for *Volo's Guide to the City of the Dead*, since it would be of interest mainly to Waterdavians—and the topic is one about which they are already intimately knowledgeable.

The City of the Dead is no drab cemetery. It is a great park of grassy hills, tended flower beds, artfully placed clusters of trees and bushes, beautiful sculptures, astounding architecture, and gravel paths that wend intriguingly through it all. Long ago, Waterdavians largely abandoned the practice of burying their dead, instead entombing them in mausoleums. For centuries, the major mausoleums here have each been connected to an extradimensional space where the dead are taken, mourned, and interred.

Those who can afford it memorialize the departed with sculptures, making the City of the Dead an open-air museum that features some of the most stunning, haunting, mournful, and downright eerie statues ever crafted in marble or bronze. Nobles and wealthy merchants have competed to erect the grandest markers for their dead, leading to a wide variety of styles and concepts created by artists at the height of their skills.

One of the cemetery's most impressive attractions is the Warriors' Monument. This intricate, sixty-foot-high sculpture depicts a circle of women and men striking down trolls, orcs, hobgoblins, bugbears, and barbarians, all of which are falling backward and outward around the warriors. Above all of them, a flying griffon rider spears a skeletal knight whose breastplate bears the symbol of Myrkul, god of the dead. But this statue is also a fountain, and the wounds on these combatants gush water! Don't try to imagine it—just go see it. And see it as Waterdavians do: pack a midday feast, have a picnic, and then take a stroll through the beauty of the place.

OUTSIDE THE CITY PROPER

There's more to the city of Waterdeep than just the wards within its walls. If you have need to visit the environs of the city, here's what you'll need to know.

FIELD WARD

This district was once a caravan yard between Waterdeep's two northernmost walls, kept free of settlement to serve as a killing field in times of war. As refugees from various calamities settled there after not being allowed into the city's wealthy northern neighborhoods, the area has grown up into a lawless town of its own.

Though not an official ward of the city, the Field Ward is commonly referred to as one. The Watch doesn't patrol this area, however, and many crimes go uninvestigated. The City Guard oversees the Field Ward from the walls around it, but its members get involved only when folk moving into or out of the city are threatened.

The area is a muddy mess, populated by the poorest people and those who take advantage of those folks' desperation. It has no sewer system and isn't served by the Dungsweepers' Guild—a fact that will be quite evident to your nose if you venture here. I don't recommend that you spend any more time here than it takes to pass through from one gate to the next.

The Guild of Butchers operates several slaughterhouses, smokehouses, and leather-making facilities in the area—noisome operations that have been pushed out of the city proper. A word to the wise: being friendly with a burly fellow who is good with a knife is one of your best defenses in the Field Ward. The other place you might solicit aid is Endshift Tavern, a popular stop for off-duty members of the City Guard, situated on the corner of Endshift Street and the Breezeway. Though the guards might not be inclined to assist you, your status as a visitor to Waterdeep technically obliges them to help you reach the city proper in safety.

THE WONDERS OF THE WAYMOOT

The place where the High Road and the Way of the Dragon meet in the south of the city is called the Waymoot. At the center of the crossroads, a high signpost stands with hanging arrows pointing toward the harbor and each of the city gates. Created by the Watchful Order of Magists and Protectors and funded by local merchants, the signpost magically directs travelers to well-known distant locations when the names of those locations are spoken into a crystal on the post. The magic of the Waymoot writes the destination onto the proper arrow of the signpost and indicates its distance from Waterdeep in miles. Folk are thereby sent out of the harbor or the appropriate gate leading north, east, or south, depending on their destination.

Unfortunately for newcomers, the Waymoot is of no use whatsoever in finding locations within Waterdeep. You will, however, find a number of enterprising individuals near the crossroads who take advantage of this fact to offer their services as city guides. Though some reputable members of this cadre will guide you true for a fair fee, plenty of citizens with nothing to lose or gain by doing so will also readily set you on the right course if you're simply polite.

UNDERCLIFF

This area of rolling grassland and small wooded areas east of the city is a rural community focused on farming and animal husbandry, and which caters to travelers. It is also the site of a large and well-protected training camp for the City Guard, and a prison farm run by the City Watch (called Amendsfarm) where those convicted of minor offenses work off their debt to the city. Many gnomes and halflings live in this region, and most buildings are built to reflect their stature.

Two noble families have estates in Undercliff. The Amcathra estate is used for the housing and final training of horses bred in the town of Amphail, many of which are sold to the City Guard. The Hothemer noble house has an estate where its members conduct business in overland trade—beyond the reach of Waterdeep's auditors.

If you visit this area, I recommend the Snobeedle Orchard and Meadery, owned and run by the Snobeedle halflings. They have a delightful drinking hall and a shop sized for larger patrons, and you can pick your own fruit when it is in season.

UNDERMOUNTAIN

Tales of this legendary dungeon below Waterdeep are told well by many in the city, but I'll provide you with the basic truths here.

Beneath the plateau of Waterdeep lies the largest and deepest dungeon in the world. It sprawls out under the city, said to plunge as many as twenty levels deep. The Melairkyn dwarves first excavated the tunnels that would become Undermountain, and the drow are said to have dug their own tunnels up from below. All were claimed, altered, and expanded by the mad wizard Halaster and his apprentices—who are believed to dwell in the dungeons to this day. What drove them deep into the earth remains a mystery, but Undermountain's allure is a siren song that still draws many. If you want to see adventurers descend into the depths, or perhaps glimpse some returning with wondrous treasures, visit the Yawning Portal in the Castle Ward.

THE CITY'S SPLENDORS

A description of each of the features that cause Waterdeep to be called the City of Splendors would require a library's worth of paper. This chapbook can't hope to encompass them all, no matter its author's expertise with a quill. However, I shall endeavor to enlighten you about several sights that have not been mentioned earlier, and to expand upon some previously covered.

AMENITIES

You'll find no city on the Sword Coast or in all the North half as civilized as Waterdeep. It's not just the law of the land that makes this so, but also the comforts that life here provides.

In most other towns and cities, you'll start with an early-morning stumble on the stairs as you carry your night soil down to deposit it outside. But in Waterdeep, many buildings are connected directly to the sewers. Public facilities for those out and about can be found all around the Market and the Field of Triumph, and

GRIFFON CAVALRY ON PATROL

near the largest city squares. In places without ready access to sewers or public outhouses, members of the Dungsweepers' Guild make multiple rounds each day, collecting urine and excrement separately—for use in industry and agriculture, respectively. Take comfort that in Waterdeep, you'll always find a pot to piss in.

Also notice how clean the streets are kept. This up-keep is due in large part to the hard work of the Dung-sweepers' Guild. Dungsweepers can be seen working their brooms and carts at every hour of the day—and for a few hours after dark—all over the city, removing not just animal dung but other refuse. This service is free to all, paid for by taxes rendered to the city—although an egregious amount of trash left for pickup does result in a separate bill from the guild.

Another amenity soon appreciated by visitors is Water-deep's water system. With public fountains and wells all about the city, clean water is plentiful. Many buildings have pumps of their own to draw water from the local supply, and some even possess taps that pour out water with the twist of a knob. This convenience is made pos-sible by the inventiveness of the Gondar, the industry of the Cellarers' and Plumbers' Guild, and the magic that Waterdeep inherited from the Illefarni elves.

Waterdeep is also a city of light. *Continual flame* spells illuminate many signs and streetlamps in the wealthier parts of the city. Elsewhere, the Guild of Chandlers and Lamplighters keeps the streets lit (excepting the Field

Ward and the most dangerous areas of the Dock Ward). Not only that, but hundreds of *driftglobes* bob about the City of the Dead at night, departing to float over the rest of the city each morning. Such is not typical behavior for *driftglobes*, I assure you!

Lastly, no city in the world is as literate as Waterdeep. Oghma's priests from the Font of Knowledge offer free instruction in reading to all who desire it, and the city has over thirty publishers of broadsheets in addition to chapbook printers and book publishers. Large paper ad-vertisements are plastered onto alley walls, and smaller ones are passed out by those hired by businesses to trumpet their services. Printed menus can be found posted in the windows of most eateries and are handed out to those who dine within. Admittedly, you'll see less reading material in the Dock Ward and the Field Ward, but this fact is notable only because of its preponderance elsewhere.

THE GRIFFON CAVALRY

Waterdeep doesn't have the fabled flying ships of Hal-ruaa, but it does deploy an aerial defense force. Brave warriors of the City Guard light out from the Peaktop Aerie atop Mount Waterdeep, riding fearsome griffons that have been bred and trained for that purpose. Each of the riders is equipped with a *ring of feather falling*—not merely to prevent death from mishap, but to allow them to perform stunning feats of aerial acrobatics.

In both martial displays and in real battles against flying threats such as manticores, harpies, and outlaw wizards, the griffon riders actually leap off their mounts into the open air! For a breath-stealing moment, they fall like stones, closing in on their targets at incredible speed. Their opponents rarely see the death blow, distracted as they are by other mounted griffon riders. When they are past the danger, the free-falling riders then suddenly halt in the air, drifting like feathers until their griffon companions swoop in and they regain their saddles. Working in concert with one another in this fashion, members of the Griffon Cavalry can rapidly eliminate any threat to the city—and even catch the body of the offender before it hits the rooftops below.

Riders of the Griffon Cavalry are trained to stay above the rooftops, not because they fear crashing into towers and weather vanes, but because the smell of so much horseflesh in the streets below can sometimes drive their griffons into a frenzy.

THE WALKING STATUES

Over a century ago, just one of these eight behemoth statues stood visible at the northern foot of Mount Waterdeep, on a bluff called Gull Leap. Ninety feet tall, it resembled a bald human staring out to sea. Later events (discussed below) caused it to be transformed into the statue known today as the Sahuagin Humbled.

When the Spellplague gripped Waterdeep in 1385 DR, six more walking statues suddenly appeared in the city, wandering to wreak havoc even as the Sahuagin Humbled remained motionless. The authorities and citizens of Waterdeep succeeded in stopping three of these new statues, breaking the Swordmaiden and the Hawk Man, and sinking the God Catcher into the street up to its waist. Then all the statues mysteriously stopped their rampage just as quickly as they had begun it. Tsarra Chaadren, the Blackstaff at the time, couldn't command them to return to their former hiding places on the Ethereal Plane. Consequently, the city repaired itself and built up around them. Much later, in 1479 DR, the eighth statue—the Griffon—emerged from the Ethereal Plane to defend Ahghairon's Tower against intrusion. It roosted there for a time before flying to its current position near Peaktop Aerie on Mount Waterdeep. Once more, this activity seemed to be outside the Blackstaff's control. Thankfully, all the walking statues have been dormant for well over a decade now, serving only as beautiful, cyclopean reminders of Waterdeep's might.

THE GOD CATCHER

This is perhaps the most famous walking statue in the city, thanks to its dramatic pose, its nearness to the Market, and the self-evident magic of its existence. The statue is of a well-muscled but impassive male human with its left leg sunk to the hip in the street, the result of a spell cast by the Blackstaff at the time of its rampage. Its left hand and right foot press against the ground as if it is trying to pull itself out. Its right arm is raised sky-

THE GOD CATCHER LOOMING IN THE BACKGROUND

ward, and above its open palm floats a sphere of stone. Its gaze looks up toward the sphere, and the pattern of bird droppings around its eyes gives it the appearance of weeping.

All about the statue, climbing up its chest and on its knee and shoulders, is a tenement that carries the name "the God Catcher." The tenement's landlord is Aundra Blackcloak, an unsociable sorcerer who is rarely seen in the city except when she alights from the door carved in the floating sphere, which serves as her home. On the rare occasions when she wants to meet with city folk (typically to purchase odd substances for magical purposes), she appears unannounced on balconies or rooftops after dark. Her dealings are polite, though, and she pays fair coin. She never confides in anyone or talks about her own doings—and if anyone but she has ever seen the inside of her spherical home, they've said nothing publicly about it.

THE GRIFFON

The walking statue called the Griffon is shaped like the beast for which it is named. Though it stands on all four legs, its back is fully twenty feet off the ground, making it a mount fit for a storm giant. Although it has shown itself to be capable of flight, with the granite feathers of its wings spreading like a bird's, the Griffon now merely stands in a regal pose near Peaktop Aerie atop Mount Waterdeep, looking to the southeast over the Dock Ward. Newcomers sometimes assume it to be a monument to Waterdeep's Griffon Cavalry, but Waterdavians know better.

THE SAHUAGIN HUMBLED

For years, the only visible walking statue of Waterdeep was known simply as "the walking statue." It stood at the foot of Mount Waterdeep near the head of Julthoon Street. Then, after its critical role in defending the city against an invasion of sahuagin in 1370 DR, Khelben Blackstaff reshaped the statue into a sahuagin. It now bows low toward the House of Heroes on bended knee—a gesture of obeisance to the city, and an acknowledgment of the sacrifice of all who fought for the city in that war.

THE GREAT DRUNKARD

This walking statue stopped its rampage as it approached the Market, then fell backward and sat upon a building. When it settled, its arms fell limp at its sides and its head tilted forward onto its chest, giving the impression that it had fallen asleep. The statue's huge stone battleaxe still stands nearby, its haft angled upright and its blade half buried in the cobbles. The rubble of the crushed building was long ago rebuilt into a broad stone stair (with railings and a ramp that drunkards are often rolled down) that ascends from the cobbles to the statue's lap. That lap now holds a two-story tavern also built from the rubble, called Gralkyn's Tankard. The unconscious pose of the statue and the tavern in its lap made the name of the Great Drunkard a natural fit.

THE LADY DREAMING

This fair lady caused much chaos when she was active. The statue has the appearance of a female elf, whose hair and clothing appeared to flow naturally as it walked through the city during the Spellplague. When the walking statues stopped, this one toppled onto its side, taking on the appearance of a titanic sculpture of a noble lady asleep in her garden.

THE HONORABLE KNIGHT

The Honorable Knight is a statue of a male warrior in plate armor with a shield and longsword. When the walking statues stopped, it bowed to those opposing it, straightened, sheathed its sword, and doffed its shield, setting it point down on the ground and upright by its side. It then ceased motion in this position, facing southwest toward the harbor, and looking for all the world like a castle guard standing at ease. The pose it assumed led to its naming, and it is viewed with respect by the citizens of the southerly wards.

THE HAWK MAN

This statue looks like a winged, hawk-headed being, and thus locals call it the Hawk Man. I can reveal that in fact it bears much resemblance to an aarakocra, one of the bird-people said to live in the Star Mounts in the High Forest. The statue's wings are folded tightly against its back and have never unfurled, leaving its flight capability uncertain. It was brought low during its rampage across the city, and now it tilts decidedly toward the northeast due to a missing right foot—long ago broken up for building rubble, along with its right arm. Its left arm is extended out toward the north, palm forward as if in a gesture to say, "Stop."

The body has been hollowed out and turned into a tower shared by several wealthy tenants, which is officially known as Sparaunt Tower after its owner. The statue's left hand extends over a courtyard to the north, wherein lies the entrance of a tunnel carved through the arm. Visitors and residents can ring a bell in the courtyard, whereupon a door guard acknowledges the ringer and lowers a rope ladder for tenants and expected guests (or a rope chair that is drawn up for guests who are infirm or laden with heavy items).

THE SWORDMAIDEN

This statue appears virtually identical to the Honorable Knight, except for its female form and open-faced helm. It was felled during the Spellplague after causing much chaos and slaughter. The residents of Waterdeep's North Ward funneled much of their frustrated and dismayed reaction to its rampage into dismantling the statue, parts of which can now be found all over the North Ward, either incorporated into buildings or as bits of freestanding sculpture.

The head of the Swordmaiden sits in a stand of tall trees in the center of the block of the North Ward bounded by Hassantyr's Street, Tarsar's Street, Whaelgond Way, and Ussilbran Street. The center of its jaw and mouth have been replaced by a door, which leads into the shop known as Thort's Findings. Undevvur Thort is a wizened ex-adventurer who leans on a cane (which some locals insist is more than just a cane). He lives in the small shop, whose many levels, staircases, and landings fill the hollowed-out interior of the head, and which is crammed with oddments sold to Thort by adventurers and other travelers. These items bear little placards in Thort's beautiful, flowing handwriting that identify them (or at least provide speculation as to their origin and purpose). Nobles and wealthy merchants who desire props for themed revels often rent some of Thort's wares as decoration—and many sages, alchemists, and wizards visit him regularly in search of potentially useful items.

CITY CELEBRATIONS

At many times of year, hardly a tenday can pass in Waterdeep without the staging of some rite, race, or rousing ceremony of civic pride. Here I briefly summarize the most widely celebrated events on the calendar, from the first of Hammer to the last of Nightal.

HAMMER 1: WINTERSHIELD

Marking the start of the new year, this observance is a widely recognized day off work, when folk sip warmed ciders and broths (often laced with herbs for health and to bring on visions) and stay inside. They tell tales of what interested them or was important in the year just done, and discuss what they intend to do or should deal with—or things that everyone "should keep a hawk's clear eye on"—in the year ahead.

Such talk inevitably leads to discussions of politics, wars, and the intentions of rulers. Maps are usually consulted, and it's widely considered lucky to possess and examine a map on Wintershield. Map sales are brisk in the tenday preceding this holiday.

ALTURIAK 14: THE GRAND REVEL

Led by the clergy of Sune, Sharess, and Lliira, the Grand Revel is a day of dancing, music, and the consumption of sweet treats of all kinds, from chocolate to red firemint candies. Although some of the dancing is wanton and performed for show, large-scale ring dances in the street for all ages are also popular. All the dancing ends at dusk, after which bards and minstrels perform at "love feasts" for families. Couples—or those desiring to become couples—slip away together to kiss, exchange promises, and trade small tokens of affection (often rings blessed by clergy with prayers of faithfulness). Even if you have no paramour, indulge a little in the dance and food of this fine tradition. The night might be cold, but your heart will be warmed.

CHES 1: RHYESTERTIDE

This holiday is named in honor of Lathander's first prophet, Rhyester, a young blind boy who was cured of that blindness by the dawn's light on this day more than seven centuries ago. That holy event occurred in the vicinity of Silverymoon, but Lathander has long had a much larger temple in Waterdeep, and a following to match. Each of the faithful dons bright garb of sunrise hues and keeps one eye covered until the next dawn in honor of Rhyester. If you want to feel like a local, catch the eye of any celebrant you see and wink. Fine friendships have grown from far less.

CHES 19: FEY DAY

The veil between this world and the faerie realm of the Feywild is thought to be weak on this day. Though this phenomenon provokes caution in rural areas (with folk avoiding woodlands, putting offerings of food on door-

---

INFAMOUS ALLEYS

Waterdeep has as many alleys as Baldur's Gate has cats, and each has a name and a story. Here are a few that you might wish to see—or should know to avoid.

Ruid's Stroll. This short avenue from Caravan Court to the Trollwall in the Southern Ward is haunted by the hooded ghost of the mage Ruid, whose touch causes deathly chills to those he meets on foggy nights. All attempts to banish or turn the spirit have failed. Those who brave its unearthly approach and allow Ruid to pass through them learn a secret truth about someone or something in their life—if they survive.

Brindul Alley. This is the lair of the Hand that Sings, a magical phantasm of a hand with a mouth in its palm. The hand is said to snatch valuables it fancies—especially magical ones—when it encounters them, and to occasionally attack folk in the darkness, strangling them or tripping them into fatal falls. Most often, though, it takes no notice of those who don't bother or follow it, eerily singing fragments of old Sword Coast ballads and love songs as it drifts through the night.

Manycats Alley. This passage crosses two city blocks and winds through the interior of a third, running between and (for the most part) parallel to Julthoon Street and Traders' Way in the North Ward. It is, unsurprisingly, home to many cats that feed on scraps from the surrounding butchers' shops, but it is also known for the many carved stone heads of people and animals that adorn the alley's buildings. Individuals who have walked the alley alone report that some of the heads whispered cryptic messages to them.

Gondwatch Lane. Found at the southern entrance to the House of Inspired Hands in the Sea Ward, this alley serves as the testing ground for inventions considered too dangerous to operate inside the temple. The locals are generally unconcerned about the risks, though, and stand watching while food vendors circulate among them.

Pharra's Alley. This alley in the Sea Ward is named after the first leader of the House of Wonder, but is more infamous for its Circle of Skulls. This infrequent and unpredictable haunting takes the form of seven floating skulls, which hover in a circle and argue with one another in whispered tones about events in the city. If they are interrupted, their reaction reportedly varies from being helpful to engaging in murderous spell-slinging.

Three Daggers Alley. This alley in the Dock Ward suffers from a magical curse that causes three daggers to appear out of thin air and attack passersby. The daggers swoop and fly about, making multiple attempts at murder before vanishing again. This magical effect, the result of a spell cast by a long-dead wizard, has resisted all attempts to dispel it. Some locals boast of how many times they've crossed the alley and lived to tell of it, but the appearance of the daggers is entirely a matter of chance, and unpredictable. So take my advice and don't test Tymora's favor.

---

steps, and the like), it is an occasion of much drinking, singing, and dancing in Waterdeep. The wealthy host elaborate masked balls, while poorer folk don costumes of their own make and travel door to door, gaining brief entry into the celebrations in exchange for performing a song or a short play. All adopt the guises of fey beings and the supposed rulers of the Feywild, such as Queen Titania, Oberon, and Hyrsam, the Prince of Fools. Those inclined to remain sullen in the face of such frivolity had best stay home, for celebrants do their utmost to evoke a smile from those they meet.

CHES 21–30: FLEETSWAKE

This festival celebrates the sea, maritime trade, and the gods of the sea, navigation, and weather. It spans the last tenday of Ches, and includes a series of boat races, the Shipwrights' Ball at the Shipwrights' House, and guild-sponsored galas at the Copper Cup festhall. According to custom, the winners of the various competitions don't keep their trophies and earnings, but deliver them to the priests of Umberlee at the Queenspire, her temple on the beach by the east entrance to the Great Harbor, at the conclusion of the festival.

The last two days of Fleetswake are the occasion of the Fair Seas Festival. During this time, there is much feasting on seafood, the harbor is strewn with flower petals, and City Guards go from tavern to tavern collecting offerings for Umberlee. Collection boxes also appear at large festival gatherings. Upon sunset of the final day, the collected coin is placed in chests and dumped into the deepest part of the harbor.

This festival has existed in a number of forms since the first trade-meets occurred here more than two millennia ago, and an uncountable amount of wealth remains sunken in what has long been known as Umberlee's Cache. The area is closely watched by merfolk guardians, whose standing orders are to kill anyone attempting to disturb it. Rumors abound that the chests have magical protections; one story tells of thieves who stole some of the collection years ago and tried to leave the city under false pretenses, only to see a squall spring up as soon as their ship left the harbor. A huge wave shaped like a hand swept the thieves overboard, but spared the ship and its crew.

TARSAHK 1–10: WAUKEENTIDE

This festival has long gathered a number of older holidays under one name, stretching those celebrations into a holiday season that lasts a tenday. Among the rituals in homage to the goddess of wealth and trade are these:

Caravance (Tarsahk 1). This gift-giving holiday commemorates the traditional arrival of the first caravans of the season into the city. Many parents hide gifts for their offspring in their homes, telling the children that they were left by Old Carvas—a mythical peddler who arrived with the first caravan to reach Waterdeep, his wagon loaded down with toys for children to enjoy.

Goldenight (Tarsahk 5). This festival celebrates coin and gold, with many businesses staying open all night, offering midnight sales and other promotions. Some celebrants and customers decorate themselves with gold dust and wear coins as jewelry.

Guildsmeet (Tarsahk 7). On this holiday, guild members gather in their halls for the announcement of new policies and a celebration of business concluded for the year. These gatherings culminate in a gala festival and dance sponsored by several guilds, which lasts from dusk till dawn and overruns the Market, the Cynosure, the Field of Triumph, and all areas in between.

Leiruin (Tarsahk 10). In times long past, Waukeen caught Leira, the goddess of illusions and deception, attempting to cheat her in a deal, and buried her under a mountain of molten gold as punishment. A commemoration of that event, Leiruin is the day for guild members to pay their annual dues and for guildmasters to meet with the Lords of Waterdeep and renew their charters for another year.

MIRTUL 6–9: THE PLOWING AND RUNNING

Rural areas around the city observe this holiday in the traditional sense of shared activities of plowing fields and moving (or "running") livestock. But within the city, the holiday is celebrated with a series of races. Foot, horse, and chariot races are run through courses in each ward, and the winners from each ward compete at the Field of Triumph. If you really want to see the wards come to life, this is the time. Pick your favorite, wear its colors, and cheer alongside its residents. Better yet, if you're of an adventuresome bent, register in your favored ward and compete! Who knows? Your name or visage might soon have a place in the House of Heroes.

KYTHORN 1: TROLLTIDE

On this day commemorating Waterdeep's victory in the Second Trollwar, children run through the city acting like trolls, banging on doors and growling, from highsun till dusk. Home and shop owners are expected to give the children candy, fruits, or small items. Those who give no treat can expect to become the target of a trick at sundown. This mischief typically takes the form of "troll scratchings" at doors and windows. Those with more malicious intent sing screechingly in the wee hours, and hurl raw eggs at windows, signs, and the heads of those who try to stop them. Have some candy on hand or some sweet rolls, and all will be calm where you live.

KYTHORN 14: GUILDHALL DAY

This day is a time of trade fairs. Most shops are closed, and street sales are suspended for all but walking food peddlers. Guildhall Day celebrates the fruits of everyone's labor with revelations of new products, innovations, fashions, and signage extolling the extent and quality of guild members' services and wares. These offerings usually take the form of glittering displays, but guilds sometimes also sponsor brief plays or other hired entertainments (jugglers, singers, magic shows put on by hedge wizards and professional raconteurs) at which prizes or free samples are distributed. Many guilds try to recruit during this time. Guildhall Day is an excellent time to browse the city's merchandise—and it doesn't matter if you can't afford what you see, because you can't buy it that day anyway.

KYTHORN 20: DRAGONDOWN

This day in Kythorn is celebrated with bonfires and rituals to "tame" or "drive down" dragons. In Waterdeep, the celebrations take the form of parades that center around effigies built of wood and cloth and filled with straw. Each effigy is named and has a traditional depiction, for it represents one of a handful of dragons the city has faced in its history. After being paraded to a square near where the dragon was defeated or driven off, the enormous effigy is burned.

The height of the celebration comes when the effigy of Kistarianth the Red is burned on the slopes of Mount Waterdeep. A dracolich version of Kistarianth is then carried up the slopes and burned as well. These proceedings symbolize the defeat of Kistarianth first by the paladin Athar, and again decades later by his son, Piergeiron. Tradition dictates that the winners of the races run during the Plowing and Running take the role of the dragons' slayers, with the champion of the chariot race representing Athar and the champion of the horse race playing Piergeiron.

FLAMERULE 1: FOUNDERS' DAY

This day commemorates the birth of the city. The Field of Triumph is the site of illusory displays that chronicle the history of Waterdeep, as well as martial exhibitions by the Guard and other worthies. Many festhalls sponsor Founders' Day costume contests, with prizes going to those who wear the best recreations of the garb of historical personages.

Once banned as frivolous and distracting, the practice of veiling Castle Waterdeep with an illusion has been reinstated. Several mages come together to produce the effect, which seemingly transforms the castle into the ancient log fortress of Nimoar. The illusion typically lasts from midday to sunset (unless someone has the audacity and magical might to dispel it) and is regarded as a stunning work of magical art.

FLAMERULE 3–5: SORNYN

Sornyn is a festival of both Waukeen and Lathander, and is used for planning business, making treaties and agreements, and receiving envoys from unknown lands and traditional foes. Much wine is drunk over this three-day occasion when, as the saying goes, "My enemy is like family to me." If you are a newcomer to the city, this time is an excellent opportunity for you to engage with new partners in business or to gain financial support for some endeavor. My agreement to write *Volo's Guide to Waterdeep* was signed on a warm Sornyn evening many years ago, so who knows where your own initiative will take you?

FLAMERULE 7: LLIIRA'S NIGHT

Originally a celebration held only in Waterdeep, this holiday has since spread up and down the Sword Coast. It has received a recent boost in popularity from the custom started in Baldur's Gate of lighting celebratory *smokepowder* fireworks—all purchased from Felogyr's Fireworks of that city, and utilized only by the City Guard, of course. This nightlong festival honors the Lady of Joy with dances and balls throughout the city.

Pink beverages, ranging from healthy juices to deadly strong intoxicants, are imbibed. The boom and crackle of *smokepowder* explosions go off all night long, so you might as well stay up with the locals and enjoy the show.

ELEASIS 1: AHGHAIRON'S DAY

Many small rituals are held throughout this day, dedicated to honoring the first Open Lord. The Lords of Waterdeep toast Ahghairon and the Watchful Order, and guildmasters toast the Lords in Ahghairon's name. Commoners leave violets (Ahghairon's favorite flower) around Ahghairon's Tower, on his statue in the City of the Dead, and atop the altars of the House of Wonder. Bards perform songs in honor of the wizard all over the city. The Open Lord visits taverns and inns throughout Waterdeep to wish the people well—giving short speeches, offering toasts to Ahghairon's memory, buying rounds of drinks, or paying for meals or accommodation. Needless to say, establishments of those sorts are generally full throughout the day.

ELEINT 21: BRIGHTSWORDS

On this day, the City Guard, the City Navy, and the City Watch—all in glittering array—conduct parades, give demonstrations of martial skill, and stage mock battles. Those desiring to join their ranks are given a chance to demonstrate their prowess, usually with wooden practice weapons in contests against veteran soldiers. Makers and vendors of weapons sell their wares openly in the markets, experts who can hurl or juggle weapons show off their skills, and the wards compete in wrestling and boxing matches. The most anticipated part of the day is when horses are cleared from the Field of Triumph and the surrounding streets so that the Griffon Cavalry can perform aerial displays over the crowds in the stadium. Members of the Watchful Order present the cavalry with illusory foes to fight, allowing the griffon riders to engage in thrilling battles as the people watch.

MARPENOTH 3: DAY OF WONDERS

The imaginative inventions of the Gondar are revealed on this day and paraded through the city. These devices range from something as humble as new cabinet hinges to massive mechanical constructs that walk or roll about. Failure is the paramour of invention, though, meaning it is a rare year when there isn't some notable disruption of the celebration. The flying chair of Marchell was one such recent oddity—a device that worked marvelously on the way up but was incapable of descending. Marchell was rescued by the Griffon Cavalry, but his flying chair drifted away and was never seen again.

MARPENOTH 7: STONESHAR

Stoneshar is an all-faiths day during which folk strive not to be idle. Even children at play are encouraged to dig holes, build sand castles, or construct crude models.

Waterdavians consider Stoneshar the best day of the year to begin construction of a building, either by digging out a cellar or laying a foundation. The common wisdom is that folk who undertake new projects on Stoneshar can expect blessings upon their works in

DAY OF WONDERS

the coming year, whereas individuals who do nothing constructive on this day can expect all manner of misfortune to rain down on them in the year ahead.

MARPENOTH 10: REIGN OF MISRULE

Swift on the heels of Stoneshar comes the Reign of Misrule. This day honors Beshaba, goddess of misfortune. People of the city are expected to break trust, belie oaths, and disobey the normal order—as long as no laws are actually broken and no rift is made that can't be later bridged. During the Reign of Misrule, nobles serve meals to their servants, children take control of schools, priests give worship to their god's foes, and any who wish to may participate in a guild's trade. Pranks are played by and on many, from simple tricks to those requiring elaborate planning. Sundown brings an end to the festivities, and most folk spend much of the night cleaning and reordering things for the following day. Many visitors decline to participate, but doing so often inspires misfortune rather than avoiding it. For fear of catching the bad luck of cynics, citizens do their best to avoid talking to anyone known to not have played along, or dealing with them in any way until Gods' Day.

MARPENOTH 15: GODS' DAY

This holiday observes the anniversary of the end of the Godswar in 1358 DR, when the gods of Faerûn returned to the heavens. Private shrines are brought out into the open, and many people wear holy symbols of their favored deities. A Gods' Day tradition in Waterdeep strictly limits the use of magic, in remembrance of the wild magic wrought during the Time of Troubles. Though not outlawed fully, spellcasting is allowable only in self-defense or in cases of extreme need.

At night, this holiday becomes solemn and serious, as many Waterdavians offer prayers in thanks for the lives they have under their gods. The Griffon Cavalry sets up an immense bonfire at the peak of Mount Waterdeep, honoring the fallen and the risen gods Myrkul, Cyric, Kelemvor, Mystra, Helm, and Ao who appeared here. In thanks for their defense during Myrkul's invasion and the resulting fires that raged through the Southern, Dock, and Castle Wards, Gods' Day is also a semiofficial "Be Kind to the Guard and Watch Day" in Waterdeep. Feel free to participate by handing out small gifts and kind words, but be aware that any gift of greater value than a few nibs might be interpreted as a bribe.

MARPENOTH 30: LIAR'S NIGHT

This holy day pays tribute to Leira and Mask. To placate those deities and ward away their attention, folk of all walks of life don masks and costumes (magical or mundane) to disguise themselves and play at being other than what they are. Commonly seen mask styles include the black mask symbol of Mask and the mirror face of the priests of Leira. But there are no bounds on the disguise you don, and the more elaborate and outlandish it is, the more celebrated the wearer.

The festivities begin in the evening, when people place candles in hollowed-out gourds or pumpkins carved with faces. Each pumpkin represents a person donning a mask, while the light inside represents the truth of the soul. For as long as the candle remains lit, lies told and embarrassing things done don't sully a person's reputation, so celebrations often descend briefly into anarchic hedonism.

Misfortune is said to come to anyone who returns to their pumpkin after celebrating to find it unlit, so buy a candle of good quality and put your gourd beyond reach of the wind. Intentionally blowing out someone else's candle or smashing someone else's pumpkin is taboo, and risks the wrath of both gods—yet it does occur.

Tricks and pranks of all kinds are common on this night, and folk expect lies and foolishness. Pickpockets are rife on this day, so few carry much coin with them, having secreted it away somewhere the previous evening. Instead, people fill their pockets and belt pouches with candies. Traditionally, a pickpocket is meant to take the candy and leave a token in return (a tiny toy, a colorful paper folded into a shape, or the like), but this has changed over the years into adults exchanging candies among themselves and simply giving candy to children who ask for it.

By custom, no deals are made nor contracts signed on Liar's Night, because no one trusts that parties will abide by them. Illusionists and stage magicians (whether through magical or practical abilities) make the rounds to entertain private parties (having been paid in advance the previous day) or to perform in public spaces, in the hopes that a good show will earn them a meal, and perhaps a place at a private party in the future.

UKTAR: SELÛNE'S HALLOWING

On whatever night in Uktar the moon is fullest, Waterdavians celebrate Selûne's Hallowing. The goddess is the focus of worship throughout the full phase, of course, but the major ceremony on this night is a parade of worshipers leaving the House of the Moon at moonrise and moving down to the harbor, where the high priestess wields the *Wand of the Four Moons* in a ceremony blessing all navigators. This holy relic is said to be the mace wielded by Selûne in her first battle against Shar, and again in a fight with her sister during the Time of Troubles. It miraculously appeared in Waterdeep after the Godswar, and has since been the focus of many divine signs. You can view it in the House of the Moon at other times of the year, but only from a well-guarded distance.

If you're lucky, you might see the *Wand of the Four Moons* weep. Droplets said to be the tears of Selûne manifest on the mace from time to time, and are collected by the priestesses for use in potions that can heal, cure lycanthropy, and be used as holy water.

UKTAR 20: LAST SHEAF

Sometimes called "The Small Feast," this day of residential feasting is held in celebration of the year's bounty. Small gifts (traditionally hand kegs of ale, jars of preserves, or smoked fish and meats) are exchanged among neighbors, and "last letters" are gathered for carriage by ship captains and caravan merchants—so called because they are the last to leave the city before travel becomes difficult. Of Waterdeep's many celebrations, this one is perhaps the most relaxed and relaxing. Plan to spend a little extra on good food and enjoy a meal with those nearest you, be they dearest hearts or the folk across the hall in the inn.

NIGHTAL 11: HOWLDOWN

In honor of Malar, members of the City Guard leave the city in groups on this day to hunt down known threats to farmers and travelers, including brigands, wolves, owlbears, ogres, and trolls that haunt the roads and wilderness. These hunts typically last no longer than a tenday. During the same span of time, the City Watch engages in its own rigorous hunt for malefactors within the city walls. If you've any reason to doubt your standing in the eyes of the law, avoid Waterdeep for at least a tenday after Howldown.

With no real hunting to do of their own, the children of Waterdeep spend Howldown engaging in mock hunts of adults dressed up as monsters, and play at the killing of these predators.

NIGHTAL 20: SIMRIL

When dusk comes on this day, folk go outside to locate particular stars that were lucky for their ancestors, or that were associated with their own births. They then attempt to stay up through the night, celebrating outside with bonfires, song, and warmed drinks. Cloudy nights often draw larger crowds than clear ones, since glimpsing your star through the haze is thought to be a blessing from Tymora. Inside buildings, service folk keep roaring fires and engage in making food to keep celebrants fed throughout the long night and into morning of the next day. If you have no particular star of your own, you'll find many vendors of star maps willing to divine which is yours—based upon your place and date of birth—and to point you in the right direction for a shard or two.

PARTING WORDS

Well, gentle readers, you've reached the end of my enchiridion. If you've yet to arrive in the city, its splendors await you. If you're reading this within its walls, please set aside this chapbook to experience the city. You might even see an extraordinarily handsome author hard at work reviewing one of Waterdeep's drinking establishments. If you do so, I greet you in advance: "Well met! Autographs cost seven nibs."

APPENDIX A: MAGIC ITEMS

This appendix describes new magic items that appear in the adventure, and which are presented here in alphabetical order.

Several of these items are found in the possession of specific NPCs:

- Aurinax has the *dragonstaff of Ahghairon*.
- Jalester Silvermane has a *badge of the Watch*.
- Jarlaxle Baenre has a *bracer of daggers*, a *feather of diatryma summoning*, a *knave's eye patch*, and a *ring of truth telling*.
- Meloon Wardragon has *Azuredge*.
- Vajra Safahr has the *Blackstaff*.

AZUREDGE

Weapon (battleaxe), legendary (requires attunement)

Forged by the archwizard Ahghairon, this intelligent battleaxe was crafted to defend Waterdeep. Its current wielder is a former member of Force Grey named Meloon Wardragon (see appendix B), but the weapon is searching for a new owner.

Azuredge has a solid steel handle etched with tiny runes, wrapped in blue dragon hide with a star sapphire set into the pommel. The axe head is forged from silver, electrum, and steel alloys whose edges constantly shimmer with a deep blue luminescence.

You gain a +3 bonus to attack and damage rolls made with this magic weapon. The *shield* spell provides no defense against the axe, which passes through that spell's barrier of magical force.

When you hit a fiend or an undead with the axe, cold blue flames erupt from its blade and deal an extra 2d6 radiant damage to the target.

Hurling. The battleaxe has 3 charges. You can expend 1 charge and make a ranged attack with the axe, hurling it as if it had the thrown property with a normal range of 60 feet and a long range of 180 feet. Whether it hits or misses, the axe flies back to you at the end of the current turn, landing in your open hand or at your feet in your space (as you choose). The axe regains all expended charges daily at dawn.

Illumination. While holding the axe, you can use an action to cause the axe to glow blue or to quench the glow. This glow sheds bright light in a 30-foot radius and dim light for an additional 30 feet.

Sentience. *Azuredge* is a sentient lawful neutral weapon with an Intelligence of 12, a Wisdom of 15, and a Charisma of 15. It has hearing and darkvision out to a range of 120 feet.

The weapon communicates telepathically with its wielder and can speak, read, and understand Common. It has a calm, delicate voice. The weapon can sense the presence of non-lawful creatures within 120 feet of it.

Personality. *Azuredge* is sworn to protect Waterdeep, and it desires to be wielded by a law-abiding person willing to dedicate everything to the city's defense. The weapon is patient and takes its time finding its ideal wielder.

If someone tries to use *Azuredge* against its will, the axe can become ten times heavier than normal, and can magically adhere to any Medium or larger object or surface it comes into contact with. Once it does so, the axe can't be wielded. Nothing short of a *wish* spell can separate the axe from the item or surface to which it is adhered without destroying one or the other, though the axe can choose to end the effect at any time.

BADGE OF THE WATCH

Wondrous item, rare (requires attunement by someone designated by the Open Lord of Waterdeep)

A *badge of the Watch* is given only to those who have earned the trust of the Open Lord of Waterdeep. The badge, signifying the rank of captain in Waterdeep's City Watch, bears the emblem of Waterdeep and is meant to be worn or carried.

While wearing the badge, you gain a +2 bonus to AC if you aren't using a shield.

If the badge is more than 5 feet away from you for more than 1 minute, it vanishes and harmlessly reappears on a surface within 5 feet of the Open Lord. While holding the badge, the Open Lord knows your location, provided the two of you are on the same plane of existence and your attunement to the badge hasn't ended.

As an action, the Open Lord can touch the badge and end your attunement to it.

BADGE OF THE WATCH

BLACKSTAFF

Staff, legendary (requires attunement by the Blackstaff heir, who must be a wizard)

The *Blackstaff* is a sentient, rune-carved staff set with thin silver veins. It is the symbol of office for the Blackstaff, the highest-ranking wizard in Waterdeep. As the rightful owner of the *Blackstaff*, Vajra Safahr is the only one who can become attuned to it. The staff can, however, choose a new owner (see "Personality" below).

The *Blackstaff* has the magical properties of a *staff of power* (see the *Dungeon Master's Guide*) in addition to the following properties.

Animate Walking Statues. You can expend 1 or more of the staff's charges as an action to animate or deactivate one or more of the walking statues of Waterdeep (see appendix B). You must be in the city to use this property, and you can animate or deactivate one statue for each charge expended. An animated statue obeys the telepathic commands of Khelben Arunsun's spirit, which is trapped inside the staff (see "Personality" below). A walking statue becomes inanimate if deactivated or if the staff is broken.

Dispel Magic. You can expend 1 of the staff's charges as a bonus action to cast *dispel magic* on a creature, an object, or a magical effect that you touch with the tip of the staff. If the target is an unwilling creature or an object in the possession of such a creature, you must hit the creature with a melee attack using the *Blackstaff* before you can expend the charge to cast the spell.

Drain Magic. This property affects only creatures that use spell slots. When you hit such a creature with a melee attack using the *Blackstaff*, you can expend 1 of the staff's charges as a bonus action, causing the target to expend one spell slot of the highest spell level it can cast without casting a spell. If the target has already expended all its spell slots, nothing happens. Spell slots that are expended in this fashion are regained when the target finishes a long rest, as normal.

Master of Enchantment. When you cast an enchantment spell of 1st level or higher while holding the staff, you can make an Intelligence (Arcana) check with a DC of 10 + the level of the spell. If the check succeeds, you cast the spell without expending a spell slot.

Sentience. The *Blackstaff* is a sentient staff of neutral alignment, with an Intelligence of 22, a Wisdom of 15, and a Charisma of 18. It has hearing and darkvision out to a range of 120 feet, and it can communicate telepathically with any creature that is holding it.

Personality. The staff has the spirits of all previous Blackstaffs trapped within it. Its creator, Khelben Arunsun, is the dominant personality among them. Like Khelben, the staff is extremely devious and manipulative. It prefers to counsel its owner without exerting outright control. The staff's primary goal is to protect Waterdeep and its Open Lord, currently Laeral Silverhand. Its secondary goal is to help its wielder become more powerful.

In the event that the holder of the office of the Blackstaff no longer serves the staff's wishes, the staff ceases to function until it finds a worthy inheritor—someone whose loyalty to Waterdeep is beyond reproach.

Spirit Trap. When the Blackstaff dies, the spirit of that individual becomes trapped in the staff along with the spirits of the previous Blackstaffs. (A Blackstaff whose spirit is trapped in the staff can't be raised from the dead.)

Destroying the staff would release the spirits trapped inside it, but in that event, Khelben's spirit can lodge itself inside any one piece of the staff that remains. The piece containing Khelben's spirit has the staff's Sentience property but none of its other properties. As long as this piece of the staff exists, Khelben's spirit can make the staff whole again whenever he wishes. When the staff is remade, the spirits of the previous Blackstaffs become trapped inside it again.

BRACER OF FLYING DAGGERS

Wondrous item, rare (requires attunement)

This armband appears to have thin daggers strapped to it. As an action, you can pull up to two magic daggers from the bracer and immediately hurl them, making a ranged attack with each dagger. A dagger vanishes if you don't hurl it right away, and the daggers disappear right after they hit or miss. The bracer never runs out of daggers.

LORD'S ENSEMBLE

DRAGONSTAFF OF AHGHAIRON

Staff, legendary (requires attunement)

While holding the *dragonstaff of Ahghairon*, you have advantage on saving throws against the spells and breath weapons of dragons, as well as the breath weapons of other creatures of the dragon type (such as dragon turtles).

A creature of the dragon type that you touch with the staff can move through the city of Waterdeep, ignoring *Ahghairon's dragonward* (see "Ahghairon's Dragonward," page 6). This effect lasts until the creature is touched again by the staff or until a time you proclaim when you confer the benefit.

The staff has 10 charges. While holding it, you can expend 1 charge as an action to cast the *command* spell. If you target a dragon with this casting, the dragon has disadvantage on its saving throw. The staff regains 1d10 charges daily at dawn.

FEATHER OF DIATRYMA SUMMONING

Wondrous item, rare (requires attunement)

This bright plume is made from the feather of a diatryma (pronounced dee-ah-TRY-mah), a Large, colorful, flightless bird native to the Underdark. If you use an action to speak the command word and throw the feather into a Large unoccupied space on the ground within 5 feet of you, the feather becomes a living diatryma for up to 6 hours, after which it reverts to its feather form. It reverts to feather form early if it drops to 0 hit points or if you use an action to speak the command word again while touching the bird.

When the diatryma reverts to feather form, the magic of the feather can't be used again until 7 days have passed.

The diatryma uses the statistics of an **axe beak**, except that its beak deals piercing damage instead of slashing damage. The creature is friendly to you and your companions, and it can be used as a mount. It understands your languages and obeys your spoken commands. If you issue no commands, the diatryma defends itself but takes no other actions.

KNAVE'S EYE PATCH

Wondrous item, rare (requires attunement)

While wearing this eye patch, you gain these benefits:

- You have advantage on Wisdom (Perception) checks that rely on sight.
- If you have the Sunlight Sensitivity trait, you are unaffected by the trait.
- You are immune to magic that allows other creatures to read your thoughts or determine whether you are lying. Creatures can communicate telepathically with you only if you allow it.

LORD'S ENSEMBLE

Wondrous item, very rare (requires attunement by a creature with a humanoid build)

The Masked Lords of Waterdeep don this ensemble when meeting with one another. This raiment renders each lord indistinguishable from the others. The ensemble consists of three pieces—a helm, an amulet, and a robe—that function as a single magic item when worn together, but only within the city of Waterdeep and its sewers. You become attuned to the ensemble as a single item.

Lord's Helm. This bucket helm covers your head and conceals your face. Screens over the eyes help to shroud your identity without blinding you. While you wear the helm, your voice is magically altered to sound genderless, and you are immune to magic that allows other creatures to read your thoughts, to determine whether you are lying, to know your alignment, or to know your creature type. Creatures can communicate telepathically with you only if you allow it.

Lord's Amulet. This amulet bears the crest of Waterdeep. It functions as an *amulet of proof against detection and location*.

Lord's Robe. This elegant robe functions as a *ring of free action*, and it creates the illusion that you have a nondescript, androgynous humanoid build and stand 6 feet tall.

PAPER BIRD

Wondrous item, uncommon

After you write a message of fifty words or fewer on this magic sheet of parchment and speak a creature's name, the parchment magically folds into a Tiny paper bird and flies to the recipient whose name you uttered. The recipient must be on the same plane of existence as you, otherwise the bird turns into ash as it takes flight.

The bird is an object that has 1 hit point, an Armor Class of 13, a flying speed of 60 feet, a Dexterity of 16

PAPER BIRD

STONE OF GOLORR

(+3), and a score of 1 (−5) in all other abilities, and it is immune to poison and psychic damage.

It travels to within 5 feet of its intended recipient by the most direct route, whereupon it turns into a non-magical and inanimate sheet of parchment that can be unfolded only by the intended recipient. If the bird's hit points or speed is reduced to 0 or if it is otherwise immobilized, it turns into ash.

Paper birds usually come in small, flat boxes containing 1d6 + 3 sheets of the parchment.

RING OF TRUTH TELLING
Ring, uncommon (requires attunement)

While wearing this ring, you have advantage on Wisdom (Insight) checks to determine whether someone is lying to you.

SMOKEPOWDER
Wondrous item, uncommon

Smokepowder is a magical explosive chiefly used to propel a bullet out of the barrel of a firearm. It is stored in airtight wooden kegs or tiny, waterproof leather packets. A packet contains enough *smokepowder* for five shots, and a keg holds enough *smokepowder* for five hundred shots.

If *smokepowder* is set on fire, dropped, or otherwise handled roughly, it explodes and deals fire damage to each creature or object within 20 feet of it: 1d6 for a packet, 9d6 for a keg. A successful DC 12 Dexterity saving throw halves the damage.

Casting *dispel magic* on *smokepowder* renders it permanently inert.

STONE OF GOLORR
Wondrous item, artifact (requires attunement)

The *Stone of Golorr* is a glossy, greenish-gray stone that fits in the palm of your hand. The stone is actually an aboleth named Golorr, transformed by magic into an object.

Random Properties. The *Stone of Golorr* has the following properties, determined by rolling on the tables in the "Artifacts" section in chapter 7 of the *Dungeon Master's Guide*:

- 1 minor beneficial property
- 1 minor detrimental property

Legend Lore. The *Stone of Golorr* has 3 charges and regains 1d3 expended charges daily at dawn. While holding the stone, you can expend 1 of its charges to cast the *legend lore* spell.

By using the stone to cast *legend lore*, you communicate directly with the aboleth, and it shares its knowledge with you. The aboleth can't lie to you, but the information it provides is often cryptic or vague.

The aboleth knows where Lord Neverember's secret vault is located. It also knows that three keys are needed to open the vault and that a gold dragon named Aurinax inhabits the vault and guards its treasures.

Failed Memory. When your attunement to the *Stone of Golorr* ends, you must make a DC 16 Wisdom saving throw. On a failed save, you lose all memory of the stone being in your possession and all knowledge imparted by it. A *remove curse* spell cast on you has a 20 percent chance of restoring the lost knowledge and memories, and a *greater restoration* spell does so automatically.

Sentience. The *Stone of Golorr* is a sentient lawful evil magic item with an Intelligence of 18, a Wisdom of 15, and a Charisma of 18. It has hearing and darkvision out to a range of 120 feet. It can communicate telepathically with the creature that is attuned to it, as long as that creature understands at least one language. In addition, the aboleth learns the greatest desires of any creature that communicates telepathically with the stone.

The *Stone of Golorr* hungers for information and prefers not to remain in the clutches of any creature for too long. Whenever the stone desires a new owner, it demands to be given to another intelligent creature as quickly as possible. If its demands are ignored, it tries to take control of its owner (see "Sentient Magic Items" in chapter 7 of the *Dungeon Master's Guide*).

Personality. The *Stone of Golorr* has an alien intellect that is both domineering and hungry for knowledge. It thinks of itself as an ageless and immortal god.

Destroying the Stone. While in stone form, the aboleth isn't a creature and isn't subject to effects that target creatures. The *Stone of Golorr* is immune to all damage. Casting an *antipathy/sympathy* spell on the stone destroys it if the antipathy effect is selected and the spell is directed to repel aberrations. When the spell is cast in this way, the stone transforms into mucus and is destroyed, and Golorr the aboleth appears in an unoccupied space within 30 feet of the stone's remains. The aboleth is incensed by the stone's destruction, and it attacks all other creatures it can see.

Appendix B: Monsters and NPCs

This appendix describes various nonplayer characters and monsters that have roles to play in the adventure. These creatures are presented in alphabetical order.

Ahmaergo

Ahmaergo, Xanathar's majordomo, has a fascination with minotaurs. Although outwardly civil, the shield dwarf is as devious and corrupt as the worst devil, yet also unflinchingly loyal to his beholder master.

After the beholder, Ahmaergo is the most influential member of the Xanathar Guild.

Ammalia Cassalanter

The vainglorious lady of House Cassalanter is schooled in the arcane arts. Like her husband Victoro, she worships Asmodeus. When they were young, Ammalia and Victoro signed a contract with the archdevil, trading the souls of their children for power, good health, and long life. The soul of Osvaldo, their eldest son, was taken immediately, and he was transformed into a chain devil. The souls of the younger twins, Terenzio and Elzerina, will be taken when they turn nine years old.

A provision in the contract allows the Cassalanters to buy their way out of it, but doing so requires a

Ahmaergo

Ahmaergo
Medium humanoid (dwarf), lawful evil

Armor Class 18 (plate)
Hit Points 143 (22d8 + 44)
Speed 25 ft.

STR	DEX	CON	INT	WIS	CHA
20 (+5)	15 (+2)	14 (+2)	15 (+2)	14 (+2)	12 (+1)

Saving Throws Str +9, Con +6
Skills Athletics +9, Intimidation +5, Perception +6
Damage Resistances poison
Senses darkvision 60 ft., passive Perception 16
Languages Common, Dwarvish, Undercommon
Challenge 9 (5,000 XP)

Dwarven Resilience. Ahmaergo has advantage on saving throws against being poisoned.

Indomitable (2/Day). Ahmaergo can reroll a saving throw that he fails. He must use the new roll.

Second Wind (Recharges after a Short or Long Rest). As a bonus action, Ahmaergo can regain 20 hit points.

Actions

Multiattack. Ahmaergo makes three attacks with his greataxe.

Greataxe. *Melee Weapon Attack:* +9 to hit, reach 5 ft., one target. *Hit:* 11 (1d12 + 5) slashing damage, plus 7 (2d6) slashing damage if Ahmaergo has more than half his hit points remaining.

Heavy Crossbow. *Ranged Weapon Attack:* +6 to hit, range 100/400 ft., one target. *Hit:* 7 (1d10 + 2) piercing damage.

Ammalia Cassalanter
Medium humanoid (human), lawful evil

Armor Class 12 (15 with *mage armor*)
Hit Points 45 (10d8)
Speed 30 ft.

STR	DEX	CON	INT	WIS	CHA
9 (−1)	14 (+2)	11 (+0)	17 (+3)	12 (+1)	15 (+2)

Saving Throws Int +6, Wis +4
Skills Arcana +6, History +6, Insight +4, Persuasion +5
Damage Immunities poison
Condition Immunities poisoned
Senses passive Perception 11
Languages Common, Draconic, Elvish, Infernal
Challenge 5 (1,800 XP)

Spellcasting. Ammalia is a 9th-level spellcaster. Her spellcasting ability is Intelligence (spell save DC 14, +6 to hit with spell attacks). She has the following wizard spells prepared:

Cantrips (at will): *friends, mage hand, mending, message*
1st level (4 slots): *charm person, mage armor, magic missile*
2nd level (3 slots): *hold person, invisibility, suggestion*
3rd level (3 slots): *fireball, haste, tongues*
4th level (3 slots): *confusion, stoneskin*
5th level (1 slot): *hold monster*

Actions

Quarterstaff. *Melee Weapon Attack:* +2 to hit, reach 5 ft., one target. *Hit:* 2 (1d6 − 1) bludgeoning damage, or 3 (1d8 − 1) bludgeoning damage if used with two hands.

tremendous amount of coin and a mass sacrifice of unfortunate people. While Victoro hunts for Dagult Neverember's lost cache of gold, Ammalia makes plans to host a poisoned feast in celebration of Founders' Day.

Ammalia is well mannered, well read, well traveled, and exceptionally shrewd. She is known for driving a hard bargain. Her hobby is lepidopterology, and her estate has the most beautiful butterfly garden. She allows her youngest children to play in the garden under her supervision.

APPRENTICE WIZARD

Apprentice wizards are novice arcane spellcasters who serve more experienced wizards or attend school. They perform menial work, such as cooking and cleaning, in exchange for education in the ways of magic.

APPRENTICE WIZARD
Medium humanoid (any race), any alignment

Armor Class 10
Hit Points 9 (2d8)
Speed 30 ft.

STR	DEX	CON	INT	WIS	CHA
10 (+0)	10 (+0)	10 (+0)	14 (+2)	10 (+0)	11 (+0)

Skills Arcana +4, History +4
Senses passive Perception 10
Languages any one language (usually Common)
Challenge 1/4 (50 XP)

Spellcasting. The apprentice is a 1st-level spellcaster. Its spellcasting ability is Intelligence (spell save DC 12, +4 to hit with spell attacks). It has the following wizard spells prepared:

Cantrips (at will): *fire bolt, mending, prestidigitation*
1st level (2 slots): *burning hands, disguise self, shield*

ACTIONS

Dagger. *Melee or Ranged Weapon Attack:* +2 to hit, reach 5 ft. or range 20/60 ft., one target. *Hit:* 2 (1d4) piercing damage.

AURINAX

Aurinax is a male adult gold dragon who can freely ignore *Ahghairon's dragonward* (see "Ahghairon's Dragonward," page 6) and reside in the city. Maaril, the archmage who last wielded the *dragonstaff of Ahghairon*, was Aurinax's friend, and invited the dragon to stay with him in the city's Dragon Tower. Shortly before the Spellplague, Maaril went mad and left Waterdeep, entrusting the *dragonstaff of Ahghairon* to Aurinax. (See appendix A for information on the *dragonstaff.*)

When Dagult Neverember became the Open Lord of Waterdeep, he cut a deal with the dragon. Under its terms, Aurinax could keep the *dragonstaff of Ahghairon* in exchange for guarding a vault beneath the city. When Neverember eventually removed the treasure from the vault, Aurinax and the *dragonstaff* could return to the Dragon Tower. As it happens, no one has come to remove the treasure, and the faithful Aurinax has remained in the vault. The vault is warded against scrying magic, and there's no one left in Waterdeep who knows about Aurinax or the whereabouts of the *dragonstaff.*

GAME STATISTICS

Aurinax is an **adult gold dragon**. He often assumes the form of an elderly gold dwarf named Barok Clanghammer, who uses the *dragonstaff* as a walking stick.

BARD

Medium humanoid (any race), any alignment

Armor Class 15 (chain shirt)
Hit Points 44 (8d8 + 8)
Speed 30 ft.

STR	DEX	CON	INT	WIS	CHA
11 (+0)	14 (+2)	12 (+1)	10 (+0)	13 (+1)	14 (+2)

Saving Throws Dex +4, Wis +3
Skills Acrobatics +4, Perception +5, Performance +6
Senses passive Perception 15
Languages any two languages
Challenge 2 (450 XP)

Spellcasting. The bard is a 4th-level spellcaster. Its spellcasting ability is Charisma (spell save DC 12, +4 to hit with spell attacks). It has the following bard spells prepared:

Cantrips (at will): *friends, mage hand, vicious mockery*
1st level (4 slots): *charm person, healing word, heroism, sleep, thunderwave*
2nd level (3 slots): *invisibility, shatter*

Song of Rest. The bard can perform a song while taking a short rest. Any ally who hears the song regains an extra 1d6 hit points if it spends any Hit Dice to regain hit points at the end of that rest. The bard can confer this benefit on itself as well.

Taunt (2/Day). The bard can use a bonus action on its turn to target one creature within 30 feet of it. If the target can hear the bard, the target must succeed on a DC 12 Charisma saving throw or have disadvantage on ability checks, attack rolls, and saving throws until the start of the bard's next turn.

ACTIONS

Shortsword. *Melee Weapon Attack:* +4 to hit, reach 5 ft., one target. *Hit:* 5 (1d6 + 2) piercing damage.

Shortbow. *Ranged Weapon Attack:* +4 to hit, range 80/320 ft., one target. *Hit:* 5 (1d6 + 2) piercing damage.

BARD

Bards are gifted poets, storytellers, and entertainers who travel far and wide, commonly found performing in taverns or in the company of jolly bands of adventurers, rough-and-tumble mercenaries, or wealthy patrons.

BARNIBUS BLASTWIND

Barnibus works for the Watchful Order of Magists and Protectors, investigating crimes that involve the use of magic. He comes across as prickly and secretive, confiding only in Saeth Cromley, a retired sergeant of the City Watch who assists in many of his investigations.

A lifelong bachelor, Barnibus has a small, tidy estate in the Sea Ward that he inherited from his grandmother. When not serving the Watchful Order, he spends his days reading and writing books in his library.

Barnibus uses spells that help him investigate crimes, pry secrets from the minds of suspects, and locate missing persons. He finds violence appalling and would never use his magic to inflict harm on others—even those who harm him.

BARNIBUS BLASTWIND

Medium humanoid (human), lawful good

Armor Class 10 (13 with *mage armor*)
Hit Points 24 (7d8 – 7)
Speed 30 ft.

STR	DEX	CON	INT	WIS	CHA
9 (–1)	10 (+0)	9 (–1)	17 (+3)	15 (+2)	11 (+0)

Saving Throws Int +5, Wis +4
Skills Arcana +5, Insight +6, Investigation +7, Perception +4
Senses passive Perception 14
Languages Common, Draconic, Dwarvish, Halfling
Challenge 2 (450 XP)

Special Equipment. Barnibus carries a *wand of magic detection*.

Spellcasting. Barnibus is a 7th-level spellcaster. His spellcasting ability is Intelligence (spell save DC 13, +5 to hit with spell attacks). He has the following wizard spells prepared:

Cantrips (at will): *blade ward, light, mage hand, message*
1st level (4 slots): *comprehend languages, identify, mage armor, shield*
2nd level (3 slots): *detect thoughts, suggestion*
3rd level (3 slots): *clairvoyance, sending*
4th level (1 slot): *locate creature, Otiluke's resilient sphere*

ACTIONS

Dagger. *Melee or Ranged Weapon Attack:* +2 to hit, reach 5 ft. or range 20/60 ft., one target. *Hit:* 2 (1d4) piercing damage.

THE BLACK VIPER

THE BLACK VIPER

The Black Viper was a notorious burglar, pickpocket, mugger, and assassin who died a century ago, after a long and nefarious career. Esvele Rosznar, a brash young noble, has recently adopted the Black Viper's persona to lead a secret life of crime. Like many other nobles, Esvele gossips about the Black Viper's exploits to lend credence to the villain's mystique.

The Rosznar family was convicted of slave trading—highly illegal in Waterdeep—and banished over a hundred years ago, but has since returned. The Rosznars' inability to regain the respect they feel they deserve rankles them. The slave trade has continued in Amn and elsewhere, and it's not like other noble houses don't have skeletons in their closets. But just because of a little family squabble that went public, the Rosznar name has been said with a sneer for a century. As part of the family's constant effort to prove this conception wrong and win others' respect, Esvele has been brought up to be the most proper noble possible, partaking in lessons of etiquette, dance, and poise as befits someone of her station.

In her younger days, Esvele openly rebelled, but that behavior led to locked doors at night and house guards

watching her every move during the day. So she taught herself how to pick locks, pluck keys from belts and pouches, clamber up walls, and sneak past guards—playing the perfect daughter by day while cutting loose at night. To hide her identity from those she met, she wore a hood and mask, exchanging her fine clothes for the kind of practical clothing her parents would never let her wear.

One of the things Esvele has learned is to embrace the legend of the Black Viper. When she throws back her cloak to reveal the costume she has put together, most folk toss their purses and flee. If that doesn't work, she usually needs only to draw her dagger. Of course, some of the nobles she targets are made of sterner stuff, so Esvele has learned how to fight as well. She knows she's playing a dangerous game, but is satisfied that at least one member of the Rosznar family is earning the respect of Waterdeep's nobility.

BLACK VIPER
Medium humanoid (human), chaotic neutral

Armor Class 16 (studded leather)
Hit Points 84 (13d8 + 26)
Speed 30 ft.

STR	DEX	CON	INT	WIS	CHA
11 (+0)	18 (+4)	14 (+2)	11 (+0)	11 (+0)	12 (+1)

Saving Throws Dex +7, Int +3
Skills Acrobatics +7, Athletics +3, Perception +3, Sleight of Hand +7, Stealth +7
Senses passive Perception 13
Languages Common, thieves' cant
Challenge 5 (1,800 XP)

Cunning Action. On each of her turns, the Black Viper can use a bonus action to take the Dash, Disengage, or Hide action.

Evasion. If the Black Viper is subjected to an effect that allows her to make a Dexterity saving throw to take only half damage, she instead takes no damage if she succeeds on the saving throw, and only half damage if she fails. She can't use this trait if she's incapacitated.

Sneak Attack (1/Turn). The Black Viper deals an extra 14 (4d6) damage when she hits a target with a weapon attack and has advantage on the attack roll, or when the target is within 5 feet of an ally of the Black Viper that isn't incapacitated and the Black Viper doesn't have disadvantage on the attack roll.

ACTIONS

Multiattack. The Black Viper makes three attacks with her rapier.

Rapier. *Melee Weapon Attack:* +7 to hit, reach 5 ft., one target. *Hit:* 7 (1d6 + 4) piercing damage.

Hand Crossbow. *Ranged Weapon Attack:* +7 to hit, range 30/120 ft., one target. *Hit:* 7 (1d6 + 4) piercing damage.

REACTIONS

Uncanny Dodge. The Black Viper halves the damage that she takes from an attack that hits her. She must be able to see the attacker.

CITY GUARD PRIVATE, CAPTAIN, AND
GRIFFON CAVALRY RIDER

CITY GUARD

The City Guard is Waterdeep's army, charged with protecting the city's walls and gates, government buildings, harbor, and officials. The City Guard also patrols the roads to Amphail, Goldenfields, and Daggerford.

RANKS IN THE CITY GUARD

Members of the City Guard have ranks. From lowest to highest, they are:

Private

Sergeant (armar)

Lieutenant (civilar)

Captain (senior civilar)

Multiple command positions, some perennial (Seneschal of Castle Waterdeep, Defender of the Harbor, Master of the North Towers, Master of the South Towers, Master Armorer), others bestowed as needed in wartime (the Lords' Hand and the Lords' Champion)

Warden of Waterdeep

The current Warden of Waterdeep is Elminster, who answers to the Open Lord, Laeral Silverhand.

The Griffon Cavalry is a special branch of the City Guard whose members are veteran soldiers trained to fly griffon mounts.

GAME STATISTICS

City Guard privates and sergeants are **guards**. Members of lieutenant rank and higher are typically **veterans**.

GRIFFON CAVALRY RIDER

Medium humanoid (any race), any alignment

Armor Class 17 (half plate)
Hit Points 58 (9d8 + 18)
Speed 30 ft.

STR	DEX	CON	INT	WIS	CHA
14 (+2)	15 (+2)	14 (+2)	10 (+0)	12 (+1)	10 (+0)

Skills Animal Handling +3, Athletics +4, Perception +3
Senses passive Perception 13
Languages any one language (usually Common)
Challenge 2 (450 XP)

ACTIONS

Lance. *Melee Weapon Attack:* +4 to hit (with disadvantage against a target within 5 ft.), reach 10 ft., one target. *Hit:* 8 (1d12 + 2) piercing damage, or 11 (1d12 + 5) piercing damage while mounted.

Dagger. *Melee or Ranged Weapon Attack:* +4 to hit, reach 5 ft. or range 20/60 ft., one target. *Hit:* 4 (1d4 + 2) piercing damage.

Light Crossbow. *Ranged Weapon Attack:* +4 to hit, range 80/320 ft., one target. *Hit:* 6 (1d8 + 2) piercing damage.

REACTIONS

Feather Fall. The rider wears a magic ring with which it can cast the *feather fall* spell on itself once as a reaction to falling. After the spell is cast, the ring becomes nonmagical.

MEMBERS OF THE CITY WATCH

CITY WATCH

The City Watch is Waterdeep's police force, charged with keeping the peace and apprehending criminals. City Watch patrols are usually four to twelve persons strong. A patrol expecting trouble might also have reinforcement in the form of a **priest** (on loan from one of the local temples) or a **mage** (from the Watchful Order of Magists and Protectors).

RANKS IN THE CITY WATCH

Members of the City Watch are called officers. Their ranks are, from lowest to highest:

Constable
Sergeant (armar)
Lieutenant (civilar)
Captain (senior civilar; leader of a watch station)
Major (ward civilar; one per city ward)
Commander of the Watch

The Watch also includes a Senior Armsmaster, who reports to the Commander of the Watch and is in charge of supplies. The Commander of the Watch reports to the Open Lord, Laeral Silverhand.

GAME STATISTICS

Most City Watch members are **veterans**. Some of the highest-ranked members are **knights**. All City Watch members wear helmets and carry clubs while on duty.

THE DOOM RAIDERS

The Doom Raiders were five unscrupulous adventurers who liked to plunder lich lairs (called "dooms" by some). They gave up adventuring to join the Black Network and came to Waterdeep three years ago with plans to establish a Zhentarim foothold in the city. In that time, they have forged alliances with various nobles and guilds and run afoul of others, all the while fending off Harper spies.

DAVIL STARSONG

Within the Waterdeep division of the Black Network, Davil is accorded the title of Master of Opportunities and Negotiations because he's good at sniffing out lucrative business deals, and he makes friends easily.

Like many sun elves, Davil has an affinity for magic and is gifted with the kind of patience that comes with a long life span. Unlike most, he's not the least bit pretentious or aloof. He keeps a room at the Yawning Portal and does all his business in the establishment's taproom. He negotiates deals with grace and aplomb, even while drunk, and uses an elven lute as a spellcasting focus.

Davil can put the characters in contact with other leaders of the Black Network's Waterdeep division, namely Istrid Horn (if they need a loan), Skeemo Weirdbottle (if they need magic), Tashlyn Yafeera (if they need weapons or mercenaries), and Ziraj the Hunter (if they need a highly skilled assassin).

ISTRID HORN

Istrid is regarded as the Black Network's Master of Trade and Coin in Waterdeep. The shield dwarf operates an illegal lending operation out of a heavily guarded warehouse in the Dock Ward, offering loans to those in need of coin. Her interest rates are comparable to those of her competitors (including noble families of bankers such as the Cassalanters and the Irlingstars), but the penalties for not paying back Istrid's loans are severe.

Istrid worships Vergadain, the dwarven god of wealth and luck. She likes having others indebted to her, and she employs thugs and enforcers to collect on her loans. If those resources prove inadequate, Istrid can call on her old adventuring companions for assistance.

SKEEMO WEIRDBOTTLE

Skeemo (see the next page for his stat block) became the Master of Magic for the Black Network in Waterdeep, setting up a cover in the Trades Ward in the form of a cramped little shop called Weirdbottle's Concoctions. Most of his potions and elixirs are nonmagical, but he crafts magical ones for his Zhent friends.

Skeemo can add "sellout" to his credentials, his services having been bought by House Gralhund and the Black Network operatives loyal to Manshoon. The rock gnome uses *paper birds* (see appendix A) to send messages both to his new friends and his old ones.

DAVIL STARSONG
Medium humanoid (elf), neutral

Armor Class 15 (chain shirt)
Hit Points 82 (15d8 + 15)
Speed 30 ft.

STR	DEX	CON	INT	WIS	CHA
10 (+0)	14 (+2)	12 (+1)	16 (+3)	12 (+1)	17 (+3)

Saving Throws Dex +5, Cha +6
Skills Arcana +6, History +6, Insight +4, Perception +4, Performance +6
Senses darkvision 60 ft., passive Perception 14
Languages Common, Draconic, Dwarvish, Elvish
Challenge 6 (2,300 XP)

Fey Ancestry. Davil has advantage on saving throws against being charmed, and magic can't put him to sleep.

Spellcasting. Davil is a 12th-level spellcaster. His spellcasting ability is Charisma (spell save DC 14, +6 to hit with spell attacks). He has the following bard spells prepared:

Cantrips (at will): *mage hand, mending, minor illusion, vicious mockery*
1st level (4 slots): *cure wounds, disguise self, sleep*
2nd level (3 slots): *crown of madness, invisibility, suggestion*
3rd level (3 slots): *nondetection, sending, tongues*
4th level (3 slots): *compulsion, freedom of movement, polymorph*
5th level (2 slots): *dominate person, greater restoration*
6th level (1 slot): *Otto's irresistible dance*

ACTIONS

Dagger. *Melee or Ranged Weapon Attack:* +5 to hit, reach 5 ft. or range 20/60 ft., one target. *Hit:* 4 (1d4 + 2) piercing damage.

TASHLYN YAFEERA

Tashlyn (see the next page for her stat block) is Master of Arms and Mercenaries for the Waterdeep Zhentarim. In this role, she provides armor, weapons, and training to sellswords on the Black Network's payroll.

Tashlyn has established a useful cover by serving as a bodyguard to Vorondar Levelstone, a dwarf magister stationed at the South Gate. She likes the dwarf and has earned his confidence, allowing her to reach the rank of captain in the City Guard. In that position, she watches over traffic that passes through the gate—and ensures that her associates in the Black Network can come and go freely.

Born to a well-off family in Calimshan, Tashlyn has an unfettered sense of superiority. Quick to anger, she hates to back down from a fight. She respects anyone who can best her in melee combat.

ISTRID HORN
Medium humanoid (dwarf), neutral evil

Armor Class 18 (plate)
Hit Points 117 (18d8 + 36)
Speed 25 ft.

STR	DEX	CON	INT	WIS	CHA
12 (+1)	10 (+0)	14 (+2)	11 (+0)	17 (+3)	13 (+1)

Saving Throws Con +5, Wis +6
Skills Intimidation +4, Religion +3
Damage Resistances poison
Senses darkvision 60 ft., passive Perception 13
Languages Common, Dwarvish
Challenge 8 (3,900 XP)

Dwarven Resilience. Istrid has advantage on saving throws against being poisoned.

Spellcasting. Istrid is a 9th-level spellcaster. Her spellcasting ability is Wisdom (spell save DC 14, +6 to hit with spell attacks). She has the following cleric spells prepared:

Cantrips (at will): *light, mending, sacred flame, spare the dying*
1st level (4 slots): *divine favor, guiding bolt, healing word, shield of faith*
2nd level (3 slots): *lesser restoration, magic weapon, hold person, silence, spiritual weapon*
3rd level (3 slots): *beacon of hope, crusader's mantle, dispel magic, revivify, spirit guardians, water walk*
4th level (3 slots): *banishment, freedom of movement, guardian of faith, stoneskin*
5th level (1 slot): *flame strike, mass cure wounds, hold monster*

ACTIONS

Multiattack. Istrid makes two melee attacks.

Maul. *Melee Weapon Attack:* +4 to hit, reach 5 ft., one target. *Hit:* 8 (2d6 + 1) bludgeoning damage.

Treasure Sense (3/Day). Istrid magically pinpoints precious metals and stones, such as coins and gems, within 60 feet of her.

THE DOOM RAIDERS (LEFT TO RIGHT): DAVIL STARSONG, ISTRID HORN, TASHLYN YAFEERA, SKEEMO WEIRDBOTTLE, AND ZIRAJ THE HUNTER

SKEEMO WEIRDBOTTLE

Small humanoid (gnome), neutral evil

Armor Class 12 (15 with *mage armor*)
Hit Points 72 (16d6 + 16)
Speed 25 ft.

STR	DEX	CON	INT	WIS	CHA
9 (–1)	14 (+2)	12 (+1)	17 (+3)	12 (+1)	15 (+2)

Saving Throws Int +6, Wis +4
Skills Arcana +6, History +6, Perception +4, Performance +5
Senses darkvision 60 ft., passive Perception 14
Languages Abyssal, Common, Gnomish, Undercommon
Challenge 6 (2,300 XP)

Gnome Cunning. Skeemo has advantage on Intelligence, Wisdom, and Charisma saving throws against magic.

Spellcasting. Skeemo is a 9th-level spellcaster. His spellcasting ability is Intelligence (spell save DC 14, +6 to hit with spell attacks). He has the following wizard spells prepared:

Cantrips (at will): *fire bolt, light, mage hand, prestidigitation*
1st level (4 slots): *detect magic, mage armor, magic missile, shield*
2nd level (3 slots): *misty step, suggestion*
3rd level (3 slots): *counterspell, fireball, fly*
4th level (3 slots): *greater invisibility, ice storm*
5th level (1 slot): *cone of cold*

ACTIONS

Dagger. *Melee or Ranged Weapon Attack:* +5 to hit, reach 5 ft. or range 20/60 ft., one target. *Hit:* 4 (1d4 + 2) piercing damage.

TASHLYN YAFEERA

Medium humanoid (human), neutral

Armor Class 18 (plate)
Hit Points 149 (23d8 + 46)
Speed 30 ft.

STR	DEX	CON	INT	WIS	CHA
18 (+4)	15 (+2)	14 (+2)	10 (+0)	14 (+2)	12 (+1)

Saving Throws Str +8, Con +6
Skills Athletics +8, Intimidation +5, Perception +6
Senses passive Perception 16
Languages Common
Challenge 9 (5,000 XP)

Indomitable (2/Day). Tashlyn can reroll a saving throw that she fails. She must use the new roll.

Second Wind (Recharges after a Short or Long Rest). As a bonus action, Tashlyn can regain 20 hit points.

ACTIONS

Multiattack. Tashlyn makes three attacks with her greatsword or her shortbow.

Greatsword. *Melee Weapon Attack:* +8 to hit, reach 5 ft., one target. *Hit:* 11 (2d6 + 4) slashing damage, plus 7 (2d6) slashing damage if Tashlyn has more than half her hit points remaining.

Shortbow. *Ranged Weapon Attack:* +6 to hit, range 80/320 ft., one target. *Hit:* 5 (1d6 + 2) piercing damage, plus 7 (2d6) piercing damage if Tashlyn has more than half her hit points remaining.

ZIRAJ THE HUNTER

Ziraj is a half-orc hunter who wields an oversized bow that shoots correspondingly large arrows. He is the Master of Assassination for the Black Network. If Ziraj sets out to kill someone, it's because one of his friends (Davil, Istrid, Skeemo, or Tashlyn) asked him to. The characters might become Ziraj's prey, or Ziraj might come to their aid to eliminate a common enemy. He's the strong, silent type.

The City Watch has received reports of a figure who haunts the rooftops of Waterdeep—a hulking shadow that glares from its perch, rains down death in the form of long black arrows, and slinks off without so much as a whisper. Where he comes from—if he even has a home—remains a mystery, as does the question of where he might show up next.

Treasure. Ziraj wears *+2 leather armor* and carries an oversized longbow. This unique weapon can be used only by a Medium or larger creature that has a Strength of 18 or higher. The bow shoots oversized arrows that deal piercing damage equal to 2d6 + the wielder's Strength modifier. Its range is the same as an ordinary longbow.

ZIRAJ THE HUNTER
Medium humanoid (half-orc), neutral evil

Armor Class 17 (*+2 leather armor*)
Hit Points 153 (18d8 + 72)
Speed 30 ft.

STR	DEX	CON	INT	WIS	CHA
18 (+4)	18 (+4)	18 (+4)	11 (+0)	14 (+2)	15 (+2)

Saving Throws Wis +5, Cha +5
Skills Athletics +7, Intimidation +5, Stealth +7, Survival +5
Senses darkvision 60 ft., passive Perception 12
Languages Common, Orc
Challenge 8 (3,900 XP)

Spellcasting. Ziraj is a 10th-level spellcaster. His spellcasting ability is Charisma (spell save DC 13, +5 to hit with spell attacks). He has the following paladin spells prepared:

1st level (4 slots): *command, protection from evil and good, thunderous smite*
2nd level (3 slots): *branding smite, find steed*
3rd level (2 slots): *blinding smite, dispel magic*

ACTIONS

Multiattack. Ziraj makes three attacks with his glaive or with his oversized longbow.

Glaive. *Melee Weapon Attack:* +7 to hit, reach 5 ft., one target. *Hit:* 9 (1d10 + 4) slashing damage.

Oversized Longbow. *Ranged Weapon Attack:* +7 to hit, range 150/600 ft., one target. *Hit:* 11 (2d6 + 4) piercing damage.

Dreadful Aspect (Recharges after a Short or Long Rest). Ziraj exudes magical menace. Each enemy within 30 feet of him must succeed on a DC 13 Wisdom saving throw or be frightened of Ziraj for 1 minute. If a frightened enemy ends its turn more than 30 feet away from Ziraj, the enemy can repeat the saving throw, ending the effect on itself on a success.

DROW GUNSLINGER

Firearms aren't widely available in the North, but some members of Bregan D'aerthe are equipped with Lantanese pistols, bullets, and packets of *smokepowder*. These drow gunslingers are expert pistoleers, as skilled with their guns as the best archers are with their bows.

FEL'REKT LAFEEN

Fel'rekt is a male drow who was born female. Unhappy with the treatment of males in his society, he petitioned to join Bregan D'aerthe. Jarlaxle took a shine to Fel'rekt almost immediately, and the young drow has since become one of Jarlaxle's most loyal lieutenants. Eager to prove himself, Fel'rekt is quick to volunteer for tasks and hurls himself into combat with verve.

Fel'rekt and Krebbyg Masq'il'yr are close friends and work as a team, trading banter and jokes at their enemies' expense. Fel'rekt lacks the cruelty common to most drow, and he won't kill an adversary unless he is left with no other choice.

DROW GUNSLINGER
Medium humanoid (elf), any alignment

Armor Class 18 (studded leather, shield)
Hit Points 84 (13d8 + 26)
Speed 30 ft.

STR	DEX	CON	INT	WIS	CHA
13 (+1)	18 (+4)	14 (+2)	11 (+0)	13 (+1)	14 (+2)

Saving Throws Dex +6, Con +4, Wis +3
Skills Perception +3, Stealth +8
Senses darkvision 120 ft., passive Perception 13
Languages Elvish, Undercommon
Challenge 4 (1,100 XP)

Fey Ancestry. The drow has advantage on saving throws against being charmed, and magic can't put the drow to sleep.

Gunslinger. Being within 5 feet of a hostile creature or attacking at long range doesn't impose disadvantage on the drow's ranged attack rolls with a pistol. In addition, the drow ignores half cover and three-quarters cover when making ranged attacks with a pistol.

Innate Spellcasting. The drow's spellcasting ability is Charisma (spell save DC 12). It can innately cast the following spells, requiring no material components:

At will: *dancing lights*
1/day each: *darkness, faerie fire, levitate* (self only)

Sunlight Sensitivity. While in sunlight, the drow has disadvantage on attack rolls, as well as on Wisdom (Perception) checks that rely on sight.

ACTIONS

Multiattack. The drow makes two shortsword attacks.

Shortsword. *Melee Weapon Attack:* +6 to hit, reach 5 ft., one target. *Hit:* 7 (1d6 + 4) piercing damage.

Poisonous Pistol. *Ranged Weapon Attack:* +6 to hit, range 30/90 ft., one target. *Hit:* 9 (1d10 + 4) piercing damage plus 11 (2d10) poison damage.

DROW GUNSLINGER

Game Statistics. Fel'rekt Lafeen is a neutral good **drow gunslinger**. In addition to his weapons, he carries four packets of *smokepowder* (see appendix A) and a pouch containing twenty pistol bullets.

KREBBYG MASQ'IL'YR

Krebbyg's house was destroyed long ago, leaving him with no connection to his old life in the Underdark. He is young and rash.

Krebbyg works closely with Fel'rekt Lafeen, and the two collaborate well despite their disparate alignments. Krebbyg prefers to follow Fel'rekt's lead, letting him do most of the thinking and talking.

Game Statistics. Krebbyg Masq'il'yr is a chaotic neutral **drow gunslinger**. In addition to his weapons, he carries four packets of *smokepowder* (see appendix A) and a pouch containing twenty pistol bullets.

SOLUUN XIBRINDAS

Soluun is a sadistic, fanatical bully who is fiercely loyal to Bregan D'aerthe, and to Jarlaxle in particular. His younger brother, Nar'l, has infiltrated the Xanathar Guild. Soluun considers Nar'l a weakling who turned to arcane magic by way of compensation, and he has never had much faith in his brother or his abilities.

Soluun has a burning hatred of surface elves and half-elves, having been taught from a young age to kill them

as opportunity permits. When not engaged in a Bregan D'aerthe operation, Soluun spends his nights haunting the darkened streets and alleys of Waterdeep, looking for solitary elves or half-elves to pick off. He conceals his nighttime escapades as well as he can, but Jarlaxle, Fel'rekt, and Krebbyg know what he's up to.

Game Statistics. Soluun Xibrindas is a neutral evil **drow gunslinger**, with these changes:

- Soluun wields a scimitar instead of a shortsword (it deals slashing damage instead of piercing damage).
- He wears a pair of drow-made *boots of elvenkind*.
- In addition to his weapons, he carries four packets of *smokepowder* (see appendix A) and a pouch containing twenty pistol bullets.

DURNAN

Durnan is the owner and proprietor of the Yawning Portal. Although he looks like a middle-aged man whose best days are behind him, Durnan has a sharp mind and can still swing a sword when he must. He doesn't like talking about his past, and he won't reveal anything about his time as an adventurer.

If Durnan has any living family members, he doesn't speak of them. He rarely says two words when one will do. He has a dark sense of humor and spares no pity on those who take the risk of entering Undermountain.

He keeps Grimvault, his magic greatsword, within reach under the bar, and can chop tables in half with it if he so desires. He also can pull out a double crossbow (a heavy crossbow with reduced range that fires two bolts at the same target). Still, if he gets involved in a brawl, he prefers fighting with fists or a well-flung tankard.

Durnan doesn't often venture far from the Yawning Portal, using his employees to run errands for him as needed. If he's feeling charitable, he might gently discourage likable "nobodies" from venturing into Undermountain, if he thinks they wouldn't survive. He can also direct adventurers toward tavern regulars who might be able to help them or offer useful information.

FLOON BLAGMAAR

Floon, a native Waterdavian in his early thirties, is a handsome fellow but not very bright. He used to work as an escort in festhalls but is currently unemployed. Several months ago, he came upon a married noble engaging in some indiscreet behavior, and now lives off the generous bribe he is being paid to keep silent.

With friends all over the city, Floon spends most of his time drinking and carousing. He gets by on his looks and doesn't know what to do with his life, and has shown little interest in working for a living.

GAME STATISTICS

Floon is a chaotic good Illuskan human **commoner** with an Intelligence of 7 (−2) and a Charisma of 13 (+1). He speaks Common.

GAZER

A gazer is a tiny manifestation of a beholder's dreams. It resembles the beholder who dreamed it into existence, but its body is only 8 inches wide, and it has only four eyestalks. The beholder can see through the gazer's eyes and uses it to spy on enemies as well as its other minions.

A gazer can't speak any languages but can approximate mimicking words and sentences in a high-pitched, mocking manner. A lone gazer avoids picking fights with creatures that are Medium or larger, but a pack of them might take on larger prey. A gazer might follow humanoids in its territory, noisily mimicking their speech and generally being a nuisance, until they leave the area, but it flees if confronted by something it can't kill.

DURNAN

Medium humanoid (human), neutral

Armor Class 16 (*elven chain*)
Hit Points 144 (17d8 + 68)
Speed 30 ft.

STR	DEX	CON	INT	WIS	CHA
18 (+4)	15 (+2)	18 (+4)	13 (+1)	12 (+1)	10 (+0)

Saving Throws Str +8, Con +8
Skills Athletics +8, Perception +5
Senses passive Perception 15
Languages Common, Dwarvish
Challenge 9 (5,000 XP)

Special Equipment. Durnan wields a *sword of sharpness* (greatsword) called Grimvault. He wears *boots of striding and springing*, *elven chain*, and a *ring of spell turning*.

Indomitable (Recharges after a Long Rest). Durnan can reroll a saving throw that he fails. He must use the new roll.

Spell Turning. While wearing his *ring of spell turning*, Durnan has advantage on saving throws against any spell that targets only him (not in an area of effect). If Durnan rolls a 20 for the save and the spell is 7th level or lower, the spell has no effect on him and instead targets the caster, using the slot level, spell save DC, attack bonus, and spellcasting ability of the caster.

ACTIONS

Multiattack. Durnan makes four melee weapon attacks.

Grimvault. *Melee Weapon Attack:* +8 to hit, reach 5 ft., one target. *Hit:* 11 (2d6 + 4) slashing damage. If the target is an object, the hit instead deals 16 slashing damage. If the target is a creature and Durnan rolls a 20 on the d20 for the attack roll, the target takes an extra 14 slashing damage, and Durnan rolls another d20. On a roll of 20, he lops off one of the target's limbs, or some other part of its body if it is limbless.

Double Crossbow. *Ranged Weapon Attack:* +6 to hit, range 60/240 ft., one target. *Hit:* 13 (2d10 + 2) piercing damage.

GAZER

Tiny aberration, neutral evil

Armor Class 13
Hit Points 13 (3d4 + 6)
Speed 0 ft., fly 30 ft. (hover)

STR	DEX	CON	INT	WIS	CHA
3 (−4)	17 (+3)	14 (+2)	3 (−4)	10 (+0)	7 (−2)

Saving Throws Wis +2
Skills Perception +4, Stealth +5
Condition Immunities prone
Senses darkvision 60 ft., passive Perception 14
Languages —
Challenge 1/2 (100 XP)

Aggressive. As a bonus action, the gazer can move up to its speed toward a hostile creature that it can see.

Mimicry. The gazer can mimic simple sounds of speech it has heard, in any language. A creature that hears the sounds can tell they are imitations with a successful DC 10 Wisdom (Insight) check.

ACTIONS

Bite. *Melee Weapon Attack:* +5 to hit, reach 5 ft., one target. *Hit:* 1 piercing damage.

Eye Rays. The gazer shoots two of the following magical eye rays at random (reroll duplicates), choosing one or two targets it can see within 60 feet of it:

1. *Dazing Ray.* The targeted creature must succeed on a DC 12 Wisdom saving throw or be charmed until the start of the gazer's next turn. While the target is charmed in this way, its speed is halved, and it has disadvantage on attack rolls.

2. *Fear Ray.* The targeted creature must succeed on a DC 12 Wisdom saving throw or be frightened until the start of the gazer's next turn.

3. *Frost Ray.* The targeted creature must succeed on a DC 12 Dexterity saving throw or take 10 (3d6) cold damage.

4. *Telekinetic Ray.* If the target is a creature that is Medium or smaller, it must succeed on a DC 12 Strength saving throw or be moved up to 30 feet directly away from the gazer.

If the target is an object weighing 10 pounds or less that isn't being worn or carried, the gazer moves it up to 30 feet in any direction. The gazer can also exert fine control on objects with this ray, such as manipulating a simple tool or opening a container.

Hlam

This venerable human monk lives in a cave halfway up the side of Mount Waterdeep. Hlam is the grand master of the Order of the Even-Handed, a small monastic group devoted to Tyr. Would-be students periodically visit him to learn the Way of the Sacred Fists, which combines cleric magic and monk training. They usually return to the city confused, bruised, and not inclined to visit again.

In times of great peril, Hlam can be called on to help. Sometimes he offers pearls of wisdom, and sometimes he descends from his cave to set things right with fisticuffs. He can show up at any point in the story as a helpful figure, and the characters can visit him in his cave if they need guidance or training. The Order of the Gauntlet considers him a staunch ally.

Hlam is immune to disease and doesn't require food or water. Although he ages, he suffers none of the frailty of old age.

HLAM

Hlam

Medium humanoid (human), lawful good

Armor Class 22 (Unarmored Defense)
Hit Points 137 (25d8 + 25)
Speed 60 ft.

STR	DEX	CON	INT	WIS	CHA
11 (+0)	24 (+7)	13 (+1)	14 (+2)	21 (+5)	14 (+2)

Saving Throws Str +5, Dex +12
Skills Athletics +5, Religion +7
Damage Immunities poison
Condition Immunities charmed, frightened, poisoned
Senses passive Perception 15
Languages all spoken languages
Challenge 16 (15,000 XP)

Spellcasting. Hlam is a 5th-level spellcaster. His spellcasting ability is Wisdom (spell save DC 18, +10 to hit with spell attacks). He has the following cleric spells prepared:

Cantrips (at will): *guidance, light, sacred flame, spare the dying*
1st level (4 slots): *detect evil and good, healing word, sanctuary, shield of faith*
2nd level (3 slots): *calm emotions, prayer of healing, silence*
3rd level (2 slots): *protection from energy, remove curse, sending*

Evasion. If Hlam is subjected to an effect that allows him to make a Dexterity saving throw to take only half damage, he instead takes no damage if he succeeds on the saving throw, and only half damage if he fails. He can't use this trait if he's incapacitated.

Magic Unarmed Strikes. Hlam's unarmed strikes are magical.

Unarmored Defense. While Hlam is wearing no armor and wielding no shield, his AC includes his Wisdom modifier.

Actions

Multiattack. Hlam attacks three times using his unarmed strike, darts, or both.

Unarmed Strike. *Melee Weapon Attack:* +12 to hit, reach 5 ft., one target. *Hit:* 12 (1d10 + 7) bludgeoning damage. If the target is a creature, Hlam can choose one of the following additional effects:

- The target must succeed on a DC 18 Strength saving throw or drop one item it is holding (Hlam's choice).
- The target must succeed on a DC 18 Dexterity saving throw or be knocked prone.
- The target must succeed on a DC 18 Constitution saving throw or be stunned until the end of Hlam's next turn.

Dart. *Ranged Weapon Attack:* +12 to hit, range 20/60 ft., one target. *Hit:* 9 (1d4 + 7) piercing damage.

Quivering Palm (Recharge 6). *Melee Weapon Attack:* +12 to hit, reach 5 ft., one creature. *Hit:* The target must make a DC 18 Constitution saving throw. On a failed save, the target is reduced to 0 hit points. On a successful save, the target takes 55 (10d10) necrotic damage.

Wholeness of Body (Recharges after a Long Rest). Hlam regains 60 hit points.

Reactions

Deflect Missile. In response to being hit by a ranged weapon attack, Hlam deflects the missile. The damage he takes from the attack is reduced by 1d10 + 27. If the damage is reduced to 0, Hlam catches the missile if it's small enough to hold in one hand and he has a hand free.

Slow Fall. Hlam reduces the bludgeoning damage he takes from a fall by 100.

Legendary Actions

Hlam can take 3 legendary actions, choosing from the options below. Only one legendary action option can be used at a time and only at the end of another creature's turn. Hlam regains spent legendary actions at the start of his turn.

Quick Step. Hlam moves up to his speed without provoking opportunity attacks.
Unarmed Strike (Costs 2 Actions). Hlam makes one unarmed strike.
Invisibility (Costs 3 Actions). Hlam becomes invisible until the end of his next turn. The effect ends if Hlam attacks or casts a spell.

HRABBAZ

HRABBAZ

Hrabbaz is a muscle-bound half-orc with a cleft palate who serves the lord and lady of House Gralhund as a bodyguard. He is well mannered and dresses impeccably—a disarming appearance that belies a murderous heart. Though he has great respect for Lady Yalah Gralhund, he is less fond of her moody husband, and wouldn't be sad to see Orond knocked down a peg or two.

HRABBAZ

Medium humanoid (half-orc), neutral evil

Armor Class 12
Hit Points 112 (15d8 + 45)
Speed 30 ft.

STR	DEX	CON	INT	WIS	CHA
20 (+5)	15 (+2)	17 (+3)	10 (+0)	14 (+2)	12 (+1)

Saving Throws Str +8, Con +6
Skills Athletics +8, Intimidation +4, Perception +5
Senses darkvision 60 ft., passive Perception 15
Languages Common, Orc
Challenge 5 (1,800 XP)

Indomitable (2/Day). Hrabbaz can reroll a saving throw that he fails. He must use the new roll.

Relentless Endurance (Recharges after a Long Rest). When Hrabbaz is reduced to 0 hit points but not killed outright, he drops to 1 hit point instead.

ACTIONS

Multiattack. Hrabbaz makes three attacks with his morningstar.

Morningstar. *Melee Weapon Attack:* +8 to hit, reach 5 ft., one target. *Hit:* 9 (1d8 + 5) piercing damage, plus 3 (1d6) piercing damage if Hrabbaz has more than half his hit points remaining.

JALESTER SILVERMANE

An earnest man in his mid-twenties, Jalester hails from the distant land of Cormyr, where he earned his spurs working for a mercenary company called the Steel Shadows. A few years ago, Jalester left the Dales and traveled to Waterdeep with several other members of the company, one of whom—Faerrel Dunblade—would become his best friend and lover.

The wizard Elminster befriended the two young men and brought them to the attention of Laeral Silverhand, who put them to work as deputies and spies. Jalester and Faerrel helped the Open Lord expose a plot to overthrow the government, but Faerrel was killed while helping bring the perpetrators to justice. Jalester remained in Waterdeep afterward, becoming one of Laeral's field operatives in the service of Waterdeep and the Lords' Alliance. He has been romantically unattached ever since Faerrel's death but longs again for love.

TREASURE

Jalester carries a *badge of the Watch* (see appendix A). If the badge is lost or taken from him, it returns to Laeral Silverhand.

JALESTER SILVERMANE

Medium humanoid (human), lawful good

Armor Class 18 (chain mail, *badge of the Watch*)
Hit Points 71 (13d8 + 13)
Speed 30 ft.

STR	DEX	CON	INT	WIS	CHA
14 (+2)	14 (+2)	13 (+1)	12 (+1)	14 (+2)	13 (+1)

Saving Throws Str +4, Con +3
Skills Athletics +4, Survival +4
Senses passive Perception 12
Languages Common, Elvish
Challenge 4 (1,100 XP)

Special Equipment. Jalester carries a *badge of the Watch*.

Second Wind (Recharges after a Short or Long Rest). As a bonus action, Jalester can regain 16 (1d10 + 11) hit points.

ACTIONS

Multiattack. Jalester makes two weapon attacks.

Longsword. *Melee Weapon Attack:* +4 to hit, reach 5 ft., one target. *Hit:* 6 (1d8 + 2) slashing damage, or 7 (1d10 + 2) slashing damage when used with two hands.

Dagger. *Melee or Ranged Weapon Attack:* +4 to hit, reach 5 ft. or range 20/60 ft., one target. *Hit:* 4 (1d4 + 2) piercing damage.

REACTIONS

Riposte. When a creature that Jalester can see misses him with a melee attack, he can use his reaction to make a melee weapon attack against that creature. On a hit, the target takes an extra 4 damage from the weapon.

H

Jarlaxle Baenre

Jarlaxle is a flamboyant, swashbuckling drow icono-clast. He leads a renegade drow faction called Bregan D'aerthe, made up of disenfranchised male drow, most of them culled from destroyed or disgraced houses. Gifted with a sharp mind, a sense of humor, puissant skill with a blade, and a wealth of useful magic items, Jarlaxle infiltrated the city of Luskan, brought a kind of order to its lawlessness, and declared himself its secret lord.

Jarlaxle likes to weave a tangled web of schemes that leave his enemies baffled—the latest of which is a plan to legitimize Luskan by making it a member of the Lords' Alliance. The city's unsavory reputation has thwarted all previous efforts, and the current leaders of the Lords' Alliance have voiced their opposition to Luskan's ad-mittance. A few have flatly declared that the city will never be welcome in the alliance. Nonetheless, Jarlaxle aims to persuade Laeral Silverhand, the Open Lord of Waterdeep, to champion Luskan's cause—even if that means losing other alliance members in the process.

Tying Luskan's fortunes to those of Waterdeep would increase Jarlaxle's political and economic power on the Sword Coast.

Jarlaxle has come to Waterdeep in the guise of an Illuskan human named Zardoz Zord. "Captain Zord" is the master of the Sea Maidens Faire, a carnival that travels up and down the Sword Coast in three ships: the *Eyecatcher*, the *Heartbreaker*, and the *Hellraiser* (all words that describe Jarlaxle). He spends most of his time aboard the *Eyecatcher*, his personal ship. The other two vessels carry members of the carnival and their parade wagons.

Jarlaxle has forged an alliance with Lantan (an island to the south), and has armed his Bregan D'aerthe lieu-tenants with Lantanese firearms that rely on magical *smokepowder* to function. He has also acquired a Lan-tanese submarine called the *Scarlet Marpenoth*. This underwater vessel is mounted below the *Eyecatcher* and kept out of sight. Jarlaxle plans on using the submarine to flee Waterdeep if his scheme unravels.

Jarlaxle's loyalties are to himself first and foremost, and to Bregan D'aerthe secondarily.

Jarlaxle Baenre
Medium humanoid (elf), chaotic neutral

Armor Class 24 (+3 leather armor, Suave Defense)
Hit Points 123 (19d8 + 38)
Speed 30 ft.

STR	DEX	CON	INT	WIS	CHA
12 (+1)	22 (+6)	14 (+2)	20 (+5)	16 (+3)	19 (+4)

Saving Throws Dex +11, Wis +8
Skills Acrobatics +11, Athletics +6, Deception +14, Perception +8, Sleight of Hand +11, Stealth +16
Senses darkvision 120 ft., passive Perception 18
Languages Abyssal, Common, Draconic, Dwarvish, Elvish, Undercommon
Challenge 15 (13,000 XP)

Special Equipment. Jarlaxle wears *+3 leather armor*, a *hat of disguise*, a *bracer of flying daggers* (see appendix A), a *cloak of invisibility*, a *knave's eye patch* (see appendix A), and a *ring of truth telling* (see appendix A). He wields a *+3 rapier* and carries a *portable hole* and a *wand of web*. His hat is adorned with a *feather of diatryma summoning* (see appendix A).

Evasion. If he is subjected to an effect that allows him to make a Dexterity saving throw to take only half damage, Jarlaxle instead takes no damage if he succeeds on the saving throw, and only half damage if he fails. He can't use this trait if he's incapacitated.

Fey Ancestry. Jarlaxle has advantage on saving throws against being charmed, and magic can't put him to sleep.

Innate Spellcasting. Jarlaxle's innate spellcasting ability is Charisma (spell save DC 17, +9 to hit with spell attacks). He can innately cast the following spells, requiring no material components:

At will: *dancing lights*
1/day each: *darkness, faerie fire, levitate* (self only)

Legendary Resistance (1/Day). If Jarlaxle fails a saving throw, he can choose to succeed instead.

Master Attuner. Jarlaxle can attune to up to five magic items, and he can attune to magic items that normally require attune-ment by a sorcerer, warlock, or wizard.

Sneak Attack (1/Turn). Jarlaxle deals an extra 24 (7d6) damage when he hits a target with a weapon attack and has advantage on the attack roll, or when the target is within 5 feet of an ally of Jarlaxle's that isn't incapacitated and Jarlaxle doesn't have disadvantage on the attack roll.

Suave Defense. While Jarlaxle is wearing light or no armor and wielding no shield, his AC includes his Charisma modifier.

Sunlight Sensitivity. When not wearing his *knave's eye patch*, Jarlaxle has disadvantage on attack rolls, as well as on Wisdom (Perception) checks that rely on sight.

Actions

Multiattack. Jarlaxle makes three attacks with his *+3 rapier* or two attacks with daggers created by his *bracer of flying daggers*.

+3 Rapier. *Melee Weapon Attack:* +14 to hit, reach 5 ft., one tar-get. *Hit:* 13 (1d8 + 9) piercing damage.

Flying Dagger. *Ranged Weapon Attack:* +11 to hit, range 20/60 ft., one target. *Hit:* 8 (1d4 + 6) piercing damage.

Legendary Actions

Jarlaxle can take 3 legendary actions, choosing from the op-tions below. Only one legendary action option can be used at a time and only at the end of another creature's turn. Jarlaxle regains spent legendary actions at the start of his turn.

Quick Step. Jarlaxle moves up to his speed without provoking opportunity attacks.
Attack (Costs 2 Actions). Jarlaxle makes one attack with his *+3 rapier* or two attacks with daggers created by his *bracer of flying daggers*.

LAERAL SILVERHAND

Anamanué Laeral Silverhand was born in the Year of the Cowl (765 DR), the fifth of seven daughters of the goddess Mystra. Each of the Seven Sisters is a powerful and ageless beauty with a penchant for arcane magic.

Long ago, Laeral ruled a kingdom called Stornanter and held the title of Witch-Queen of the North. After that, she led a band of adventurers called the Nine. She met and married Khelben Arunsun, who would later become the Blackstaff, the Lord Mage of Waterdeep. After Khelben died, Laeral retired from public life. She resurfaced after the Spellplague and the Sundering, weakened by Mystra's death, rebirth, and withdrawal from the world.

Laeral's magic isn't as great as it once was, though she does her utmost to hide this fact. Only Elminster, her trusted friend and advisor, knows the extent of her decline. Despite her diminished abilities, Laeral remains a formidable, clear-headed wizard with plenty of magic at her disposal.

A few years ago, Dagult Neverember was ousted as Open Lord of Waterdeep. Laeral reluctantly stepped into the vacancy at the request of the Masked Lords, and has served as Waterdeep's Open Lord ever since. Initially overwhelmed by the demands of the nobles and guildmasters, she has settled nicely into her new role. She uses her magic sparingly and relies on trusted advisors and deputies. As time allows, she likes to venture outside the Palace of Waterdeep in disguise, just to clear her head or check up on old friends (and enemies).

Laeral's relationship with Vajra Safahr, the current Blackstaff, has its challenges. For one thing, Laeral is much older, much wiser, and much more powerful than Vajra, whom she views as an insecure child. In addition, Vajra wields the *Blackstaff*, which has Khelben Arunsun's soul and the souls of all the other Blackstaffs bound inside it. Laeral covets the staff, because it con-

---

LAERAL SILVERHAND
Medium humanoid (human), chaotic good

Armor Class 18 (*robe of the archmagi*)
Hit Points 228 (24d8 + 120)
Speed 30 ft.

STR	DEX	CON	INT	WIS	CHA
13 (+1)	17 (+3)	20 (+5)	20 (+5)	20 (+5)	19 (+4)

Saving Throws Int +11, Wis +11
Skills Arcana +17, History +17, Insight +11, Perception +11, Persuasion +10
Damage Resistances fire
Damage Immunities poison
Condition Immunities poisoned
Senses truesight 60 ft., passive Perception 21
Languages Common, Draconic, Dwarvish, Elvish, Giant, Infernal
Challenge 17 (18,000 XP)

Special Equipment. Laeral wears a white *robe of the archmagi* (accounted for in her statistics). She wields a *flame tongue* longsword.

Magic Resistance. While wearing her *robe of the archmagi*, Laeral has advantage on saving throws against spells and other magical effects.

Spellcasting. Laeral is a 19th-level spellcaster. Her spellcasting ability is Intelligence (spell save DC 21, +13 to hit with spell attacks). Laeral has the following wizard spells prepared:

Cantrips (at will): *light, mage hand, minor illusion, prestidigitation, ray of frost*
1st level (at will): *detect magic, disguise self, magic missile, shield*
2nd level (at will): *detect thoughts, invisibility, misty step*
3rd level (3 slots): *counterspell, fly, sending, tongues*
4th level (3 slots): *banishment, greater invisibility, Otiluke's resilient sphere*
5th level (3 slots): *cone of cold, geas, Rary's telepathic bond*
6th level (2 slots): *globe of invulnerability, mass suggestion*
7th level (1 slot): *prismatic spray, teleport*
8th level (1 slot): *feeblemind, power word stun*
9th level (1 slot): *time stop*

ACTIONS

Multiattack. Laeral makes three attacks with her silver hair and *flame tongue*, in any combination. She can cast one of her cantrips or 1st-level spells before or after making these attacks.

Silver Hair. *Melee Weapon Attack:* +11 to hit, reach 5 ft., one target. *Hit:* 7 (2d6) force damage, and the target must succeed on a DC 19 Constitution saving throw or be paralyzed for 1 minute. The target can repeat the saving throw at the end of each of its turns, ending the effect on itself on a success.

Flame Tongue. *Melee Weapon Attack:* +7 to hit, reach 5 ft., one target. *Hit:* 5 (1d8 + 1) slashing damage plus 7 (2d6) fire damage, or 6 (1d10 + 1) slashing damage plus 7 (2d6) fire damage when used with two hands.

Spellfire (Recharges after a Long Rest). Magical, heatless, silver fire harmlessly erupts from Laeral and surrounds her until she is incapacitated or until she uses an action to quench it. She gains one of the following benefits of her choice, which lasts until the silver fire ends:

- She can breathe underwater.
- She can survive without food and water.
- She is immune to magic that would ascertain her thoughts, truthfulness, alignment, or creature type.
- She gains resistance to cold damage, and she is unharmed by temperatures as low as –50 degrees Fahrenheit.

While the silver fire is present, she has the following additional action options:

- Cast the *cure wounds* spell. The target regains 1d8 + 5 hit points. After Laeral takes this action, roll a d6. On a roll of 1, the silver fire disappears.
- Cast the *revivify* spell without material components. After Laeral takes this action, roll a d6. On a roll of 1–2, the silver fire disappears.
- Release a 60-foot line of silver fire that is 5 feet wide or a 30-foot cone of silver fire. Objects in the area that aren't being worn or carried take 26 (4d12) fire damage. Each creature in the area must succeed on a DC 21 Dexterity saving throw, taking 26 (4d12) fire damage on a failed save, or half as much damage on a successful one. After Laeral takes this action, roll a d6. On a roll of 1–3, the silver fire disappears.

LAERAL SILVERHAND

MANSHOON

Referred to in this adventure simply as "Manshoon," this clone of the ancient archwizard infiltrated Waterdeep years ago and has been hiding out in Kolat Towers ever since, in the city's Southern Ward.

The original Manshoon was one of the founders of the Zhentarim. Evil to the core, he made enemies all across Faerûn, including other powerful spellcasters such as Khelben Arunsun and Elminster. Fearing that he might be destroyed by his foes, Manshoon magically crafted several clones—but a mishap caused all of them to be awakened at once, whereupon they tried to destroy one another in a series of conflicts that came to be known as the Manshoon Wars.

Now the original Manshoon is dead, and it's widely believed that all his clones were destroyed as well. In fact, at least three are still alive. The one presently in Waterdeep escaped death by hiding out in Undermountain, where he eventually ran afoul of Halaster Blackcloak. After a brief spell duel, Halaster captured Manshoon and amputated his left arm at the elbow for reasons unknown. Manshoon escaped imprisonment and fled Undermountain, taking refuge in the city above. Attempts to magically regenerate his severed limb failed, forcing him to craft an artificial arm and hand for himself.

Manshoon took control of Kolat Towers, a crumbling residence in the Southern Ward that was abandoned years ago by the two wizards who built it. The edifice is surrounded by a magical barrier that has the properties of a *wall of force*. Manshoon rarely leaves the towers and uses a teleportation circle when he must do so, and thus is never seen entering or leaving.

Manshoon aims to rule Waterdeep and replace the City Watch with Black Network mercenaries that are loyal to him alone. By bribing and blackmailing the Masked Lords, he hopes to oust Laeral Silverhand as Open Lord and take her place, kill the Blackstaff, reduce the Masked Lords to mere vassals, and declare himself the Wizard-King of Waterdeep. Once the city is firmly in his clutches, Manshoon will then turn his attention toward Undermountain, destroy Halaster once and for all, and claim the dungeon's riches.

MANSHOON SIMULACRUM

Manshoon uses the *simulacrum* spell to create a magical duplicate of himself as needed. He has customized the spell to increase his simulacrum's hit points at the expense of its spellcasting ability.

Manshoon can have only one simulacrum at any given time, and he uses it as a subordinate to command his Zhentarim minions in the field. If his simulacrum is destroyed, Manshoon creates another. Each simulacrum has the statistics of **Manshoon**, with these changes:

- The simulacrum has no special equipment. Consequently, it has AC 12 and lacks the Magic Resistance trait and the *Staff of Power* action option.
- It loses all spell slots of 6th level and higher.
- It has a challenge rating of 8 (3,900 XP).

tains all that's left of her husband. Not surprisingly, the two mages avoid each other as much as possible.

In times of great need, Laeral can command Vajra to unleash Force Grey. Until that order is given, Force Grey isn't allowed to conduct operations in Waterdeep, though Laeral's spies tell her that Vajra has secretly activated members of the elite order and sent them on a number of unauthorized missions. Laeral is reluctant to confront Vajra on the matter, and rationalizes her inaction by framing it as a test of Vajra's competence.

A FLYING SNAKE OF
THE ZHENTARIM

MANSHOON
Medium humanoid (human), lawful evil

Armor Class 19 (*robe of the archmagi*, *staff of power*)
Hit Points 126 (23d8 + 23)
Speed 30 ft.

STR	DEX	CON	INT	WIS	CHA
10 (+0)	14 (+2)	12 (+1)	23 (+6)	15 (+2)	16 (+3)

Saving Throws Str +2, Dex +4, Con +3, Int +13, Wis +9, Cha +5
Skills Arcana +11, History +11
Senses darkvision 60 ft., passive Perception 12
Languages Common, Draconic, Goblin, Infernal, Orc,
  Undercommon
Challenge 13 (10,000 XP)

Special Equipment. Manshoon wears a black *robe of the arch-magi* and wields a *staff of power* (both accounted for in his statistics). Roll 2d10 to determine how many charges the staff has remaining.

Magic Resistance. While wearing his *robe of the archmagi*, Manshoon has advantage on saving throws against spells and other magical effects.

Spellcasting. Manshoon is an 18th-level spellcaster. His spellcasting ability is Intelligence (spell save DC 21, +15 to hit with spell attacks). He has the following wizard spells prepared:

Cantrips (at will): *fire bolt, light, mage hand, prestidigitation, shocking grasp*
1st level (4 slots): *detect magic, mage armor, magic missile, shield*
2nd level (3 slots): *detect thoughts, mirror image, misty step*
3rd level (3 slots): *counterspell, lightning bolt, sending*
4th level (3 slots): *fire shield, greater invisibility, polymorph*
5th level (3 slots): *Bigby's hand, scrying, wall of force*
6th level (1 slot): *flesh to stone, globe of invulnerability*
7th level (1 slot): *finger of death, simulacrum*
8th level (1 slot): *feeblemind, mind blank*
9th level (1 slot): *imprisonment, power word kill*

ACTIONS

Metal Fist. *Melee Weapon Attack:* +6 to hit, reach 5 ft., one target. *Hit:* 4 (1d4 + 2) bludgeoning damage.

Staff of Power. *Melee Weapon Attack:* +7 to hit, reach 5 ft., one target. *Hit:* 5 (1d6 + 2) bludgeoning damage, or 6 (1d8 + 2) bludgeoning damage when used with two hands. Manshoon can expend 1 of the staff's charges to deal an extra 3 (1d6) force damage on a hit.

MARTIAL ARTS ADEPT

Martial arts adepts are disciplined monks who have extensive training in hand-to-hand combat. Some protect monasteries; others travel the world seeking enlightenment or new forms of combat to master. A few become bodyguards, trading their combat prowess and loyalty for food and lodging.

MARTIAL ARTS ADEPT
Medium humanoid (any race), any alignment

Armor Class 16
Hit Points 60 (11d8 + 11)
Speed 40 ft.

STR	DEX	CON	INT	WIS	CHA
11 (+0)	17 (+3)	13 (+1)	11 (+0)	16 (+3)	10 (+0)

Skills Acrobatics +5, Insight +5, Stealth +5
Senses passive Perception 13
Languages any one language (usually Common)
Challenge 3 (700 XP)

Unarmored Defense. While the adept is wearing no armor and wielding no shield, its AC includes its Wisdom modifier.

ACTIONS

Multiattack. The adept makes three unarmed strikes or three dart attacks.

Unarmed Strike. *Melee Weapon Attack:* +5 to hit, reach 5 ft., one target. *Hit:* 7 (1d8 + 3) bludgeoning damage. If the target is a creature, the adept can choose one of the following additional effects:

- The target must succeed on a DC 13 Strength saving throw or drop one item it is holding (adept's choice).
- The target must succeed on a DC 13 Dexterity saving throw or be knocked prone.
- The target must succeed on a DC 13 Constitution saving throw or be stunned until the end of the adept's next turn.

Dart. *Ranged Weapon Attack:* +5 to hit, range 20/60 ft., one target. *Hit:* 5 (1d4 + 3) piercing damage.

REACTIONS

Deflect Missile. In response to being hit by a ranged weapon attack, the adept deflects the missile. The damage it takes from the attack is reduced by 1d10 + 3. If the damage is reduced to 0, the adept catches the missile if it's small enough to hold in one hand and the adept has a hand free.

MELOON WARDRAGON

Meloon is a handsome, formidable warrior in his prime, who serves the goddess Tymora and loves a good fight. His friends—among them Renaer Neverember and Vajra Safahr—describe him as honest, optimistic, and extraordinarily lucky. Until recently, he was a member of Force Grey and reported directly to the Blackstaff. In recent months, Meloon has spent much of his time at the Yawning Portal.

Three months ago, out of boredom, Meloon accompanied a fledgling band of adventurers on an expedition to Undermountain. There, his luck ran out. While resting in the dungeon, the adventuring party was attacked by monsters unleashed by Xanathar—including a number of intellect devourers. One of the creatures succeeded in magically devouring and replacing Meloon's brain, turning the champion of Tymora into a puppet. After finishing off his unsuspecting companions, Meloon returned to Waterdeep as a Xanathar Guild spy.

The intellect devourer that inhabits Meloon's skull was bred by Nihiloor, a mind flayer in Xanathar's employ. It knows everything Meloon knew, and Meloon behaves much as he did before his descent into Undermountain. He hangs out at the Yawning Portal, tries to bond with adventurers, and offers a helping hand whenever doing so feels appropriate. The intellect devourer's primary goals are to steer adventurers away from Undermountain and get them to undertake quests that further the aims of Xanathar. Such quests usually involve the eradication of Xanathar's enemies, and Meloon is all too eager to fight alongside those who fall for his ruse.

ADJUSTED GAME STATISTICS

If Meloon is killed and raised from the dead, his true self is restored and his statistics change as follows:

- Meloon is neutral good.
- He loses his telepathy, and his ability to speak and understand Deep Speech.
- He can attune to *Azuredge* (see appendix A).

MIRT

Once known as Mirt the Merciless and the Old Wolf, Mirt made a fortune and carved out a reputation as an adventurer and philanderer. Today, an older and wiser Mirt serves as one of the Masked Lords, a Harper, and a close advisor to Laeral Silverhand. The years have not worn him down, and though he has grown soft in the flesh, he remains deceptively strong, vigorous, and clear of mind. Mirt has survived the passing of centuries by means of magic, and of all the Masked Lords, he is the least concerned with concealing his identity.

Despite his prodigious girth, Mirt can move with good speed when he must, and he hasn't let his adventuring skills wither. His wife, Asper, passed away several years ago, and his rambling mansion has seen better days. Mirt spends his days embroiled in politics and whiles away his nights in drink and debauchery.

MIRT

MELOON WARDRAGON

Medium humanoid (human), neutral evil

Armor Class 18 (plate)
Hit Points 143 (22d8 + 44)
Speed 30 ft.

STR	DEX	CON	INT	WIS	CHA
20 (+5)	15 (+2)	14 (+2)	10 (+0)	14 (+2)	15 (+2)

Saving Throws Str +9, Con +6
Skills Athletics +9, Survival +6
Senses darkvision 60 ft., passive Perception 12
Languages Common, Deep Speech, telepathy 60 ft.
Challenge 9 (5,000 XP)

Special Equipment. Meloon wields *Azuredge* (see appendix A) but can't attune to it, and thus gains none of its benefits.

Indomitable (2/Day). Meloon can reroll a saving throw that he fails. He must use the new roll.

Second Wind (Recharges after a Short or Long Rest). As a bonus action, Meloon can regain 20 hit points.

ACTIONS

Multiattack. Meloon makes four attacks with *Azuredge*.

Azuredge. *Melee Attack:* +9 to hit, reach 5 ft., one target. *Hit:* 11 (1d12 + 5) slashing damage.

TREASURE

Mirt has access to magic items of all kinds, but keeps only a few on his person. He can equip himself with other magic items as the need arises.

In addition to his other magical gear, Mirt owns a *Lord's ensemble* (see appendix A). He dons the ensemble only when meeting with other Masked Lords in an official capacity.

MIRT

Medium humanoid (human), chaotic good

Armor Class 16 (*bracers of defense*)
Hit Points 153 (18d8 + 72)
Speed 30 ft.

STR	DEX	CON	INT	WIS	CHA
18 (+4)	18 (+4)	18 (+4)	15 (+2)	12 (+1)	15 (+2)

Saving Throws Dex +8, Wis +5
Skills Acrobatics +8, Athletics +8, Perception +5, Persuasion +6, Stealth +8
Senses passive Perception 15
Languages Common, Dwarvish
Challenge 9 (5,000 XP)

Special Equipment. Mirt wears *bracers of defense* and a *ring of regeneration*. He wields a *+1 longsword* and a *+1 dagger*.

Brute. A melee weapon deals one extra die of its damage when Mirt hits with it (included in the attacks below).

Evasion. If he is subjected to an effect that allows him to make a Dexterity saving throw to take only half damage, Mirt instead takes no damage if he succeeds on the saving throw, and only half damage if he fails. He can't use this trait if he's incapacitated.

Sneak Attack (1/Turn). Mirt deals an extra 14 (4d6) damage when he hits a target with a weapon attack and has advantage on the attack roll, or when the target is within 5 feet of an ally of Mirt's that isn't incapacitated and Mirt doesn't have disadvantage on the attack roll.

ACTIONS

Multiattack. Mirt makes three attacks: two with his *+1 longsword* and one with his *+1 dagger*.

+1 Longsword. *Melee Weapon Attack:* +9 to hit, reach 5 ft., one target. *Hit:* 14 (2d8 + 5) slashing damage, or 16 (2d10 + 5) slashing damage when used with two hands.

+1 Dagger. *Melee or Ranged Weapon Attack:* +9 to hit, reach 5 ft. or range 20/60 ft., one target. *Hit:* 10 (2d4 + 5) piercing damage when used as a melee weapon, or 7 (1d4 + 5) piercing damage when used as a ranged weapon.

REACTIONS

Parry. Mirt adds 2 to his AC against one melee attack that would hit him. To do so, Mirt must see the attacker and be wielding a melee weapon.

NAR'L XIBRINDAS

Xanathar's advisor is a nervous and conniving male drow named Nar'l Xibrindas. Nar'l's house was wiped out long ago, but he and his elder brother Soluun survived and joined Bregan D'aerthe. A year ago, Nar'l was given the difficult task of infiltrating the Xanathar Guild and getting as close to the beholder as possible. Not only did he succeed, but in the course of gaining Xanathar's trust, he managed to convince the beholder to eliminate its other advisors. The beholder's paranoia will eventually cause Xanathar to question the drow's loyalty, though, and Nar'l has become increasingly worried about his future. If forced to decide between himself and Bregan D'aerthe, he'll choose the former and betray his drow allies to save his own skin.

Xanathar is aware that something is off with Nar'l, and recently assigned him a **grell** bodyguard. The grell has instructions to dispose of Nar'l at the first sign of disloyalty.

GAME STATISTICS

Nar'l Xibrindas is a **drow mage**. He prepares and casts the *sending* spell whenever he needs to communicate with his brother. In addition to his other gear, Nar'l carries a vial containing three doses of eyescratch, a contact poison. A creature that comes into contact with the poison must succeed on a DC 14 Constitution saving throw or be poisoned for 1 hour and blinded while poisoned in this way. A *lesser restoration* spell or similar magic ends the effect.

NAR'L XIBRINDAS AND
GRELL BODYGUARD

Nihiloor

The illithid Nihiloor works for Xanathar, spending its days creating intellect devourers and setting them loose in the sewers of Waterdeep. Each intellect devourer attacks the first humanoid it encounters, using its victim as a puppet to spy on the city and relay information back to Nihiloor. Occasionally, an intellect devourer is instructed to seek out a particular kind of target, such as a member of the City Guard or the City Watch. Sometimes its instructions will include orders to capture specific Waterdavians and bring them to Skullport, where they can be enslaved or ransomed.

Nihiloor has an alien mind, and it considers itself Xanathar's equal. It has no interest in supplanting the beholder, however, preferring to operate in the shadows and pursue its own fell schemes.

Game Statistics
Nihiloor is a **mind flayer**.

Nihiloor

Nimblewright

A nimblewright is a magical construct created to serve as a guard or assassin. Composed predominantly of lightweight wood and powered by magic, it can pass for humanoid while wearing clothing. Some nimblewrights wear plain clothing, while others are clad in flashier attire. A nimblewright is emotionless, its face frozen in whatever expression was given to it by its creator.

Duelist. A nimblewright moves like a dancer and fights like a swashbuckler, using dodges and parries to avoid damage while deftly skewering its foes.

Constructed Nature. A nimblewright doesn't require air, food, drink, or sleep. Damage it takes can be repaired with *mending* spells, but a nimblewright reduced to 0 hit points is permanently destroyed.

NIMBLEWRIGHT
Medium construct, unaligned

Armor Class 18 (natural armor)
Hit Points 45 (6d8 + 18)
Speed 60 ft.

STR	DEX	CON	INT	WIS	CHA
12 (+1)	18 (+4)	17 (+3)	8 (−1)	10 (+0)	6 (−2)

Saving Throws Dex +6
Skills Acrobatics +8, Perception +2
Damage Resistances bludgeoning, piercing, and slashing from nonmagical attacks
Condition Immunities exhaustion, frightened, petrified, poisoned
Senses darkvision 60 ft., passive Perception 12
Languages understands one language known to its creator but can't speak
Challenge 4 (1,100 XP)

Magic Resistance. The nimblewright has advantage on saving throws against spells and other magical effects.

Magic Weapons. The nimblewright's weapon attacks are magical.

Repairable. As long as it has at least 1 hit point remaining, the nimblewright regains 1 hit point when a *mending* spell is cast on it.

Sure-Footed. The nimblewright has advantage on Strength and Dexterity saving throws made against effects that would knock it prone.

Actions

Multiattack. The nimblewright makes three attacks: two with its rapier and one with its dagger.

Rapier. *Melee Weapon Attack:* +6 to hit, reach 5 ft., one target. *Hit:* 8 (1d8 + 4) piercing damage.

Dagger. *Melee or Ranged Weapon Attack:* +6 to hit, reach 5 ft. or range 20/60 ft., one target. *Hit:* 6 (1d4 + 4) piercing damage.

Reactions

Parry. The nimblewright adds 2 to its AC against one melee attack that would hit it. To do so, the nimblewright must see the attacker and be wielding a melee weapon.

NIMBLEWRIGHT

After she was passed over, Orond became insanely angry, and he has remained that way ever since.

Less than a year ago, the Gralhunds were approached by agents of the Zhentarim loyal to Manshoon, and the nobles formed an alliance with them. House Gralhund gives the Zhents coin and allows them to use the family's noble villa as a refuge. In exchange, the house reaps all the benefits that the Black Network offers, including intelligence that its spies have gathered. So while the Zhents use House Gralhund as a shield, the Gralhunds are using the Zhents to ascertain the identities and weaknesses of the Masked Lords.

Orond doesn't fully grasp how entwined the Black Network and his family have become—it is now next to impossible to separate one from the other. It's no secret in Waterdeep that the Black Network has firmly rooted itself in House Gralhund. But what's not generally known is that the Zhents in House Gralhund are agents of Manshoon. Neither Orond nor any other member of his family knows about the wizard's clone. As far as Orond and his wife are concerned, the local leaders of the Black Network (with Urstul Floxin chief among them) reside with them in the family villa.

Orond is a short, stocky man who dresses well and is easy on the eyes. When he opens his mouth, his boorish nature, inflated sense of self-importance, fragile ego, and despicable opinions about "the common rabble" come to the fore, and his charm quickly dissipates. When not in his wife's company, he is prone to excessive boasting and temper tantrums. When he must speak to strangers, he keeps his half-orc bodyguard Hrabbaz close by, for fear that others might attack and rob him at

Noska Ur'gray

Noska is a ruthless enforcer in the Xanathar Guild. A green slime in Undermountain dissolved his left hand and forearm, and the lost appendage has been replaced with a heavy crossbow that attaches to the stump.

Game Statistics

Noska Ur'gray is a shield dwarf **thug**, with these changes:

- Noska is neutral evil.
- He has these racial traits: His walking speed is 25 feet. He has advantage on saving throws against poison and resistance to poison damage. He has darkvision out to a range of 60 feet. He speaks Common and Dwarvish.
- He has disadvantage on Strength checks made to climb, due to his disability.

Orond Gralhund

The Gralhunds are nobles who trade in arms and mercenaries, and whose family motto is "We see both sides." Orond is the patriarch, but he's not a quick-thinking or cultured sort—and deep down, he knows it. He leaves most of the plotting and socializing to his wife, Yalah, to whom he is devoted.

When several of the Masked Lords were assassinated in quick succession some years ago, Lord Gralhund had expected his wife to fill one of the vacancies. That never happened, though, despite many promises and bribes.

NOSKA UR'GRAY

OTT STEELTOES

OTT STEELTOES

The dwarf Ott Steeltoes has the nerve-wracking task of tending to Xanathar's pet fish, Sylgar. In his spare time, he worships Zuggtmoy, the demon queen of fungi, and cultivates mushrooms, spores, and molds. He wears a leather skullcap stitched with fake beholder eyestalks.

GAME STATISTICS

Ott is a shield dwarf **cultist**, with these changes:

- Ott is chaotic evil.
- He has these racial traits: His walking speed is 25 feet. He has advantage on saving throws against poison and resistance to poison damage. He has darkvision out to a range of 60 feet. He speaks Common and Dwarvish.
- He has an Intelligence of 6 (−2) and Religion +0.

any moment. While in Yalah's presence, Orond becomes an altogether different person: quiet, almost timid, and happy to let his wife have the spotlight.

Orond relies on Yalah to manage the Zhentarim. He spends his days watching mercenaries train, paying bills, and ranting about the cost of doing business in the city. Although he is human, Orond was born with a tiefling's tail. The tail was amputated when he was a young boy, but the scar on his backside remains.

GAME STATISTICS

Orond Gralhund is a Tethyrian human **noble**, with these changes:

- Orond is neutral evil.
- He has an Intelligence of 9 (−1).
- Never one to bother learning other languages, he speaks only Common.

OSVALDO CASSALANTER

Ammalia and Victoro Cassalanter traded the soul of their eldest child for power. Stripped of his humanity, Osvaldo was chained up in Cassalanter Villa and slowly transformed into a devil (and an insane one at that). Now a creature of pure evil and hate, he has no hope of regaining what was taken from him.

GAME STATISTICS

Osvaldo is a **chain devil**.

REMALLIA HAVENTREE
Medium humanoid (elf), chaotic good

Armor Class 12 (15 with *mage armor*)
Hit Points 66 (12d8 + 12)
Speed 30 ft.

STR	DEX	CON	INT	WIS	CHA
10 (+0)	14 (+2)	13 (+1)	18 (+4)	15 (+2)	17 (+3)

Saving Throws Int +8, Wis +6
Skills Arcana +8, Deception +7, History +8, Persuasion +7
Senses darkvision 60 ft., passive Perception 12
Languages Common, Draconic, Dwarvish, Elvish, Halfling
Challenge 9 (5,000 XP)

Special Equipment. Remallia has a *figurine of wondrous power* (silver raven).

Fey Ancestry. Remallia has advantage on saving throws against being charmed, and magic can't put her to sleep.

Spellcasting. Remallia is a 13th-level spellcaster. Her spellcasting ability is Intelligence (spell save DC 16, +8 to hit with spell attacks). She has the following wizard spells prepared:

Cantrips (at will): *dancing lights, mage hand, mending, message, ray of frost*
1st level (4 slots): *alarm,* mage armor,* magic missile, shield**
2nd level (3 slots): *arcane lock,* invisibility*
3rd level (3 slots): *counterspell,* dispel magic,* fireball*
4th level (3 slots): *banishment,* stoneskin**
5th level (2 slots): *cone of cold, wall of force*
6th level (1 slot): *flesh to stone, globe of invulnerability**
7th level (1 slot): *symbol,* teleport*
*Abjuration spell of 1st level or higher

Arcane Ward. Remallia has a magical ward that has 30 hit points. Whenever she takes damage, the ward takes the damage instead. If the ward is reduced to 0 hit points, Remallia takes any remaining damage. When Remallia casts an abjuration spell of 1st level or higher, the ward regains a number of hit points equal to twice the level of the spell.

ACTIONS

Dagger. *Melee Weapon Attack:* +6 to hit, reach 5 ft. or range 20/60 ft., one target. *Hit:* 4 (1d4 + 2) piercing damage.

REMALLIA HAVENTREE

Remallia (Remi to her friends) is the lady of House Ulbrinter and a guiding light for the Harpers in Waterdeep. She became an active force for good in the city after assassins killed her husband, Arthagast Ulbrinter, and destroyed his remains. A sun elf, she has two adult children (a half-elf son named Arthius, who is studying music in Silverymoon, and a half-elf daughter named Serenore, who lives on the Moonshae island of Alaron with her husband and daughter). Lady Haventree retains a handful of loyal servants and spies.

Remi holds secret Harper meetings in her villa, which is warded by all manner of spells. She uses a silver raven *figurine of wondrous power* to deliver messages to Harper spies scattered throughout the city.

RENAER NEVEREMBER

Renaer is the estranged son of Dagult Neverember, the former Open Lord of Waterdeep and the current Lord of Neverwinter. Father and son detest one another, and Renaer is least happy when he finds himself forced to deal with some mess his father left behind. Qualities that both share include striking good looks, a love of drink, and a flair for diplomacy. What Renaer lacks is his father's belligerence, ill temper, and bad judgment.

Renaer lives off a sizable inheritance left to him by his mother. Approaching middle age, he has given up adventuring and settled down somewhat. As a Harper, he spends a lot of time defending Waterdavians against those who, like his father, would deprive them of their coin and rights. He owns Neverember House, a four-story residence in the Sea Ward. Renaer spends as little time there as possible, however, since it's constantly under surveillance by spies loyal to his father. His friends have an open invitation to use the house as they please, while Renaer spends most of his free time in taverns and festhalls.

Some believe that Renaer's estrangement from his father is nothing but an act, and that anyone who bears the Neverember name is an enemy of Waterdeep. Renaer just shakes his head at such accusations and gets on with his life. He has many powerful friends to watch his back.

GAME STATISTICS

Renaer Neverember is an Illuskan human who has the statistics of a **swashbuckler** (see page 216), with these changes:

- Renaer is chaotic good.
- He speaks Common.

RENAER NEVEREMBER

SAETH CROMLEY

Saeth Cromley is a retired sergeant of the City Watch, a likable fellow with a sharp, sarcastic wit. He occasionally comes out of retirement at the request of Barnibus Blastwind, and he assists the mage in investigating unusual crimes in the city. Cromley helps Barnibus relate to the common folk, and he is good at coaxing information out of them. Though Cromley was once a strict proponent of Watch regulations and dress codes, he has grown a bit lax in both matters now that he's officially retired.

GAME STATISTICS

Saeth Cromley is an Illuskan human **veteran**, with these changes:

- Saeth is lawful good.
- He has a Charisma of 14 and Intimidation +4.
- He speaks Common.

SWASHBUCKLER

Swashbucklers are charming ne'er-do-wells who live by their own codes of honor. They crave notoriety, often indulge in romantic trysts, and eke out livings as pirates and corsairs, rarely staying in one place for too long.

THORVIN TWINBEARD

Thorvin serves as Xanathar's chief engineer and trapsmith. He also serves the Harpers as a paid informant, keeping that faction apprised of Xanathar's plans as well as he can. Thorvin uses the ruse of maintenance inspections to cover up secret meetings he holds with Harper spies in Skullport and elsewhere.

Thorvin wears iron-rimmed spectacles and carries a large, heavy wrench that doubles as a club. He also carries mason's tools, smith's tools, and thieves' tools, and has proficiency with all three.

GAME STATISTICS

Thorvin is a shield dwarf **commoner**, with these changes:

- Thorvin is lawful neutral.
- He has these racial traits: His walking speed is 25 feet. He has advantage on saving throws against poison and resistance to poison damage. He has darkvision out to a range of 60 feet. He speaks Common and Dwarvish.
- He has an Intelligence of 16 (+3).

THORVIN
TWINBEARD

SWASHBUCKLER

Medium humanoid (any race), any non-lawful alignment

Armor Class 17 (leather armor)
Hit Points 66 (12d8 + 12)
Speed 30 ft.

STR	DEX	CON	INT	WIS	CHA
12 (+1)	18 (+4)	12 (+1)	14 (+2)	11 (+0)	15 (+2)

Skills Acrobatics +8, Athletics +5, Persuasion +6
Senses passive Perception 10
Languages any one language (usually Common)
Challenge 3 (700 XP)

Lightfooted. The swashbuckler can take the Dash or Disengage action as a bonus action on each of its turns.

Suave Defense. While the swashbuckler is wearing light or no armor and wielding no shield, its AC includes its Charisma modifier.

ACTIONS

Multiattack. The swashbuckler makes three attacks: one with a dagger and two with its rapier.

Dagger. *Melee or Ranged Weapon Attack:* +6 to hit, reach 5 ft. or range 20/60 ft., one target. *Hit:* 6 (1d4 + 4) piercing damage.

Rapier. *Melee Weapon Attack:* +6 to hit, reach 5 ft., one target. *Hit:* 8 (1d8 + 4) piercing damage.

URSTUL FLOXIN

Urstul Floxin works for Manshoon, and he is the highest-ranking member of the Zhentarim squad stationed at House Gralhund. Urstul is a glorified thug with all the charm and breeding of a snake, but the Gralhunds tolerate him because he feeds them useful information culled from his spies throughout the city. Urstul takes his orders from Manshoon's current simulacrum, which comes and goes from House Gralhund by way of a *teleportation circle* (connected to the circle in Kolat Towers).

Urstul is a large, heavyset man in his forties. He storms about House Gralhund like he owns the place. He has a collection of black **flying snakes** that he uses as couriers to deliver messages to underlings throughout the city.

GAME STATISTICS

Urstul Floxin is an Illuskan human **assassin**, with these changes:

- Urstul is lawful evil.
- He speaks Common and Orc and knows thieves' cant.

VAJRA SAFAHR

Vajra is a capable wizard in her mid-thirties, the youngest person ever to hold the position of Blackstaff. As the High Wizard of Waterdeep, she is charged with using all the magic and resources at her disposal to defend the city against threats. She was handpicked for the job by Khelben Arunsun, and wields the *Blackstaff* from which

Khelben derived his name and the title of the office. Vajra isn't the city's most powerful wizard, but she can hold her own. Despite her many gifts, she still questions her ability to meet the demands of her role, and she rarely makes a decision without first soliciting the advice of the *Blackstaff*, which contains Khelben Arunsun's spirit as well as the spirits of all the other Blackstaffs who preceded her. She also gets intelligence from many other sources, both through her own network of spies and from Harper agents.

Vajra runs Blackstaff Academy, a school for mages, out of Blackstaff Tower in the Castle Ward. She is also in charge of Force Grey, an order of highly skilled adventurers who are called upon to defend the city in times of need. Vajra is always looking for new adventurers to fill the ranks of Force Grey, and she is particularly interested in those who can bring unique skills, abilities, or spells to the mix.

Several of the older and more seasoned wizards in Waterdeep consider Vajra an upstart, but they are smart enough not to challenge her. Only the Open Lord, currently Laeral Silverhand, can strip Vajra of her title.

VAJRA SAFAHR, THE BLACKSTAFF

VAJRA SAFAHR

Medium humanoid (human), lawful neutral

Armor Class 14 (*Blackstaff*; 17 with *mage armor*)
Hit Points 126 (23d8 + 23)
Speed 30 ft.

STR	DEX	CON	INT	WIS	CHA
10 (+0)	14 (+2)	12 (+1)	20 (+5)	11 (+0)	16 (+3)

Saving Throws Str +2, Dex +4, Con +3, Int +12, Wis +7, Cha +5
Skills Arcana +10, History +10
Senses passive Perception 10
Languages Common, Dwarvish, Elvish, Giant, Halfling, Undercommon
Challenge 13 (10,000 XP)

Special Equipment. Vajra wields the *Blackstaff* (see appendix A), accounted for in her statistics. Roll 2d10 to determine how many charges the staff has remaining.

Magic Resistance. Vajra has advantage on saving throws against spells and other magical effects.

Spellcasting. Vajra is an 18th-level spellcaster. Her spellcasting ability is Intelligence (spell save DC 18, +12 to hit with spell attacks). She has the following wizard spells prepared:

Cantrips (at will): *fire bolt, light, mage hand, message, prestidigitation*
1st level (4 slots): *detect magic, identify, mage armor, thunderwave*
2nd level (3 slots): *invisibility, misty step, web*
3rd level (3 slots): *counterspell, fly, sending*
4th level (3 slots): *banishment, fire shield, stoneskin*
5th level (3 slots): *Bigby's hand, geas, telekinesis*
6th level (1 slot): *chain lightning, globe of invulnerability*
7th level (1 slot): *forcecage, prismatic spray*
8th level (1 slot): *antimagic field, power word stun*
9th level (1 slot): *imprisonment*

ACTIONS

Blackstaff. *Melee Weapon Attack:* +7 to hit, reach 5 ft., one target. *Hit:* 5 (1d6 + 2) bludgeoning damage, or 6 (1d8 + 2) bludgeoning damage when used with two hands. Vajra can expend 1 of the staff's charges to deal an extra 3 (1d6) force damage on a hit.

VICTORO CASSALANTER

The lord of House Cassalanter is a devilishly handsome half-elf who likes coin and power. He and his wife gained both by cutting a deal with Asmodeus—which involved trading away the souls of their three children.

VICTORO CASSALANTER
Medium humanoid (half-elf), lawful evil

Armor Class 15 (*glamoured studded leather, ring of protection*)
Hit Points 97 (15d8 + 30)
Speed 30 ft.

STR	DEX	CON	INT	WIS	CHA
13 (+1)	13 (+1)	14 (+2)	16 (+3)	17 (+3)	18 (+4)

Saving Throws Con +6, Wis +7
Skills History +7, Insight +7, Persuasion +8, Religion +7
Damage Immunities poison
Condition Immunities poisoned
Senses darkvision 60 ft., passive Perception 13
Languages Common, Draconic, Elvish, Infernal
Challenge 10 (5,900 XP)

Special Equipment. Victoro wears a *ring of protection* and *glamoured studded leather* disguised to look like fine clothing. He carries a *rod of rulership* shaped like a ruby-tipped cane.

Fey Ancestry. Victoro has advantage on saving throws against being charmed, and magic can't put him to sleep.

Spellcasting. Victoro is a 15th-level spellcaster. His spellcasting ability is Wisdom (spell save DC 15, +7 to hit with spell attacks). Victoro has the following cleric spells prepared:

Cantrips (at will): *guidance, light, mending, spare the dying, thaumaturgy*
1st level (4 slots): *charm person, command, detect magic, disguise self, protection from evil and good, sanctuary*
2nd level (3 slots): *augury, lesser restoration, mirror image, pass without trace, spiritual weapon*
3rd level (3 slots): *blink, clairvoyance, dispel magic, magic circle, protection from energy*
4th level (3 slots): *banishment, dimension door, divination, freedom of movement, polymorph*
5th level (2 slots): *dominate person, flame strike, modify memory, insect plague*
6th level (1 slot): *heal*
7th level (1 slot): *divine word*
8th level (1 slot): *earthquake*

ACTIONS

Multiattack. Victoro makes two attacks with his rapier.

Rapier. *Melee Weapon Attack:* +5 to hit, reach 5 ft., one target. *Hit:* 5 (1d8 + 1) piercing damage.

Cloak of Shadows (2/Day). Victoro becomes invisible until the end of his next turn. He becomes visible early immediately after he attacks or casts a spell.

Summon Devil (Recharges after 9 Days). Victoro summons a **barbed devil**. The devil appears in an unoccupied space within 30 feet of Victoro, acts as Victoro's ally, and can't summon other devils. It remains for 1 minute, until it or Victoro dies, or until Victoro dismisses it as an action.

Victoro is a priest of Asmodeus, though his devotion to the Lord of the Nine Hells is a secret known only to his wife and his closest friends. Most Waterdavians know him as a successful banker, philanthropist, and worshiper of Lathander. Some of his business profits go toward feeding and sheltering the poor. But behind this veneer of generosity, Victoro is a self-serving beast.

The soul of Victoro's eldest son, Osvaldo, is forever lost and can't be saved. To allay his guilt, Victoro has forged a plan to win back the souls of his young twins, Terenzio and Elzerina. Under the terms of the contract, their souls will be forfeit on their ninth birthdays, and that day is fast approaching. But Victoro can buy his way out of the obligation by providing, as the contract states, "one shy of a million gold coins and the sacrifice of one shy of a hundred unfortunate souls."

Victoro is well schooled, suave, slow to anger, and blessed with good health, long life, and immunity to disease. He dresses in the latest fashions and walks with a ruby-tipped cane, though not because he needs to. This cane has the magical properties of a *rod of rulership*.

VOLOTHAMP GEDDARM

The bombastic world traveler Volothamp Geddarm is enjoying some downtime in Waterdeep following a successful book tour promoting his latest work, *Volo's Guide to Monsters*. He spends most of his free time in the taproom of the Yawning Portal, reuniting with old friends and mulling over his next book project.

Volo has an inflated opinion of himself and his importance in the world, but he's not without his charm. There is nothing he won't do to help a friend in need.

VOLOTHAMP "VOLO" GEDDARM
Medium humanoid (human), chaotic good

Armor Class 11
Hit Points 31 (7d8)
Speed 30 ft.

STR	DEX	CON	INT	WIS	CHA
9 (–1)	12 (+1)	10 (+0)	15 (+2)	11 (+0)	16 (+3)

Saving Throws Con +2, Wis +2
Skills Animal Handling +4, Arcana +4, Deception +5, History +4, Insight +2, Investigation +4, Perception +2, Performance +7, Persuasion +7, Sleight of Hand +3, Survival +2
Senses passive Perception 12
Languages Common, Dwarvish, Elvish
Challenge 1/4 (50 XP)

Spellcasting. Volo is a 1st-level spellcaster. His spellcasting ability is Intelligence (spell save DC 12, +4 to hit with spell attacks). He has the following wizard spells prepared:

Cantrips (at will): *friends, mending, prestidigitation*
1st level (2 slots): *comprehend languages, detect magic, disguise self*

ACTIONS

Dagger. *Melee or Ranged Weapon Attack:* +3 to hit, reach 5 ft. or range 20/60 ft., one target. *Hit:* 3 (1d4 + 1) piercing damage.

WALKING STATUES OF WATERDEEP

Scattered throughout Waterdeep are eight enormous statues that can defend the city in times of great peril. Because they are so destructive, the walking statues are used only to fend off armies and seemingly insurmountable foes.

Each statue has a name and a unique appearance (see "The Walking Statues," page 182), but in terms of statistics they are similar. The statue known as the Swordmaiden is too broken to be animated, and only the wielder of the *Blackstaff* (see appendix A) can animate the other seven.

Landmarks. Over the years, Waterdavians have built structures around and on top of several of the statues, believing them to be little more than landmarks at this point. In their inanimate state, the statues pose little danger—but any structures attached to a walking statue are destroyed the first time it animates.

Constructed Nature. A walking statue doesn't require air, food, drink, or sleep.

WALKING STATUE OF WATERDEEP

Gargantuan construct, unaligned

Armor Class 17 (natural armor)
Hit Points 314 (17d20 + 136)
Speed 60 ft.

STR	DEX	CON	INT	WIS	CHA
30 (+10)	8 (−1)	27 (+8)	1 (−5)	10 (+0)	1 (−5)

Saving Throws Con +14
Damage Immunities cold, fire, poison, psychic; bludgeoning, piercing, and slashing from nonmagical attacks not made with adamantine weapons
Condition Immunities charmed, exhaustion, frightened, paralyzed, petrified, poisoned, stunned
Senses truesight 120 ft., passive Perception 10
Languages —
Challenge 18 (20,000 XP)

Crumbling Colossus. When the statue drops to 0 hit points, it crumbles and is destroyed. Any creature on the ground within 30 feet of the crumbling statue must make a DC 22 Dexterity saving throw, taking 22 (4d10) bludgeoning damage on a failed save, or half as much damage on a successful one.

Immutable Form. The statue is immune to any spell or effect that would alter its form.

Magic Resistance. The statue has advantage on saving throws against spells and other magical effects.

Siege Monster. The statue deals double damage to objects and structures.

ACTIONS

Multiattack. The statue makes two melee attacks.

Slam. *Melee Weapon Attack:* +16 to hit, reach 5 ft., one target. *Hit:* 29 (3d12 + 10) bludgeoning damage.

Hurled Stone. *Ranged Weapon Attack:* +16 to hit, range 200/800 ft., one target. *Hit:* 43 (6d10 + 10) bludgeoning damage.

Xanathar

Xanathar is the name given to the beholder crime lord that lives in the dungeons under Waterdeep. It isn't the first beholder to claim this mantle, nor will it be the last.

Like all beholders, Xanathar is a paranoid tyrant that charms and bullies its minions into servitude. The Xanathar Guild is made up of some of Waterdeep's most disreputable folk, as well as monsters forced into subservience or drawn to the beholder by the promise of treasure, food, or power. Treachery within the ranks of the guild is common as servants vie for the beholder's favor and affection. Such boons are fleeting, though, as the beholder is quick to distrust those who finagle their way into its good graces.

Xanathar lives in a dungeon under Skullport, a subterranean settlement connected to Undermountain's third level. The place resembles a ramshackle town, built inside a giant cavern connected to an underground river. Members of the Xanathar Guild haunt Skullport's dilapidated buildings, and flameskulls patrol its streets.

The only creature Xanathar truly cares about aside from itself is a fish, named Sylgar, that it keeps in a large glass tank. Xanathar has minions that look after the fish constantly, but even their ministrations can't keep such a creature alive forever. Whenever the fish dies, panic spreads through the occupants of the lair as minions try to replace the fish before Xanathar realizes what has happened. Luckily for them, the beholder can't tell one fish from another.

Xanathar is extremely fond of gold. A few years ago, its spies stole the *Stone of Golorr*, which contained information that led to the discovery of a dwarven vault under Waterdeep. Xanathar was able to open the vault, but was forced out by the dragon inside the place. Recently, someone stole the *Stone of Golorr* from where it was hidden inside its lair, and the beholder is convinced that the Black Network is behind the theft.

The beholder is caught up in the unbreakable grip of its own paranoia. It sees enemies everywhere, and lashes out at anyone it suspects of being a Zhentarim spy or assassin. Adventurers who attract its attention by dealing with known or suspected Black Network operatives are quickly branded as enemies that must be destroyed.

Game Statistics

Xanathar is a **beholder** that wears magic rings on three of its eyestalks. It is attuned to all three rings, which don't alter the beholder's challenge rating. It wears a *ring of invisibility* on its fear ray eyestalk, a *ring of mind shielding* on its sleep ray eyestalk, and a *ring of resistance* (force) on its slowing ray eyestalk.

Xanathar's beloved fish, Sylgar, has the statistics of a **quipper**, except that it lacks the Blood Frenzy trait.

Yalah Gralhund

The lady of House Gralhund is no fool. She has a keen mind and the wisdom to discern friend from foe. She also has a husband who worships her (see "Orond Gralhund," page 213) and a house that has the resources of the Black Network at its disposal.

Yalah stays abreast of events in the city, keeps a tight rein on her children, and uses her station and her family's wealth to pry secrets from the lips of nobles, guildmasters, and commoners alike. Though her previous attempts to become a Masked Lord have been thwarted, she believes it's only a matter of time until that honor is bestowed on her. Once she knows the identities and secrets of enough Masked Lords, Yalah is confident that she can bribe, blackmail, or extort her way into their ranks. From there, she plans to effect changes in the government that will ensure House Gralhund's prosperity for generations to come.

Yalah shares the services of a half-orc bodyguard with her husband, although Hrabbaz (see "Hrabbaz," page 205) is more loyal to her than to him. She also uses the Zhentarim who are based in House Gralhund as her personal spy network, not realizing that the Zhents' true master is Manshoon. Most of her dealings are with the Zhent master assassin Urstul Floxin (see "Urstul Floxin," page 216), whom she treats as an underling.

Game Statistics

Yalah Gralhund is a Tethyrian human **noble**, with these changes:

- Yalah is neutral evil.
- She has an Intelligence of 16 (+3).
- She speaks Common and Infernal.

YALAH AND OROND
GRALHUND

Appendix C: Handouts
Yawning Portal Friendly Faces

Durnan
Human proprietor

"I'll give you a free flagon of ale if you don't talk to me about the weather."

Bonnie
Human barmaid

"Many adventurers pass though the Yawning Portal on their way to greatness. All of them try the ale."

"Threestrings"
Human bard

"Anyone can play *The Three Flambinis* on a lute, but try playing it with just three strings!"

Jalester Silvermane
Human patron

"Want to know what's going on in our fine city? Grab a stool. Stay a while."

Meloon Wardragon
Famous human adventurer

"Heroes, am I right? Maybe one day you'll join Force Grey. Can I buy you an ale?"

Obaya Uday
Human cleric of Waukeen

"The wonders of Waterdeep are something to behold. I tell you, I've never seen so much money in my life!"

Yagra Stonefist
Half-orc mercenary

"Want to arm wrestle? Hope you're stronger than you look."

The Code Legal

Punishment for a crime can include one or more of the following, based on the nature of the crime, who or what the crime is committed against, and the criminal record of the convicted:

- Death
- Exile (for a number of years or summers)
- Flogging (a set number of strokes)
- Hard labor (for a period of days, months, or years depending on the seriousness of the crime)

- Imprisonment in the dungeons of Castle Waterdeep (for a period of days or months depending on the seriousness of the crime)
- Fine (payable to the city; inability to pay the fine leads to imprisonment and/or hard labor)
- Damages (payable to the injured party or victim's kin; inability to pay damages leads to imprisonment and/or hard labor)
- Edict (forbidding the convicted from doing something; violation of an edict can result in imprisonment, hard labor, and/or a fine)

I. Crimes against Lords, Officials, and Nobles

Assaulting or impersonating a Lord: death

Assaulting or impersonating an official or noble: flogging, imprisonment up to a tenday, and fine up to 500 gp

Blackmailing an official: flogging and exile up to 10 years

Bribery or attempted bribery of an official: exile up to 20 years and fine up to double the bribe amount

Murder of a Lord, official, or noble: death

Using magic to influence a Lord without consent: imprisonment up to a year, and fine or damages up to 1,000 gp

Using magic to influence an official without consent: fine or damages up to 1,000 gp and edict

II. Crimes against the City

Arson: death or hard labor up to 1 year, with fines and/or damages covering the cost of repairs plus 2,000 gp

Brandishing weapons without due cause: imprisonment up to a tenday and/or fine up to 10 gp

Espionage: death or permanent exile

Fencing stolen goods: fine equal to the value of the stolen goods and edict

Forgery of an official document: flogging and exile for 10 summers

Hampering justice: fine up to 200 gp and hard labor up to a tenday

Littering: fine up to 2 gp and edict

Poisoning a city well: death

Theft: flogging followed by imprisonment up to a tenday, hard labor up to 1 year, or fine equal to the value of the stolen goods

Treason: death

Vandalism: imprisonment up to a tenday plus fine and/or damages covering the cost of repairs plus up to 100 gp

Using magic to influence an official without consent: fine or damages up to 1,000 gp and edict

III. Crimes against the Gods

Assaulting a priest or lay worshiper: imprisonment up to a tenday and damages up to 500 gp

Disorderly conduct within a temple: fine up to 5 gp and edict).

Public blasphemy against a god or church: edict

Theft of temple goods or offerings: imprisonment up to a tenday and damages up to double the cost of the stolen items

Tomb-robbing: imprisonment up to a tenday and damages covering the cost of repairs plus 500 gp

IV. Crimes against Citizens

Assaulting a citizen: imprisonment up to a tenday, flogging, and damages up to 1,000 gp

Blackmailing or intimidating a citizen: fine or damages up to 500 gp and edict

Burglary: imprisonment up to 3 months and damages equal to the value of the stolen goods plus 500 gp

Damaging property or livestock: damages covering the cost of repairs or replacement plus up to 500 gp

Disturbing the peace: fine up to 25 gp and edict

Murdering a citizen without justification: death or hard labor up to 10 years, and damages up to 1,000 gp paid to the victim's kin

Murdering a citizen with justification: exile up to 5 years or hard labor up to 3 years or damages up to 1,000 gp paid to the victim's kin

Robbery: hard labor up to 1 month and damages equal to the value of the stolen goods plus 500 gp

Slavery: flogging and hard labor up to 10 years

Using magic to influence a citizen without consent: fine or damages up to 1,000 gp and edict

TROLLSKULL MANOR AND TAVERN

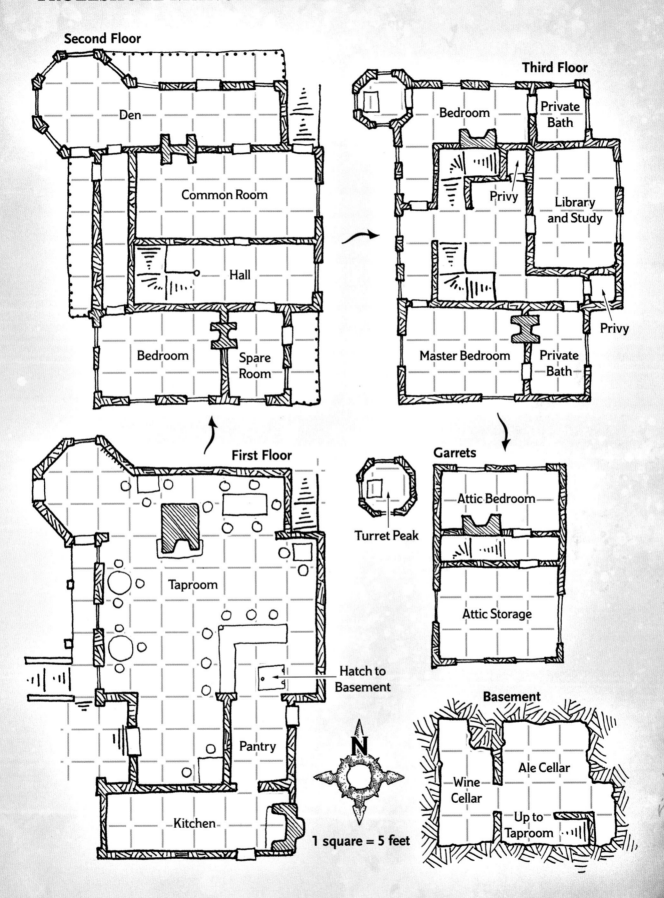

Second Floor

Den

Common Room

Hall

Bedroom

Spare Room

Third Floor

Bedroom

Private Bath

Privy

Library and Study

Master Bedroom

Private Bath

Privy

First Floor

Taproom

Hatch to Basement

Pantry

Kitchen

Garrets

Attic Bedroom

Attic Storage

Turret Peak

Basement

Wine Cellar

Ale Cellar

Up to Taproom

N

1 square = 5 feet

KEY TO THE YAWNING PORTAL

Here are the names of the numbered characters featured in the Yawning Portal illustration on pages 18–19.

1. Victoro Cassalanter
2. Ammalia Cassalanter
3. Vajra Safahr
4. Renaer Neverember
5. Laeral Silverhand
6. Mordenkainen
7. Qilué Veladorn
8. Alustriel Silverhand
9. The Simbul
10. Elminster
11. Harkle Harpell
12. Storm Silverhand
13. Syluné Silverhand
14. Dove Falconhand
15. Florin Falconhand
16. Illistyl Elventree
17. Jhessail Silventree
18. Merith Strongbow
19. Lanseril Snowmantle
20. Artus Cimber
21. Volothamp Geddarm
22. Minsc and Boo

23. Krydle
24. Delina
25. Vartan Hai Sylvar
26. Priam Agrivar
27. Ishi Barasume
28. Minder
29. Foxilon Cardluck
30. Shandie
31. Obaya Uday
32. Manshoon
33. Yoshimo
34. The Nameless One
35. Valygar Corthala
36. Abdel Adrian
37. Hexxat
38. Pikel Bouldershoulder
39. Ivan Bouldershoulder
40. Cadderly Bonaduce
41. Hrolf
42. Drizzt Do'Urden
43. Guenhwyvar
44. Ruqiah

45. Reginald Roundshield
46. Krebbyg Masq'il'yr
47. Spider Parrafin
48. Arkhan the Cruel
49. Tyril Tallguy
50. Dagny Halvor
51. Jamilah
52. Hitch
53. Dragonbait
54. Brawlwin Chainminer
55. Durnan (proprietor)
56. Skip Brickard
57. Diath Woodrow
58. Evelyn Marthain
59. Strix
60. Alias
61. Akabar Bel Akash
62. Olive Rustkettle
63. Mirt
64. The Black Viper
65. Artemis Entreri
66. Joppa

67. Fel'rekt Lafeen
68. Soluun Xibrindas
69. Jarlaxle Baenre
70. Danilo Thann
71. Paultin Seppa
72. Calliope
73. Ziraj the Hunter
74. Skeemo Weirdbottle
75. Davil Starsong
76. Tashlyn Yafeera
77. Istrid Horn
78. Nihiloor
79. Noska Ur'gray
80. Nar'l Xibrindas
81. Ahmaergo
82. Thorvin Twinbeard
83. Ott Steeltoes
84. Xanathar
85. Matthew Mercer

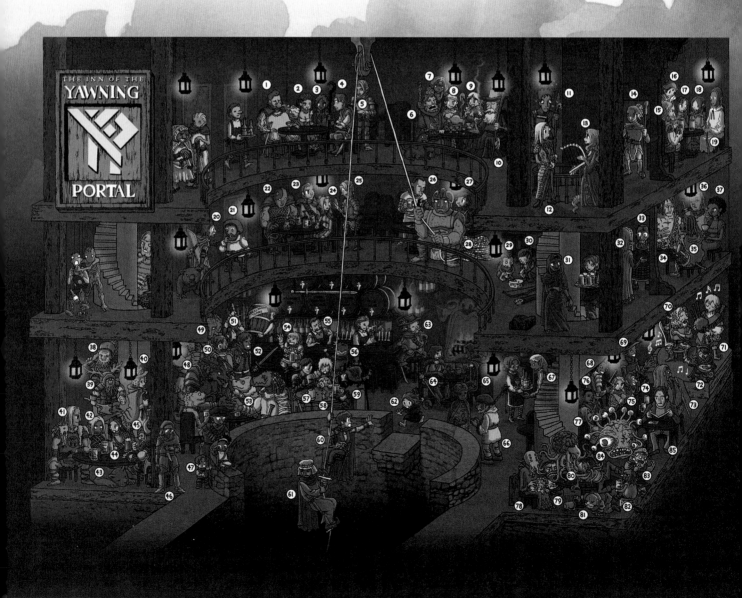